I0674331

WIZARDS OF DRAGON KEEP

BOOK THREE, DARK UNDERMASTER SAGA

C.T. PHIPPS

So, I was at a government black site. Possibly. I mean, I'd never been to one before and for all I knew this could have been just the interrogation room for something else. Of course, I might be interrogated here then dumped into a much, much worse place. Such was the life of Aaron Bartkowski, Dark Undermaster.

Me.

You may wonder why I'm beginning the story here as we last left me in a very different place, but I feel the need to let you know things are going to go in another direction. What with my being on Earth and all. We'll get back to how I got in this predicament back on my homeworld soon. Well, soonish. In any case, I was feeling nostalgic in this moment. I'd spent the past year in the fantasy world of Mokosh and I had obviously missed out on some events back on my homeworld.

Among these events seemed to have been the existence of magic being revealed, the evil god Veles becoming president of the United States, a plague of zombies, and absolutely everything going to shit. Yeah, that was a lot. Time had apparently passed a lot faster here and I'd missed almost thirty years compared to the one I'd spent trying to save Mokosh,

Right now, I was sitting with my left hand handcuffed to a metal table in a spartan white room with a two-way mirror. I was still dressed in my Dark Undermaster Master Ranger's armor, which made me look like I was cosplaying. They'd taken my weapons but hadn't done anything to suppress my magical abilities, assuming they could, so I had some advantages. Unfortunately, I was pretty sure that said advantages wouldn't do much if they unloaded assault rifles into me.

CHAPTER ONE
ARRESTED BY THE GOVERNMENT

So, I was at a government black site. Possibly. I mean, I'd never been to one before and for all I knew this could have been just the interrogation room for something else. Of course, I might be interrogated here then dumped into a much, much worse place. Such was the life of Aaron Bartkowski, Dark Undermaster.

Me.

You may wonder why I'm beginning the story here as we last left me in a very different place, but I feel the need to let you know things are going to go in another direction. What with my being on Earth and all. We'll get back to how I got in this predicament back on my homeworld soon. Well, soonish. In any case, I was feeling nostalgic in this moment. I'd spent the past year in the fantasy world of Mokosh and I had obviously missed out on some events back on my homeworld.

Among these events seemed to have been the existence of magic being revealed, the evil god Veles becoming president of the United States, a plague of zombies, and absolutely everything going to shit. Yeah, that was a lot. Time had apparently passed a lot faster here and I'd missed almost thirty years compared to the one I'd spent trying to save Mokosh,

Right now, I was sitting with my left hand handcuffed to a metal table in a spartan white room with a two-way mirror. I was still dressed in my Dark Undermaster Master Ranger's armor, which made me look like I was cosplaying. They'd taken my weapons but hadn't done anything to suppress my magical abilities, assuming they could, so I had some advantages. Unfortunately, I was pretty sure that said advantages wouldn't do much if they unloaded assault rifles into me.

I took a moment to check my stats, conjuring them up in front of my eyes even if no one else could see them.

ARAGORN "AARON" BARTKOWSKI

LVL: 17
CLASS: UNDERMASTER SORCERER (MASTER RANGER)
ALIGNMENT: GRAY
AGE: 34
SEX: MALE
RACE: HUMAN (Demigod)

STR: 12 (19)
AGI: 10 (11)
CON: 11
INT: 30
WIS: 11
COM: 15 (16)
CHA: 15

ARMOR CLASS: 27
ATTACK: +9 (+19 to ATTACK, 1d10+19/23 [Undead] DAM, *Sword of Perun* [Lightning, Holy, INT bonus])
HEALTH: 96
DIVINITY: 7

FEAT: Taunt, Sword and Shield, Two Handed Fighting, Tracking, Craft Magical Items/Recharge Magical Items, Leadership
SPECIAL ABILITIES: ARCANE FIRE (1d6+13 INT bonus, Eldritch Damage, x3 Staff of Dragon Kings, Critical Hit Possible), BLOCK (requires shield), LESSER MAGIC (unlimited times per day),

COUNTERSPELL, DIVINE ENHANCEMENT [Push]

SPELL LIST (MAX/5/5/5/5/5/3/3/2)

LESSER MAGIC EFFECTS: CLEAN SELF, CREATE FOOD, CREATE FIRE, CREATE WATER, MINOR ILLUSION, REFRESH, TELEKIESIS (1 Kilo per INT bonus), VENTRILOQUISM, MEND, TORCHLIGHT, SILENT WALK, IDENTIFY MAGICAL OBJECT, LESSER SENDING (Party Only), BLESS, SOOTHE ANIMAL

[1] ARMOR, CURE, FRIENDSHIP, JUMP, PUSH [+++]

[2] ANIMAL SUMMONING, ENTANGLE, SILENCE, WEB

[3] CURE (II), LESSER CHARM, LIGHTNING BOLT, NEUTRALIZE POISON, SUGGESTION

[4] BANISHMENT, CURE (III), POLYMORPH OTHER, DIVINE BOW, REMOVE CURSE

[5] CURE (V), DRAGONBREATH, IMPROVED LIGHTNING BOLT, REVIVE, SUNSTRIKE

[6] CHAIN LIGHTNING, GLOBE OF INVULNERABILITY, HEAL

[7] AARON'S AWESOME BATHHOUSE, RAINBOW BLAST, RESURRECTION,

[8] MASS UNDEAD SLAYING, PLANESHIFT

SPIRIT SUMMONS: STOMPY, THISTLE, RUSALKA, ZORYA DAWNBRINGER, ZORYA NIGHTBRINGER, SPARKY, LEGALLY DISTINCT COPY OF ASH FROM *EVIL DEAD*

STATUS EFFECTS:

* *Alchemical Stone* (White): You recover 20 HP after a short rest and status ailments

* Blessing of Zorya Dawnbringer: +1 to STR, +1 to AGI

* *Ring of Ogre Strength:* STR is 19 when wearing this

* *Boots of Speed:* Double Movement Speed, Dodge Roll Bonus

* Ranger's Mark: +4 to hit/damage against Undead

* +4 to all Saving Throws [Divine]

* Can cast PERUN'S DIVINE LIGHTNING BOLT once per day

* DIVINE SENSES [Always Active, No Penalties to Environment]

* Can grant 1st and 2nd level spells to priests and answer PRAYER [ACTIVE]

Level 17 to 18
2,000,000/3,000,000

Almost 18th level.

Impressive.

Sort of.

I'd never expected to make it past 12th level and that had been after I'd defeated the Wind Demon. That had all happened in the first month of my time in the world of Mokosh. The next eleven months had been spent on busy work of monster slaying, petty questing, and level grinding while trying to build up an army capable of fighting Veles. Now I was trapped here on Earth away from most of my allies.

Not good.

I was thinking about where they might be when the door to the interrogation chamber opened. A man in a black suit with mirror shades who bore a not-inconsiderable resemblance to Agent Smith from *The Matrix* walked in. He sat down across from me and put down a manila folder full of photos and documents.

"Ah, Mr. Bartkowski," the man said, shaking his head. "It seems that you have gotten yourself in a spot of trouble, haven't you?"

"Yeah," I said, annoyed. "Listen, the world is in terrible danger—"

"Mm hmm," the man said. "So you've said. You claim that Epic Dungeoneering™, the video game company, is plotting to conquer the world with the help of its former CEO, Andrew Veles. The president of the United States. A man you claim is really the Slavic god of evil."

"Yeah, how did that happen?" I asked. "The president part, I mean. He's not even an American citizen. Also, does no one notice that Andrew Veles looks exactly like Peter Stormare? That should be a big tip off right there."

"I'll be asking the questions here," the man said. "So you claim to have been on another world this entire time."

"Yes," I said. "Mokosh. Earth's sister planet."

"Where magic is real," the man said, sarcastically.

"You guys threw fireballs at me and captured me with SILENCE spells," I said, remembering how humiliating it had been.

"Yes," the man said, drawing out the word like it was something foul in his mouth. "Your associates managed to escape from what is believed to have been an act of terrorism. I don't suppose you have an excuse for what you were attempting to do."

This was probably going to go nowhere but I had to try. "Listen, those big tower things—"

"The universal magical conductors," the man explained. "The UMCs. They're the source of magic in our world. They've solved the energy crisis across the planet, global warming, and quite possibly will end scarcity."

Mostly I knew them as a key part of Veles plan to destroy the universe. Not just Earth or Mokosh but everything everywhere.

I stared at him. "Right, yeah. If the billionaires let you do that. Which they won't."

I wasn't normally political. Well, political about Earth politics. I'd had enough problems trying to keep the lights on in my apartment without worrying about things way above my pay grade. However, Veles was the president now and not worrying wasn't an option when a literal god of evil was ruling Earth's largest economy. It wasn't quite full-on Antichrist stuff but that was only because the Devil was a fallen angel while Veles was an actual god. Yes, I'm saying it was actually worse.

"You were saying about the towers?" the man asked. "The ones you wanted to blow up?"

I glared. "I should be asking for a lawyer. So, I'd like one please."

"That's hilarious," the man said. "Please go on."

Yeah, no surprise that under Veles the rights of prisoners hadn't exactly thrived. I sighed, trying to figure out how to convince the authorities I wasn't insane. At least I didn't have to convince them that magic was real. "The UMCs are part of a big, planned ritual that is going to destroy two worlds. He's—"

"Andrew Veles," the man said. "The man you claim is actually the Slavic god, Veles. The president."

I balled my fists. "Yes, *him*. He's one of the creator gods and more powerful than almost any other in this galaxy."

This was getting me nowhere but as long as I was a prisoner here, I couldn't exactly do much. Veles would probably order my execution as soon as he was recovered enough to do so. Yeah, that was a story by itself. I was lucky they seemed to be unaware of that fact or uncaring. Either way, if my friends didn't bail me out, I wasn't sure how I'd turn this around. Slight problem with that: most of my friends were either gone or dead. That was a *really* long story.

"Interesting," The man said. "You *also* claim to be a god, as I understand it?"

I hadn't mentioned that in my early attempts to talk my way out of this. It seemed high charisma only got you so far when dealing with government bureaucracy. "That's complicated."

"Uncomplicate it," the man said.

"I'm a god but the Diet Coke version of one," I replied. "All of my power is borrowed and all of my worshipers are on Mokosh."

I stared at the two Marks of the Champion on my arms. They were the creations of Larry C.C. Weis AKA the Wiseman and each contained a fragment of Perun's divine essence. They were the last of the existing marks and if I absorbed them, well, then I'd cease to be a demigod. Instead, I would become a full-fledged god. Probably not anywhere near as powerful as Perun had been at his height but something beyond human.

Which is why I hadn't.

Was it selfish? Probably. I'd developed a life in Mokosh that transcended what I'd lived here on Earth. I was married to Ania, in spirit if not law, and my family was living there as well. If I became a god, I was afraid I would lose the fundamental things that made me human. Worse, I was worried that it wouldn't be enough to defeat Veles. There were other gods out there, Mythras and Svarog for example, but they hadn't taken up the fight against Veles. Still, the temptation was there, and I had to admit it was hard to resist when we seemed so close to defeat despite all our accomplishments.

"Of course," the man said, contempt in his voice. "Tell me, Mr. Bartkowski, do you really think that your group *Dungeons and Dragons* heroes have the slightest chance of defeating the United States military?"

I stared at him. "I don't need to fight the United States military. I just need to get to Veles."

The man snorted. "You really think that's an option. Oh, Aaron, you have always been an insufferable idealist."

I stared at him. Something was very wrong here. "What is this? Who are you?"

Before I could get a response, the lights turned off and everything became a foggy gray around me. One of the benefits I got from being a demigod was DIVINE SENSES, which amounted to the fact that I could see in the dark and never be confused by noise or distractions.

That was when the man across the table pulled out a set of keys and unlocked my handcuffs. "Okay, we've got to get going!"

"What the hell?" I asked, confused as fuck.

"Psych! It's me!" Jon's voice spoke from the secret agent's mouth. "How did you like my Agent Smith impression?"

Jon was clearly enjoying his dragon ability to shapeshift.

"I fricking hated it!" I said, staring at him. "Is this a jailbreak?"

"Yes!" Jon said, throwing his hands in the air. "We need to get going!"

I was about to comment on how utterly stupid it was to try to infiltrate a government base before I realized, oh wait, I was the only member of my party who had a problem with getting in a fight with the United States government. Everyone else was either from another planet or thought they were living in a real live version of *Red Dawn*.

Before I could express how upset I was at this development, I heard gunfire followed by the explosion of magical blasts. Alarms started going up across the base and I knew things had gone from bad to, "Yeah, we were now trapped in a *Call of Duty* level."

Reacting as reasonably as I could in the situation, I reached across the metal table and grabbed Jon by the shirt before pulling him across the table. "What the hell do you think you're doing?"

"It's okay!" Jon said, smiling in a way that made me think Hugo Weaving had grounds to sue. "All the people in the base are already dead!"

"What?" I asked, staring at him.

"Yeah, it turns out that Veles is turning huge chunks of the planet into wights with a super advanced version of deathrot," Jon explained. "So, there's like no moral issues whatsoever with blowing the hell out of them on our way out."

I stared in horror.

The two-way mirror in the room was smashed open as a trio of scientists wearing lab coats dropped their glamours and revealed rotting, hideous, undead faces on the other side. It was like something from *Resident Evil* or, well, zombie mode from *Call of Duty*.

Jon pulled out a pistol and aimed it straight forward. "Die, you mothersuckers!"

He fired a half-dozen bullets in a few seconds, pulling down the trigger as he attempted headshots on all three.

All his shots missed.

I stared at him.

"Sorry!" Jon said, looking ashamed. "I've never actually used one of these before."

The three wights climbed over the broken glass and charged me. Their expressions were unified in their desire to kill me.

"PUSH," I said, absently, lifting my hand and blasting the three of them with a massive blast of kinetic force that splattered them like rotten bananas against the back of the room. "So, just so we're clear, I let myself get captured for nothing and the US government is probably now composed of a bunch of mind-controlled undead?"

"You let yourself get captured?" Jon asked.

"Yeah," I said, annoyed. "I was hoping to inform the authorities so we could resolve this peacefully."

Which was totally true and not me trying to cover up I'd been taken down by a bunch of magic-equipped DC cops. Seriously, I hadn't wanted to hurt them, and I'd already exhausted myself fighting Veles.

Jon stared. "Wow, Aaron, you are the smartest man in the world and such an idiot at the same time. Yes, the government is compromised, and the people are completely unprepared. Really, the UMCs blowing up the world is probably a quicker death than the zombie virus thing that Veles will do otherwise."

I frowned. "Well, I guess it's time we get out of here and finish blowing up those things."

Jon nodded. "The first intelligent thing you've said since we started this. We need you to finish this race, Aaron."

I slapped my best friend on the shoulder. "You got it."

"Otherwise, who am I going to make incest jokes about?" Jon asked. "Speaking of which, have I mentioned your daughter is the one who made the plan to rescue you? The one who isn't technically blood related to you?"

I cast SILENCE on Jon.

So, how *did* we get here?

I'll start from closer to where we left off.

CHAPTER TWO
JUST A WEE BIT OF A BACKTRACK

Yeah, I probably jumped ahead too much.

Suffice to say, things are going to get a bit anachronic. You know, like *Pulp Fiction*, this whole thing is going to be told out of order. Why? Well, reality is going to get/did get/is getting broken because of a bunch of things I don't even know where to begin explaining. Magic. Veles. World-hopping. Really, it's like *Final Fantasy*, you think you've got a good idea as to what is happening before the plot starts becoming completely nonsensical. Anyway, back before my entire world was falling apart—say about a month before—I was still relatively in control of the situation. Things were much more normal.

Okay, that's a lie.

Things were normal only in the sense of normal being the life of a LitRPG hero or high fantasy protagonist.

Which I was.

Technically.

I was travelling with my adventuring party through the air-filled parts of an underwater city underneath Śniardwy, which was the largest lake in Ledziana. It notably shared the same name and location as the largest lake in Poland, which was another sign that Larry C.C. Weis was completely unoriginal. One element that was different was the one in Poland had a depth of about twenty-one meters. Which was deep, don't get me wrong, but it had nothing on its Ledzianan counterpart. The Śniardwy in Ledziana was closer to a kilometer deep and, as mentioned, contained a vast city which was inhabited by the Rusalka, mutated humanoids, and a variety of other aquatic creatures.

The city was the former Grand Temple of Water and the final location for our war against the Old Gods. It was composed of beautiful spiral towers, Grecian buildings made of marble, and a bunch of twisted structures that had no real human architectural equivalent. It was also wholly corrupted by the influence of Belobog AKA Cthulhu. Yes, I was calling him Cthulhu. Why? Because he was a giant humanoid squid monster god with batwings. Some things didn't need a deeper meaning.

At that moment, my party was in the middle of the Grand Temple's antechamber to Belobog's summoning room. In two of the three previous temples, wits and deception had gotten us past most of the defenses. (We'd skipped the third.) This time, we'd pretty much had to brute force our way through. My seven-man group had fought our way through mermen, kelpies, water horses, naga, vodniks, living oozes, slime monsters, mud monsters, elementals, and what I was pretty sure was Ursula from *The Little Mermaid*.

We were almost to Belobog now, so the forces of the Water Demon had regrouped to throw everything they had at us. But the numbers game wasn't working out in their favor. We'd taken on the other three Old Gods and level grinded to become more than enough to deal with these guys. I'd been completely overwhelmed fighting Chernabog and Zorya Nightbringer, but here? Here, I was doing great. So was everyone else. Which, of course, meant something was about to go disastrously wrong.

"Belobog fhtagn!" One of the squid priests shouted as he shook his coral staff at me while displaying his bare chest through his drenched robes. A seashell necklace hung around his neck. "Ph'nglui mglw'nafh Belobog wgah'nagl fhtagn!"

The antechamber was a four-story tall room with a giant pair of golden doors facing north, a bunch of moist red tapestries hanging from the walls, and a set of stone steps with a moldy red carpet leading up the doors. Dim lighting was provided by glowing crystals on the wall. Yeah, the Grand Temple of Water had seen better days. You get what you pay for when you make a city underwater. Ask Andrew Ryan for you *Bioshock* fans.

We were being swarmed by dozens of squid-faced ogres under the command of the mutated priests of Belobog. There were also a few slime monsters that were totally not shoggoths as well as, I shit you not, a few evil giant starfish. How did I know they were evil? Because they kept trying to eat me.

"Okay, this is bullshit," I said, hacking through the tentacle-faced ogres that the squid priest was siccing on me. "What is with all the Cthulhu Mythos nods? I gave Belobog that name as a joke! What the hell does H. P. Lovecraft have to do with Polish mythology? The guy feared Welsh people, let alone Eastern Europeans. At least Robert E. Howard wasn't afraid of slightly less Anglo people than medieval Londoners."

"Just go with it, Aaron!" Jon said, punching his fist through the head of one of the ogres. He was now relishing his new shapeshifting abilities and had assumed what I suspected was an idealized version of his human self. He looked a bit like a young Keanu Reeves dressed in a white gi like Ryu from *Street Fighter*. That he was a dragon now should have meant he was less useful in human form but, well, he'd been an 18th level bare-fisted monk before he died. "You'll enjoy this world a whole lot more once you stop questioning how little sense it makes!"

"I dunno," Bloodstorm said, hacking and slashing with his golden axe given to him by Mythras. "I wonder about the intricacies of all this. Was H. P. Lovecraft inspired by this world or did Veles decide to mutate his son into something resembling the author's most famous creation? Is it perhaps an attempt to harness the collective psyche of Earth's modern mythology to make a more effective evil?" Bloodstorm was a seven-foot-tall black man of mixed ogre and elvish ancestry that looked like an Adonis of muscle if you ignored his large bull horns and slightly pointed ears. He'd let his hair grow out long and was dressed in a new set of armor that mostly looked like belts with a loin cloth.

"What is wrong with you people?" Ania said, wearing a tight leather catsuit with a cleavage-exposing top that looked equally impractical for combat but had been enchanted with magic to work like Kevlar. She was a beautiful redheaded woman who I had been crushing on, at least her fictional version, since I was a teenager. "Focus on the task at hand!"

"Talking is a free action according to the rules of the divine concordat!" Rachel Morning, my sort-of daughter, said. She was a beautiful girl with her own distinct resemblance to Ania, red hair and pale skin, but a goofier girl next door sort of beauty. Rachel was wearing a red witch's hat and robes while carrying a crystal-tipped staff.

Oh, and she was a reincarnated goddess of war as well as sex.

Rachel blasted one of the giant starfish that attempted to engulf her, exploding the thing into so much chum. She had replaced Agata as our chief spell lobber and could throw down with the best of them. Unfortunately, her presence caused a lot of questions and misunderstandings. After all, she hadn't existed until less than a year ago and was vulnerable to corruption by the Twisted Gods.

The penultimate member of our group was a white-haired girl with pig tails wearing a hooded white robe trimmed with gold and solar symbols. A group of ogres were attempting to bang their clubs against her but a glowing shield surrounded her, providing a lot of room for us to maneuver while they were distracted. That was Pope Joan the First of the Church of Mythras, a fifteen-year-old girl who I hated bringing into battle but was every bit as powerful a wizard as me.

"We are close to facing down the Water Demon!" Joan said, proudly. "We must reserve our strongest spells to defeat him!"

"Easy for you to say!" Jon said, kicking an ogre with an impractical somersault that made me wonder where he'd learned these crazy martial arts or if they were just another sign of how ridiculous this world is.

"Screw it," I said, seeing that there were even more monsters coming in. "CHAIN LIGHTNING!"

The chief squid priest shouted a warning of alarm before trying to COUNTERSPELL the effect, only for him to get a knife thrown into his throat from seemingly nowhere. That was my cousin, Alek, who had used his ring of invisibility to clear a way through much of the Grand Temple ahead of us only to botch the final stretch due to an ALARM spell put on the privy.

Those always seemed to screw us in the end.

Either way, the lightning shot from my fingertips and leapfrogged from one ogre after another as well as several other unidentifiable creatures. The blast took down almost a dozen in the end and gave my team the edge they needed to rush on the wounded to finish them off. From there, I cast WEB against the door the reinforcements had been coming through. The steel-like spider goop wouldn't hold them forever, but it might allow us to finally get to Belobog's chamber. Which was, when you thought about it, an insane thing to hope for. We *wanted* to bring the giant corrupted god's avatar to us from whatever dimension he was residing in so we could kill him. It was the only way to finish off the last of the Elemental Demons and stop Veles from feasting on Mokosh's power.

Ania took a moment to pause for breath before staring at the many corpses in front of us. "Did anyone else think that was too easy?"

Jon turned to look at her. "Hell no!"

"I agree," Bloodstorm said, frowning. "That was way too easy. This temple should be crawling with Veles forces but is strangely underpopulated."

"Underpopulated?" Jon asked, shaking his head. "We've probably killed two hundred guys since the alarm started."

"Which is pretty small for a city full of evil monsters," Ania said. "Agata and the dwarvish navy were supposed to lure their forces out so we could strike Belobog but there's nothing more than a token force guarding this place."

"I hate to agree with Ania on this but she's right," Alek said, disengaging his *Invisibility* spell. Unlike Tolkien's One Ring, it wasn't perfect and worked more like the Predator's light-bending effect. Super-duper camouflage rather than actual invisibility. The real Alek dressed in army fatigues, a bandana, and resembled a bearded version of me. Which wasn't surprising since we were biological brothers despite being raised by different parents. No, you don't get to call us brother-cousins.

"Shut up," Jon said, looking at Alek. His look was one of disgust and anger, which I'd hoped would have gotten better over our time together but hadn't. "You don't get to contribute to this conversation. You're like our Scrappy Doo. No one wants you here and we're only tolerating you because Aaron likes you."

"I like him!" Rachel said, cheerfully.

"You can't fuck your uncle either, Rachel," Jon said.

"Aww," Rachel said, always undercutting Jon's attempt to gross her out by acting like she was into that sort of thing. "He looks so much like Dad, too."

At least I hoped she was acting.

"Seriously, both of you are horrible," I said.

Rachel smirked.

"Personally, I think of myself as more your sixth Power Ranger," Alek said, smirking.

Everyone stared blankly.

"Seriously, no one watched *Power Rangers*?" Alek asked.

"Sorry," I said. "Never saw a single episode. That's the one with the girl from *Felicity*, right?"

Alek sighed. "Never mind."

"You got it," I said.

"Even with the much-diluted forces we've faced here, we've expended a large amount of magic fighting them. We might not have the remaining strength to fight Belobog," Joan said, remaining laser-focused on our goal.

"I have some potions of refreshment," I replied. "We should take some of those before we make a direct assault. Either that or take some time to hang around in AARON'S AWESOME BATHHOUSE."

"Did you have to name it that?" Ania asked, staring at me.

"What?" I asked. "It's a sauna."

"Yes, full of elemental sexy people," Jon said. "You realize it's a wizard spell for sex, right?"

"It's for relaxing!" I said, frowning. "Safety at night rather than a campfire. Maelor taught it to me and said it was a perfectly valid military resource."

"Soldiers like to fuck too, Aaron," Alek said.

"Are we not supposed to have sex with the bathers?" Ania asked, unwittingly paraphrasing the Eddie Murphy classic *Coming to America*. "It's not cheating if they're spirits. Err, not that I am. Because Aaron and I are monogamous."

Everyone looked at her.

"You're not fooling anyone," Bloodstorm said. "My sister Angelica has told me you've managed to break Aaron out of his shell. Her, Winter Chill, Shakra the Goblin, and Theresa Miller. It's all over Dragon Keep."

"Mrs. Miller?" Jon asked, mocking me. "For shame, Aaron! She is a married woman!"

"Her husband turned out to be gay," I said, defensively. "Ania and I were just providing a comforting service."

"Oh wow, you believed that?" Ania asked. "No, Klaus is just terrible at sex."

I stared in mock horror.

"Yeah, your attempts to win Ania over from the Charlie Sheen/Lindsay Lohan lifestyle aren't working great," Jon said. "Real bang-up work in converting her."

"I'm going to say mocking him for that isn't the flex you think it is," Alek said, crossing his arms. "It's a bit like insulting Vin Diesel for being badass and a *Dungeons and Dragons* nerd."

"Yeah," Jon said, sighing. "Just doesn't have quite the same punch as the incest jokes. Also, shut up, because you suck. You're the *Star Trek: Discovery* of our franchise."

"I don't even know what that means," Alek said.

"You suck!" Jon said.

"I like *Discovery*," I muttered. "I mean it's no *Star Trek: Lower Decks* but..."

"No one likes *Discovery*!" Jon said.

That was when there was an enormous creaking that didn't take much to figure out was coming from the giant golden doors in the chamber. Suspecting we were about to fight Belobog or more of his minions, all of us assumed battle stances. From within, there was an eerie incandescent white light that obscured anything beyond.

That was when a spectacularly beautiful older woman with a voluptuous figure, long black hair, and olive skin stepped out of the light. She was dressed in a single wrap around her body that displayed her belly and was almost translucent. On her head was a five-pointed crown covered in purple sapphires that glowed with witchfire. Her fingers were also all covered in rings.

I recognized the woman from when I'd had to work on her digital model for several months while still employed by Epic Dungeoneering™. It was the Witch Queen of Angho'horak, most powerful of all magicians in the Southern Kingdoms after (possibly) the Wise Man. She was notably the ruler of the Thirteen and the first death lord, which really took away a lot of her attractiveness. She was, even more than a vampire, a very pretty corpse.

"Well, this is going to make fighting Belobog harder," I muttered, lifting the Sword of Perun.

"Hey, Suzie!" Jon said, waving.

I glared at him. "Suzie?"

"You didn't think her name was Witch Queen, did you?" Jon asked.

"I hadn't really given it any thought to be honest. Suzie?" I asked, confused. I was, however, ready for the fight of my life. The Witch Queen had destroyed whole armies with her magic and come perilously close to conquering Mokosh on multiple occasions. I'd say she was the Saruman to Veles' Sauron, but I wasn't sure that she wasn't the Sauron to his Morgoth.

"Do not fear, Aaron Bartkowski," the Witch Queen said, "I do not come here as an adversary."

"You created the death rot," Ania said. "You killed millions. Also, you slept with Jon and I'm not sure which is worse."

"Hey!" Jon said, irritated. He paused before turning back to her. "Okay, I admit, that's actually pretty funny."

"Where's Belobog?" I asked.

"Preparing to attack Crossroad with all the armies of darkness," the Witch Queen said. "Veles has abandoned this world and gone to yours."

I blinked. "Okay, maybe we should start from the beginning."

See, I told you this was going to get confusing.

CHAPTER THREE
WE'VE BEEN SUCKERED

"What do you mean he's attacking my world?" I asked, staring at the Witch Queen in horror.

"Technically, she said he's attacking Crossroad with Belobog leading the armies of darkness," Alek corrected. "Suzie just said that Veles went to your world. For all we know, he's just decided to retire in Florida."

"Not helping, Alek," I muttered.

"He'd fit right in," Jon said, pausing. "Which isn't me being political. I meant that Veles is old and prone to doing weird stuff."

"Don't ever explain the joke," I said, looking at Jon before turning back to the Witch Queen. "Also, back to my world being attacked."

"Your parents are at Crossroad," Ania said, reminding me of its importance. "So are your sister and nephew."

"Which is why I'm not worried too much about it," I said, somewhat exaggerating my feelings.

The Witch Queen stared at us, a look of barely contained fury in her Monica Belluci-esque eyes. "The god of evil has betrayed his followers. With the tides of battle turning against us and the alliances forged among the Five Races, he summoned his power to transport himself across oceans of space to Mokosh's sister world."

"Yeah, who could have possibly seen that coming," Ania said, sarcastically. "What with him being the god of evil."

Yeah, I loved her attitude. I didn't think it was going to help with the 60th level wizard, though. They planned to buff her for the next expansion too.

The Witch Queen didn't seem offended, though. "I expected to be taken with the rest of the followers he brought with him across the Star Bridge on Bald Mountain's summit. Instead, Belobog and I have been left to merely provide interference for you. To soak up the wrath of the gods and their minions—you—while Veles moves to his plan to destroy the two worlds."

"Yeah, that's a pretty awful plan," I said.

"I didn't object to it when I was going to survive," the Witch Queen replied. "Once you know an afterlife objectively exists, it takes some of the sting out of murder."

I grimaced. "*Should it,* though?"

The Witch Queen did not acknowledge me but continued as if I had been silent. "But I was abandoned like so much refuse despite having been my master's most faithful follower since the first Great Darkness. I did not wish to believe he was corrupted by the Twisted Gods but his oath breaking and betrayal of our marriage can have no other explanation."

"Either that or he's just not into you," Rachel said.

"It's terrible," Jon said. "I offer my body for your comfort."

"Seriously, she's a death lord," Ania said. "That's necrophilia."

"If I can't tell, I don't care," Jon said.

"And yet you mock Aaron for wanting to bang his spiritual daughter," Bloodstorm said, shaking his head.

"I do not!" I snapped. "Also, seriously, you don't get to make incest jokes. That's restricted to Jon and Rachel."

"Why Rachel?" Ania asked, confused.

"Because she's a deeply scary person despite looking like a guest star on *Critical Role*," I replied.

Rachel waved her hand as if acknowledging she was there while we talked about her. "I based my appearance on Aaron's sexual partners from when he was con clubbing."

"Kill me now," I muttered. "Except you, Witch Queen, because I worry that you'd take that offer seriously."

"What an odd group," the Witch Queen said, blinking once. "I find it very difficult to believe you defeated three of the Old Gods and have driven Veles from this world. Nevertheless, it is difficult to argue with results. I come here to bring a warning of the attack as well as to propose a detente."

"I'm listening," I said, staring at her face and trying to see past the glamour to the corpse below.

"You can't be serious," Ania said. "She's one of history's greatest monsters."

"Let's focus on Hitler before worrying about Stalin," I said. "Any war where one party chooses to bow out is one where you should let them."

"First, that's not actually true if the enemy intends to take you out after you exhaust yourself fighting their enemies," Alek said. "Second, Stalin didn't really work out well for Poland. You know, my homeland."

"I'll happily negotiate on our behalf!" Jon said, cheerfully.

"Do not think I come here empty handed," the Witch Queen said, conjuring a large, weathered scroll held together by a black ribbon with a tiny rat skull. She handed it to me.

"What's this?" I asked, reluctantly taking it.

"It is the true names of the gods you slew," the Witch Queen said. "It took me millennia to find them and give Veles power over his offspring."

"Gee, thanks," I said, unsure what I could do with it.

"It's why the Zoryas needed to change their identities on a basic level," Rachel explained. "Every time they were defeated, Veles just asserted his will over them and reinfected them with the Twisted Gods' power."

"Ah," I said, still not sure. "But Rachel and Nightchilde aren't affected by this anymore. Right?"

"No," the Witch Queen said. "But it should allow you to not only summon shadows of their past avatars but also Belobog once you defeat him. Chernabog will not be able to be summoned because you destroyed his spirit. It will be a century or more before he regenerates."

"Yeah, couldn't have happened to a nicer guy," I muttered. "Why would you give this to me versus keeping it for yourself?"

"Aaron, don't look a gift scroll in the Evil Queen who gave it to you's mouth," Jon said. "Just accept that Maleficent here is on our side."

"For now," Ania muttered.

"They're worthless to her," Rachel explained. "The kind of summoning she's describing could only be performed by someone with sufficient divine blood."

"Just another sign of privilege in action," Jon said. "Wait, Bloodstorm, Alek, Ania, Rachel presumably... am I the only one here who isn't a demigod?"

"I'm the Chosen of my God," Joan said. "But just the bastard daughter of royalty."

"Oh boo hoo for you, Schoolgirl Daenerys," Jon said. "You're lucky I have standards or you'd be subject to vicious mockery."

"You have standards?" Joan asked, appalled.

"Hey, I haven't once made a jailbait wait joke—" Jon started to say before I blasted him in the face with a minimum power ball of Arcane Fire. "Ow! What the hell?"

"Pavlov had a solution for you," I replied. "We'll see if it works. But Witch Queen—"

"Susanos," the Witch Queen corrected.

I blinked. "Really? Um, okay, sure. I'm not sure I'm really comfortable with a gift of controlling the ghosts of dead gods."

"You are facing one of the creator gods," Susanos said, as if talking to an especially slow child. "Being able to summon the lesser deities may prove to be the difference between triumph and defeat for the Two Worlds. Besides, the gods will be incredibly grateful to you for freeing them."

"So, we could summon Zorya Dawnbringer for a threesome?" Ania asked, very deliberately exaggerated in her horniness. "Ooo, maybe

Zorya Nightbringer for a foursome now that she's no longer insane? I worshiped her for a while, y'know."

"Ooo sounds great," I said. "What if we invite some priestesses of Mokosh or Dark Moon priestesses?"

"Nah, we need to keep it reasonable for our bed size," Ania said. "Three times a day for sex is enough. Maybe with REFRESH, though..."

"Gah!" Jon said, covering his ears and walking away, saying, "Lalalala."

I smirked, watching him leave earshot.

"Do you think we should ever tell him that we're not actually screwing other people?" Ania asked, watching Jon leave.

"No, it drives him crazy since he found out that dragons only have a month out of every five years mating cycle," I said, amused. "Like Vulcans."

"Yeah, I know that island," Ania said, nodding. "Rachel is a devious mastermind."

"Thank you," Rachel said, curtsying.

"You guys are evil," Alexi said, smirking. "The fun kind."

"Happy to help with the rumors," Bloodstorm said. "Though I don't get what's weird about any of that."

"Are you sleeping with anyone but Agata now?" Ania asked. "Your wife?"

Bloodstorm looked to one side. "That is completely different."

Yeah, they were married now. I was jealous. Just a bit.

Rachel looked to me. "As hilarious as I find this whole conversation, I should note that the scroll of true names would also contain the methods for summoning other spirits aligned to you."

"Other spirits?" I asked.

"Thistle, the Bastard Knight, Francine Dubois..." Rachel trailed off.

"Ehh," I said, pausing. "I'm not exactly fond of any of those people right now."

Rachel sighed. "Stompy."

"Oh God, yes," I said, clutching the scroll tighter. "I've missed him so much."

Rachel rolled her eyes.

"Yes, the perfect justification to start employing the dark arts: you want your horse back," Ania said, pausing. "Okay, yeah, that makes sense."

"Stompy is a good horsey!" I said, feeling a little like a kid in a Western.

Susanos cupped her face with both hands and sighed despite having nonfunctional lungs. "I'm afraid we're going to have to wrap this up."

"We don't want your help, Susanos," Ania said, turning to her. "You're as much a threat to this world as Veles. I'll gladly see you stay out of this war, though."

"You will need my help if you want any chance of destroying the armies of Belobog," Susanos said. "Veles only took a few hundred agents with him as well as some of his most powerful artifacts. The rest of his vast empire of corpses, mercenaries, and slave soldiers have been sent on to Crossroad. It's nothing more than a distraction that will lay waste to Ledziana and maximize the casualties of the people."

It was a reminder that Veles, despite how charismatic and congenial he was in person, was a real pile of crap. I could imagine the armies of Mordor straight out of Peter Jackson's films moving through Ledziana, destroying and burning everything in their path. A military assault that would do nothing more than serve as a spiteful genocide that would distract us from chasing him. Well, if we were lucky. It was more likely it would kill us all. We'd have to gather all of the forces we'd forged alliances together to defend Crossroad and that would be like herding cats.

"What do you get out of this?" I asked, still wondering what angle she was playing.

"Revenge," Susanos said. "That is enough, but there is also the knowledge that if Veles falls then there will be a place for a new Dark Lord to replace him. I can't rule the world if he destroys it and if I am not to be Queen of Hell, I'd rather be Queen of Everything."

I was about to say that wasn't very reassuring when the entirety of the temple chamber rocked. Little bits of dust started falling from the ceiling as water began to drip from holes sprouting across the walls.

"Well, that's not good," I said, looking down to my ring of water breathing as well as my belt of super swimming. All of us were sporting them. These had been invaluable for our attack down here.

"No, it is not," Susanos said. "The fanatical priests of the Water Demon have started undoing the spells protecting the city to try to drown and crush you under the lake's immense pressure."

"You got the spell to keep us from suffering the bends, right?" I asked Joan.

Joan nodded. "I admit, decompression sickness wasn't something I normally think about memorizing spells for."

"Smartest man on Mokosh," I said, tapping the side of my head. "We need to fast travel out."

"You won't be able to do that," Susanos said. "The Water Demon's priests are also the least of your worries."

"What do you mean?" I asked, looking at the death lord in confusion.

"This is a trap," Alek said, cursing under his breath. "Veles knew we'd eventually come here to slay Belobog, so he arranged for us to get to the central chamber before bringing the whole place down on us."

"Yes," Susanos said. "But to make absolutely sure you don't escape, he also placed a thermonuclear device in Belobog's summoning chamber."

Alek and I stared.

"Veles has nukes now?" Jon asked. "Why the hell hasn't he used them already?"

"He only had the one," Susanos said. "Again, my husband is a very spiteful being."

I stared at the golden doors and started to march to them. "We have to disarm it."

Susanos stopped me with her hand held up, palm facing outward. "It is too late for that, Aaron Bartkowski. The only thing preventing your total obliteration now is my TIME STOP spell over it."

I stared. "How long?"

"Less than a minute," Susanos said. "Now do we have an accord or do I teleport away by myself?"

I stared behind her and saw there was, in fact, the top of a Soviet ICBM. Veles certainly didn't scrimp when he decided to go all out.

"We have an accord," I said.

Ania clenched her teeth. The others looked like they trusted me, which should have been more reassuring.

"Good," Susanos said, waving her staff just as everything went white.

CHAPTER FOUR
ROYAL PAINS

"Oh, mother sucker!" I said, clutching my eyes. Everything was white and I still couldn't see a damn thing. Which wasn't a good thing when you saw a nuclear explosion.

"It's alright," Joan said, beside me. "You're just blind."

"Just blind?" I asked, stunned by her insensitivity. Then I remembered she was a woman with access to casual magical healing. Hopefully, magical healing will work in taking care of my issue.

"Yeah, hold on," Joan said, placing her hands on me. At least I thought it was Joan from her voice. "CURE BLINDNESS."

That was when everything slowly moved its way back to shapes and then colors. I blinked several times as I looked down upon Joan. "Okay, it really is much better to have magical healing than the alternative. Though I am ninety percent sure my mother's plan to introduce penicillin to Ledziana is a good idea."

"Is that her weird idea that we need to eat powdered fungus?" Joan asked, holding the side of my head. "Because I'm still not down with that."

"You have pizza in the Empire," I said, looking at her. "You also put mushrooms on everything."

"That is completely different!" Joan said.

"Ahem," Ania cleared her throat. "We have bigger issues to deal with right now."

I shook my head and turned around to see my party had teleported to the edge of the lake where there was a massive waterspout from the center.

The Śniardwy was surrounded by a vast forest and we were not that far from the camp where King Ivan III and King Wotanson had assembled their forces.

"I'm pretty sure that an explosion a kilometer underwater wouldn't cause that," I said, pausing. "But I admit I do not know the exact science of nuclear physics as related to magical fantasy worlds."

"Hold up your thumb!" Jon said, having assumed his raven form and sitting on my shoulder. "Also, if it blinded you, what's the chances you are utterly cooked with radiation? And by you, I mean me, since we're focused on what's important here."

"You were caught mid-teleport but while light struck you, actual radiation did not," Susanos said, drawing my attention.

Susanos had dropped her glamour and no longer looked like a glamorous southern European movie star. Instead, she looked more like the horrifying desiccated corpse she was. Susanos was still dressed in her wrap and crown but in the words of the great Ash Williams, she'd got real ugly.

"Yeah, but light is radiation," I pointed out, walking over to the lake's edge and splashing my face a few times. I dropped the scroll of true names on the ground because, well, it was not as important as whether I'd be dead of cancer tomorrow.

"Try shapeshifting a few times," Rachel said. "That should reset your genetics."

"Would that work?" I asked.

"It's an interesting puzzle," Rachel said, adjusting her witch's hat. "Magic fundamentally obeys the laws of physics in the context of simply being a new element of cause and effect adding to the existing world."

"Yeah, it works like programming language," I said, picking up the scroll. "You fuck with the engine too much and it breaks, but it works fine if you acknowledge how it all works together."

Ania put two fingers in her mouth and whistled. "*Please.* Can we focus on the end of the world? Or worlds in this case?"

"We're always focused on the end of the world," Bloodstorm said, taking a deep breath. "I also don't want to die of poisonous magical energy. So I'm all down for any folk remedies that will cure us. Turn me into a dog and then back. I like dogs."

"Ha!" Jon taunted. "I'm surviving this no matter what. The crow wins."

"Are you a crow or a raven?" Rachel asked, curiously. "You identify as both but they're distinct birds."

"Yeah, but the thing that distinguishes them most is the sounds they make," I pointed out. "Jon speaks English."

"Crows and ravens can speak some English."

"Not enough to discuss why the *Star Wars* sequels suck."

"True, but they also differed in tail, bill, flight pattern, and size," Rachel said. "I'd argue he's kind of weirdly in-between and that was before he became a dragon."

"Maybe we could get him his own species name, *Ledzianan corvus*," I suggested.

Ania stared. "So, yeah, clearly we aren't focusing on the end of the worlds despite my request. How long do we have until the Crossroad is attacked by Belobog?"

"Three days," Susanos said. "The armies of the dead do not tire, hunger, or thirst. Belobog mindlessly marches to his master's tune because he has been the one most affected by the Twisted Gods' corruption. He only desires to cause as much pain and suffering for his master as possible before being put down."

"Great," I muttered. "What kind of help can you offer us?"

I'd been under duress when I'd agreed to an alliance with the Witch Queen, but war was rarely a situation where you got to do things without duress. Indeed, virtually every treaty and surrender were made under some form of it. You didn't agree to these things just because. Right now, we needed to figure out how to deal with whatever Veles was doing on my world. I had visions of *The Walking Dead*, nuclear war, and worse dancing through my head.

Like most evil dictators, Veles couldn't be counted on to act in a perfectly rational and sensible way. Much of our struggle against him had been defined by the fact he was treating all of this as an enormous game. I wasn't even the person he was playing against. Veles had been playing against Larry C.C. Weis. I'd even wasted a wish (way back when I'd won a game of Pwiffle against the god of evil), trying to get Veles to follow the rules. Basically, we had no idea of knowing what he'd do next.

"I have assembled the surviving members of the Thirteen," Susanos said. "I have destroyed the ones who refused to accept my leadership. That, unfortunately, gives me only a tenth of the undead forces assembled by Belobog. I am working on convincing the goblin kings of the Death Mountains to join me as well. That is hard."

"Why?" I asked.

"Because they are too busy celebrating their god leaving," Susanos said. "They also sensibly believe that if Belobog destroys much of Ledziana then they can claim the depopulated surface for themselves."

"They may find that humanity decides to pay them back for that," Bloodstorm said. "Assuming, you know, other humans don't invade them for the exact same reason."

I grimaced as that was a reference to our biggest failure so far in the past year. Something so bad that if I survive to write a LitRPG trilogy detailing my adventures, I would leave it off page. We'd tried to recruit the Viking Rus to join our army and Bloodstorm's people had proven to be utterly intractable. For a so-called proud warrior race, none of the jarls or petty kings wanted to waste their soldiers on something like saving the world.

Not even bribery and playing them against one another had accomplished anything. I had thought I was pretty good at winning people over but, in the end, the Rus had beaten us through the power of sheer selfishness. We'd had more luck recruiting the Empire and elves to our cause. The dwarves had joined us immediately.

"They will accompany my forces because of another race of Veles' creation accompanying them," Susano said, surprising me.

"Who?" I asked, confused.

"The ratkin," Susano said. "They are a vast empire underneath the ground, one with uncounted numbers but no desire to serve anyone until now. They will join the cause of defending your race, but you have to pay their price."

"Me?" I asked.

"Yes," Susano said, her skull face unreadable. "They wish you to be their god."

"Their...god," I said, making sure I understood her properly.

"Nice work if you can get it," Jon said. "Sit around on your ass all day and take credit when things go right, but when things going wrong they're mysterious ways."

"Which is absolutely true," Joan said.

"You poor thing," Jon said.

"You remember you have divine blood too, right?" I asked Jon. It was a requirement to use the Marks of the Champion properly.

"Nope! Completely forgot," Jon said.

"You're dodging the question," Susano said. "The ratkin are deeply impressed with you for some reason."

"I stopped a few genocides and forced Ivan to repeal the bounties on their heads," I replied. "Killing them is now murder. It apparently wasn't before."

Susano was silent for a moment. Her eye sockets glowed with eerie witchfire. "I didn't think there would be a reason. Curious."

"Yeah, they even had a holy war underneath Crossroad," Bloodstorm said. "Kept the population numbers down when they couldn't decide whether Aaron preferred *Star Wars* or *Star Trek*."

"None of them even knew what those movies were," I muttered, feeling immense guilt about the whole thing.

"Another sign you make a great god," Jon said.

"Except you are not a god," Susano said. "Not yet. You have not claimed the power of the marks."

"It's complicated," I said, looking at Alek.

"Is it?" Alek asked, giving me no support.

Alek had given me his Mark of the Champion and essentially forfeited his collective divine power and chance to be a god. I hadn't absorbed its energy, though, for multiple reasons. One, I'd nearly been overwhelmed by the previous attempts. Two, I figured it would get Veles to take off the kid gloves and just straight up kill me. A reason that had never been particularly convincing even before Veles had started throwing nukes at us. Third, I didn't want to be a god.

You may not believe the last one, but it was true. I didn't want to return to my boring humdrum life of being an office drone, but I didn't want to be a god. That seemed like way too much work.

"It is the nature of fools to believe the seeking of power is somehow immoral by itself versus how that power should be used," Susanos said.

"No offense, lady, but that would come across a lot more sincere if it wasn't from the second in command to Veles," I replied.

"Told you that the *Star Wars* worshiping ratkin were right," Rachel said to Jon. "That is Aaron's preferred series."

"You haven't seen Aaron drink one beer and then go into a lengthy rant about smashing both Kira and Jadzia from *Deep Space Nine*," Jon said. "I almost respected him after that. It makes me wonder what sort of statues the ratkin will build in their cathedral sewers."

"I told you that in confidence," I muttered to Jon, pausing. "Admittedly, in front of an entire bar of inebriated patrons."

"It wasn't exactly a secret," Ania muttered. "Thanks to you I know far too much about shows I will never watch."

Not the least because there was no such thing as television on Mokosh. The only one that existed had belonged to the late Valentin and broke when I'd accidentally thrown an eldritch blast at it while exercising.

"Yeah, you're not going to make it as a couple," Jon said, shaking his head. "He could handle the fact you're an assassin, but not being able to keep up with his Trekkie-dom? Oof."

I ignored the obvious bait. "Let's focus on the Susanos issue here, people. Defeating Veles is my top priority. Do you know what his plans are for Earth?"

Susanos chuckled, which sounded like a cartoon villain with a reverb. "I know that he wishes to destroy both worlds but in such a way that all the souls of both realities come to him and empower him to be as powerful as Triglav."

"Who is Triglav again?" Alek asked.

"God," I replied. "With a capital G, or at least legally indistinguishable from our mere mortal perspective."

"Technically, I suppose he'd be considered closer to the Demiurge of Gnostic mythology in that he'd be—" Rachel started to explain.

"No other gods would be able to stop Veles if he ascended to overgod status and he would be able to rewrite reality as he sees fit," Susanos said. "An ambitious plan if not for the fact that if the Twisted Gods have truly corrupted his heart, then he will simply end up destroying all reality."

"It would have been so much better if he just intended to conquer the universe by killing it," Ania said.

"Yes," Susanos said. "You will have to return to your world, Aaron Bartkowski. However, you must thwart Belobog's actions here first."

"Why?" I asked, knowing that it probably wasn't because she was afraid that millions would otherwise die.

"Because I live here," Susanos said, lifting a skeletal hand. "For the value of living when you're undead."

"Right," I said, staring at her. "You bring your army and tell the ratkin they'll get what they want."

"Aaron..." Ania trailed off.

"The only delay will be dealing with Veles," I said, staring.

"Excellent," Susanos said, before vanishing. No puff of smoke, no flash of light, or even a swarm of bats. Nope. Just one second she was there and then wasn't.

Ania looked at me. "Are you going to just agree to work with every awful person as long as it brings us closer to Veles' defeat? Maybe? Are you willing to sacrifice your future?"

I stared at her. "I learned it from you. You said we should do everything in our power to defeat him. Even if it meant our deaths. You said there was nothing beyond it."

Ania blinked, opening her mouth then closing it. "Maybe that was before I had something to lose, Aaron."

I shrugged. "Yeah, it seems to be that way, doesn't it?"
I walked off to talk with the kings and Great Mother.

CHAPTER FIVE
THE DEVIL YOU KNOW

The camp for the Grand Allied Ledzianan Army was a collection of mercenaries, conscripts, volunteers, refugees just glad to have a job that fed them, and hangers on. It was, in simple terms, not exactly the biggest bunch of winners you'd ever seen assembled to fight the good fight. However, professional armies were also a distinctly modern invention and getting them up to even this level had been a product of months.

If nothing else, sparing Alek's life had gone a long way to organizing the military as his expertise had proven invaluable. It had cost me dearly as a lot of people hated Alek and justifiably considered him a war criminal.

But you didn't betray family.

No, I wasn't imitating Vin Diesel with that thought.

Much.

One interesting thing about the Grand Allied Ledzianan Army was it was mobile. In addition to horses, a huge chunk of its facilities were wagons and carts aided by magical means. Thanks to the defeat of Zorya Nightbringer, the Sorcerers of the Wind Temple had added their power to the Priestesses of Mokosh as well as the Elf Battlemages. That meant that, logistically, things moved far faster.

I just wasn't sure they'd be fast enough.

Walking into the circles of wagons, tents, and extradimensional houses was a bit like entering into a Renaissance fair or a circus. There were colorful flags, banners, and even cages with enchanted animals. There were other Dark Undermasters and while none of them were as experienced as Ania, my parents had done a pretty good job of recruiting and putting them through boot camp.

"I don't trust the Witch Queen," Ania said, leaning in and whispering to me.

"No kidding," I said, wondering if she thought I did.

"I just hope you're not going to do your thing," Ania said.

I stopped mid-step. "My...thing?"

"Sleeping with relatives?" Jon asked, having resumed his human form.

"That happened once!" I said, referring to Zorya Dawnbringer before I remembered Zorya Nightbringer. Both goddesses were my relatives due to Perun being my great-great-grandfather and the Zoryas being his daughters. "Twice."

"Like I said, sleeping with anyone of divine ancestry is not incest," Rachel said. "Not that I'm dropping hints."

I sighed. "You are so funny, Rachel. But if we're going to hash this out, what do you mean?"

Ania frowned. "I mean, you're not going to try to recruit her, are you?"

"You mean the Witch Queen?" I asked. "No! I draw the line at genocidal dictators."

"Do you?" Ania asked.

"Yes!" I replied.

"Good," Ania said, crossing her arms. "Because I was worried you might try to redeem Veles. I saw the ending of *Return of the Jedi*."

"Veles isn't my father," I said.

"And the *Rise of the Skywalker*," Ania said.

"Dammit, Aaron, why would you do that to her?" Jon asked.

"I'm not Adam Driver either," I replied, remembering how much I hated that movie. "Apparently, genocide can be overlooked when you're sufficiently hot."

"Suzie's a very hot monster!" Jon said, raising his hand. "I offer my services to seduce her back to the side of good."

"She's a skeleton, Jon," Alek said. "The fleshy bits are where the fun is."

"No one asked for your opinion, Solid Snake," Jon said.

"Is that supposed to be an insult?" Alek asked. "Because Solid Snake is awesome."

"I'm trying to figure out one that doesn't make Aaron look awful too. Stupid ridiculously handsome warrior dude. Grumble, grumble," Jon muttered.

Yes, he said "grumble".

"Aaron! You're alive!" A familiar voice spoke, drawing my attention. "Praise Mokosh!"

There were three figures standing nearby, well, eight, including the Royal Guard in their helmeted red plate mail. The person speaking was none other than the Great Mother of the Sisters of Mokosh, Agata Rose. She was a tall and beautiful raven-haired woman wearing a shimmering blue gown that emphasized the fact she was visibly nine months pregnant.

In defiance of the rule that Sisters of Mokosh were not supposed to get married, Agata had broken her oath for a second time and wedded Bloodstorm in secret. Thankfully, it wasn't against the rules anymore since she was now the head of her religion.

Sisters of Mokosh could now get married with special dispensation from the Great Mother. Which, hey, worked out for them. Another reason was that I was jealous of Bloodstorm and Agata. Their marriage and impending parenthood, I mean. It was also why she hadn't been adventuring with us for the past nine months. No, she just had the easier job of leading armies. Man, the gods made the Rose family tough.

Standing beside Agata was King Ivan the Third AKA Ivan Crookback. Ivan was dressed in a military uniform that more resembled a WW1 officer than a medieval fantasy despot. He did, however, have a silver crown that marked him as head of Ledziana. Ivan wasn't the "real" Ivan from the books but a kind of hybrid with the late Prince Cezary. Either that or just a brainwashed Cezary wearing Ivan's old body. He was, however, our ally and someone who'd followed all my "suggestions" on how to win the war.

The third was Captain Crunch.

No, seriously.

Sort of.

King Krunch Wotanson was dressed in a bright blue uniform and a broad Napoleonic hat. While he had no beard, he did possess a gloriously thick white mustache. He was the Lord Admiral of the Dwarvish Navy (they had a lot of ships in the underground oceans of Mokosh) but preferred to go by Captain when on one of his vessels. I'd been certain I was being punked when he first showed up but Captain Crunch had ignored all my vague cereal references. Mostly because there hadn't been an equivalent to John Harvey Kellog here to make breakfast cereal a thing.

"We bid thee greetings, Overmaster," Ivan said, using the royal wee.

"Ahoy, laddies!" Captain Crunch said, waving. "Are ye responsible for the giant forking wave of scalding hot water that splashed me and my ships? If ya were gonna blow up da damn underwater city, I'd wish ya'd told me! I wouldna bothered to break out the wessels."

Yes, that was how he talked. It was the kind of accent that wandered from Pavel Chekov to Scotty with no actual real-life equivalent. It was, however, how dwarves seemed to talk in Ledziana or at least under it.

"That was Veles making use of, uh, an anti-material bomb," I said, deciding not to mention anything about nuclear physics around anyone here. Despite their mostly medieval aesthetic, Ledziana was closer to a magical steampunk society ala Discworld or Eberron when it wasn't suffering a decade long civil war alongside a zombie apocalypse. The idea its sorcerers could figure out how to split the atom with magic and start lobbing nukes at one another wasn't likely, but I'd accidentally triggered a volcanic explosion in my time here, so it wasn't beyond the realm of possibility either.

"Don't worry, we managed to deal with at least a few soggies," Jon said, clearly still finding humor in a joke I thought was long beaten to the ground.

"Ugh," Captain Krunch said, scowling. "Ah forking hate dem damned things. Da naked water spirits and their fornicating filthy flabbing aboot."

Okay, now he was sounding Canadian.

Jon grinned, apparently missing that Captain Krunch was assuming "soggies" was a slur against Rusalka. "In any case, we managed to get all the way to Belobog's chamber before Veles blew the place up. Thankfully, we were rescued by—"

I raised my hand. "By my and Ania's quick thinking."

I wasn't going to be able to hide allying with the Witch Queen from the other monarchs, especially if she showed up with her own personal army of the dead. However, I'd learned a few lessons about diplomacy in the past year and one of them was to never share more information than you must until the ink is dry on any agreement.

Literally.

I was happy to tell Agata and Ivan, but I'd want to speak with Captain Crunch (seriously, I couldn't think of him any other way—I'd tried) in private along with the other monarchs. I just needed the best way to phrase it like, "There's a civil war among Veles forces and we should let them fight like Godzilla versus the Tarrasque." Probably without specifically mentioning those beings in the context of the explanation.

"I mean I was referring to the Witch Queen coming to tell us that Veles has left Mokosh and gone to our home planet," Jon said, completely missing my hint. "Belobog
was left behind with the majority of Veles' undead army, though, so we have to stop him before he destroys Crossroad and then presumably the rest of Ledziana. On the plus side, she's agreed to bring her own horrifying forces to help us against Belobog's minions in a way that in no way probably will result in her backstabbing us at the eleventh hour."

Goddammit Jon.

Agata moved to embrace Bloodstorm before exchanging a short glance with him then turning back to me. "That is a lot, Aaron. Please tell me you haven't decided to pardon the Witch Queen and attempt to redeem her."

"Thank you!" Ania asked, as if agreeing with her sister for the first time in her life.

"No!" I said, offended. "Why does everyone keep asking that?"

"Because it's a very 'you' thing to do," Agata said. "Like the fact you invited our aunt's murderer to join the party."

"I assume you're referring to me," Alek said.

"Sometimes I even imagine I can hear him," Agata said, ignoring Alek. "You also invited Jorg the Bastard Knight who tortured Ania."

"I didn't invite him," I said. "I invited Francine who invited him."

"You forgave your own rapist," Ania added.

"Thistle didn't sexually assault me," I said, pausing. "She just bit me as a vampire-succubus."

"Vampire bites cause immense pleasure as a means of disabling victims," Bloodstorm said. "I'm pretty sure that qualifies. We don't actually nitpick these things on Mokosh."

"Mostly, we just toss vampires on the barbie," Captain Crunch said, now inexplicably Australian sounding. "Burn, baby, burn."

"Oh, and you made Ivan king," Ania said. "Despite him also torturing us."

I paused. "I didn't *make* Ivan king."

"You really did," Ivan said, chuckling. "You could have been the one wearing the crown but you're so allergic to power that you preferred to put the nearest body on the throne versus attempting to rule yourself."

I stared at him. "You also might want to recall the oath you made to do what I say. Especially given what preceded it."

Possibly the worst thing I'd ever done in my life was an act of torture that would have made Spawn or the Punisher blanch. Specifically, I'd killed Ivan before using my newly acquired RAISE DEAD ability to bring him back. It had put the fear of god—or demigod in my case—into him. I wasn't proud of what I'd done but it had gotten Ivan to cooperate on a lot of things.

"I recall it," Ivan said, frowning. "But you should also know that our positions have changed a great deal. You can't just threaten the king."

I stared down at him.

Ivan looked at his bodyguards who looked aside.

"Really?" Ivan asked, clearly disappointed. He should have checked to note that they'd all been hired by Agata.

"Sorry," I said. "But it occurred to me that we may not actually be able to trust you."

Ivan sighed. "It seems I must continue to be your marionette for some time."

"I like your style, Garland," Captain Crunch said. "Wicked and cruel. So, we've got the Skull Bitch on our side and Veles isn't here? That's nothing but good news as far as I'm concerned."

"Not if we can't assemble all our forces to defend Crossroad," I said, frowning.

"Your hometown isn't the war, lad," Captain Crunch said. "Crossroad being lost would be a tragedy but you should also be prepared to lose it."

"Let's burn that bridge after we cross it," I said, noting that I'd spent the past year pouring vast amounts of recovered wealth into building it up into the kind of fortress that could stand against Veles armies.

"Mobilizing all of our forces to arrive in time is going to be the biggest issue," Agata said. "Your attempts to get the Old King's portal network means that we'll be able to get about half of our forces there in time. But I'm not sure we can stand a siege, and everyone else will be cut off then. Destroying Belobog might be the only way to disperse the army."

"My people's navy travels through magic," Captain Crunch said. "But we won't be able to help much in a landlocked city."

"You got them up here," I said, pausing. "Which is more than I expected."

"Sacrificing Crossroad is perhaps the best thing we can do as long as the capital remains intact," Ivan said, showing the kind of attitude that I'd come to expect from him. The irony was Ivan was much better than most aristocrats about the fate of their peasants.

"The capital is past Crossroad," Alek said, pointing out a simple fact of geography. "We can possibly assemble our forces to defend Crossroad, but we can't do it for Akoa. Honestly, the best hope we can have for the capital is hoping the armies of Belobog ignore it to destroy Crossroad. But it's very likely they could smash it on the way."

Ivan stared. "Godsdammit."

"We should have tried to get the nuke from Veles," Jon said, haphazardly. "I think all moral considerations regarding nuclear warfare go out the window when fighting Cthulhu and his army of zombies."

"Eh, if you nuke Cthulhu, he comes back after four rounds and is now radioactive," I sighed. "I don't need to remind you that this is probably a distraction from whatever Veles is planning."

"You're right to worry about your world, Aaron," Ania said, looking at me. "But you should also realize your family is here."

She reached up and touched my face.

"I know," I replied.

Ania kissed me passionately and I kissed her back.

"Ugh, romance," Captain Crunch said. "It wouldn't be so bad if y'all humans weren't so weirdly proportioned."

I pulled away. "I have one more card left to play."

"Ah, yes, the Pwiffle card game," Captain Crunch said, nodding. "I've been wondering if I would get a chance to challenge you to a match."

I took a deep breath. "Not quite. Joan, Rachel, Agata, could you accompany me to the Temple tent? I think we need to contact the gods."

CHAPTER SIX
THE GODS MUST BE CRAZY

The Tent of the Gods was, as you probably could guess, the mobile temple of the Ledzianan army. This was a bit of a sore spot since Mythras worshipers were monotheists, traditional Ledzianans were polytheists, Rus worshiped the Aesir, elves worshiped the three goddesses, and the dwarves of this world only worshiped Svarog even though he was part of a pantheon of his relatives. The Temple of Mythras having been on a "convert by the sword and flame" kick for the past couple of generations hadn't improved relations between the groups either.

Really, the result of my efforts to create peace among the religions had achieved great things. The clerics of virtually every faith believed I was a heretic now and called for my head. It had gone a long way to legitimizing King Ivan III, Agata as Great Mother, and Joan the First of the Temple of Mythras.

Why?

Because every single bad decision and mistake they made could be attributed to my evil influence. I called it "The Rasputin Effect." Well, technically, they were still attributing it to Garland and the Dark Undermasters as a whole. It turned out Dark Undermasters weren't the most popular group in the world, which you'd think it would be since it literally hunted human-eating monsters for a living, but a bunch of dark magic using knights tended to invite paranoia. If we managed to defeat Veles, we'd probably end up suffering the same fate as the Knights Templar. The burned at the stake part, not the becoming Ubisoft villains part.

Either way, my solution for the Tent of the Gods was to basically make it resemble a hospital chapel. Which was to say include a bunch of vaguely spiritual things like candles, altars, and pews while not actually putting in any explicit references. It offended everyone who was genuinely religious, including people in my party (*cough* Agata, Joan *cough), so I knew I was doing something right. There were a couple of people currently praying here and one Mythran priest preaching that every single person who worshiped another god than Mythras was going to die.

"Alright, everyone out!" I said, entering through the tent flaps. "Private meeting for the people out to save the world."

An old toothless grandmother who helped with the army's wash spit on the ground in front of me and said something in a language not even the Mark of the Champion could translate before walking past me.

The red priest pointed at Joan and said, "You have disgraced the faith of the god and lay down with heretics, False One! Our god will punish you with eternal damna—"

"POLYMORPH OTHER," I said, pointing at him.

The red priest transformed into a rabbit before my eyes, looking scared and confused before hopping away.

"Aaron!" Joan said, looking up. "That was not good."

"At some point, I stopped giving a shit," I said, trying to access my mark's menu and only getting static. "Anyway, I set the polymorph to wear off after a few minutes. Hopefully, no one will turn him into hassenpfeffer in the meantime."

"I think that was one of the more liberal Mythran priests," Agata said, watching him depart.

"Good job, Aaron!" Rachel said, cheerfully. "You're finally getting into the spirit of being a god."

Joan sighed. "A split among the Mythrites seems inevitable. I don't know how the faith is going to survive if we do not possess unity."

I paused. "Yeah, I've got some news for you, I'm pretty sure that religions fighting one another is normal. Yes, including ones that worship the same god and who are arguing over nothing."

Joan looked up. "That makes no sense."

"Yes, you'd think their god would intervene," Agata said, appalled.

Jon flew into the tent and landed on a nearby pew's back. "Yeah, well, second hottest pregnant lady after Demi Moore, our world operates by different rules."

"I was wondering when you'd get around to that one," I said to Jon.

Agata looked annoyed, which was her natural state anyway.

"I was saving it until she was showing enough," Jon said. "Fun fact: birth-related mortality is almost zero in this world because of magic.

"Yes, we've established your world is terrible. Especially for women," Agata said, illustrating the old proverb about the grass always being greener.

Except the opposite of it.

"Hey, some women have it good," Jon said, pausing. "I'm pretty sure Madonna is okay. Jennifer Lopez is doing well. The Queen of England."

"She died," I pointed out.

"What?" Jon asked. "No! What will happen to her dogs?"

I shook my head. "Let's focus on what we're here for."

Great, now I was wondering if the dogs had been buried with her like the Pharaohs.

"Which is?" Joan asked, looking up.

"You want to summon the other gods," Agata said. "As if they were individuals who were yours to bring forth."

I shrugged. "It's more like a family chat."

"Do you really think they'd answer?" Agata asked.

"They will," Rachel said, surprising me. "Joan has the ability to summon her god for an audience and my mother will come for Aaron."

Agata frowned.

"He is as close to Perun as exists right now," Rachel interrupted. "You could probably summon her as well, Great Mother."

"I'm hesitant..." Agata muttered. "I have broken my sacred oaths twice."

"I do not believe my mother would hold your marriage against you," Rachel said. "After all, she was married twice. She would probably bless your child as well."

Agata smiled. "Thank you."

"She'd also probably want to have sex with you and your husband," Rachel said.

Agata's eyes widened.

"Not to question the physics of how sex at this stage works but is it like a medicine ball between you and Bloodstorm or...AH!" Jon said.

This time, it was Joan flinging a book at him. She'd picked it up from one of the pews. I was really surprised at how many books they had in the Southern Kingdoms. Apparently, the printing press was one of the steampunk (Clockpunk? Powderpunk? Sailpunk?) things that separated it from the medieval era.

"We're running out of time and while prayer is usually a last resort, I want to see if we can get any help we can," I said, before adding, "Besides, with Veles gone, they might be more willing to directly intervene."

"You realize that's directly accusing the gods of cowardice, right?" Rachel said, raising an eyebrow.

"I'm not accusing them of cowardice," I said. "I'm accusing them of *apathy*."

Yeah, I'd gone from being an atheist to a believer to a guy deeply frustrated with the divine. I liked some of the gods, Mokosh and Rachel in particular, but only Perun had shown himself willing to get their hands dirty in the fight against Veles. Admittedly, this had resulted in Perun dying and being unable to be reborn. So maybe they had a reason to be wary about trying to fight a creator deity head on.

"They'll also accuse you of cowardice and apathy," Rachel said, softly.

"Is that your opinion?" I asked, knowing Rachel was a god.

"You are not a coward, Aaron," Rachel said. "You are, however, afraid of godhood."

"We need a new Perun," Agata said. "Perhaps you are the one who is destined for that role."

I stared at her, trying to figure out how to respond without yelling. "I'm not Perun."

"No," Rachel said. "You're not nearly as big an asshole as my other father."

Joan drew a line in the dirt in front of the tent flaps and cast a barrier spell in the language of the Empire. She'd learned how to cast spells by just saying their name—

something that should be impossible for anyone but a mark wielder—but defaulted to the "old" style of elaborate incantations when she had time to do them.

"There, that should keep any unexpected visitors from arriving," Joan said, looking at Jon. "Well, other than the ones we already have."

"You're going to rule high school when you grow up dear," Jon said. "Regina George will have nothing on you."

"Aaron showed me that movie on his magic box," Joan said. "The one who looked like Ania apparently became an alchemical powder addict?"

"Eh, I don't see the resemblance," Jon said. "Eh, other than hot redhead who would rule the local prison."

I sighed and walked up to the center of the tent. "Okay, here goes nothing. HEY YOU GUYS, CAN WE TALK!"

All the other tent occupants looked at me with skepticism.

"What?" I asked.

Jon covered up his face with a wing.

"We're here," spoke a surprising voice, a male with a slight Imperial accent.

Standing there in front of the tent altar were three figures. The first of them was a spectacularly handsome golden-skinned man with black hair and eyes with glowing golden irises. He was ripped in a way that would make most body-builders envious and sported the armor of an Imperial Centurion. A pair of laurels rested around his head despite the fact he was a Persian deity rather than a Roman one. Well, originally. Mythras was an imported deity the same way the

Abrahamic God was. I didn't think anything of it since I was an immigrant to Ledziana. I admitted, though, there was a humorous element in that he distinctly resembled Tom Cruise and was a little on the short side, despite having a ripped body.

Next to Mythras was the ravishing beauty of Mokosh, Goddess of Love, Motherhood, and the world that carried her name. Mokosh was notably an idealized beauty for the standards of her world as opposed to Western sensibilities back on Earth. Which was a sideways way of saying Mokosh was short, plump, and had plenty in both the front as well in the back. She was dressed in a sheer toga. Modesty was not a quality that she possessed or had passed to any of her children.

I'd only seen the third figure in visions but never actually met in person. The resemblance to Mythras was tremendous in terms of how they were built but utterly absent in the face. It was Svarog, who was a bit on the homely side and resembled John Rhys Davies' Gimli. He was bare-chested save for a forgemaster's leather apron and he wore a pair of dirty linen pants. Unlike Mythras, he also proudly boasted many scars and burns across his torso, something he might have avoided if he'd worn a shirt while forging. I couldn't tell what his eyes looked like because he had a pair of anachronistic blackened goggles on his face.

Joan and Agata got on their knees. Rachel stood.

"Hey," I said, waving.

"You could at least bow, Aaron," Mokosh said. "Really? Hey?"

"Sorry," I said. "But you didn't exactly go all out on this either. No angels, no 'be not afraid', or burning bush."

"You also summoned us in the middle of a non-denomination tent by shouting," Mythras said. "The least you could have done is sacrifice a bull."

"Seriously, what is with you and bulls?" Svarog asked.

"I hate bulls," Mythras said. "They're ornery, smelly, and nasty creatures."

"Yeah, but you can't have a barbecue without them," Svarog said, clearly not being a pork or chicken man. "In any case, Aaron, consider this a onetime acknowledgement of your heroism. If you want to seek our counsel again, you'll have to come to us."

"You want me to come to Heaven?" I asked.

"Sky Realm," Mokosh explained. "Which is their home not mine. I live here on Mokosh. Sky Realm is the home of the gods. Heaven is where good humans go and that's in the Underworld. Seriously, Christianity is like 50% wrong in terms of the planes and it's all Dazhbog's fault."

"I don't acknowledge that name anymore," Mythras said. "Also, they were ripping me off! I could have been huge, but Constantine just had to see that damn cloud shaped like a cross.

Wow, that was a deep cut.

"Try a game called *Planescape*," Mokosh said, pointing at me. "It's a setting by the board game people and is 85% how reality actually works."

"That is horrifying," I said, without missing a beat. "Wait, is Odin going to show up? He's the only other god I know and I was hoping he'd involve himself."

I'd met him briefly during the whole Rus incident and things had gone badly when Freya had decided to make him jealous.

And Thor's mom.

Who was Mokosh.

Yeah.

Awkward.

"Wotan is sitting this one out," Mythras said, annoyed. "He's still pissed at you for preventing the apocalypse."

"He's mad at me for *preventing the apocalypse*?" I asked, confused.

"There's only so long you can wait for the end of the world before you want to get it over with," Mokosh explained. "They've been torturing Veles' avatar in Loki for centuries and his escape should have been the start of things."

"No kidding," I said, not even bothering to note that Veles and Loki had no connection in normal mythology. Same with Mythras and Dazhbog. Sometimes I honestly thought the gods were less the actual beings they claimed to be and more like the Vorlons. You know, aliens who were pretending to be gods and just claiming the names of whoever was convenient.

All three of the gods stared at me.

Rachel facepalmed.

"Right," I said, looking away. "I need to learn to block my thoughts, don't I?"

"Yes, Aaron," Mokosh said. "Either way, we're willing to help you against Belobog and his armies. However, there's a quid pro quo necessary to maintain universal balance."

Why was I not surprised?

"We can transport all of your armies through portals to Crossroad and allow you to fight them directly," Mokosh said. "You know, despite the fact that you made my sacred lake radioactive for the next hundred years."

"That was Veles!" I said. "I mean, probably. I'm pretty sure the Witch Queen arranged that whole thing."

Svarog nodded. "You're on the money there, Aaron. We knew after Veles and Mokosh divorced that he was going to do something stupid. Hooking up with a gold-digging Goth chick, though? I knew that she was going to end up fucking him over in the end. She was always in the mood for a magical sugar daddy."

"So much of the world makes more sense now that I know what the gods are like," Jon said. "It was a real mistake having religion depict you guys as perfect non-anthropomorphized beings."

"Blame Mythras," Mokosh said. "Seriously, it's his hanging around the Romans. All the ego of the Greek gods and then trying to whitewash the flaws away. No, Ares, I'm not going to forget what a douchebag you were just because you're calling yourself Mars now."

Mythras glared at her.

Joan whispered to Agata. "Do the gods just appear this way because it's how Aaron sees them?"

"Yes," Agata said. "That is what I'm telling myself at least."

"We will also send you—after you have defeated Belobog—to Earth along with your friends," Mokosh said. "My sister, Mat Zemalya, has been bound by Veles magic. He gained enough strength from me to be able to hold her down while also blinding us from what is going on there."

"How do you know what he did if he blinded you?" Jon asked.

"Magic," Mokosh said, in an "ask a stupid question, get a stupid answer" way.

"Ah," Jon said.

"What do you want in exchange?" I asked, suspicious of their generosity.

"We are almost restored," Mokosh said. "But I want my daughter back. For that, we need a new host for Zorya Nightbringer. Agata, you have a child on the way."

Agata's eyes widened in horror.

CHAPTER SEVEN
YOUR FIRST BORN

I didn't get a chance to react to the outrageous statement by the gods before Agata, the most noble and self-sacrificing of us, answered for us.

"Get fucked!" Agata growled, hissing at the deities.

"Yeah," Jon said. "I think the story in the Torah went slightly different. Mind you, I imagine in the original Hebrew, Abraham was told by God that it was 'just a prank, bro.'"

I looked at Jon. "Honestly, that actually is how it ends."

"Really?" Jon asked.

"With a lamb and everything," I replied. "It also has the historical context of being a statement that the Hebrew wasn't going to require human sacrifice unlike the contemporary Assyrian and Canaanite faiths."

"Shut up!" Agata said, looking at me. "We are not giving up my child."

I looked at her confused before remembering my neuroatypical qualities could sometimes be construed as callousness. "No, obviously not. Sorry, that's a dealbreaker and I stand by Agata."

"You would put the life of a single unborn child up against the tens of thousands of people who will die otherwise?" Svarog asked.

I paused. "Yeah."

"All because she is your friend?" Svarog asked.

"I mean, I'd probably not be down with human sacrifice either way," I replied. "We're also pretty far along development wise and she's protective of her child to be so that kind of eliminates any grey area—"

"Don't drive away half your audience, Aaron," Jon said.

"Right," I said, sucking in my breath. "I have Agata's back and I think if you start compromising your values on one thing, you'll start compromising them on—"

"Take me instead," Joan said, standing up. "I will gladly give up my life for the people of Ledziana."

"No," Mythras said. "I am not sacrificing my Chosen One so that my cousin, Zorya Nightbringer, can live again."

"I failed you, milord," Joan said, looking down at the ground. "I was willing to make a deal with that odious harlot in order to bring back my deceased mother. I must atone and will do anything to prove myself again."

"So, your idea of atoning for working for Nightchilde," I said, referring to her by her human avatar's name, "is to help resurrect her?"

Joan blinked.

"Also, it would be the second inappropriate body that a goddess Aaron banged would be stuck in," Jon said.

"Who is he?" Svarog asked.

"Aaron's court jester," Mokosh replied.

"Ah," Svarog said. "I thought some random village idiot had wandered in that somehow transformed into a raven."

"I am not random!" Jon interjected. "The rest is a fair cop."

"Yes," Rachel said. "Aaron should sire a child so it can become the new Nightbringer."

"Wait, what?" I asked.

"Don't worry, I'm not volunteering to bear the child," Rachel said. "That would be weird."

"Oh, yes, *that's* what would make it weird," I said, appalled.

"I seem to recall humans being less insolent in the old days," Svarog said.

"What old days?" Mythras asked. "You predate the human race by billions of years."

"Pfft," Svarog said. "I'm older than that."

"Only two of them are human," Mokosh said, referring to the odd mixture of our group.

"Which is absolutely nothing if they cannot defeat Veles," Svarog said. "Mokosh might be arguing that the new Nightbringer might be raised over decades with love and affection, but we need her now if we're going to defeat my brother."

I paused. "No offense intended—"

"But you're about to say something offensive," Svarog said, crossing his arms.

I raised my hands in surrender. "Probably. No offense but, uh, what have you guys been doing until now?"

Agata, Joan, and Rachel looked horrified.

Mokosh smirked.

Mythras glared in anger.

Svarog just gazed at me for a long time before bursting into laughter. "You wonder if we've just been sitting on our asses during your battle with our brother."

"Yeah, kinda," I said, pausing. "I mean, Mokosh at least provided some help."

"Sexual healing," Jon said, nodding. "Marvin Gaye. Bow chicka wow, wow."

Svarog took a deep breath. "The answer to your question is that I have been keeping the Twisted Gods imprisoned. Perun sacrificed much of his power to bind them but with him being, you know, dead, it required me to step up to prevent them from escaping again. I also didn't realize my brother was corrupted by them until recently."

"You didn't realize your brother was corrupted by the anti-gods even when he was openly talking about killing everyone in the universe to rule the dead?" I asked.

"He was always an asshole," Svarog said. "To be honest, threatening to dominate the living and the dead was always in his wheelhouse."

I didn't want to comment on the fact Svarog probably should have taken notice of

what Veles was up to after he'd killed Perun. However, as we'd found out with the gods, they tended to have a slightly less human attitude toward death and rebirth than, well, humans. "Okay, I'm going to admit keeping the Twisted Gods imprisoned is probably a good thing."

Mokosh and Svarog both noticeably gave Mythras side-eye. It would have been hilarious if we weren't dealing with terrifying temperamental beings that might obliterate us with a stray thought.

"Oh, we're wondering what I'm doing now?" Mythras said. "What deeds my glorious empire has been doing to hold back the tide of darkness?"

"Yeah, kinda," I said.

To be honest, Mythras was the wild card in all of this. I was bitterly disappointed the Aesir weren't even showing up for battling Veles' forces but that was mostly because Marvel comics had predisposed me to believing they weren't a bunch of selfish assholes. No, it turned out the people who had favored raiding all of Europe for centuries weren't necessarily heroic protectors of the innocent.

Mythras, however, had traditionally been a god of heroism. He slew the bull, which was Veles' symbol, and had been a god of soldiers. Unfortunately, despite everything Joan had done, I hadn't seen much from him. Dazhbog, his other identity, had been the sole second generation god who had avoided being corrupted into one of the elemental demons. As for the Holy Eastern Empire? Well, they'd proven to be more like the Galactic Empire than, I dunno, some theoretical empire that wasn't full of dicks.

Mythras stared at me. "I've been biding my time."

"Biding your time?" I asked, staring.

"Aaron, please don't insult my god," Joan said.

"No, I actually am with the fake Garland on this," Svarog said, showing a hint of his real opinion of me. "What *have* you been doing, son?"

"Refer to Aaron by his true name, Father. Garland never killed gods," Mokosh said, coming to my defense. "Aaron's accomplishments exceed those of the Black Rose."

"Yeah, the Steel Rose," Svarog said, making air quotes with his fingers. "He sounds like a hair metal band frontman."

Svarog had an odd awareness of music genres. Then again, as a creator god, he probably knew more about everything than I'd ever know.

"I mean, that is true," Jon said, throwing in his two cents.

"Garland could have slain gods," Agata said, looking down. "Please don't insult my late husband."

"He was a good man," Mokosh said, pausing. "I mean, good-ish. Like, it took him an hour to cheat on you."

"Wait, what?" Agata asked.

"When he woke up after your consummation, he ended up in the local river with some Rusalka," Mokosh said. "The rest of the week was worse. He cavorted with succubus Nikkole, the tavern maiden where you got married, her sister—"

Agata stared in horror.

"This is why every married couple should never include vows of monogamy," Mokosh said, pointing at her. "It's just messed up. You should know this as one of my priestesses."

"I wanted him to be sleeping with *me*!" Agata said, crossing her arms.

"So, back to Mythras," I said, horrified at that entire line of conversation. It explained so much about the state of Ledziana.

"Veles is a far more powerful god than me," Mythras said, calmly. "I couldn't trust my father to aid me against him."

"That's cold, son," Svarog said. "But fair."

"I would only get one shot," Mythras said. "I probably would lose in a battle with him after Perun's defeat, but I could perhaps cripple him. The threat of that allowed me to maneuver Veles and keep him from making some of his more overt moves. At least until he was strong enough to crush me outright. In the meantime, I empowered individuals to work against him on my behalf and protected Veles' enemies."

"The Wise Man," I said, pausing. I still didn't know how I felt about his death. He'd put me in this situation and manipulated countless people to do his bidding, getting a lot of good people killed, but the guy had been doing it to save the world. Also, he was a formative part of my teenage years' reading (probably not a good reason to ignore the murders).

"Yes," Mythras said. "Between Mokosh and me, that's a large reason why Veles was forced to do his ridiculous quest game against the champions."

"Mostly me," Mokosh said. "It is a sign of just how far Veles has gone that he no longer feels obligated to obey the oaths he made to both you and the Wise Man in order to finish the fight between your proxies. It was a duel of honor made between champions and his fleeing the field of battle forfeits any claim of honor."

"Yeah," I said, pausing. "I'm sure that was his chief concern when destroying all life. How honorable it would be."

Mokosh smirked.

"Speaking of the Wise Man, uh, where is Larry?" I asked, looking around.

"The Wise Man is the one who opened the gates to your world to let Veles leave," Svarog said.

"What?" I asked, staring.

"Yes, what?" Agata asked.

"Plot twist!" Jon said, spreading out his wings.

"The Chosen of Perun was only interested in playing the game as long as he was the one directing the pieces," Svarog said, his voice disdainful. "The moment that you proved far more intractable than the other champions was the moment that the Wise Man began to look for alternative pawns."

That was a kick in the butt. "So, just because I wasn't completely controllable, he decided to join up with the person who he is opposed to?"

"I assume that Larry thinks that he's playing a deeper game," Mokosh said. "But Veles' cunning is greater than the last druid's."

Svarog shook his head. "It's also possible that he simply sees getting Veles to your world as a way of winning. After all, it is officially not his problem."

"My theory is that he's so sick of people wanting the next book out that he's decided to have Veles destroy Earth," Rachel said.

Everyone looked at her.

"What?" Rachel asked. "The next manuscript was still being written when Garland died. Andrzej Sapkowski has gotten like three books out for *The Witcher* saga while we waited for the next Dark Undermaster book. Just release the goddamn thing."

I decided to try making a big speech. "Listen, the people of the Southern Kingdoms need your help. Now is not the time to hold back or make deals. You love your followers, I know this, and are all exemplars of what mankind can be. Show the people of the world that you have their back and they will worship you. Restore their faith in you by providing them the miracle they need, not necessarily one they deserve."

"Okay," Mokosh said.

"Sure, why not?" Svarog said.

"Yeah," Mythras said.

I blinked. "Oh, well, thanks."

That was when Joan and Agata vanished.

Jon squawked in surprise.

Rachel didn't look surprised in the slightest.

"What the..." I trailed off.

"They've been sent to Crossroad with the rest of the armies," Mokosh explained. "It's best if they don't know the truth."

"The truth?" I asked.

"Yes," Mokosh said. "I was trying to disguise the fact that Zorya Nightbringer has already been merged with her child."

I stared in horror. "Please don't take her child away from her."

Mokosh shook her head. "Never."

"Provided you do what we say," Svarog said. "The needs of the many and all that. War destroys thousands of lives and whatever brings it to a close the fastest is almost inevitably the greatest good."

"What do you want me to do?" I asked.

"Defeating Belobog is important," Svarog said. "Restoring him will cut off Veles from the last of his support on this world. However, we can't take the chances that he might have an agent working both sides of the equation. Before we transport you and your team's survivors back to Earth to save it, we need you to eliminate the Witch Queen."

"Betray her before she betrays us," I said, feeling disgusted by all the backstabbing around me.

"Yes," Svarog said.

"We also want you to kill the Wise Man but that's a lower priority," Mythras said.

Yeah, I didn't like the gods anymore.

"Right," I said, reluctantly agreeing.

With that, they vanished, and Jon and I were left alone in the Temple.

Jon looked at me. "You know, with allies like these, who needs enemies?"

"I agree, bird," I said, sighing. "I agree."

CHAPTER EIGHT
CONFRONTING MY ENEMY

I took a deep breath. "So, just so we're clear, Weis is working with Veles now."

"Uh huh," Jon said, flying onto my shoulder. "Though he's probably doing some three-dimensional chess thing because the alternative is he's being a complete moron or traitor. Neither of which fits with my concept of the guy."

I wasn't sure about it either way because Larry had done a lot of shady things in our short association, up to and including bringing me to Mokosh in the first place. Unfortunately, events taught me that Larry was no different than most of the people in charge of the supernatural on this world. The gods were, in simple terms, shady as shit. The problem was that didn't necessarily make them wrong as even my attempts to be Captain Superman of Paladinland™ (to quote Jon) hadn't always shielded me from having to do things I was disgusted with myself for,

Indeed, Veles and I had once had a conversation where he'd said that was the inevitable destiny of all so-called heroes in the Southern Kingdoms. The world was so toxic and full of hate that it would eventually corrupt me.

"We're working with the Witch Queen," I said, pointing out a fact I was already uncomfortable with before we got to the next bit.

"Yes, but we're going to betray her because nothing says heroics like stabbing your allies in the back," Jon said.

"Yes," I replied. "Even if I should feel okay about it because she's really, really bad."

"You are telling me that or are you telling yourself?" Jon asked.

"Yes," I replied.

I sighed and decided to use Fast Travel to transport myself and Jon back to Crossroad Keep. Unfortunately, I found myself blocked from using it. Worse, the entirety of the interface was flickering and static-ky, which was confusing since it wasn't an electronic device but a magical approximation of one.

Perun, in our short time together, had stated that he'd made it so the Mark of the Champions functioned like a video game RPG because it was the easiest way he could communicate how he was strengthening me via his magic. The idea—at least as much as you could call it one was—that it'd be a waste of Perun's dwindling power to just give it all to someone that looked like they'd make a good hero only for them to switch sides like Valentin had.

Instead, the whole leveling-up thing was based on the idea that heroes had to earn their power-ups. The more heroics they did, the more they would be rewarded with power. This would also have the side benefit of restoring at least some of Perun's power in the process. Him being the god of heroism and all that.

All in all, the whole thing had proven to be a terrible idea, and I was now the last of the champions. Alek was still alive, but he'd surrendered his mark to me. Jon was alive-ish but he'd given up his humanity to become a dragon (assuming you counted going from being a raven/hawk/storm crow thing to a dragon as losing your humanity). Neither of them wanted the remaining marks back and were encouraging me to become a "full" god.

Probably so they didn't have to.

"On that you are correct, my dear nephew," a voice that chilled my blood spoke nearby. It was a voice that had haunted my nightmares despite the brave front that I'd put up since I'd come to Fantasy Poland™.

I looked up. "Veles."

Standing there in the Temple of the Gods was the Peter Stormare avatar of the evil god. He wasn't dressed as he was before with his thick beard and robes but, instead, was clean shaven and in a finely tailored white business suit. He even had a Panama hat and looked like one of those drug lords Mel Gibson or Arnold would kill in the Eighties.

"Indeed," Veles said, adjusting himself. "I see you've managed to avoid getting burnt to a cinder."

"Yeah, well, I'm hoping I'm not thoroughly riddled with cancer either," I replied. "Are you responsible for the mark acting up?"

He smirked. "I imagine the copious doses of radiation are doing more to achieve that than anything else. Elemental forces are one of the few things that can mess with the power of the gods. You probably should have absorbed that divine energy earlier. Now who knows what might happen when you try."

"I'm in no rush to be a god," I said, staring at him. "I thought you were on Earth now."

"This is a mere fragment of a fragment," Veles replied. "Even a creator god can have difficulty projecting his consciousness across vast swaths of the cosmos. Still, I thought I'd provide you a goodbye."

"I'm coming after you," I said, coldly.

"How?" Veles asked, sounding as threatened by my promise as he would be by a mouse. "You don't really think the other gods are going to let you travel to Earth, do you?"

I stared at him. "I'm pretty sure they know you'll continue to be a threat to them, what with the whole desire to wipe out life on two worlds."

Veles smirked. "A thing you'll have to learn, Aaron, is that there's no such thing as a good billionaire and every god is fundamentally many times richer. My brother was the only one willing to die for this world and the others are too interested in covering their own ass to risk their powers. Now that I'm no longer on Mokosh, they'll do their best to keep you here until they can seal off any avenues back to your world. I know because they're already doing it."

I shook my head. "You'll forgive me if I call bullshit. You haven't exactly done much to convince me of your trustworthiness."

Jon's beady little eyes stared at him. "Yeah, you've kind of rage-quit the game, That's just poor sportsmanship, dude."

Veles chuckled. "In the end, the game was only as valuable as the promises I made to play fair. Once that meant a great deal to me, promises and fair play. However, something has eaten away at that feeling. The Modern Age is not one where a deal is a deal anymore. The dream of honoring one foes is dead. Instead, there is only victory."

I shook my head. "It's the Twisted Gods' influence, Veles. You must see that. You tried to use their power against them, and it's been rotting your mind just like the other Old Gods. We need to purge it so you can..."

"Oh, Triglav Above," Veles said, shaking his head. "You're actually doing it."

"What?" I asked.

"Now I have to pay Larry a free resurrection," Veles said, snorting. "I suppose he'll need it."

"I don't understand," I said.

"He said you'd actually try to redeem me," Veles said, staring at me. "That you'd make some sort of half-hearted speech about there still being good in me and that I should return to the light side or whatnot."

"Is it working?" I asked.

"No," Veles said.

"Darn," I said, not really surprised. "Also, it's not half-hearted. It really is an appeal to end this now. If you can stop this whole thing, you should."

Veles stared at me. It was like having frozen lightning bolts shot through my chest. If that makes no sense as a metaphor, take note that having your soul gazed through by a god of evil isn't easy to describe. "Aaron, did it ever occur to you that this isn't some mystical hogwash about brainwashing from even eviler gods? That I simply grew disgusted with humanity's constant never-ending idiocy and decided to try something new? Modern humanity has had a hundred thousand years to finally get itself in order and it has gotten worse. My plan to destroy the existing worlds which I created with my brothers and then stick their occupants' souls in the realm of the dead where things will be properly ordered isn't new. It is the promise of most apocalyptic religions. Fulfilling this problem is a decision which I reached after careful deliberation."

"Humanity has potential it is only now reaching!" I said, staring. "We've gone—"

"No speeches, Aaron, please," Veles cut me off. "I am not Q and you are not Captain Picard."

I was silenced. "What are you doing to my world?"

"Fixing it," Veles said, amused. He pulled on the folds of his jacket. "I'm president of the United States now."

I stared at him. "Bullshit."

"Hail to the Chief," Veles said, sarcastically.

"You can't do that!" Jon said, pointing at Veles with one of his wings. "You weren't born in the United States!"

"I know!" Veles said, covering his mouth with his palm. "I lied. While you were distracted preparing for the big final battle with us that was never going to come, I decided to transfer my elite followers to your world. It doesn't take much to cause a crisis in your world. Humans, no matter what world they inhabit, are scared little monkeys who seek out the strongest among them to protect them whenever things go wrong. The return of magic was the perfect event to plunge your world into chaos."

Veles filled my mind filled with images of monsters tearing through cities, creatures rising from the dead, and the appearance of powers among the public. It was a full Marvel Cinematic Universe of chaos that I'd been missing. There was a massive crater where the National Mall had previously been and big black banners hanging from the White House. If this was a lie pushed by Veles then he'd thought it out very clearly.

"Why?" I asked. "Why want to be president?"

"I mean, you'd be better than some in living memory but while I support your bring back magic policy, I don't support your kill everyone course of action," Jon replied. "Also, is this meant to be political? Because if Larry C.C. Weis has decided to go political, I think he should avoid dating it. That whole Dragon Queen takes over a city and it's like the Iraq Occupation was the worst part of the last Dark Undermaster book. He should have kept the planned time skip. No wonder the sequels took so long."

I shook my head. "You're planning, what, to nuke the planet?"

"Nukes are far too 1950s," Veles said. "Even if I did help invent them in hopes that you would destroy yourselves. No, Aaron, I have something far more special planned."

"What?" I asked.

"Oh, like I'm going to tell you," Veles said, rolling his eyes. "Seriously, do I look like a comic book villain?"

I stared at him.

"Don't answer that," Veles muttered.

I narrowed my eyes. "So, what, this is whole Bond villain thing you're doing here is just to gloat?"

"Kind of, yes," Veles said, shrugging. "You've come farther than any of the other champions and actually put me on the back foot for a bit. You deserve an 'attaboy' and a 'good dog' for that. However, I do want to let you know you won't be able to do a damn thing to stop this now."

"Uh huh," I said, shaking my head. "Somehow I think if you could have killed me, you would have."

"Don't get cocky." Veles pointed at me. "You're doomed but here is one thing you should note: you do have an out."

"An out," I said, not changing my earlier opinion of him. I was only talking because he'd failed to kill me so far.

"You have all the remaining Marks of the Champion," Veles said. "Absorb them, become a god and take some of the people you care about to Sky Realm. Do the whole Biblical Rapture thing and spare them their horrific deaths. You'll be able to claim at least a partial victory, and I'll let you be."

"This is just the Architect scene from the *Matrix Reloaded*," Jon said. "The Wachowski Sisters never should have made any sequels."

"I'm not going to abandon the fight," I said, staring at him. "Which you know. So, I wonder what you're up to here."

Veles smirked. "My motivations are beyond your comprehension, nephew. However, if you need a reason then note that it amuses me. When I finally hold your broken, battered, and disillusioned body before me. When I have crushed your friends, shattered your dreams, and made you aware of just how utterly worthless it all was, I want you to know that you could have saved your beautiful harlots and minions from damnation. Instead, they will be imprisoned with the worst of oath breakers and scum for all eternity."

I gave him a golf clap. "Very nice. I give it an 8.5 on the monologue scale."

Veles frowned. "You've grown more insolent over the past year."

"I know," I said. "I blame success."

"Also, admitting you're an oathbreaker while you are punishing oathbreakers is pretty hypocritical," Jon said. "Are you sure you're not brainwashed? Because if you are, we can have you defeat Darth Malak and return to the Light Side."

"Darth Malak, really?" I asked. "Not Vader or even Kylo Ren?"

"I feel like the original trilogy is too obvious a reference and the sequels suck eggs," Jon said. "So, I decided to go with *Knights of the Old Republic*. Darth Revan gets Bastilla or Carth and lives happily ever after despite being Space Napoleon."

"Goodbye, Aaron," Veles said. "Allow me to leave you a parting gift. One to let you know just how utterly doomed you are."

I made a "yap, yap, yap" gesture with my fingers. Veles was on the run now and that was not something I was going to let him take away from me. He'd been mocking me and dismissing me since the beginning of our situation. The tables had turned, though, and I was confident we could cross the finish line with him.

That was when Veles dropped the glamour, and I saw the portly form of Larry C.C. Weis. However, the man had been subjected to horrific torture as blood covered every inch of his body. He'd been stabbed, burned, flayed, and maimed. His body fell to the ground in front of me, lifeless, and broken.

"The next time, this will be you," Veles said through Larry's mouth. With that, Veles' presence vanished.

"Larry," I said, going to his side.

I tried CURE, RAISE DEAD, and more. I even attempted to contact his soul by prayer, which wasn't a thing I could do without the proper spells but was worth a try.

Nothing worked.

"Huh," Jon said, looking down at the corpse of the Wise Man. "I guess we're never getting those books finished now. I wonder if we should ask Brandon Sanderson to finish them."

"Not right now, Jon," I said, looking at the man who had brought me to Ledziana. "He deserved better than this."

"Did he?" Jon asked. "I ended up pretty okay but what about the rest of his enslaved ravens? My friend, Becky? A lot of good people tried and died to save this place. His final act was to help Veles move to Earth. I'm going to say that was a dick move to go out on."

I checked his body.

"Be careful, corpses crap themselves when they die," Jon said.

"I've seen enough to know that," I replied.

"Right." Jon said. "What are you looking for? It's not like the guy is going to be left with—"

I pulled out a letter that said, "To Aaron in the Case of My Death."

"Oh, you've got to be kidding me," Jon said.

I opened it up to read.

CHAPTER NINE
LETTERS FROM THE DEAD

Veles was an asshole.

This was something that he'd already established with his whole "kill the world" philosophy and contemptuous attitude toward everyone. Plus, there was the constant low-level cheating that he'd engaged in throughout our attempts to overthrow him. Cheating that had graduated to incorporating nukes and rage-quitting. However, doing what he'd done to Larry C.C. Weis dug the hole a bit deeper and cost me my little remaining respect for the man.

My feelings regarding the Wise Man were complicated. As Jon said, he'd done a lot of shady stuff that had resulted in needless suffering for numerous people. Perhaps I was too forgiving. Which, honestly, was a bit like saying that Mario jumped a lot or Link liked green hoodies, but I was willing to overlook quite a bit. Yet, Larry had killed the Dragon Queen because he didn't think she had what it took to defeat Veles. This had driven my cousin insane with revenge and led to the deaths of many of Larry' allies. He'd also set me up to become lovers with Zorya Dawnbringer and reincarnate her but only after forcing me to kill her. Explicitly making me the murderer of the mother of my child (however much Rachel denied she was my daughter in any way).

Larry had also done something worse than both of those things—at least from my perspective—in that he'd undermined his own cause by refusing to trust anyone with the whole picture. If Larry had really wanted to save Mokosh then he should have shared what he had planned with the people he was trying to maneuver. Instead, he'd kept it all extremely close to his chest and now I wasn't sure what he'd been planning.

Except what was in this letter that I was now opening. "Maybe this holds the key to his plans."

"Did you learn dialogue from Writing 101?" Jon asked. "Also, please tell me you don't believe that letter is actually from Weis."

"Maybe it's his last message to me," I said, offended.

"That Veles didn't notice when he was torturing him before wearing his body like a condom?" Jon asked.

"I don't think that last metaphor was needed," I replied. "You think this is a trap?"

"I think that our insides might still be liquifying because Veles used a nuke on us after planting it in the penultimate boss chamber," Jon said. "At this point, I wouldn't be surprised if Veles paid your ex-girlfriend to reveal your secret identity so she could do porn and buy drugs."

"Nice *Daredevil* reference," I said, referring to the original Frank Miller *Born Again* run. "I wonder if they cancelled the remake while I've been here in Mokosh."

"Godsdammit," Jon muttered. "If he's responsible for that, he's eviler than we thought! FYI, you need to be clear with me if you are monogamous with Ania or just playing head games. Because if we do save the world, we can pretty much get any man or woman we want. Deborah Anne Woll, Matthew Cox, the guy who does the stunt work—"

"Comments like that are why I play head games," I said, opening the letter. A glowing yellow wisp of gold flew out and transformed into a translucent ghostly apparition of the Wise Man.

"Huh, it seems Larry is now cribbing from *Spaceballs*," Jon said. "Sure, why not. Aaron is a prince, and he can marry Princess Vespa."

"I'm sorry, Larry," I said, looking at his ghost with sympathy. "I should have moved quicker. Maybe if I'd beaten Belobog immediately after defeating Zorya Nightbringer, I might have been able to beat Veles before he escaped."

"He can't hear you, Aaron," Jon said. "This is a prerecorded message. It's also, again, almost certainly a trap."

"It's not quite as prerecorded as you might think, Jon," Larry said, surprising me by speaking in a sad but respectful tone. "Perun elevated me to his Chosen before his death. As such, the states of being alive and dead are somewhat fluid when dealing with me. Even Veles can't touch the cycle of life and death without the consent of the people involved."

"I'm so glad Evil Dark Lord Von Badness cares so much about consent," Jon said. "Oh, Aaron, can we bury Larry? I'd like to piss on his grave."

"You shit on my shoulder way too often for me to take that any way but literally," I replied.

"Ravens don't have bowel control!" Jon said, defensively. "It's nothing personal. I'd be in human form when I pissed on his grave."

"We'll cremate you unless you have any other wishes," I said, having adopted that as a policy throughout Ledziana. Tombs couldn't really be afforded these days when the dead were refusing to stay that way. The only exceptions were individuals who were marked for being raised and since only Joan, Agata, and I could do that, there wasn't much demand for. Rachel might have been a god, but it didn't seem like healing, let alone resurrection, was her purview.

"What happens to my remains now doesn't matter, though I wouldn't be surprised if Veles left something on the body to deal with you," Larry said, unaware of what just happened. "He might not sound like it, but you have him scared and it is part of the reason he's accelerating his plans so quickly. You remind him too much of his brother and while they are buried deep, there are feelings of both guilt as well as doubt within Veles."

"Aaron reminds Veles of Perun? The Chris Hemsworth Thor with slightly better magic?" Jon asked. "Yeah, I suppose I could see it."

I rolled my eyes. "Jon thinks this message is the trap."

Larry shook his head. "The letter is just a representation of me and is composed purely of Perun's essence. It is sent along the marks and cannot be seen by him. This is a conversation just between us."

"Which is exactly what a trap would say," Jon said.

"I'm listening," I said.

"You will go to the Dagobah System," Larry said, waving his hand. "There you will learn from Yoda, the Jedi Master who instructed me."

"Okay, I'm gone," I said, getting up. "Clearly, I am the most serious person here and that is just tragic."

Larry let out a Santa Claus-esque laugh, which probably shouldn't have been surprising since in addition to being the Southern Kingdom's discount Gandalf, he also was apparently the guy who delivered toys to all the good little pagan girls and boys during the Winter Solstice. The weird shit you find out about alternate worlds. That also meant, of course, that in addition to all the other evil things he'd done, Veles had ruined Christmas.

"I'm kidding, Aaron," Larry said. "No more training do you require. However, I made the choices I made with the knowledge that they'd lead to my death. I hope the information I can pass on will mean the difference between victory and defeat."

"Oh, so you dying and depriving us of the strongest wizard on Mokosh was part of the plan," Jon said. "Great job. Real brilliant planning there, Sun Tzu."

"Throw your soldiers into battle from which there is no escape, and they will prefer death to flight," Larry said, quoting the *Art of War*. I'd never read it but I was familiar with the Sabaton album of the same name. "That's the strategy I chose to follow when bringing the champions to this world. It forced you to become the heroes we needed. Which includes you too, Jon."

Jon raised a wing in what I assumed was a flipping off gesture.

"What's the message, Larry?" I asked.

"Three parts," Larry said. "The first of which is that you have to be on top of Bald Mountain in three days."

"*Three days?*" I asked. "I can't be on top of Bald Mountain in three days. I have to fight Belobog."

Larry shook his head. "Belobog doesn't matter right now. He's a mindless force of destruction and it might take an army or three to defeat him. Thousands may die, maybe tens of thousands, but the world will recover. Veles is the real danger. The portal between Earth and Mokosh that is located there will only be open on Walpurgis Night, however. All the other times it can be opened will require an archmage of which, well, we're distinctly lacking. Either because they're loyal to Veles or because Alek killed my students."

"Yeah, he's real sorry about that," I said, sarcastically. "Some asshole murdered the woman he loved and replaced her with an imposter."

Larry frowned. "I see your opinion of me isn't that much better than Jon's."

"I just don't like people who hurt my family," I said, sighing.

"Family," Jon grunted in his best faux-Vin Diesel.

"Second, Veles plan is to unite the worlds," Larry explained. "That is his endgame and what you have to prevent on Earth. The Old Gods warping the Elemental Temples was the groundwork he needed to achieve this on Mokosh. He's had decades to do it and will have to work much faster on Earth, so at least his works will be big and obvious."

"This isn't going to be like the original *Final Fantasy* where we have to refight all the bosses in a row is it?" Jon asked. "Or *Castlevania: Symphony of the Night* where we're going through the castle again upside down?"

I ignored Jon. "By uniting the worlds, do you mean—"

"He will literally combine their timelines and reality to create a massive explosion of magic that will allow him to absorb all of the other gods as well as the billions of souls on both worlds into himself," Larry said. "It will transform him from a creator god, already one of the most powerful beings in the universe, into a new Triglav. An anti-Triglav if you will. As close to an opposite of the traditional interpretation of the Abrahamic God as exists. Then nothing will be able to stop him. If any other overgods exist in the universe, I do not know of them."

I didn't bother asking if the Abrahamic God would qualify as I wouldn't trust Larry's answer regarding old Eli. Instead, I nodded. "Right, so Veles plan is still to kill everyone but he's going to do it in a way that makes him even more of a god than before."

"More *Final Fantasy* rip-offs," Jon said. "The villain is always trying to be a god in the end but here, he's already a god so it's just hack writing."

"Reality, unlike fiction, doesn't actually have to follow the rules of good storytelling," Larry said. "Veles' own followers have been deceived about his plan. As the Twisted Gods' influence poisons his mind, his usually rock-solid willingness to honor his promises diminishes. The Thirteen, Epic Dungeoneering™'s executives, and many others are expecting to be rewarded for their service. The fact that Veles plans to destroy the world would result in many of them questioning their loyalty."

"The Witch Queen has already shown up to us and offered to help us against her master," I said.

Larry's expression became unreadable. "You shouldn't trust her."

"No kidding," I said, dryly.

"I trust her as far as my dick," Jon said. "Which can be pretty far now that I can become a dragon. Seriously, you can bash someone's head in with that thing now."

"The Witch Queen wants to be a goddess and Veles' equal," Larry said. "However, she was cheated by Veles when they first made their bargain during the early days of humanity. Becoming a death lord, or indeed any sort of undead, precludes a person from ascension to divinity. Your soul is permanently bonded to Veles and reduced in nature. All of their power is channeled from him as well so while they may be vast in personal magic, they are no longer truly free-willed beings and permanently subject to his will."

"And we're back to ripping off Tolkien," Jon said. "You act like that's really profound but it's derivative. Sauron wants to conquer Middle Earth while Melkor wants to spite Eru. The Ringwraiths were kings of men but they're now Sauron's busboys. No one can destroy the One Ring willingly. Do you have any original ideas?"

"Given this is all the history of a living world, no," Larry said, showing remarkable honesty. "I deserve credit for turning your dialogue, Jon, into something even remotely readable. What I mean to say is the Witch Queen covets the Marks of the Champion. She may also seek other means of ascending to the divine as well."

"You mean like stealing Veles power?" I asked.

"No," Larry said.

I cursed as I knew what Larry was getting at. "Agata and Bloodstorm's baby."

Jon flapped a bit in alarm. "Hey, she's not the kind of person who would steal a baby."

Larry and I both looked at Jon, though in my case it was more turning my head.

"Okay, she's exactly the sort of person to steal a baby," Jon said, looking down. "Probably so she could put her in a tower and harvest her golden hair but that doesn't mean she's a bad person."

"Amazing," Larry said. "Even Aaron has a better opinion of the women he sleeps with."

"Given he killed one of them, I'm not sure that qualifies," Jon said. "That's going to be a red flag on your dating profile forever after. I mean, Agata is probably not going to seek you for comfort after she and Bloodstorm inevitably break up."

"What?" I asked, appalled.

"Oh, sorry, no, that was my plan," Jon said. "But you were thinking it. Single moms need love too!"

I decided that when I got back to Dragon Keep, I'd develop a permanent *Silence* spell for Jon. "What was the third thing you were going to tell me? At this point, I'll take any advice I can get since everyone seems to want Veles defeated but they're already starting to feud about how."

It was a sobering moment because there had been many wars that had been close to victory before infighting snatched it away. We were far from close to victory.

Much to my annoyance, Larry didn't respond. Indeed, his image was frozen in place with no response.

"Hello, hello," Jon waved his wing at the archwizard. "Is this thing on? Great, he's crashed. Do we need to reboot him or what?"

"I don't think that's an option," I said, annoyed. "What are the odds the third thing he had to tell us was, by far, the most important?"

"Given the quality of the writing so far, I'd say about 100%," Jon replied. "Do you think we should move to another universe with better material? Maybe superheroes? I know the MCU has taken a dive, and I doubt it's gotten better while I've been gone but maybe they finally let Zach Snyder finish his work."

"James Gunn is in charge now," I said.

"Really?" Jon asked. "Well, it's too bad Satan is probably going to ruin that too."

"Towers..." the image of Larry C.C. Weis slurred. "Deathrot... Reincarnation."

With that, his image winked out of existence.

"Well, that was useless," Jon said. "Is your mark acting up?"

"'Fraid so," I replied. "I can't see any of my stats."

"But that's the entire appeal of LitRPG and RPGs in general!" Jon said, appalled. "Seeing the little numbers go up is addictive like crack! It's why we shell out seventy bucks or even more for these games!"

I sighed and noted the letter in my hands was now just blank. Well, blank if you didn't count the bloodstains. "We need to figure out a way to get to the portal on Bald Mountain while not betraying everyone we've assembled to fight Veles' forces."

"You don't think that they'll be fine without you?" Jon asked before bursting into laughter mixed with caws. "Oh, yeah, no, they'll be at each other's throats in minutes. They almost fell apart the first time you went to the bathroom. Ivan will start chopping off heads the moment you're not looking over his shoulder and Agata is going to go nuts the moment she finds out that her goddess betrayed her."

There was a crack of thunder outside the tent.

"I mean asked a great sacrifice of her," Jon said, nervously.

"Come on, let's go," I said. "I need to tell the rest of the group. Secrets are poison."

"Said no man in any successful relationship ever," Jon said.

That was when Larry C.C. Weis' corpse got up off the ground and threw a fireball at my face.

CHAPTER TEN
ANOTHER AMBUSH. REALLY?

Yeah, this one is on me, isn't it?

I was stupid and believed that Larry had left a final message for us. I believe he did. I also believe Veles knew about it and decided it was worth using as yet another cheap shot. Given he'd been willing to use an actual nuke against me, I had to admit that it was starting to look like I was the idiot for continuing to give him opportunities.

Now, normally, I'd have cast COUNTERSPELL, but the gods of luck were not kind to me today and I got smacked in the face with what amounted to a concentrated blast of flame. Now, if this were me pre-Mark of the Champion, this would have been a game over. (Anyone miss game over screens? I do. I feel like something has been lost from just showing the continue without something to remind us we needed to get better.)

Anyway, I was blasted in the chest and set on fire before rolling across the ground. I wasn't dead, though. I was no longer just a human being, I was a demigod infused with the power of a dozen other champions now. Perun's magic had altered me so that I was more like a comic book superhero. If I wasn't Superman, I was at least Spider-Man in terms of durability. The spells woven into the fabric of my Dark Undermaster armor also blunted some of the damage. It hurt, don't get me wrong, but more like touching a hot stove than having boiling grease thrown in my face.

My interface also sprang to life enough to acknowledge what had happened too, which was a sign it wasn't completely busted.

YOU HAVE SUFFERED 32 POINTS OF DAMAGE.

"This is why you need to double tap the bodies!" Jon shouted, flying out of the way of the spellcasting zombie. "Be like John Wick!"

Larry C.C. Weis' corpse stood up and stared at me with a malevolent glare. He then spoke in a shrill Saturday Morning cartoon villain's voice, complete with reverb. "You perfidious little worm! I curse the day that I met you! Your existence has been a plague on mine in a way that I cannot think of a single other being matching."

I blinked. "Larry?"

This seemed to piss off the rotting corpse, and he growled at me. "No!"

I paused. "I'm sorry, you're going to have to be a bit more specific then. I've killed a lot of people since coming to Ledziana and quite a few of them have been evil wizards."

"Is it Valentin?" Jon asked, slowly transforming behind an overturned set of pews.

"Valentin was a warrior, not a mage," I pointed out. "Also, he was a lot more frat boy than faux Shakespeare."

Valentin had been the first of the champions and the first of them to go bad. I still didn't know what Lary had been thinking recruiting the guy since he'd not only been a janitor at Epic Dungeoneering™ but a serial killer.

"Ooo, maybe it's that Boris Poppy guy," Jon said. "I felt like he was an underused villain for a cursed dragon!"

"Also, not a wizard," I said, remembering Valentin's dragon ally that we'd tricked Chernabog into slaying at the Earth Temple.

"I am Hellmaster Pollux, the Verminlord!" the corpse that had once belonged to Larry C.C. Weis shouted.

"Oh yeah, you," I said, remembering him. "You were the guy who tried to ambush us on the back of a flying skeleton steed."

"Very Metallica album cover," Jon said. "Less so riding around in the corpse of a hack fantasy author. That's more Sam Raimi."

"Dead by dawn! Dead by dawn!" I said, waving my hands in the air.

Pollux, despite his body being nothing more than the remains of a far better man, looked confused. Clearly, this conversation was not working out the way he expected. "What in the world are you two idiots—"

"SUNSTRIKE!" I said, blasting the death lord in the face with a spell designed for the slaying of the undead.

Hellmaster Pollux the Verminlord was a death lord like the Witch Queen but significantly lower down the rankings, Still, like the adage went, what did you call the worst student at a medical school's graduating class? "Doctor." Well, in this case, the worst Sith Lord was still a Sith Lord (with apologies to Darth Maul). Hellmaster Pollux was one of the Thirteen and apparently the sole one who hadn't joined Susano or been taken out by her. It made me call into question everything else she'd said to me.

The blast that flew out of my hands into Pollux's (or Larry's) face was one of glowing light, but it didn't disintegrate his body. No, the death lords were infused with Veles' power the same way I was infused with Perun's, and that meant that we could exchange blows like comic book characters. Instead of being disintegrated by the blast, he just looked a little extra crispy.

Hellmaster Pollux glared at me with his now-empty eye sockets that began to glow with blue-white witchfire.

"Oh, that's dirty," Hellmaster Pollux said, chuckling. "I am starting to see why the master believes you were the only one worthy of succeeding Garland."

"I am me, no more no less," I said, pulling out Perun's sword and causing it to crackle. It was as large as a great sword and as thick as a two-by-four but as light as a piece of plastic now that I'd settled into my power. It crackled with lightning from the Sky Realm. "Which is way more than you can handle."

"Points for trying to be badass but a little off on execution," Jon said. "I give it a 6.0 out of 10.0."

Hellmaster Pollux let out an ear-splitting cackle. "You actually think you can take on me, fool? I was old when your country of birth was new. I waited until—"

"Are you taking credit for Veles dumping your ass here to attack me after he delivered his message and then waiting until Weis delivered his?" I asked. "Because from my perspective, that makes you just a mailman."

Hellmaster Pollux snarled, blood leaking from his mouth. "I am the last of the faithful death lords."

"Which doesn't make me respect you," I replied. "It means you're the only one of the lich kings that was too stupid to realize he was being played. Because if you really were so beloved a ringwraith then why did Super Sauron leave you here to be an annoyance?"

Hellmaster Pollux didn't initially respond. "I will end you, Bartkowski."

Why did people keep saying that?

I was trying to delay him to figure out a proper way to deal with a death lord. As significant as the upgrades I'd made were, I was still pretty much outmatched. The problem was that the best way to fight him would have been with the rest of my team and I didn't want to take for granted that this guy was a centuries-old archmage.

"DISINTEGRATE!" Pollux shouted, having switched to the same "name the spell and done" type of magic I used, presumably a gift from Veles. I had to admit I wasn't fond of it since, well, it was a lot easier to fight guys who had to spend at least a few seconds reciting a spell.

"COUNTERSPELL!" I said, managing to barely bring up enough power to diffuse the spell that otherwise would have been an instant kill. Even so, I felt it wash over me like a tidal wave, threatening to drown me in magic that wanted to tear me down to base molecules.

"Oh, how cute, you fancy yourself a wizard," Pollux said, looking more annoyed than intimidated.

I pointed my sword at him. "PERUN'S LIGHTNING BOLT!"

It was my biggest and most powerful spell to throw at anyone, since I'd inherited it from my absorption of divine energy versus an ability

I'd learned. It was basically Zeus' thunderbolt but, well, Perun's, and could be felt even by gods.

From my fingertips and channeled through the Sword of Perun flew a massive bolt of blue-white energy that sailed outward at Pollux like a hungry monster. It had the potential to backfire or cause unpredictable magical effects whenever I used it but, at this point, I was willing to take the risk.

"PORTAL!" Pollux said, conjuring a hole before me.

Oh shit. I knew where I'd make the other end of the portal open if I was doing this. Throwing myself to the side, I barely managed to avoid being struck by my own lightning bolt as the exit to the portal Pollux had conjured up appeared right behind me. The blast continued onward and went over the death lord's shoulder. I had to give all my training credit. This was a triumph, I'm making a note here: huge success.

That was when Pollux pointed one long bony finger at me, much of Larry's flesh having been seared off by my SUNRAY spell. "ANTI-MAGIC FIELD."

What happened next was like someone stuffing a wet rag down your throat and pouring a pitcher of ice-cold water down past it. Waterboarding for the soul. I could still talk but it would be like choking out words through the water that kept coming. I couldn't feel my magic anymore and as powerful as a demigod as I was supposed to be, Pollux was stronger in pure mastery of the art. Still, I managed to spit out the words, "You... can't... cast... while... disabling me."

Hellmaster Pollux kept pointing at me while grinning his rictus grin. "Oh, stupid boy, you don't know the benefits of actually learning the true art of sorcery rather than having it downloaded into your brain like one of your insipid computer programs. I am ambidextrous in my spellcasting. POISONOUS GAS CL—"

Hellmaster Pollux was caught mid-spell by a dragon breathing its napalm-like breath on him, catching him in the face much as Sparky had done before. Since the only dragon present was Jon, I was glad he'd decided to finally intervene. Did that sound catty? Maybe it was. It destroyed the tent around us but I was honestly surprised it had lasted as long as it had.

Hellmaster Pollux was reduced to a flaming skeleton but stood there, growling as his now bony appendages shook with rage. "You think this will stop—"

"RAINBOW BLAST!" I said, hitting him with a prismatic spray of red, yellow, blue, orange, and green energy blasts. Each of them struck the death lord one after the other, forcing him to his knees. Well, if he had knees. His patella.

"I am empowered now with the status of Chosen One by Veles!" Hellmaster Pollux said, lifting his finger bones. "I shall cast you—"

"PUSH!" I shouted, aiming my hand forward and sending the death lord flying into the air like a cartoon character.

"PULL!" Jon shouted before hitting him with a second blast of dragonfire, this one causing the death lord to explode like a miniature death star. A shockwave of mystical energy exploded from the dead Chosen One's body and showered the tent with little sparkles. It was beautiful in a, "we just killed a guy" sort of way.

"Do you think he'll stay dead this time?" I asked, looking up to the spot where he'd exploded. The tent was now on fire, and I wasn't planning on staying inside for long.

"Probably," Jon said, stepping forward to reveal a large blue dragon the size of an RV. He casually knocked away the pews or crushed them with his girth. "I get the impression that Veles isn't big on second chances to begin with. Honestly, bringing him back in the first place feels like fanservice."

I sighed. "We're in a 'death of the author' situation, Jon. Except literally. It doesn't matter what happened before. There's no storyline being written and no rules anymore. Everything now is like actual history, which, unfortunately, does not require things to make sense."

"How much EXP did you get for killing skull face here?" Jon asked. "Again."

I tapped the side of my right hand's mark.

Nothing but static.

"No idea," I said, pausing. "I'm not even sure I'm getting experience anymore."

"That would suck if you maxed out right before the climax," Jon said, his body being pelted with bits of burning cloth from above our heads. Thankfully, that didn't bother a dragon. "Mind you, that happened in *Baldur's Gate 3*. You can only get up to 12th level before you're finished. What was your level last time you checked?"

"14th," I muttered. "No, I had enough EXP for 15th before the nuke."

"Eh, not bad but not good, either," Jon said. "I managed to get all the way to 18th before I died."

"I know, Jon," I said, tapping the side of the interface before trying to fast travel us. "So you've told me, many times."

"I'm just saying that if it's a choice between a guy who is 18th level and a dragon," Jon said. "Versus, well, you, maybe we should rethink who is the leader of this group."

I hesitated at using the fast travel system because, again, I wasn't sure whether Veles had been lying about the radiation affecting the marks or if it was something else. I also really hoped I wasn't dying of radiation sickness and unaware of it. I'd find out soon, though, especially if the whole shapeshifting thing didn't work.

There was also the time limit factor that I had to consider. I believed Larry's message and didn't think it was a kind of reverse, double bluff idiotic twist like the revelation that the Machines were responsible for the creation of Zion in *The Matrix 2*. That had just been shitty writing because the Wachowskis hadn't been allowed to make one sequel and one prequel.

I only had three days to deal with Belobog's armies, or I was going to be stuck on Mokosh. Which wouldn't have been such a bad thing except that I had some lingering fondness for Earth. Oh, and I was sure Veles would figure out a way to destroy this planet too. It really wasn't a temptation to stay here. I needed to take out the god of evil, hubristic statement as that might be, or I'd be living the rest of my life wondering when he would finish the job.

"Ready to go?" I asked Jon, ignoring his attempt to try to take over. I was pretty sure the only person who thought he'd do a better job than me was Jon himself.

"Uh," Jon looked at me uncomfortably. "I think I'll just fly back if you don't mind. Maybe take a detour down to the nearest portal and use it. You know, until we can confirm the magic hasn't been effected."

"I don't have time for that," I said, uncomfortable. "But suit yourself."

I pictured Dragon Keep and commanded myself to appear there. Light surrounded me as usual, but it began to twist, turn, and shatter into a rainbow. After a few seconds, I found myself in an endless white void like, ironically, the Architect's chamber in the movie I'd just derided a few seconds ago.

There was nothing surrounding me.

Nothing.

Forever.

"Ah crap," I muttered.

CHAPTER ELEVEN
HOW DO YOU TALK TO AN ANGEL?

"Great," I said, surveying the featureless white void around me. "I've accidentally clipped outside the map."

Intellectually, I knew I wasn't inside a video game. As much as the powers I wielded were like those I used to program into characters, the fact was that the Southern Kingdoms were as real as Earth. It was just that Perun, or Perun's ghost, really loved *Dungeons and Dragons* as well as the rules for its magic. He'd also wanted the nerds he recruited to understand how to do sorcery quickly, so he'd had the actual sorcery we'd been empowered with follow the game's rules. Okay, it sounded stupid when explained that way. Still, I couldn't help but feel a mild panic as I found myself surrounded by nothingness. I immediately tried to fast travel back to my original location then tried Dragon Keep.

Nothing.

Crap.

The prospect of dying here in the middle of a lonely nothingness wasn't great. Would I need food, water, or sleep here? Did demigods? I'd never actually bothered to go without any of them, and it wasn't like my condition had come with an instruction manual. Indeed, it was possible I might end up imprisoned here forever. Sanity might be the first thing I lost.

I ended up sitting down with my arms around my knees, staring into my surroundings while retreating into my consciousness. I played the *Star Wars* movies over in my head and grew a beard as loneliness and isolation consumed me. Time lost all meaning, and I became a broken wreck of my previous self.

That was when I hallucinated Thistle in front of me. Thistle was a beautiful but harsh Dark Moon elf who had a distinctly punk look to her features. She had with facial tattoos as well as multiple piercings. This version of her was more like a heavy metal album cover than punk, though, as she was wearing metal armor with, uh, exaggerated proportions and missing pieces that showed off her curves. Oh, and she also had a pair of black wings and a flaming sword.

I stared at her. "I admit, you were not who I expected to see first when I lost all touch with reality."

"Aaron—" Thistle started to speak.

"I suspect it's guilt talking," I said, shaking my head. "After all, while you were trying to murder me in order to take my blood, I was letting you. Which is cheating on Ania. Except, well, she didn't believe we were exclusive, and you were brainwashing me."

"Aaron—" Thistle started to speak, clearly annoyed.

"You are a bad person," I said, shaking my head. "I don't care if I did brainwash you. I'm pretty sure if you weren't elvish Joan Jett, I would have killed you. Killed you!"

Thistle stared. "Are you finished?"

"Begone spirit!" I said, getting up and waving my hands in the air. "This is my mind, and you have no power here! If I'm going to hallucinate anyone, it'd be Ania! That or Mary Jane Watson Parker and Felicia Hardy. Probably played by the Zoryas because I admit, they've kind of buried themselves in my brain."

Thistle pinched the bridge of her nose as if trying to stave off a migraine. "Oh, for the love of you. Aaron—"

"I said, begone!" I shouted.

Thistle slapped me across the face with her free hand.

I blinked. "Oh, you're actually here."

"Yes," Thistle said.

"Ah," I said, rebooting my brain. "How many years have I been trapped in this snow-colored purgatory?"

"Nine hours," Thistle said.

I paused. "Wow, I wouldn't make it in prison."

It also explained why I'd only made it to the middle of the sequels. Which might be why I'd started to have my mental breakdown.

"Probably not," Thistle replied. "You are in Sky Realm."

"The home of the gods," I said.

"Yes," Thistle said. "It is not the afterlife of mortals, which is under the domain of Veles for both the good and the bad. No, it's where Perun once held dominion."

"Uh huh," I said, pausing. "Gotcha. Like Olympus or Asgard."

"Or Sky Realm," Thistle said, unhappy. "This is your section of it."

I took a moment to look around the void before turning back to her. "I'm going to be honest, I think we need to make an IKEA run."

"Aaron—"

"Seriously, I know I probably got this unfurnished, but they could have at least installed a bathroom." I waved my hand absently in a random direction.

KERTHUNK. A port-a-potty fell out of the sky before landing right in front of me.

"Huh," I said, staring. "So, what, I can mod this zone like *Fallout 4*?"

"I don't know what that is," Thistle said.

"Creation Kit rules!" I said, concentrating and creating a reproduction of my fortress from the *Dark Undermaster 3* DLC. It was an enormous stone castle that was surrounded by the Lake of Despair and had numerous crafting stations. It wasn't quite as cool as Dragon Keep but I'd added my electricity and a hydroelectric dam from the Mothership Zetan mod. Oh, and bits from the New Reno set that a friend of mine had made after his bachelor party. No reason for your medieval fantasy realm not to have a jukebox and neon signs after all.

Thistle sighed. "I am going to have to interrupt you again, aren't I?"

"Quiet, modding," I said, transforming the empty void into a masterwork of nerd construction. "I think the neon signs should go over here..."

"Perun wants to speak with you," Thistle finally said.

I'd already conjured a backdrop of a verdant rural environment with a Sun, mountains, and babbling brook nearby the crumbling fort. Why was the fort crumbling? Because it looked cool. However, the mention of Perun's name immediately deflated me from my sudden outburst of energy.

I sighed. "That guy is awfully active for someone who is meant to be dead-dead."

"You have weakened Veles enough that his brother is capable of manifesting,"

Thistle replied. "He is only able to manifest here in your soul, though."

"My what now?" I asked, turning my head to her.

Thistle sighed. "Imagine you're ripping off *He Who Fights with Monsters*."

"You read that?" I asked.

"I have been trapped in your subconscious with no one but a talking horse for months," Thistle said. "I am now familiar with most of your pop culture, childhood, and masturbation fantasies. I hate it."

I stared at her. "Never share that thing with Agata. In my defense, I once woke up with her naked in my bed. That puts thoughts in your head."

Thistle stared at me. "Do you want me to assume her form?"

I blinked. "What? No!"

"It is your prerogative as my god," Thistle said.

"Way to make this even creepier," I said. "Wait, did you say a talking horse?"

"If that's your preference, I may have chosen the wrong god," Thistle said, crossing her arms.

I narrowed my eyes. "No, I'm saying, is Stompy back? Can I talk to him?"

"Yes," Thistle said, sighing.

With that, there was a crack of thunder and a cloud of black smoke before I saw my beloved horse. Stompy was a demon steed, mare if you played D&D, and a beautiful example of a stallion but as removed from mortal breeds as succubi were from women. He had red eyes and a set of black leather wings that were new.

I opened my arms and tried to hug him. "Stompy, I am so glad to see you."

Stompy took a few steps backward. "Just because I died to save you doesn't mean we're in the hugging territory, Lord Aaron."

"I'm not a lord," I said.

"You're a god," Stompy said. "That means that you're a lord. Perhaps the least god of the pantheons of Mokosh but a god, nevertheless."

It was a conversation point that made me uncomfortable. So, I turned to Thistle. "You say that Perun wants to speak with me?"

"Yes," Thistle said. "He will appear when you will it."

"Well, I will it," I said. "Also, is my unconscious making you dress like Rob Liefeld dressed you? If so, I apologize."

Before Thistle could respond, there was a crash of thunder and a flash of lightning before a two-story tall bare-chested man appeared. He was wearing a loin cloth and a helmet that sported the stereotypical horns that no Viking helmet had ever actually possessed in real life. In one hand was a maul that was like a cinderblock on a metal pole. It fit into his hand like he was holding a hammer for pounding nails.

He was tanned and blonde with a thick beard. "Immigrant Song" by Led Zeppelin played in the background with his appearance, which highlighted that there was no situation too dire in the world that you couldn't make it ridiculous.

"Perun," I said, looking up. "Nice to see you again. Aren't you supposed to be dead?"

Mind you, he'd been showing up in my brain for some time. Dead didn't mean the same thing to gods as it did to us mortals. Well, mortals. I wasn't sure where I ranked on the spectrum between human and god these days.

"Veles stopped preventing me from resurrecting!" Perun said, saluting me with his maul. "I've been following your activities. Honestly, I have notes."

"Uh huh," I said. "I'm kind of on a time crunch here, Perun. The other gods also want me to kill the Witch Queen."

"Yeah, good luck with that," Perun said. "Honestly, I think you've been kind of dragging your feet. Trying too hard to level up to be able to defeat Veles. Level grinding. Maxing out your crafting. Really, it shows signs that you're not willing to take the risks necessary to get the job done."

I stared. "I'm sorry, call me crazy, but I thought the goal of this mission was to win. So, I want to maximize my chances."

"Bah!" Perun said, dismissively. "There's no chance you'll ever be powerful enough to defeat Veles on your own, so it's really just how suicidally brave you want to be when you assault him."

I stared at him. "What do you want, Perun?"

"To give you some advice," Perun said.

"A lot of that going around," I muttered, sarcastically. "Everybody wants to tell me how I should handle this."

"Success has many fathers, but failure is an orphan," Thistle said. "Old elvish proverb. You were alone when you were losing but now that you are winning, everyone wants to direct your activities."

"Go ahead," I said, wondering what sage advice the Lord of Surfer Dudes (as I thought of Perun) would say.

"Trust your gut," Perun said, surprising me. "My brother can't understand you because he's used to playing every possible angle while manipulating people. Even before the Twisted Gods got into his head, he was always someone who treated every relationship as transactional. The mercy you've shown your enemies is something he assumes is designed to be strategic. But he doesn't think of you as just trying to do the right thing and helping as many people as possible. He doesn't get that and it's allowed you to run circles around him until now."

"Until now," I said.

"He's on Earth now and that means he's on the second worst planet in the universe for corruption and backstabbing after Mokosh," Perun said. "Worse, the public is eager to embrace the kind of power he offers.

He is spreading all of the magic he stole from Mokosh via universal magical conductors or UMCs. Stop them and you can stop Veles."

"It's that easy, huh?" I asked.

"I mean, he's still a creator god and you're totally outmatched but yes," Perun said. "Especially since you've been irradiated and the magic inside your remaining marks has been utterly fucked."

I blinked. "What?"

"Don't worry, you're immune to radiation unlike the rest of your group," Perun said. "Comes with being a sky god. However, the marks are useless right now. You need to recharge them."

"How the hell do I do that?" I asked.

"Gimme the marks," Perun said, holding out his hand.

Even though Veles was a Trickster god, I handed them over as I was certain he had already exhausted his cheap shots for the day. Perun set down his maul and took the marks. He held them in the air. Both glowed before he handed them back.

"Thanks," I said, taking them. "So, they work now?"

"No," Perun said. "They'll need to be recharged, as I said. However, they'll absorb the essence of a divine being if you slay it."

"Yeah, because there's plenty of those running around," I said, having learned that I had a lot of sass toward the divine these days.

"Belobog," Perun said, as if that made it any better. "They can absorb his essence and, if you choose to take that into yourself, it might give you the edge you need."

I stared at him. "At what cost?"

"Everything that makes you who you are," Perun said, not mincing words. "You tell me if it's worth it to protect all the people you love."

I didn't answer.

"You should be prepared for the Witch Queen's treachery, Lord Aaron," Thistle said. "She is only helping you because she believes she can somehow steal your divinity."

"Can she?" I asked.

Perun shrugged. "You never know with magic. When you're rewriting the rules of reality that we, the gods, wrote, it's always up in the air. Are you ready to go back to Mokosh?"

I looked up at Perun. "One more question: why are you and the other gods so dead set on me joining your ranks?"

Perun's expression didn't change but he looked at Stompy and Thistle. "You have good friends, Aaron."

"I would question numbering Thistle among my friends," I said. "Is she still brainwashed into being my slave?"

"Being in your head has cured me of any lingering adoration," Thistle said. "But I will fight by your side to protect the elvish race."

"Good luck," Perun said, waving his hand. "With what I've done for the bracelets, I won't be able to fully regenerate for a century. I hope I'll live long enough to see a pair of liberated worlds."

"Yeah, yeah," I said, looking up. "Listen, it was good to see—"

That was when Perun picked up his maul and pointed it at me. Everything went white and I was suddenly falling a few hundred feet over Crossroad Keep.

Oh, and Belobog's army was already attacking it.

Mothersucker!

CHAPTER TWELVE
THE BATTLE OF DRAGON KEEP

A t this point, I was about done with gods. I hadn't believed in them before I'd found out they were real, but I'd swiftly come to appreciate them once I'd started receiving help from them. Was I influenced by the fact some of the "help" seemed to be in the form of attractive, charismatic, scary as hell women? Yes, I'll admit that. To everyone but Ania because she's even more scary than the goddesses. However, Perun and Larry managed to cause no end of trouble for me even though both were dead now.

Currently, I was falling from the height of several hundred feet in the air. This was not the worst situation I'd ever found myself in but was probably in the top ten. That was before I took in the sight of Belobog's massive two-hundred-foot-tall frame nearby in all his cyclopean glory. Belobog was an enormous tentacle-faced horror with bililous skin, wings, and an aura of mind-chilling terror that washed out from around him to the point that only undead soldiers were able to surround him.

Cthulhu.

He was basically Cthulhu.

Or maybe Cthulhu was basically him.

The armies that the last of the Old Gods had gathered around him were everything the Witch Queen had said they would be. He'd assembled a horrifying host of wights, zombies, skeletons, goblins, humans, and magically created monsters to lay siege to my home. They shouldn't have been here, not for days, but I really didn't know how long I'd been in Sky Realm. Either way, they were descending on the walls of Crossroad Keep like a swarm of ants with a particularly ugly *kaiju* in the center.

Ironically, by some definitions of ironic at least, my last sight on Earth (or Mokosh as the case may be) wasn't necessarily one of imminent defeat. I'd spent a massive amount of treasure upgrading Crossroad village and Dragon Keep's defenses across the past year. So much so that I'd not only filled out the original set of upgrades but the second and later a third tier of them. So much so that cannon, wand-wielding wizards, and musketeers were firing into the horde of monsters assaulting the place. Catapults shot rune-covered rocks over the walls while ballista fired glyph-marked javelins which exploded when they landed.

Then there were the dragons.

Dragons, as all fantasy fans knew, were the apex of monsters. Others might be bigger, faster, stronger, or weirder but it always came back to the giant lizards with human mythology. Dragon Keep had been created by giants in the ye olden days of Mokosh to raise dragons for the gods before passing it down to the Rose family so they could do the same for Ledziana's kings.

Our version had been less animal husbandry and more a mad scientist's experiment as we'd discovered the secret of turning people into dragons. Creating an army of flying WMDs probably wasn't the smartest move we could have made but it was the most effective. The lines of the enemy army burst into flames as they were dive bombed with mystical napalm. It was devastating and helped create openings in the front lines for the armies we'd teleported in to fight.

Unfortunately, the dragons weren't enough to win the battle as I saw Belobog reach down and grab two by the neck with his enormous fists. He crushed their necks, and their bodies hung limp like he was strangling chickens. Not that I had any experience seeing chickens being strangled but it was a sight to behold.

Well, time to die.

Before I was about to hit the ground—or at least a bunch of spear wielding goblin soldiers—I was grabbed in the claws of a very familiar figure. He'd grown into an adult dragon across the past year and was now a brilliant red-scaled monster.

"Sparky!" I shouted, feeling agony as the dragon's claws bit into my side but not willing to complain.

"Hi!" Sparky said, his voice now deeper.

Sparky was the child of the Poppy Family that had lived an extended life as a cursed adolescent before we'd broken the spell upon him. As a result, he'd started resuming his natural growth. Possibly even faster than usual with a growth spurt that made up for the fact he was as old as, if not older than, Ania and Agata.

"I seem to have missed the battle!" I shouted, barely able to be heard over the conflict as Sparky swerved around back toward Dragon Keep.

"No, it's still happening!" Sparky said. "Big Squid Guy decided to come through a giant hole in the sky."

Great, a portal. "Yeah, that'll do it!"

Sparky took me over the enhanced village—well, city—of Crossroad and I could see that it was jam-packed with refugees from all over Ledziana. The armies we'd assembled were also present, holding back for the inevitable fall of the wall. After all, despite all of the eventualities we'd prepared for, a giant squid monster hadn't been one of them. I had to admit, in the face of something like that, I didn't think our chances were good.

Sparky took me toward the center of town where the heart of the Dark Undermasters was located, as well as our (small) dragon army. It was a beautiful castle that stretched far in the sky and had massive towers, an extensive moat, and plenty of magical defenses that, unfortunately, couldn't be applied to the town itself.

Dragon Keep had been sacked multiple times under the previous champions and been rebuilt just as many times but had never been as strong as it was now. It was also the place my family was located and I had to admit I was more scared for them than the tens of thousands of people defending it. It wasn't exactly heroic, but I freely admitted to it.

Either way, saving everyone was the best way to save a specific someone. Stupidly idealistic as that may be, it was my way of life.

"So, where were you?" Sparky asked, as the wind blasted against us both.

"Sky Realm!" I replied. "I was adding neon lights there, crafting tables, and slot machines!"

"Sounds good!" Sparky said. "Have you built a place for the ratkin to live in?"

I paused. "I don't think they go to my realm when they die, Sparky."

"You need to work on that!" Sparky said.

"I'll think on it!" I said, more focused on the fact that the sky had cracked open and was now releasing a horde of winged serpents who weren't quite dragons but were close enough for government work.

Finally, we managed to arrive at the tallest tower of Dragon Keep where I saw Ania, Agata, Ivan, Bloodstorm, and Captain Crunch gathered. There was no sign of Rachel, and I had to wonder if she was among the many individuals choosing to fight closer to the front. I didn't think she was dead—I was pretty sure I'd have felt something if that was the case—but I still couldn't help but worry despite the unconventional nature of our relationship. Jon was missing too but I figured whatever he was up to, he was probably causing more mayhem than solving it.

"Aaron!" Ania said. "You're alive."

"You ever doubted it?" I asked, right before Sparky dropped my body on the tower stone with a thud.

"Yes!" Ania said, rushing to my side. "Belobog arrived early!"

"Yeah," I said, climbing up and whispering a *Cure* spell. "I noticed."

"Do you have a plan for getting rid of this thing?" Bloodstorm asked, looking at me. "Because, honestly, I got nothing."

"He's far more powerful than he should be," Agata said, clutching her staff tightly. "Belobog was less powerful than the Nightbringer, yet this version seems to be able to shrug off all of our spells like water droplets."

"I think you guys are far too dependent on me," I said, making a half-hearted joke. "We should work on some training programs to get pinch hitters to take over in my absence."

"I think—" Ivan started to speak.

"Not you," I replied. "Veles must have given Belobog a boost on his way out. I don't suppose our unexpected ally showed up?"

"No," Agata said, "But she cast a spell that has proven useful."

"What spell is that?" I asked, almost regretting doing so. I was at the point where I was genuinely sick of surprises.

Belobog lifted his massive arms above his head and conjured an enormous ball of ice large enough to flatten Dragon Keep and hurled it in our direction. The ball had to be fifty or sixty feet in diameter, glowing with magical energy. It sailed over the attacking army before smashing into a magical dome that shattered it into little, tiny pieces that rained down onto Belobog's own forces. The dome, however, shuddered from the effort.

"Huh," I said, looking at the results. "I'm going to say that is a good thing."

"It doesn't work against flying creatures," Agata said, looking at Sparky. "Which has its benefits and drawbacks. Our dragon advantage should have won us the day decisively, but Belobog is immune to dragonfire."

"That's... not good," I said, trying to figure a way to turn this around.

Yeah, I had nothing.

"The armies have been pushed back behind the barrier," Captain Crunch said. "Thousands dead. But we've made them bleed for every step of the way. Unfortunately, that's the downside of dealing with a necromancer. The death lords loyal to Veles keep bringing back their own fallen alongside ours, which has meant that our advantage keeps getting whittled down. We might be able to smash the dark armies for good here but not if that giant pile of seafood breaks through the barrier."

"At least they bypassed the capital," Ivan said, smiling.

Everyone glared at him.

"I'm a king!" Ivan said. "It's my job to keep up morale!"

Captain Crunch rolled his eyes. "I prefer minstrels for that, lad. A king's primary job is to keep the kingdom intact. If you do that, you're fine in the annals of history."

Ivan adjusted his crown. "Well, then I'm an objectively terrible leader."

"Ivan the Terrible?" Ania asked. "Nah, that would never stick."

Ivan glared at her.

"I'm going to blame this all on my awful advisors, starting with your boyfriend," Ivan said. "Assuming there is anyone left to record history after today."

I pulled out the scroll that the Witch Queen had given me. "I have an idea."

"Oh thank the gods, we're saved," Agata said, sounding a lot more sarcastic than she really should have under the circumstances.

"Hey, give me a little credit," I said, pausing. "I've got us this far."

Ania looked at the monster as it hurled another giant ball of ice at the dome, causing the barrier to shudder again. "Aaron, I love you, but you have to wait until the race is over to take your bows. Stumbling in the final stretch isn't going to do anyone any good."

Unfortunately, she had a point.

"Do you know where Jon is?" I asked.

"Unfortunately," Ania said, frowning. "He decided that he would help the Witch Queen and keep an eye on her."

I stared at her in horror. "He does know she's evil, right?"

Bloodstorm chuckled. "To think we were worried about *you* thinking with your dick."

I shook my head, knowing I'd have to adjust what little plans I had on the fly. "What about Joan and Rachel?"

"They're with the rest of the sorcerers trying to reinforce the barrier," Agata said, wondering where I was going with this.

"Okay," I said, looking over at the large number of teleported boats spread across the side of the river and saw the dwarves' largest one. "Can you guys combine your might to do something like, I dunno, lift up something really heavy?"

"Yes, Aaron," Agata said, following my gaze. "But if you think we can take out Belobog with just a boat thrown at his head, I think you overestimate its effectiveness."

"Trust me, Cthulhu hates boats going through his head," I said, making a reference only Jon would have gotten. "But I'm actually thinking of drawing from an old *Star Trek* episode called 'Arena'."

I explained my plan.

Everyone stared at me as if I'd lost my mind.

"Uh huh," Ania said, frowning. "That is the dumbest thing I have ever heard in my life. Are you sure you're alright, Aaron?"

"Absolutely not," I replied, taking a deep breath. "But I have good news! My plan gets even dumber."

"I don't think that's possible," Bloodstorm said.

I only wished that were true. "We need to ride dragons around Belobog and weaken him enough to hit him with my suicide ship. Sort of like how the lions in Voltron have got to do some battle with big monster first before pulling out the blazing sword."

"That doesn't sound terribly stupid," Ania said, looking like she was waiting for another shoe to drop.

So was I.

I finished memorizing the scroll. It should have taken hours but that was the benefit of having maxed out my divine intelligence. "Yeah, well, I'm going to bring back the Zoryas. I really hope I have the juice to summon both."

Silence reigned.

"Yep," Bloodstorm said. "I stand corrected. That actually makes the plan dumber."

"You do recall we went to elaborate lengths to kill both of those gods, right?" Ania asked.

"Technically, Aaron just fucked and killed Dawnbringer by himself," Agata said.

Everyone looked at the pregnant priestess.

"What?" Agata asked.

"Huh," Captain Crunch said, shaking his head. "You are a very strange group."

"You're just now getting that, huh?" I asked. "In any case, we need all the help we can get and I find nothing at all suspicious about the fact that the Witch Queen gave me this spell nor that it summons two people that might hate me."

"Or that it summons someone who is already reincarnated," Ania said, showing she was aware of Agata's child's true nature. "How does that work?"

"That too," I said.

"You probably should be suspicious," Sparky said, not quite able to comprehend my level of sarcasm yet.

"Thank you, Sparky," I said, patting him on the snout. "I wouldn't have figured that out on my own."

"You're welcome!" Sparky said, cheerfully.

And with that, the dome fell.

CHAPTER THIRTEEN
SUMMONING SOME OLD ENEMIES

"Well, that's not good," I said, staring at the shattered defenses which meant a kaiju was now coming directly at us.

"Oh no," Agata said, her look one of abject horror. "I should have been down there! I could have lent my own power! We could have—"

Bloodstorm came up behind his lover and put his arms around her shoulders. "You would have added a few more minutes. Nothing more. Now our fates lie in Aaron and his incredibly stupid plan."

"No pressure," I said, shaking my head.

"Actually, consider yourself under an immense amount of pressure," Bloodstorm said, looking up to me. "The lives of both the woman I love and our child-to-be are at stake. If you don't save this, I promise I'm going to haunt you from beyond the grave."

I'd have taken that as a particularly black bit of humor except I knew he was probably serious. "Don't worry, B. If this plan fails, I can assure you that it is because I've already died myself."

"That's not reassuring," Ania said. "What we want is to figure out a plan that will succeed."

Yeah, that caused me to wince. I'd, justifiably or not, managed to earn the reputation as a master planner who pulled victories out of nowhere. Some people even thought I was the smartest man in the world, just not one of the wisest. The thing was that there was only so much you could do with the ability to quickly process information. For example, no matter how smart you were, you couldn't make two plus two equal five and that was the case with Squidzilla over here. Technically, since Godzilla meant Lizard God, it was Godika, but I wasn't going to fret over details.

"Do you want me to lie?" I asked Ania.

"Absolutely," Ania deadpanned.

I nodded. "Yes, I absolutely have this in the bag. You don't have to worry about anything."

"Good," Ania said, nodding. "Aaron has got this."

Bloodstorm laughed.

"Let's go kick some ass!" Sparky said, blowing a tiny blast of flame.

I held the scroll in my hands as I decided on my next move. "Ania, Bloodstorm, I need you to both get flying mounts. Dragons preferably. Please also get Rachel and Joan if you can. We're going to need all the magical juice we can squeeze."

"You lost me with your metaphors, lad," Captain Crunch said. "But if you're going to take that monster head on, I wish the blessings of Svarog on you. Because you're going to need them."

"I hope you don't expect me to fight," Ivan said, sucking in his breath.

I didn't disagree. "I need you and the dwarf king to take care of stage two of my plan. Please hurry."

Ivan nodded, probably just as glad to get away from the frontlines as he was to try to do something involving alchemy (which my plan depended on). Unfortunately, there was no real safety to be had if my stupid plan didn't work. The siege of Dragon Keep was about to become a full-on assault and there was not a damn thing we could do about it. Indeed, the next giant ball of ice sailed into Crossroad and landed on a set of houses, crushing dozens of people to death. A lot more would die before I could even begin my counterattack.

As everyone rushed to do their part, I proceeded to begin my summoning. I'd have to trust Susano's "gift" here because we flat out didn't have a chance if she was lying. They would go from slim to nonexistent if this was a trick of some kind. Which was the real reason I was so gracious to my enemies. An enemy turned to a friend was infinitely better than just slaying an enemy and rarely backfired. Well, I mean, forgiving his enemies worked out terribly for Julius Caesar but he was the exception.

Ahem.

"In the name of Aaron, God of Push, I beseech you echoes of those who have passed before! Through my power and will, I summon you not from the realms of the dead but the realms of memory! Come forth, Zorya Nightbringer, lover and enemy both! Come forth, Zorya Dawnbringer, lover and daughter both! I command it."

I really hoped no one heard the lover and daughter part because that would be hella awkward to explain.

Sparky, meanwhile, looked at me. He was still behind me on the battlements and hadn't left. "Lover and daughter both?"

"There is a perfectly valid explanation that I do not have time to give right now!" I said to my dragon companion.

"Is this like you fucking Rachel?" Sparky asked, cocking his saurian head to one side.

"I am not fucking Rachel!" I snapped, irritated. "Also, who taught you that kind of fucking language."

Sparky somehow rolled his eyes, which was something I never expected to see a dragon do in my lifetime. Mind you, up until last year, I'd never expected to see a dragon alive and in the flesh, either.

Nothing happened for the first few seconds, and I was worried that this had been all for nothing, especially when one of Belobog's giant ice balls slammed into the side of Dragon Keep. Thankfully, the magic woven into the castle walls caused the ice to disintegrate before it could kill everyone here. That magic, too, had its limits.

The Witch Queen had given me *something*, though, as the scroll started to glow, and I felt an immense amount of energy leave my body. So much so that I was forced to my knees and felt like all my "divine power" was gone. I was, instead, just poor ordinary Aaron again. Well, poor, ordinary Aaron and still a wizard.

There was that.

Two glowing blue-white translucent figures appeared in front of me, and they were instantly recognizable. The first was a beautiful elvish-looking woman with a witch's hat, voluminous robes, long black hair, and an enigmatic smile. The second was a tall, muscular, and yet still incredibly sexy Asiatic woman in armor with a ponytail so long that it went down past the end of her back. To be frank, they looked more like they belonged in anime than they did medieval fantasy, but I wasn't going to complain too much. Err, because they were incredibly powerful goddesses we needed the help of, not because they were hot.

Honest.

"Hi," I said, getting up and waving. "Nice to see you two again. Sort of."

"Ghosts!" Sparky said, rearing back. I was afraid he was going to blast both and cost us our advantage but he, thankfully, stayed his attack.

"Yeah, kind of," I admitted. "Okay, Zoryas, this is going to be awkward to explain but—"

"You killed us," Nightbringer said. "Which, to be fair, I kind of had coming. As much as I was able to purge the Twisted Gods' influence from my mind, it was not enough to prevent them from bringing my worst qualities to the forefront."

Dawnbringer looked at her sister. "I mean, honestly, you were always an enormous bitch. The big difference between you and Veles was that you were happy to have the living worship you."

Nightbringer glared. "At least I didn't trick my lover and student into siring a child on me so I could merge with it. That's disgusting even by my standards."

"Actually, your mother may have made it so you'll reincarnate in Agata's child," I said, pausing. "Which means that you'll be my niece when I marry Ania."

Both Zoryas looked at me in shock.

"That is messed up," Nightbringer said, reminding me that she'd lived in my world as a punk rocker.

"I know!" I said, throwing my hands out in the air and unsure how I could rush this along.

"Agata's baby is going to be your girlfriend?" Sparky asked, once more surprising me by reminding me of his existence.

"No!" I said, grimacing. "Forget you heard that! It's a secret."

"I wish I could forget it," Sparky muttered.

I'd say the gods hated me, but I'd already had ample proof. "Okay, listen, I don't know how this works—"

"We're drawing energy from you to manifest avatars based on our past selves," Dawnbringer said. "Unfortunately, we're limited by the amount of divine energy you possess."

"If you'd absorbed it all we could do a lot more," Nightbringer said. "Your hesitation to become a true god may be a crucial factor."

Man, was I getting sick of everyone telling me that. "Yeah, well, the wrist bands are radioactive. They got EMP blasted or something. Either way, it's not an option right now. At any minute, Belobog is going to stop hurling rocks and realize he'd be better off just knocking over the walls to let his army into Crossroads. So, we need to go kill him. You up for that?"

"When there is war, I am there to inspire those about to die," Dawnbringer said, puffing up her (ample) chest.

"That is a terrible motto," I said, staring at her.

"I always hated my brothers," Nightbringer responded. "I'm in."

"Good," I said, taking a deep breath. "Let's roll."

I could already feel myself becoming winded from sharing so much power with the pair of them and had no idea if I'd be able to sustain them in full combat. I was glad to have both women by my side rather than in my path, though.

Both women raised their hands together simultaneously and conjured demon steeds for them to ride upon. I felt agonizing pain as they did so, more energy passing from my body. It passed quickly, though, and I moved to mount on Sparky's back.

"Mind carrying me on top rather than in your claws?" I asked, patting Sparky on the side.

"You okay with me fighting now?" Sparky asked.

That was a complicated question because Sparky and Joan were both still children from my perspective, teenagers at best and adolescents at worst. I didn't want to be the kind of monster who put children into battle but, bluntly, I wasn't sure there was a choice to save everyone. "No, but if you don't fight, you'll probably die anyway. So, yeah, we fight together now."

"Super!" Sparky said, hearing none of the nuance. "Let's kick some ass!"

He reminded me way too much of my nephew for this to be anything but uncomfortable. "Yeah, let's do that."

Sparky proceeded to take into the air as I cast WEB to make sure that I was sealed to his back. It would prevent me from doing something insane like leaping off Sparky to stab Belobog but, well, that would have gotten me killed anyway. Both Zoryas joined me in the sky, and I sucked in deep breaths as they conjured weapons: a magic staff for Nightbringer and a giant sword for Dawnbringer.

In the sky around Crossroad, I could see other dragons had taken to flight and were readying for an assault on Belobog. There were a few less than when we'd started this battle, and it was clear that they were not the game changer we needed them to be.

Belobog had started his charge toward Crossroad, stomping like an earthquake as he prepared to destroy the walls and let his army into the city. It wouldn't be an instant loss for our side because there were a lot of soldiers waiting for his forces, but if Belobog stomped on them then there wouldn't be much we could do about it.

That was when Belobog let out an enormous roar that echoed across the battlefield. It was agonizing and partly mystical in nature, striking at the hope and confidence of everyone who heard it.

"Aaron Bartkowsi! Come face me! I am the Lord of Good Fortune, and it is my blessing to share with you the gift of a swift death! All those you cherish will be smashed beneath my feet and all those you love will be slaughtered to the last! This is only mercy that can be shown them for Veles' reign is at hand!"

The wave of despair that poured out with Belobog's words had an instant effect on a huge chunk of the army. Veteran soldiers that were willing to stand against the two-hundred-foot-tall thing threw down their weapons and ran for safety while terrified conscripts curled into fetal balls. Peasants and nobles screamed alike while mothers clutched their children in fear.

Me?

I was just pissed off. "Sparky I'm going to need you to get close."

"How close, Lord Aaron?" Sparky asked, dodging away from spells fired from the ground by undead sorcerers like they were fantasy artillery. Which I supposed they were. Explosions were roaring all around us.

"Really close," I said. "Close enough to shave."

I swear Sparky grinned.

Belobog's eight eyes looked up, each of the crimson orbs zeroing in on Sparky and me. That was when he focused his despair-generating voice on me. "You have come a long way to die, Champion. You will never know the touch of your lover again. You will never know peace. All to try to win a pointless war with a foe you could never have beaten. When you die, you will be raised as an undead horror that will be tortured every day for the rest of eternity as punishment for your hubris. You will be—"

"Shut. The. Fuck. Up," I said, summoning every bit of my willpower and hoping that my time in Sky Realm counted as resting.

I raised the Sword of Perun up as Sparky charged right at the monster and I cast PUSH on the hilt of the sword as I aimed it with my telekinesis. It was the same tactic I'd used against the Wind Demon, and the blade flew into one of Belobog's eyes.

Belobog reared back and let forth a below that threatened to shatter my eardrums. The sword sunk deep into his bilious flesh. The squamous horror (which I'd always wanted to say) didn't die, though. Instead, he just looked pissed off and that was impressive since you normally couldn't tell what a giant demon was thinking by their face.

"We got it!" Sparky said. "He's hurt!"

"If it bleeds, we can kill it," I said, quoting Arnold in *Predator*.

"Demons of the Sky! I call upon you!" Belobog bellowed, raising a tentacle-like set of fingers to the sky. "Smite these fools in my name!"

It was funny how Belobog had gone from being a silent menace to a chatty Cathy. I was focused on dodging out of the way as storm clouds rolled over the battlefield and began pelting lightning bolts at me. It was ironic that I, the descendant of a thunder god, was now struggling for my life against a bunch of electrical attacks. Sparky was good at avoiding the first few blasts, but the rain of lightning didn't stop and we started veering downward. I cast a Globe of Invulnerability around myself and Sparky that knocked away a few of the attacks. It took almost everything I had because the goddesses began their attacks.

"Have at thee, brother!" Nightbringer shouted, redirecting Belobog's own lightning bolts back upon him. A dozen or more of the lightning re-orientated and blasted into the monster. It was hard to imagine the two of them being related but that was gods for you.

"BLADE OF HEAVEN'S STRIKE!" Dawnbringer cried out, conjuring a spear the size of a football field before hurling it through Belobog's chest.

My heart pounded as my eyes watered. I'd exhausted every bit of my divine power and the spells they were hurling were now drawing on my lifeforce.

"Aaron, are you okay?" Sparky asked.

"No," I whispered. "I think I'm dying."

That was when the rest of my team arrived on dragonback, guarding a flying galleon sporting the flag of the Dwarvish Empire on its sails.

Belobog was not impressed. "I will smack your airship out of the sky!"

That was when the galleon smashed itself into the chest of the Old God, igniting the hold full of every bit of alchemical powder and flaming oil that we had in our reserves. Which was a lot given I'd built an alchemy factory in the city.

The explosion was beautiful, detonating Belobog from the torso upward and sending his gooey-god parts in every direction.

It also knocked Sparky out of the sky. I lost consciousness with the magic of my marks returning as they absorbed Belobog's power.

A great voice spoke in the air, **"GOD SLAIN."**

CHAPTER FOURTEEN
DEVIL WITH A BLUE DRESS ON

I laid face down in the mud of the battlefield, surrounded by huge chunks of dead god. It weirdly reminded me of the ending of *Ghostbusters* where they'd successfully destroyed Gozer's avatar, only to cover all of Manhattan in marshmallow goop. Belobog was dead and I could feel the divine energy coursing once more through my marks.

All around me, the army of Belobog was in full retreat and our forces were charging out of Crossroad rather than waiting to be assaulted. Dwarves, elves, and humans joined together to slaughter the undead that were as disorientated as a dog after chasing its own tail.

There was also more going on than I could see with the sound of the ground bursting open in many places. Turning my head to one side, I saw thousands, if not tens of thousands, of ratkin pouring into the battle to slaughter the remaining forces under Veles' command. It was the arrival of my "followers" and made what was already going to be a costly victory into the total slaughter of the enemy. I just hoped the ratkin didn't get into a fight with our existing forces.

"I don't feel so good, Mr. Aaron," I heard Sparky's voice nearby.

Slowly, I managed to pull myself together and stood up. The world wobbled around me and a kobold with a pocketknife could have probably shanked me. Both Zoryas were gone, and I was glad of that since I doubted I could have sustained them in my current state.

Sparky... didn't look great.

The red dragon was spread out with broken wings as well as a compound fracture on his leg. He was barely breathing, and I couldn't tell if he was able to shapeshift. We'd managed to take down Belobog, but the consequences were severe.

"Don't worry, Sparky, I've got you," I said, hobbling over to the side of the dragon and casting HEAL. It made me fall to my knees again and spit up blood, which wasn't a good sign. It was another reminder that I had wasted every single ounce of my strength conjuring the goddesses. Still, I focused on trying to heal Sparky's injuries.

"It's okay, Mr. Aaron," Sparky said, sounding distant. "I'm okay dying heroically."

"Sparky, do me a favor," I said, concentrating with every ounce of my power.

"Yes, Mr. Aaron?" Sparky asked.

"Shut up while I work," I said.

"Right, sorry."

That was when my newly recharged Mark of the Champion started spitting various updates from my time since the assault on the Water Temple. The sheer number of EXP awards beggared description and were overgenerous, rapidly moving me up several levels at once. That resulted in all my injuries healing as well as my magic strengthening.

ACHIEVEMENT UNLOCKED: THE NEW DAWN
(A) - 50 - Slay the last of the Old Gods

ACHIEVEMENT UNLOCKED: SIEGEBREAKER
(A) - 50 - Successfully defend Crossroad from the invading army.

ACHIEVEMENT UNLOCKED: UNITED WE STAND
(A) - 50 - Reunite Ledziana as a single kingdom

REWARD:
+ 150,000 EXP (Discover way to Water Temple)
+ 100,000 EXP (Mermen)

+ 50,000 EXP (Kelpies)
+ 25,000 EXP (Naga)
+ 25,000 EXP (Vodniks)
+ 40,000 EXP (Living Ooze)
+ 15,000 EXP (Mud Monsters)
+ 45,000 EXP (Water Elementals)
+ 100,000 EXP (Temple Ogres)
+ 50,000 EXP (Belobog High Priests)
+ 50,000 EXP (Water Demon Priests)
+ 20,000 EXP (Giant Starfish)
+ 200,000 EXP (Escape Veles' nuke)
+ 150,000 EXP (Reborn Verminlord)
+ 1,000,000 EXP (Enhanced Belobog)
+ 1,000,000 EXP (Win the Battle of Crossroad)
+ 500,000 EXP (Win the Battle of Crossroad without losing Dragon Keep or Crossroad)
+ 1,000,000 EXP (Reunite Ledziana)
+ Mask of Belobog
+ Robes of Belobog
+ Specter of the Twisted Gods
+ Ring of Madness
+ 1,000,000 GP

MAIN QUEST(S) COMPLETED:
DEFEAT THE OLD GODS SERVING VELES (4/4)
DEFEND CROSSROAD (1/1)
DEFEND DRAGON KEEP (1/1)
MAIN QUEST UPDATED:
JOURNEY TO BALD MOUNTAIN (0/1)

Healing Sparky wasn't instantaneous, but I was able to draw from that sudden burst of energy to successfully cast the HEAL spell but also

CURE IV and CURE III spells. Enough that not only wasn't he dying but he'd probably suffer no long-term damage.

"Can you shapeshift?" I asked Sparky.

"Sure," Sparky said, slowly resuming his appearance as being an adorable golden-brown corgi.

"You don't want to be a young man?" I asked. "Because if there was any doubt, you're a Dark Undermaster, it's gone now."

"I'm good," the dog said. "Being a young man is hard. Being a dog is fun."

There was something to that at least. I took a second to update my levels, noting that I'd almost reached the maximum of being a demigod. In Ledziana, only demigods could reach 18th level and reaching 20th level was the limit of all mortal beings. Checking my enhanced magic, I took a moment to cast MASS UNDEAD SLAYING and wiped out a remaining couple of dozen fleeing skeletons.

REWARD:
2500 EXP (Skeletons)

ARAGORN "AARON" BARTKOWSKI

LVL: 17
CLASS: UNDERMASTER SORCERER (MASTER RANGER)
ALIGNMENT: GRAY
AGE: 34
SEX: MALE
RACE: HUMAN (Demigod)

STR: 12 (19)
AGI:: 10 (11)
CON: 11
INT: 30
WIS: 11

COM: 15 (16)
CHA: 15

ARMOR CLASS: 27
ATTACK: +9 (+19 to ATTACK, 1d10+19/23 [Undead] DAM, Sword of Perun [Lightning, Holy, INT bonus])
HEALTH: 96
DIVINITY: 7
FEAT: Taunt, Sword and Shield, Two Handed Fighting, Tracking, Craft Magical Items/Recharge Magical Items, Leadership
SPECIAL ABILITIES: ARCANE FIRE (1d6+13 INT bonus, Eldritch Damage, x3 Staff of Dragon Kings, Critical Hit Possible), BLOCK (requires shield), LESSER MAGIC (unlimited times per day), COUNTERSPELL, DIVINE ENHANCEMENT [Push]
LESSER MAGIC EFFECTS: CLEAN SELF, CREATE FOOD, CREATE FIRE, CREATE WATER, MINOR ILLUSION, REFRESH, TELEKINESIS (1 Kilo per INT bonus), VENTRILOQUISM, MEND, TORCHLIGHT, SILENT WALK, IDENTIFY MAGICAL OBJECT, LESSER SENDING (Party Only), BLESS, SOOTHE ANIMAL
SPELL LIST (MAX/5/5/5/5/5/3/3/2)
[1] ARMOR, CURE, FRIENDSHIP, JUMP, PUSH [+++]
[2] ANIMAL SUMMONING, ENTANGLE, SILENCE, WEB
[3] CURE (II), LESSER CHARM, LIGHTNING BOLT, NEUTRALIZE POISON, SUGGESTION
[4] BANISHMENT, CURE (III), POLYMORPH OTHER, DIVINE BOW, REMOVE CURSE
[5] CURE (IV), DRAGONBREATH, IMPROVED LIGHTNING BOLT, REVIVE, SUNSTRIKE
[6] CHAIN LIGHTNING, GLOBE OF INVULNERABILITY, HEAL

[7] AARON'S AWESOME BATHHOUSE, RAINBOW BLAST, RESURRECTION,
[8] MASS UNDEAD SLAYING, PLANESHIFT
SPIRIT SUMMONS: STOMPY, THISTLE, RUSALKA, ZORYA DAWNBRINGER, ZORYA NIGHTBRINGER, SPARKY, LEGALLY DISTINCT COPY OF ASH FROM *EVIL DEAD*

STATUS EFFECTS:
* Alchemical Stone (White): You recover 20 HP after a short rest and status ailments
* Blessing of Zorya Dawnbringer: +1 to AGL, +1 to AGI
* Ring of Ogre Strength: STR is 19 when wearing this
* Boots of speed: Double Movement Speed, Dodge Roll Bonus
* Ranger's Mark: +4 to hit/damage against Undead
* +4 to all Saving Throws [Divine]
* Can cast PERUN'S DIVINE LIGHTNING BOLT once per day
* DIVINE SENSES [Always Active, No Penalties to Environment]
* Can grant 1st and 2nd level spells to priests and answer PRAYER [ACTIVE]

Level 17 to 18
1,002,500/3,000,000

"So, we won, Mr. Aaron?" Sparky asked, looking around to the bloody battlefield and the losses surrounding us.

None of the troopers had bothered to approach me when I was down in the mud, possibly because of the presence of a nearby dragon but just as likely because there was no way to tell me from the hundreds of other Dark Undermasters that had been trained in the past year. The reasons kings wore crowns was because you couldn't recognize most people by sight unless they had the regalia to let you know.

We'd managed to win a crushing victory today and everyone had a right to celebrate but the fact was that hundreds, thousands, of people on "our" side had died. There were also victims on the side of the genocidal monsters too, like the living that had been pressed into service or transformed into sentient undead against their will. Ledziana was now free of the curse of Veles but who knew for how long.

"Sort of," I said, being honest with myself. "War isn't exactly the way they speak of it in the songs."

"You killed a giant god with an exploding ship while riding a dragon," Sparky said.

"Well, yes," I said.

"Two goddesses were fighting by your side, both of whom were your lovers," Sparky said.

"You're too young to be thinking about that," I said, annoyed.

"It is exactly how the songs are," Sparky said.

"Right," I said, noting he was probably right. "Yeah, I don't do this for fame."

"I mean, everyone will attribute it to Garland of Nowhere and not you so that's not why you do it," Sparky said, joking around.

I snorted. "Yeah, well, someday people will write a true story of war and all of its costs."

"Probably not," Sparky said. "Then people wouldn't want to do it."

That struck me as very funny in the moment before I shook my head. "I'm going to go talk with the commanders of our armed forces and try to see who is in charge of the ratkin. Maybe we can keep everyone from attacking one another."

"Good luck, Mr. Aaron," Sparky said. "Can I tell Ms. Ania to come down to see you?"

"Please do," I said, really looking forward to spending some more time with her. Hopefully, I still had a couple of days to get to the portal on Bald Mountain.

Unfortunately, that was something I was going to have to broach with the others. I was 90% certain that they would all agree to come with to finish off Veles, but there was still a 10% uncertainty. Agata had other responsibilities to look after now and so did Bloodstorm. I didn't want to drag Sparky and Joan into war at their age. Ania would be by my side come hell or high water, but Earth wasn't her home. I hadn't really gotten to know Rachel that well in our time together despite—or more likely, because of—our unusual relationship. About the only person that I could 100% rely on with any certainty was Jon and that was just a depressing thought.

Sparky was about to take flight, and I was soon to be left alone in the mud among the corpses and large chunks of dead god.

"It seems my faith was well placed in you, Lord Bartkowski," A familiar voice spoke from my side.

"Great," I said, turning around to see the beautiful but sinister form of Susano. Jon was sitting on her shoulder. She was wearing a loose blue dress that showed a generous amount of everything. The effect was diluted by the fact that I knew she was a mummified corpse that just so happened to have a pleasant appearance.

Sparky stopped his retreat.

"Hey, Aaron!" Jon waved a wing at me. "I wanted to help you during the whole apocalyptic battle thing, but Susano said not to. For some reason that seemed really important."

I checked Jon's character status on my interface.

JON SNOWAN [Status: Charmed]

Oh crap.

"It is time for us to go," Susano said.

"What, now?" I asked.

"Yes," she said.

CHAPTER FIFTEEN
JOURNEY TO BALD MOUNTAIN

"What if I don't want to go with you?" I asked, not exactly feeling up to the whole business of solo questing with the Witch Queen.

Jon stared at me like I was an idiot. "I don't think this is exactly an offer you can refuse, Aaron. Believe me, I understand you want to. Personally, I wish you would. I can handle this femme fatale and all her wily ways. Two's company, three's a crowd."

"I thought *Three's Company* was the name of the TV show," I said, staring. "My dad used to date the woman who did the Thighmaster."

Jon stared. "I have so many questions about how the Most Interesting Man in the World™ had a son as dull as you."

"Those commercials really are based on him," I said, remembering one of my dad's stories about how the beer licensed his life's rights. "That and the Chuck Norris jokes. My dad and Chuck were apparently sparring partners."

Jon raised a wing to ask another question.

"We're going now, or you won't go at all," Susanos said, coldly. "Do you want to defeat Veles or not?"

"I do," I said, pointing to all the devastation around us. "I'd do anything to keep this from happening again."

"Should I blast the woman?" Sparky asked, making a boneheaded statement only matched by some of the things I'd said.

"Nope," I said, patting him on the snout. "All I'm saying is, Susanos, that I think I'm a package deal with my fellows. If we have a chance to defeat Veles then it probably will be a team effort."

"You're talking about defeating the god of evil, not coaching little league," Jon said.

I frowned, wondering if it would be possible to break Jon of his curse. The problem was that under her influence, he would probably fight for Susanos against me. I still remembered my time under the control of Mrs. Grubb and while it sounded hilarious, "Haha, a hag woman lures adventurers to screw her instead of investigate all the people she murdered.", it had been objectively terrifying.

Okay, it didn't sound that hilarious either.

I'd been hanging around Jon for too long.

Maybe it was the fact she'd looked like Jennifer Connolly.

"Which is why I think everyone would be onboard," I replied to Susanos, not really addressing Jon at all.

"Is this because you think I'm going to betray you, and you worry that you won't have any backup when it happens?" Susanos asked.

I blinked. I hadn't seen directly addressing that issue coming. "Err, kind of."

Susanos looked bored. "Believe me, Aaron Bartkowski of Michigan, I do not have any interest in you. If I did, I would have killed you now and tried to seize the marks on your wrists. They would elevate me to the status of a petty god should I figure out how to harness their power and slay you. However, I have no interest in being a petty god."

I blinked. "So, your argument is you absolutely would betray me if it was worth your time but I'm too basic for you to stab in the back."

"You are, in simple terms, too under-leveled in your gear," Susanos said. "You've moved up considerably but we're talking sixties and seventies versus nearing twenty."

It was weird hearing her use RPG speak. "You'd do well at Epic Dungeoneering™."

I was presently debating whether to try to fight Susanos now that I'd defeated Belobog. It would have been an objectively stupid move to fight her alone, but I had Sparky at my side, and the others were nearby. I might be able to survive fighting her long enough for the others to join in and if we could beat Cthulhu, I was pretty sure we could beat her. Excepting, of course, that it'd taken throwing a boat full of magical gunpowder and dynamite at him.

A bigger consideration, though, was that I'd been given a direct task to kill Susanos by the gods. I hadn't suddenly become religious. I liked some of the gods, but I liked Jon and Maelor the Black too, however I didn't want to be taking orders from them. The gods had pretty much proven they were all manipulative sons of bitches like the late Larry C.C. Weis. Even Mokosh.

However, the situation here was a classic RPG dilemma of who to side with. Like in *Dragon Age: Origins* when you can either help the elves, help the werewolves, or figure out a way to do both. I didn't see the last option happening despite my enhanced intelligence. I also knew where I stood with the Southern Kingdoms' gods in a way that I didn't with the Witch Queen.

"I'm the CEO of Epic Dungeoneering™ or, I was, at least, until Veles overthrew me," Susanos said. "At least I used to be. I was the one who came up with the idea that we should lure Larry C.C. Weis into writing Garland's story before turning it into a multimedia franchise."

I blinked. "So, you're Zuzanna Czarownica."

I'd never met Zuzanna Czarownica in person, but she was on the walls of the studios where I'd worked as well as the occasional issue of *Wired* or the website (not the magazine) of *Forbes*. She hadn't sought publicity despite building a multi-billion-dollar empire out of a video game company. The woman in the picture had also been touched up enough that I hadn't made an immediate connection. That and I was just terrible with faces.

"Yes, her name was literally Susan the Witch," Jon said. "Not really making much effort to hide her identity."

"No, I wasn't," Susanos said. "Working with the Wise Man allowed for a steady supply of faith to be poured into the Old Gods as well as Perun himself. Enough to create the Marks of the Champion as well as feed Veles. The idiotic veneration of people buying comics, action figures, and wasting hours of time in front of the idiot box was not as pure as true faith but quantity has a quality all its own. *Dark Undermaster 3* sold fifty million units alone and that's not including the TV show's audience. When the Kingdom of Poland existed during the Middle Ages, it had a million and a half people."

I stared at her. "So, you were plotting against Veles for some time."

"I was hedging my bets," Susanos said. "Whatever the case, it also created a bond between Veles and Earth that would eventually allow him to manifest on your world. Which is why your world is in danger and why we must go now. Veles knows that the public is fickle and with no more books coming from Larry—who realized what we were doing was empowering Veles as well as the champions—this will be his last opportunity to carry out his plan."

"Ow," Sparky said, blinking his big draconic eyes. "That makes my head hurt."

"Mine too, buddy," I said.

"But to put it simply, I only need you, Aaron," Susanos said, simply.

"The rest of your team is Destiny's Child while you're Beyonce," Jon said. "You know, except not nearly as hot, cool, or capable of doing multiple musical genres."

"I have my own group. Which you are now a part of," Susanos said, snapping her fingers.

There was a flash of light, and I found myself standing next to Susanos. Sparky was gone and we were on the top of a mountain as the skies shuddered with thunderclouds, pouring down a chilly rain. No sunlight penetrated, and the only illumination was the lightning that crackled every few seconds mixed with glowing crystals growing on the rocks around us. The mountaintop was about the size of a football field's interior and there were shattered ruins of a temple and tombs spread throughout.

It reminded me of one of the final levels of *Eldritch Ring* where you were supposed to face down the Death God/Goddess. There was a sense of oppression to the air and I couldn't help but feel chilled from more than the rain. This was a place of great evil and far more corrupt and twisted than any of the warped Great Temples.

"Where the hell am I?" I asked, turning around in confusion. "Where's Sparky?"

My mark began to rapidly ding, letting me know my status was being updated.

SPARKY HAS LEFT THE PARTY
ANIA ROSE HAS LEFT PARTY
AGATA ROSE HAS LEFT PARTY
KRAGEN BLOODSTORM HAS LEFT THE PARTY
POPE JOAN THE WISE HAS LEFT PARTY
IVAN CROOKBACK HAS LEFT PARTY

SUSANOS THE WITCH QUEEN HAS JOINED THE PARTY

"You know where you are," Susanos said, chuckling. "As for the dragon boy, we don't need him. Nor do we need your other associates. I hope my teleporting you against your will shows that I can be trusted."

"How's that?" I asked, furious. I knew, at least, where I was: Bald Mountain. Veles' former domain.

The place that was supposed to be where we had our final showdown. I knew this not just because it was the most logical place, but because "Night on Bald Mountain" from Disney's *Fantasia* started to play on my mark.

"I could have teleported you to space or the bottom of the ocean," Susanos said. "The differences in our power are of type than amount. You will require my power as well as that of my associates to survive even a second against Veles."

"Right," I said, accepting her logic for now. "You're not really convincing me I don't need my party."

"Hey, man, it sucks to be them," Jon said, flapping his wings while remaining on Susanos' shoulder. "However, look at the bright side, Agata is going to be able to have her baby in peace."

"I induced labor before we left," Susanos said. "That should provide us with a distraction until we have left this plane."

"Or she's going to be absolutely miserable for the next few day," Jon replied. "Then miserable for the next eighteen years because kids suck."

I took a deep breath. "I guess I don't have a choice at this point, do I?"

"You did, until now," Susanos said.

ACHIEVEMENT UNLOCKED: THE LESSER EVIL IS STILL EVIL
(A) - 50 - Side with the Witch Queen over the Gods

Well, that wasn't reassuring. It seemed that this quest was on a timer and I'd screwed up by not making a decision fast enough. What was the adage? Not making a decision is a decision by itself?

"Right," I said, sighing. "So, what now?"

Susanos smiled.

That was even less reassuring.

"Now we go meet the others I've gathered," Susanos said. "A more... appropriate party than the one you have assembled for yourself."

"They're going to be a bunch of psychopaths and serial killers, aren't they?" I asked, adjusting my hood to keep out the rain. That was one good thing about Dark Undermaster gear: it was very good at keeping the elements away.

"Some of them," Susanos said. "But I prefer not to deal with complete monsters."

"The regular kind?" I asked.

Susanos laughed at that and turned around to head into the temple ruins. Veles had either trashed the place on the way out or hadn't bothered with the upkeep over the past thousand years. It was far more like Castle Dracula than Castle Bloodmoon, with webs everywhere, broken statuary, and no sign that anyone had been there for years.

Nevertheless, the webs parted for Susanos, and we headed into the heart of the central chamber, revealing a desecrated temple like the one inside Dragon Keep. Except Perun and Mokosh's heads had been chopped off, and the smaller gods had been replaced with their Old God demon forms. It was about as close to, "This is a Temple of Evil" as you could probably get without being the literal Temple of Doom. Man, that movie was inaccurate with Hindu religious practices.

Focus, Aaron!

The temple had a portal circle in the back, radiating power that dwarfed anything I'd experienced up to this point. The portal network had once been a mainstay of the Southern Kingdoms and had elevated society to something closer to steampunk (magicpunk) instead of the medieval hellhole it had been since the 1940s and the Great Darkness. That was when the deathrot plague, Twisted Gods, and literal Nazis had kicked everyone back to the Dark Ages. I'd restored a few of the temples but this was akin to a nuclear reactor while I'd just been fiddling with steam engines.

There were other people present in the central chamber of the Temple, though. Some of whom I recognized and some I did not. The first two figures that came to mind were ones that I'd fought alongside already: Alek and Rachel.

"Hi, Aaron!" Rachel said. "Or should I call you daddy around here?"

"Seriously, she's doing it deliberately," Alek said. "You realize that, right?"

"I wish she'd develop another personality trait," I muttered.

"Do you?" Jon asked. "Because I question that."

Next was Maelor the Black, vampire brothel owner and former king of the elves. He'd been so bad at it that they'd sworn off monarchy forever and become anarchists. Mind you, his turning himself into a vampire via a pact with Veles had probably helped. He was wearing a special suit of black armor that incongruously had a Green Goblin-esque cap on top. Bloodstorm's father was an unusual addition here.

"Hello, Aaron," Maelor said. "It seems I'm out of retirement."

A woman was standing next to him, dressed in a black leather corset and carried two silver *tonfas* that had blades attached to their ends. She was quite curvaceous, had long black hair and looked almost identical to Agata only twenty years or so older. It took me a second to realize she was Maria Rose, the sisters' mother, who had gone from grande dame to Bloodrayne since her transformation to the undead.

"Oh, uh, hi," I said, feeling very awkward about this meeting.

"Is this the man sleeping with my daughters?" Maria asked.

"The naked healing thing doesn't count! I mean, I'm only sleeping with one! Now! Sleeping not s... fuck," I said, pointing at her. "Anything I say will just make it worse."

Maelor laughed.

Maria glared.

Alek chuckled.

Rachel just beamed brightly, like she didn't have a care in the world.

The final member of the group was a man in Dark Undermaster Master Ranger armor like me. His skin was gaunt, pale, and saggy, and his eyes were glowing. That would have been disconcerting enough even if we didn't have the same face.

I knew him in an instant.

"Meet your own personal Suicide Squad, Aaron," Jon said. "The bad, the worse, and the nasty."

MARIA ROSE JOINED THE PARTY
MAELOR THE BLACK HAS JOINED THE PARTY
GARLAND OF NOWHERE HAS JOINED THE PARTY

CHAPTER SIXTEEN
MEETING THE TEAM

G arland of Nowhere was alive.
  Alive-ish.

Dude looked pretty much like a Death Knight from *World of Warcraft* and it wasn't a good sign for him to be a potential ally here. I would have been relieved by Alek and Rachel's presence but, well, Alek had already proven to be morally flexible at the best of times while Rachel's agenda was inexplicable.

"So, the reason you wanted me to break away from my team is because you had a bunch of your own people to substitute and we can't all fit into one party, huh?" I asked.

"Also, to isolate you from your allies and make you dependent on me," Susanos said.

"Ha, ha," Jon said, stretching out his wings and accidentally hitting her in the head. "Such a kidder. A real gut-bustingly hilarious Maleficent wannabe, isn't she?"

"Please, Maleficent is based on me," Susanos said, without a hint of irony. That scared me. Veles was already a self-aware villain and that was one too many. "I shall begin opening the portal to your world, Ser Aaron. In the meantime, feel free to meet with your associates. I'm sure you have much to discuss."

"Really? What does the damned have to say to the damned?" I asked, quoting Brad Pitt from *Interview with a Vampire*.

"Ooo, good one!" Rachel said, clapping her hands together. "Did you make that one up?"

I paused. "Yes, yes I did."

Alek rolled his eyes and walked over to me. "Listen, Aaron, this is probably confusing."

"You made a deal with another evil overlord when I wasn't looking and left the battle against Belobog to come here," I replied.

"Okay, maybe not confusing," Alek said, sighing. He wasn't nearly as witty as other members of the family but could still hold his own. "I failed to protect Celestyne and my quest for revenge against Weiss failed."

"Yeah, he's dead," I said, dropping that bomb. "Veles killed him. This is our last chance to stop him."

Rachel followed Alek and frowned. "Aw, that sucks. Now the books will never be finished."

We were having this conversation a lot.

"Guys," Alek said, interrupting. "I know that Aaron likes to run his parties like a sitcom—"

"More like the Marvel Cinematic Universe," I said. "Most sitcoms don't have giant monster fights."

Alek sighed, clearly losing his patience. "But this is important. More important than you could possibly imagine. We have to defend our world."

"Yes, as opposed to defending this one," I said, less than pleased. "My family and fiancé are here, Alek. I also don't see that much difference between the people of Mokosh and the people of Earth. At the end of the day, they're both humans."

"Except for all the people that are, in fact, not human," Rachel said, interjecting.

"Everyone is human," I said, quoting Captain Kirk.

"Yeah, that's just objectively wrong," Rachel said, humorously. "Either way, I've got your back during this."

"Thank you," I said, meaning it. "I'm pretty sure Jon is brainwashed."

"Yeah, boobs will do that," Alek said, not realizing I was speaking literally.

"Undead boobs," Rachel said. "I know plenty of guys don't care about that, but there really is a difference between living and undead. Trust me, I know, I'm a goddess of love."

"You look like one of those Nineties movie girls who shows up to make a boring corporate guy's life better by showing him how to have a good time," Alek said.

"Yeah, I know," Rachel said. "Honestly, Aaron, you have issues."

I rolled my eyes. "I refuse to be judged for the weird shit you did to me."

"Zorya Dawnbringer and I are both the same as well as different," Rachel said. "You can't blame me for anything bad she did. However, I can take credit for everything good she did."

"Sounds like some of my ex-girlfriends," Alek said.

Rachel leaned into Alek. "Looking for a new one?"

Alek gently pushed her away. "Biologically, you being my niece is kind of a turn off."

"Kind of?" I asked.

Alek glared at me.

Rachel put her hand over her heart. "My apologies if I ever make you uncomfortable. It's just how I am with everyone. Love goddess, again."

"Right," I said. "I don't believe that in the slightest."

"You probably shouldn't," Rachel said. "In any case, the Witch Queen's powers have limitations. She can control Jon but probably can't Maelor or you with all of your enhancements."

"Probably?" I asked.

"I can protect Alek," Rachel said. "But that means Maria Rose is probably vulnerable. I can't say on Garland."

"Should we be talking about this in public?" I asked.

"Absolutely not," Rachel said. "But she knows that we know while we know that she knows so that's a thing we both know."

I stared at her. "Gods above and below, you really are a Manic Pixie Dream Girl."

"I don't know what that is," Alek said. "I'm also afraid to ask."

"I'm just saying we're prepped," Rachel said, looking at me intently. "But the thing you should realize is we all do want to destroy Veles. He made a lot of promises to Susanos a long time ago. Promises that became meaningless once he was corrupted by the Twisted Gods. I believe her when she says she wants to destroy him. You should trust that."

"Woman scorned and all that," I replied. "The thing is that I'm also pretty sure she wants to take Veles' place as god of evil."

"Well, duh," Rachel said, rolling her eyes. "Just because she's the enemy of my enemy doesn't mean she's our friend. She's still a bad guy."

I sighed. "I used to have a lot more faith in redeeming bad guys."

I didn't comment on the fact that that included Alek. I'd tried to reconnect with my brother-cousin, as Jon called him, but we had remained somewhat divided despite everything. Perhaps too much water had flowed underneath the bridge, or some crimes were unforgivable. There was also the possibility that Alek had gotten so used to me as his adorable dork of a relation that he really couldn't parse that I'd managed to beat the Old Ones. After all, he had been meant to be the big hero before me and had utterly botched the job before pursuing personal vengeance. Not even my parents still liked him. Only my sister, Wendy, still came to his defense and I kind of wished she was here instead of him.

"Yeah, that was probably before you started shooting them in the face with magic and then raising from the dead," Alek said. "Hardcore."

I suppressed my response. I had no desire to point out that had been the lowest point of my life. Instead, I tried to think of the situation from his perspective. "Weis is gone."

"So, you've said," Alek said, his expression unreadable.

"That means it's over," I replied. "Celestyne is avenged. We must focus on Veles."

I was referring to the Dragon Queen who had been the co-protagonist of the Dark Undermaster books.

"Larry C.C. Weis was killed by someone entirely different than me for reasons unrelated to her murder," Alek said, his voice cold and without emotion. "There's no avenging her. He got away with what he did until he died of unrelated causes."

I opened my mouth to point out that there were a lot of innocent people who had died because of Alek's actions, allies of the Wise Man or not. However, there would be no point. I had a very simple philosophy regarding justice/vengeance: it was alright to pursue it but it shouldn't come at the expense of the living. The primary concern I had right now wasn't whether the Witch Queen had razed kingdoms to the ground or was directly responsible for creating the possibility of Veles entering my world in the first place. No, it was the fact that I didn't trust her to not backstab us before we were victorious. Assuming even with her help that we had a snowball's chance in hell. Maybe I needed to find another nuke and give Veles a taste of his medicine.

"I'm going to go talk to the others," I said. "Maybe I can raise their approval ratings enough to get a loyalty quest or two out of them."

"You realize you don't have to continue to pretend this is a video game, right?" Alek asked. "We're going home."

"Your home, Alek, not mine," I said, sighing. "I hope I'll be able to come back after this but I'm not sure that'll be an option."

That was another reason I was worried about taking the plunge here. Larry C.C. Weis was strong enough to send people from one reality to another, and Veles knew how to bring Epic Dungeoneering™ staff here. Bloodstorm had even made the journey to our world and back. However, everyone else seemed to think interstellar travel was almost impossible. If we did defeat Veles and the Witch Queen didn't betray us—let alone if she did—I had no guarantee there would be a way to return to Mokosh. It would be worth it to save so many lives, but I'd still be fucked over by it.

"So, uh, Lady Rose—" I started to say, approaching her and Maelor. Both seemed pretty cozy despite events.

"I have no desire to speak with you." Maria Rose said.

"That's rather rude," I muttered, unsure what else to say.

Maria turned to me. "You look identical to my stepson, who seduced both my daughters and married one despite the fact that it turned her into an oathbreaker. You've since followed the same path."

"Technically, I suppose," I said, pausing. "However—"

"You have also usurped the home of the family I married into," Maria said. "While working in the name of the gods who cursed it."

I paused. "I'm really not going to win you over, am I?"

"Probably not," Maelor said. "I have encouraged my beloved to seek out her daughters over the past two decades. To make peace with the perilous circumstances that have befallen them. However, each time she has rejected my advice."

"I do not wish them to see me as this," Maria gestured to herself, though I could only see her looking pretty rad. Seriously, I was a big fan of the Bloodrayne games and thought she was due to a revival.

That was when the rest of my brain realized I was checking out my future mother-in-law and I decided to quickly retreat.

"Right," I said, unsure how else to respond. "So, you're coming with us, Maelor?"

"Veles will destroy the entirety of the universe in his present state," he said. "The rest of the gods can team up against him and cast him down but will ignore him until he's inflicted unforgettable damage on everything. I made my pact with a very different Veles and regretted it ever since."

"And the Witch Queen?" I asked.

"She cannot rule a world that does not exist," Maelor said, dramatically. "Tell me, how is my grandson to be?"

"Being born last time I checked," I said, unsure how to relate the fact she was probably going to be a reincarnated goddess. "I think Bloodstorm makes Agata very happy and the two of them would make good parents. I don't think that circumstances are going to allow them to be so, at least with this child, though."

"You are very bad at equivocation, Ser Aaron," Maelor said, sighing, "But I actually appreciate you trying to warn me. I know the truth of what is going to happen to the heir to the Rose family. Something I think only you are in a position to understand."

I looked back at Rachel. "Understand may be stretching things. I should have told her before I left."

"Yes, you should have," Maria said, staring at me. "Now my daughter will give birth to an abomination."

She was being harsh. Then again, the previous Zorya Nightbringer incarnation had tried to kill me multiple times. How much of that was on the Twisted Gods' corruption wasn't something I could really judge.

"You were kidnapped," Maelor said, defending me. "But Agata and Bloodstorm will survive."

"Will they?" Maria asked. "Agata has been forced to be strong, but she has ever been more sensitive than her sister."

"That's like saying compared to a bear, I have less hair," Maelor said. "I have faith in your daughters, though. In my son. In Aaron's *hanse*. His companions that he loves as family. They will pick up the cause if we fail and if we don't, we have given them the greatest gift we could: a future."

"You are a really good dad for a former evil dictator turned pimp," I said, offering a fist bump.

He left me hanging.

"Gotcha," I said, giving a thumbs up and heading over to the last of the people here. "Yo, Garland! Whassup!"

"Hello, Aaron," Garland said, speaking a throaty deep voice that was close to the one from the video games.

"Oh, you know me," I said, pausing.

"You have slain the four Old Gods," Garland said. "You slew the Lord of the Vampires."

"He wasn't a real vampire," I said, remembering the fight with Radu.

"You married my sister," Garland said.

"We're still engaged," I said, pausing. "You know, not wanting to do anything with the looming threat of ultimate evil."

"Plus, you broke the curse on my adopted father's ghost and homeland," Garland said. "Yes, I know who you are, Aaron."

"I'm glad you remember that more than the fact I've been pretending to be you for a year," I said, pausing. "Sorry?"

"Better you than me," Garland said, sighing. "I was never capable of doing the things that the Wise Man wanted me to. I'm a professional trapper and hunter of monsters but I wasn't a diplomat, tactician, or leader of men."

"I think you underestimate yourself," I said.

"No, I didn't," Garland said. "Maybe if I'd had Celestyne's help then we could have pulled it off, but you know that she was not one to be dominated by anyone, man or god. Once she was replaced by the Nightbringer, I knew the quest was an exercise in futility. So, I opted out."

"Opted out," I said.

"Died," Garland said, shrugging. "I was killed by my own men, Aaron. Men who followed you, thinking you were me. Believe me, you are a better Garland than I ever was."

It was a strange situation being praised by a fictional character you'd been reading about since you were fourteen. Also, being praised for things you were pretty sure had been achieved by a combination of dumb luck and rules exploits. "Err, thanks, I guess. You were pretty set on staying dead, though, Garland. What happened?"

Garland turned to me with his glowing eyes. "There's a revolt in Hell."

CHAPTER SEVENTEEN
YOU CAN'T GO HOME AGAIN

"A revolt in *Hell*?" I asked, skeptically.

"The creator deities are lodestones of the universe," Garland said, as if that meant anything to me. "When the universe was created, parts of it came awake and coalesced into the first deities. If there was anything beforehand, I don't know who or what they might be, nor do I care. However, the creator gods are a fundamental part of everything that—"

"Yeah, they're gods," I interrupted, confused as to why he needed to point that out. "You're describing the definition of them."

"Well, there's gods and gods," Garland said, shrugging. "Just like Perun being absent affected things on how the universe fundamentally worked, Veles is the same way. He's pretty much the incarnation of the Underworld for humans."

I hadn't been religious before coming to Mokosh and still wasn't fond of the concept, but I wasn't militant either. Still, it was hard to ignore all the fundamental truths of reality I'd been exposed to. One of them being that the creator deities: Veles, Svarog, and Perun were among the earliest beings in creation. There were others, but they'd been there at the beginning. They could also combine into an entity called Triglav who, if not God, was a good Demiurge analog. Unfortunately, with Perun dead and Veles corrupted, there was no Triglav to keep all the other deities on point.

"The Underworld is Heaven, Hell, and everything in between," I said, remembering how it had been described to me. "At least afterlife-wise. Sort of one big Greek-style real estate rather than a bunch of separate ones."

"Yeah," Garland said. "There're other death deities but they're all under his purview."

"And Veles going utterly insane hasn't helped matters," I said, trying to follow his logic. "Which bleeds over into the entirety of all the various realms. Is that what you're saying?"

I was imagining fluffy cloud Heaven under assault from the forces of a burning Hell like a particularly weird *World of Warcraft* expansion. It was hard enough imagining an afterlife but doubly so to imagine that they could be compromised like this.

"It's more that breaking his oath has ruined things," Garland said, his voice taking on an echoing quality. "Veles being evil could be tolerated but oathbreaking when you're the embodiment of the Underworld? That's something else entirely. Up becomes down, right becomes left, and the supposedly immutable parts of the universe are all changed. Veles has abandoned the Underworld for Earth and that means there are uprisings of souls from all over. The individual death gods can maintain their realms but their power weakens the longer he's absent."

Well, that didn't sound good.

"So, it's like Kevin Smith's *Dogma*," I replied. "Except when God was proven fallible, that would result in the universe being unmade."

I hoped that wasn't in the cards but, at this point, I wouldn't have been surprised. It seemed that every step forward we took only ended up revealing that the road had gotten longer. This should have been the end of our journey, confronting Veles here on Bald Mountain, but now we were heading back to Earth. It was like the Kefka-devastated world in *Final Fantasy VI* or the revelation of the upside-down castle in *Symphony of the Night*. I didn't want to purely communicate in video game terms but it was hard not to after a year of living in one.

"Yeah, I didn't watch a lot of movies while dead," Garland said, pointing out an obvious fact. "I mostly spent it having sex and fishing."

"Oh," I replied. "Fishing? Really?"

"I like fishing," Garland said. "You should try it sometime."

"I don't like hurting animals," I replied. "Just eating them."

Garland snorted before chuckling. It was the most human I'd seen him. "In any case, I was enjoying my afterlife when everything went to shit. The afterlife for the good was soon full of zombies, the afterlife for the middling was at war with itself, and the Hells for the wicked? Well, honestly, they're pretty much the same. So, when Larry arrived in the afterlife and set things as right as he could, I agreed to be sent back as his champion. We have the afterlife to save now."

"Great," I muttered. "No pressure."

"He also wanted me to take over from you," Garland said.

"Wait, what? He sent an entire message to me about how I was the only hope!" I said, appalled.

"Yeah, well he's a lying bastard," Garland replied. "I would have killed him for what he'd done to Celestyne but he was already dead, so I didn't see the point."

"Yeah, how is she doing?" I asked.

"Fine," Garland said. "I mean, still dead."

"Oh," I replied. "Right. Well, Alek and I—"

"Celestyne and I reunited in death," Garland said, cutting me off. "You should probably tell your cousin that his romance with her is not going to go anywhere else."

"Yeah, about that..." I trailed off. "I'm going to be marrying your stepsister. Ania and I are together now. I hope you understand that your marriage with Agata is probably done too. Til death do you part and all that."

"We actually don't have that in our vows," Garland pointed out. "Couples are expected to stay married in the afterlife."

"Oh," I said, pausing.

"Divorce is very easy, though," Garland said. "You just agree before an altar of Mokosh."

"Really?" I asked.

"I was a shitty husband to Agata," Garland said, pausing.

"You don't say," I said, not wanting to comment on the fact he made her an oathbreaker and had a child with the Dragon Queen while she was married to a Mongol warrior that was supposedly Garland's friend. There was also his relationship to Ania.

Garland frowned. "You didn't have to agree so quickly."

"I mean, there's not much room for argument," I said. "I only know your adventures from the books in my world. You were a great hero but kind of a cad."

"'Kind of' is understating matters," Garland said, pausing. "I was an unwanted bastard growing up in the house of an incredibly honorable man. A man who loved a goddess and worshiped her but also honored his vows to his wife."

I was about to interrupt his story by saying that I knew all that, but he kept going.

"In the end, his own honor destroyed him when he tried to make peace between the old king's daughters and the Poppy family," Garland said, calmly. "Being a Dark Undermaster was more a place I ended up rather than embraced. It was a way of escaping the horrors of the past, but you can't run from your past forever. My sisters were prisoners at the Royal Capital and my stepmother the bride of a monster—"

"I heard that!" Maelor the Black called from across the room.

Garland didn't seem to pay him any attention. "I sought to lose myself in the petty heroism of a monster hunter. I didn't realize, though, that the overweight bard who accompanied me was the Wise Man. That he was collecting stories of me and spreading them around in hopes of forging me into his tool against Veles."

"I don't know why you're telling me this," I said, genuinely confused. I wasn't exactly good at social engagements. Even with my boosted CHA score, I still struggled to understand what people wanted from given conversations. There was a reason I hadn't done a big Mel Gibson speech to all the troops preparing to fight the undead horde.

"You need to know that you exist as a weapon," Garland said, softly. "The Wise Man, Perun, and now the Witch Queen all try to make you the tip of the spear they are wielding against Veles because gods are inherently creatures of stories. They believe that if you occupy the role of hero then you will beat Veles and save the world."

"Is that true?" I asked, oddly trusting Garland more than anyone else in the group, at least in telling me how it was.

"No," Garland said, simply. "It is a superstition no truer than vampires detest garlic or that kings are appointed by divine right."

"Gods don't play favorites there?" I asked.

"They love whoever is supporting them at the time," Garland said, sarcastically. "But their favor is mercurial and swift to change. As the number of dead champions proves—as I prove—nothing prevents the gods from killing any hero who seeks to overthrow them. Prophecies are more like a set of instructions than actual readings of the future."

"Joan mentioned that the Wise Man, Veles, and she all had the gift to see the future," I said. "However, that just meant that the future was always changing since the people involved could adjust what was going to happen to their liking."

I found that existentially terrifying since it meant everyone who couldn't see the future was effectively a pawn to those who could. It was some real Muad'Dib *Dune* shit.

Garland's expression changed at the mention of the world's littlest pope. "How is Joan, anyway?"

"Cursed with a heavy burden that she has no business possessing," I said, thinking about as much about Joan being Mythras' chosen as I did the gods merging Nightbringer with Agata and Bloodstorm's child. "She's remarkably well adjusted for a person who has to deal with people trying to kill her every day of her life, though. Ania has taken to treating her like a kid sister or adopted daughter, though. If she makes it through this, well, she'll probably have to deal with even more challenges rebuilding the trust of the people."

The Temple of Mythras was pretty hated throughout the Southern Kingdoms thanks to the fact that its policy for the past couple of generations had been to burn anyone who worshiped the Old Gods or had slightly other-than-the-norm lifestyle choices. I didn't necessarily believe that it was better to reform an institution like that than burn it to the ground, but Joan had done her best and managed to get the

Empire on our side. At least most of the Empire. Quite a few lords and priests had the view Mythras didn't know what he was talking about regarding Mythras' will. Which sounds funny until you realize its real-life people being murdered over the issue.

"I failed her as well," Garland said, once more ruminating in his own guilt.

"To be fair, you were dead for most of her life," I replied, not sure if that was the best thing to bring up. Garland had been dead for ten years of Mokosh time and the only reason the world hadn't moved on from his legend was because people had continued to walk around claiming to be him. He was the Mokosh version of Robin Hood or King Arthur but with a dozen claimants to the name, each adding to his story. In a way, he was right, he wasn't the only Garland of Nowhere anymore. Garland of Nowhere was larger than all of us, including the original. That would drive me insane. Well, insaner. I wasn't sure I had much claim to sanity these days given all the things I'd done.

Garland smiled. "That is true."

"You can still visit her," I replied, frowning. "After this. Be her father."

Garland looked at me as if I'd said the stupidest thing imaginable. Which was an impressive thing since his eyes were glowing and couldn't really express normal emotion. "You know that's not going to happen. Besides, I doubt the amount of parental attention she'd get from me would equal the kind she'd get from another man with my face."

I frowned. "I'm getting less of a compliment to my capacity as a hero now and more that this is just a way of indulging in your self-loathing."

"You sound like a priest," Garland said.

"Your priests do a lot of pop psychology?" I asked.

Garland shrugged. "Whatever that means. Ania is lucky to have you."

"She should be here," I replied.

"Because she would have your back?" Garland asked.

"Because she's going to kill me for not letting her be part of the mission to kill Veles," I said, knowing I hadn't had much choice.

"Probably," Garland said, frowning. "But from what I hear, the Ania you know is different from the one I knew. Softer."

"Maybe just sharper in a different way," I replied.

That was when Susanos spoke. "It is time! The portal is ready!"

"Oh joy," I muttered, about as excited as a kid who just found out Santa had brought him socks.

"Good luck, Aaron," Garland said. "We're going to need it."

I didn't dispute his statement as I gathered with the others in front of the portal. It wasn't too late to try to contact the others, to make sure they knew where I was going and why but I couldn't figure out a way to do it. Especially since they'd been removed from my party.

E-MAIL OTHER PLAYERS? Y/N

I blinked at the message appearing in my mind's eye.

I hit Y.

A keyboard and empty page appeared in front of my face as I thought a very simple message.

> WENT TO BALD MOUNTAIN WITH THE WITCH QUEEN. THE PORTAL IS GOING TO EARTH. GOING TO KILL VELES. RACHEL, ALEK, MAELOR, MARIA ROSE, AND JON ARE HERE. SOMEONE ELSE THAT WOULD TAKE TOO LONG TO EXPLAIN.
>
> OH, FAIR WARNING, NIGHTCHILDE'S POWER IS IN AGATA'S BABY. LIKE, I DON'T WANT TO SPRING THAT ON YOU BUT I HOPE YOU'LL FIGURE SOMETHING TO DO ABOUT IT. I'M PRETTY SURE SHE'S NOT POSSESSED OR ANYTHING, THOUGH. LIKE RACHEL ISN'T EVIL. JUST KIND OF INCESTUOUS.

Okay, I needed to wrap this message up because it was already going to go down in history as the worst e-mail of all time. There also wasn't much else to say. Well, maybe one last thing.

I LOVE YOU, ANIA.

I hit SEND.

Susanos began chanting a language I didn't understand as the portal began to swirl and shimmer like it contained a miniature hurricane. It reminded me a bit of the special effects for *Stargate*, but I supposed that was inevitable when dealing with interstellar (Interdimensional? I had no idea if Mokosh was in "our" universe or not) portals. Eventually, the effect changed to show an image of Washington DC.

Except Washington DC. had changed. It no longer resembled the one I'd seen in countless photos and visited that one time for Mock Trial in high school. Instead, it looked like some sort of twisted cyberpunk reimagining of America's capital.

It was nighttime and the sky was blanketed with storm clouds. There were black skyscrapers with red lights running along the side, one emblazoned with the Epic Dungeoneering™ E on the side, while the Washington Mall was nothing but a burnt-out crater. The White House was unharmed but now sported a set of red and black banners with a coiled dragon in the center. It looked like a hack's idea of a fascist takeover of the country.

"Man, Larry C.C. Weis' books are probably better off unfinished if this was where they were going," I muttered, staring at the sight.

With that, we headed into the portal.

I somehow knew I was never going to see the Southern Kingdoms again.

CHAPTER EIGHTEEN
DAYS OF FUTURE PRESENT

The arrival in Washington DC was less cataclysmic than I expected. I was getting used to the sense of queasiness that accompanied portal transportation, but it was still like going on a roller coaster for about thirty minutes. Whether interdimensional or interstellar, the distance between Mokosh and Earth was immense.

The world around me was utterly confusing and I briefly wondered if I wasn't going back to my Earth, but some sort of alternate version of the planet like in *Star Trek* or *Doctor Who*. At this point, the idea of parallel Earths wouldn't have shocked me.

The place looked like I'd stepped into *Cyber Dragons 2080*, the video game I'd worked on for Epic Dungeoneering™ with the premise of Earth falling into a cyberpunk dystopia and magic returning. I'd wanted to work on the Dark Undermaster games, but it turned out that when you became a game designer, you didn't choose when and where you'd apply your creative talents. Also, they'd work you like a dog with no overtime pay until they could replace you with someone cheaper and not yet disillusioned.

"How can all this be happening?" I muttered, staring at the sights around me. "It's like we're in Hell or something."

"No, it's Hill Valley. Although I can't imagine Hell being much worse," Jon replied, having moved from Susanos' shoulder back to mine.

Our group had arrived in the middle of a back alley in the shadow of one of the skyscrapers that couldn't have been constructed in the time I'd been away from the city, at least with normal means. There was a homeless guy lying in a group of newspapers that I didn't realize people still read and he looked so drunk that he didn't seem to notice the arrival of a bunch of adventurers from another world.

The walls were plastered with a bunch of flyers announcing President Andrew Veles' re-election campaign, to watch your neighbors, and a bunch of zombies attacking US soldiers with the tagline: THE LIVING VERSUS THE DEAD. TRUST YOUR GOVERNMENT. Which was perhaps the single most ominous flyer and not because of the zombies. The air also felt "charged" for lack of a better term and I was surprised I could still feel magic in the air. I had become accustomed to the feeling of sorcery while living in Mokosh and it was always there, like humidity in the air. You may not pay much attention to it but when it was absent, you felt it.

It was not absent.

It might even have been stronger.

Which was not a good sign.

My bracelets both pinged and I saw that I'd received let's just say a substantial reward.

MAIN QUEST UPDATED:
JOURNEY TO BALD MOUNTAIN (1/1)
ARRIVE AT EARTH (1/1)

REWARD:
+ 400,000 EXP
+ 500,000 EXP

Level 17 to 18
1,902,500/3,000,000

It was a rather substantial reward for just getting teleported and walking through a portal. However, it was entirely possible I was receiving a reward for what the rest of my "party" had done, which was clearly a lot of slaughtering and mayhem to get Bald Mountain clear of enemies. It was also possible that, like with the Fire Temple and Wind Temple, I was doing massive skipping of Veles' intended "plot."

One thing that I'd learned while living out my personal RPG journey was that if you had the freedom to sequence break around massive amounts of combat like so many speed-runners did, you absolutely would. Even with the fact you were rewarded for all the combat and dungeon crawls, most human beings were wired to avoid death-defying situations if they could. You needed a special kind of person like Bloodstorm—I'm not going to say psychopath—and a more *Spider-Man versus Wolverine* story. Jesus, what was with all the Spider-Man references lately?

It had mostly served me well and I'd probably avoided being killed multiple times because of my prudence but I couldn't help but feel like I was under-leveled as a result. Indeed, that was a reason why I'd spent the last year vacillating on going after Belobog. I'd wanted to level grind and make sure I was strong enough to defeat Veles.

Maybe I had just been a coward. Maybe it had just taken beating three gods and all the other craziness to make me realize just how insane it all was. Either way, I still felt under-leveled and unpowered for this throw down. Worse, my hesitation had clearly allowed him to change my world. People had suffered for my desire to get a slightly higher bonus to attack rating on my sword.

"How the hell did Veles do this all-in-one year?" I asked,

"He didn't," Susanos said, looking around with utter disdain. "This is the result of Veles dominating your world for the better part of a decade."

I paused. "What?"

"Time moves differently between Mokosh and Earth," Maelor said, as if it was the most normal thing in the world. "You're lucky your loved ones ended up being moved as they would have been top targets for the Deceiver."

"They still were," Alek said, looking around. "It's like they always say, you can't go home again."

I shook my head, still blown away by all this. "This was not what I agreed to."

Never mind that I hadn't really agreed to anything. Larry had me sign a contract but he'd made sure it had been in Polish without any chance to go over it. I'd been so blinded by the prospect of reading the next book that I hadn't bothered to note how utterly weird it had all been.

"Yeah, who would have thought that Larry C.C. Weis would lie to us!" Jon said, flapping his wings a bit.

I rolled my eyes. "So, the entire time I was gone, Veles was laying the groundwork for his takeover."

I felt like such a fool. I should have seen this coming. Hell, I'd had hints about what Veles was doing the entire time. He'd been harvesting magical wood at the Earth Temple and with workers from Earth. Bloodstorm had once worked at an Epic Dungeoneering™ shipping plant before being replaced with the undead. He'd been building up his resources here the entire time and I'd been too focused on Mokosh to follow up on it.

"Yes," Susanos said, raising her hands and muttering something incomprehensible.

Instantly, everyone's armor changed its appearance to clothing more appropriate for the setting that made us all look like we were gang members from the Eighties. Susanos was the sole exception, who found herself in a business suit dress that screamed corporate.

"Huh," I said, looking at my ripped blue jeans and leather jacket over a band t-shirt. None that I recognized. "I don't think this is going to get us into the White House."

"Veles rarely spends time in the White House," Susanos said. "What with it being in front of a giant crater and all that. If he is anywhere at all, it is usually the Epic Dungeoneering™ building. That is protected by his finest mercenaries and the death lords I was unable to persuade to switch sides. We must focus our attention on the UMCs in order to lure him out."

"The what now?" I asked.

Susanos pointed out past the city skyline to something in the distance that looked like a bunch of Eiffel Tower-sized metal constructions. They were being constantly hit by red lightning bolts and looked like something out of cyberpunk Mordor, which I supposed America had become in my absence.

"Wow, cell phone towers have really changed since we left," Jon said.

"These towers are bringing in magic from the æther and changing the fundamental physics," Susanos said, absently. "It is part of the crisis that allowed Veles to seize control over this country and others. People panic at the sight of things they do not understand. People morphing into elves, goblins, or dwarves will certainly do that. So will the appearance of dragons and magic."

"Veles must be a fan of *Shadowrun*," Jon muttered. "I love those games. The NES, Genesis, and computer versions I mean."

"I used to play the tabletop game," I admitted.

"Pfft, nerd," Jon said.

"Standard political philosophy for democracies," Maelor said. "Break everything and then say only you can fix it."

"It's why it's a silly system," Maria said, wearing a tight black leather dress that didn't come down to her knees. She also had poofy black hair and makeup that made me think fashion had gone back to the Eighties. My parents would love it.

"What is with Ledzianans and hating democracy," Jon muttered. "Where did the voting both touch you?"

"Democracy has its flaws," I said, ignoring Jon. "But you're really running a crap shoot with the whole king thing. Your child inheriting things is no guarantee of a good king."

"Which is why you should have an immortal god king. Hint, hint," Rachel said, leaning in on me. She was wearing mesh hose with a red dress that exposed generous amounts of cleavage. Her hair was every bit as large as Maria's.

"We need a six-inch rule, Rachel," I said, looking at her.

"Six inches of what?" Rachel asked, fluttering her eyelashes.

"*Distance*," I said, annoyed that she'd apparently inherited some weird combination of her mother's horniness and my snark.

Rachel pouted. "Fine."

"Immortal rulers certainly seem like a good idea," Maelor said, shrugging. He had a headband covering his ears, a blue jean jacket, a tank top shirt, and pants like mine. "Particularly when you're the immortal ruler. Believe me, I should know. However, in the end, it becomes all too easy to fall into bad habits."

"Like turning your nobility into bloodsucking horrors?" Garland asked. He was wearing a plain grey hoodie, tracksuit pants, and sunglasses.

"Yes," Maelor said. "It's better to be like the Sith Lords, only a master and an apprentice. That way you keep your rivals all in one place, but they keep you on your toes."

Before I could ask how Maelor knew about Sith Lords, Susanos cleared her throat. "If I may interrupt the inane banter portion of the evening, allow me to direct us back to our plan."

"You want to attack the big magical electrical towers, blow them up, and hopefully lure Veles out for a straight fight," I said, following her logic. Somewhat. "Which seems like a lot simpler plan than I'm really comfortable with."

"The simplest plans are best," Susanos said with a lot more confidence than I think was warranted.

"And you don't think he's going to just drone strike us," I said, referring to the fact we now had to deal with modern military tactics. Would we have to fight US soldiers? The police? What kind of resources could Veles bring to bear here now that he'd had a decade to consolidate his power?

"That is not his way," Susanos said. "Believe me, I have known him for thousands of years."

"You knew the old Veles," I replied. "The old Veles who hated oath breakers and wasn't actively trying to kill everyone everywhere."

"Like Morgoth in the *Silmarillion*," Jon said, showing he wasn't completely under Susanos' control. "Except Morgoth also wanted to destroy the afterlife, which Veles doesn't want to do. Yet."

Susanos' stare could have frozen water. Apparently, she wasn't entirely happy with us telling like it was with Veles. That didn't bode with.

"Right," I said, pausing. "I guess we should go with your plan then."

"We might not have time to come up with another," Garland said, surprising me.

"What do you mean?" I asked, confused.

"Veles is the god of your world now," Garland said, putting a neat little bow on how fucked we were now. "There may be other gods here, but he's managed to place himself on the throne of your most powerful nation."

"Not the first complete asshole to do so," Jon said, making a comment both sides of the political spectrum could agree on, if not the specifics.

"Which means?" Maria asked, looking at Garland rather than me. It seemed the only thing she hated more than her bastard stepson was me.

"It means that Veles may well know what we're doing anyway," Garland said. "He probably sensed our entrance the moment we opened a portal from Mokosh."

"Well, that's not good," I muttered, contemplating the very likely possibility that we were screwed before the mission had begun.

Susanos stared off in the distance. "All the more reason to do what we need to do. Quickly and with decisiveness."

"Halt! Put your hands up!" said a voice coming from the end of the alleyway.

Turning my head, I saw two police officers—a white man and a black man—standing there in leather jackets with a V patch on their lapels. Both had their guns drawn. I could see their police cruiser not far behind them at the beginning of the alley. I hoped they'd been close by or Veles already had our number.

"Oh goddamnit," I muttered.

One of them pulled out his walkie talkie and put it to his mouth. "We've got a Zero-B-Eleven incursion, sir. They're seven people who look like they stepped out of *The Warriors*. You know, the musical that's based on the old Eighties musical. My wife and I—"

"Die," Susanos said, extending a single bony finger toward the pair.

"No!" I shouted, trying to stop her.

But it was too late. The two of them froze up and collapsed to the ground like puppets whose strings had been cut. It was a reminder that I was travelling with casual killers and monsters.

"That was unnecessary," I said, wondering if I had enough juice to raise one from the dead.

"Do it and I'll kill them again," Susanos said. "We don't have time to deal with the local constabulary."

I turned around and hissed. "Yes, because killing cops is going to make it so much easier for us to operate!"

"How many guards and soldiers have you killed on my world?" Maria asked, looking at me with a dismissive look.

I didn't have a good answer for that. "Let's go blow up the fucking towers and have the final boss fight."

"That's the spirit!" Jon said. "None of this bullshit about endless doorstopper books where the story just keeps going on and on. No, sir, we're going to wrap this up, one and done with enough room to maybe do a trilogy but no more."

I stared down at the bodies of the dead cops on the ground, knowing they'd already called reinforcements. There was nothing I could do now, and I had to focus on the mission if I wanted to make their deaths worth it.

"Alright," I said, taking a deep breath. "Let's go blow up those towers and see if they summon the Devil."

"Oh, he is so much worse than the Devil," Maelor said. "We could have handled Old Scratch at level 12 or 13."

"I really would love to know what people in-universe think of RPG mechanics," Jon said.

"Bring them up and die," Susanos said, waving her hand in the air.

With that, I felt my center of gravity lift and I was hurtling into the air.

CHAPTER NINETEEN
THE BATTLE OF THE TEN THOUSAND TOWERS

I have made a horrible mistake.

These are undoubtedly the words that will be printed upon my tombstone. Well, assuming I had a tombstone. At this point, I gave even odds that I ended up as a mindless undead servant, was buried in an unmarked grave by the US government or was blown to pieces when Veles ate Earth like Galactus.

Was Veles going to eat Earth like Galactus? I had no idea. He said he was going to kill everyone to achieve his insane idea of paradise. Was he going to do it with nukes? Exploding the sun? Zombie plague? The last one seemed likely and that was almost a relief.

I mean, zombies were slow and easily killed monsters. There was no way things would end like they had in *World War Z*. Even if the initial outbreak was everywhere, surely the governments of the world would know how to handle a pandem... Okay, I hear what I'm thinking now.

Either way, I was now travelling with a bunch of supervillains and we'd arrived at the scary ominous towers with little resistance. The place was being guarded by a bunch of rent-a-cops when I'd been expecting dragons or the National Guard.

"Run you idiots!" I shouted, hoping to save them from getting annihilated when Susanos descended with the rest of us floating around us.

Some did.

The cops pulled out their pistols and suicidally fired, their bullets bouncing off the protection spell that Susanos had conjured. I wondered whether I would have to fight my so-called companions to save these poor fools.

Fortunately, or unfortunately, depending on your perspective, that didn't turn out to be necessary. As mentioned, there were barely any defenses for the huge field of towers that were channeling sorcery from the cosmos onto my home planet. It wasn't really a sight that inspired awe, looking like a combination of electrical towers and oil rigs really, but I could tell just how much it was doing, just how much the air crackled with magic.

It was, in a real way, the moment I accepted I was never going to come back to "my" Earth because it no longer existed. Veles had used the massive amount of resource stripping and experimentation he'd been doing on Mokosh to prepare my world to become more hospitable to him. He'd spread the stories by Larry C.C. Weis—even though he was the bad guy—because it made a place for Veles among Earth's mostly silent pantheons.

I didn't know the exact specifics of how this all worked but I had the suspicion that Earth would always be a place of magic now. The problem was that the only people trained in it were those already sworn to the god of darkness. My story was no longer an *isekai*, if it was, because Earth was now a fantasy world too. Why did that prospect fill me with dread? Even without gods of darkness putting their finger on the scale? God, I had become cynical over the past year.

Maelor was the first person to attack the fifty-foot-tall structures around us, unleashing a black shadowy tendril which tore the tower in half. There was brief explosion in its center as equipment caught fire and the erection fell to one side.

"Destroy them," Susanos said, simply. "Destroy them all. We must make as much noise as we can to lure the Worm of the Underworld to battle."

"And hope it's not a dinner bell," Jon said flying into the air and transforming himself into a dragon.

NEW QUEST ADDED
DESTROY UNIVERSAL MAGICAL CONDUCTORS 1/10,000

I didn't have much hope for this plan's success, but it certainly seemed to be working. Susanos, Maelor, and Rachel blasted the towers with their powers. Garland and Maria used blades that slashed through the steel beams like they were tissue paper before pushing them over, resembling were anime heroes or superheroes. Alek used a ring to conjure packages of C4 explosives that he applied strategically, one after the other and detonated in the most peculiar merger of magic and science I'd seen so far. Jon? Well, Jon was burning them from the sky because he was a frigging dragon.

`Me?

I was more hesitant because I wanted to make sure there were no remaining workers or security guards around. I may not have been able to stop my Brotherhood of Evil Mutants-esque brethren from killing anyone who stood in their way, but I could certainly get any survivors away. I hesitated to go all out but not because blowing up a bunch of government property was a bad idea, but because I felt like wasting all my spell energy on towers was a bad idea if this was going to be just a prelude to our showdown with Veles.

Real magic didn't work 100% like in *Dungeons and Dragons* but was closer to *Final Fantasy*'s early depiction of sorcery. You had spell "slots" and only X amount of them per day as a representation of just how much juice you were able to channel through your body. The stronger a wizard you were, the more you could throw down. Blasting away at all these towers seemed like we were wasting a lot of energy before the big fight like running down the entrance to ringside before a big match. Which probably was the only MMA reference I was ever going to make.

Indeed, the more I thought about it, the more that I realized my biggest issues here were how utterly half-cocked this all was. I didn't know if Susanos had packed potions of refreshment or not. It wouldn't have surprised me if she did or had another way to restore our expended power. But that was the real rub: I didn't know any of her plans regarding attacking Veles, how to fight him, or other essential plans.

I mean, I made most of my plans up on the fly—which prevented them from being called plans at all really—but I normally liked to make some sort of outline of a strategy. I knew my team and their capabilities. Susanos had been deliberately vague with details and only introduced me to the others literally an hour before.

Was this some sort of trap? That didn't make sense either since Susanos could have taken me out at Crossroad. Even Sparky couldn't have stopped her if she'd wanted to. Hell, before Crossroad, she'd had us at the Elemental Temple of Water. Maybe I was overestimating her power level, but I somehow suspected I wasn't.

I was still pondering the idea when I heard someone calling out. "Please, someone—anyone—help!"

All around me there were exploding towers and displays of magic as well as combat that defied description. Maria leapt dozens of feet in the air to swing around a glowing whip that bisected the tops of towers off while Garland used freezing spells before shattering them with his own version of PUSH. It was very noisy and distracting but I still heard the words.

"Damnit, why did I have to choose to be neutral good?" I muttered, looking for the survivor and knowing that they probably weren't going to think I was coming to rescue them. What with me being involved in multiple felony murders and what was probably terrorism by the laws of our new Orwellian state.

But I had to try.

It didn't take long, thankfully, to find one of the security guards trapped under a piece of fallen tower that had just barely managed to avoid crushing him. He was in his thirties, had a five o'clock shadow, and a bit of a belly. Certainly, he didn't look threatening, and his gun was several feet away where he'd dropped it. He also looked terrified.

"Okay, you're not going to like me, but I need you to stop screaming and stand still," I said, trying to be as calming as possible.

The security guard screamed at me. "AAAAAAAH!"

"Oh, for Pete's sake," I muttered. "FRIENDSHIP. LESSER CHARM. SUGGESTION. I need you to stand still and let me rescue you."

Using all three spells was overkill and probably the exact opposite of preserving my energy but I was also trying to save a life here. Thankfully, overkill or not, it worked, and the security guard froze up with his hands over his head.

"Thank you," I said, taking a deep breath. "PUSH!"

The metal flew into the air and scattered nearby, thankfully not hitting the security guard along the way. I wasn't naive. (Much as that sentence would cause Ania and Alek to laugh at me.) I'd been fighting a war for over a year now and it had cost innocent people their lives. There was no such thing as a clean war, even when you were fighting against annihilation. People died who you didn't want to.

The security guard stood up then, seemingly confused that he wasn't dead. "Thank you."

"You're wel—" I started to say.

Unfortunately, no sooner did I open my mouth than the security guard's face twisted into a horrific corpse-like visage. The face was rotted through and one of his eyes was missing. His mouth was full of greenish pus and teeth that were twisted into little, tiny daggers of bone. He was a deathrot wight and coming at me with fingers that ended in claws jutting out through his flesh at the tips of his fingers.

I sliced his head off with the Perun sword, cutting through bone and flesh like they were air.

The wight promptly fell over and disintegrated into powder. It had successfully hidden itself from my so-called divine senses and made me realize just how screwed Earth possibly was. The deathrot plague had almost wiped out the Southern Kingdoms and left some places looking like *Resident Evil 4*.

This? This was worse.

The zombies were among us, capable of acting like regular human beings, and I was without a pair of sunglasses to see their true form like Roddy Piper in *They Live*. No sooner did I finish contemplating this than my bracelets pinged.

QUEST UPDATED
DESTROY UNIVERSAL MAGICAL CONDUCTORS 58/10,000

Yeah, we weren't destroying these things nearly fast enough. I decided to put my maximum demigod intelligence towards figuring a way we could start a chain reaction or overload the devices so they could all be detonated at once. It was a long shot but we might be able to make this go from being a pointless exercise in destruction to a very pointed one.

Spotting the only building in this massive field, I ran up a set of metal steps and across a catwalk to the door leading inside. The door was locked but that didn't mean anything to someone who had a magic sword.

Inside, I saw, thankfully, all the staff had run for their lives and there were no more survivors or wights pretending to be them. Some had even left behind their coffee and donuts. I grabbed an untouched one and some of the coffee before sitting down at one of the computer terminals. It was still logged on and I took advantage of that.

Figuring out a wholly unique system that incorporated magic into it should have been impossible. However, I recognized the programming style. The computers all ran on repurposed Epic Dungeoneering™ bullshit software and apparently things hadn't gotten any more advanced in the past ten years than what I'd been working with back in Michigan. My mind also worked at an astoundingly faster rate. It was, to press my luck, easy.

Too easy.

WARNING - DANGEROUS REACTION OVERLOAD WILL OCCUR IF YOU REMOVE SAFETIES. DO YOU WISH TO CONTINUE?
Y/N?
Y.

YOU HAVE TRIGGERED A DANGEROUS OVERLOAD. THIS AREA WILL DETONATE WITHIN TEN TO TWELVE MINUTES.

PRAISE VELES.

I didn't have any problem believing Veles would make it relatively easy to blow up the place. He was, after all, a man who had absolutely zero fucks to give about the safety of his minions. He was going to eventually kill them all as well, I assumed, or at least turn them into undead. Still, I was grateful when the alarms started blaring around the facility. That meant it would be easy enough to convince everyone else in the building to evacuate.

So, I ran out of the steps waving my hands. "Hey, everyone! The place is going to blow! We need to get the hell out of here!"

No one paid any attention.

Ah, goddammit.

QUEST UPDATED
DESTROY UNIVERSAL MAGICAL CONDUCTORS 115/10,000

Yeah, we weren't going to get this done before things went to hell.

"It's going to blow!" I shouted.

With that, Jon came down and turned back into his human form. He was wearing a Nirvana t-shirt and ripped jeans. He looked like he'd just come from a cover band concert.

"What was that?"

"The field of towers! I've set them to overload!" I shouted.

"I'm right here, dipshit!" Jon said, annoyed.

"I'm not..." I sighed. "We need to get the hell out of here."

"We're waiting for—" Jon started to say.

That was when the sky split. A terrifying crack in the fabric of reality opened to a greenish-black, sickly-looking dimension where I could see spectral phantasms swirling around dark clouds. Hovering in the sky was the Eye of Providence in front of a pyramid, just like on the back of a dollar bill. It was the kind of visual you saw at the climax of bad Eighties horror movies only with a much higher budget. Descending from the sky was a cloaked figure that crackled with power as far above the other gods I'd fought as they'd been above me.

NEW QUEST ADDED
SURVIVE 0/1

"Meep," Jon said, sounding like a cartoon character.

"Ah," I said, looking up. "I guess I underestimated Susanos' plan. It was stupid but worked. Veles is here."

CHAPTER TWENTY
THE WRATH OF VELES

Veles descended from the sky like an angry god. Okay, not *like* an angry god, but just *as* an angry god. As much as I despised the man for all the evil shit he'd done to Mokosh and me personally, he still possessed the power to awe my mere mortal heart.

Demigod or not.

I'd faced Veles before, in a dream, but he'd never actually made a move to fight me. Really, he'd just showed up, terrified off the Wise Man and then sent Valentin to kill me. I'd always wondered why he hadn't just snapped his fingers and caused me to die then and there. Now I understood. Pride.

Veles also wasn't a coward, no matter the fact that he'd chosen to flee Mokosh. No, he'd shown up here directly with none of his armies. Veles was ready to hash it out with us and that took courage. Mind you, it was the kind of courage required by Andre the Giant fighting the Seven Dwarves, but courage it was.

Veles settled down close to me rather than any of the others among the destroyed towers and lowered his head before conjuring a staff that suspiciously resembled Skeletor's from the Eighties *Masters of the Universe* cartoon.

"Oh Aaron, still fleeing from the godhood of my brother?" Veles said. "I was hoping you'd take my warning and not do something incredibly stupid."

I shrugged. "What can I say? High INT and low WIS score."

"Veles!" Susanos shouted, floating over with her fists crackling. Each of them contained a lightning bolt and the fury in her eyes made me think, death lord or not, there was something still very human inside her.

"Ah, the ex," Veles said, sighing. "This is going to be awkward."

"I challenge you, false god!" Susanos called out, her mouth frothing with rage. "I challenge you for the betrayal of our love, your worshipers, and all the thousands of promises you whispered before breaking them! I challenge you for the divinity promised and denied! In spite's name, for hatred's sake, I come to bring you the death you have brought millions of others!"

"Khaaaaaaan!" Jon said, sounding desperate to find some distraction from the two titans about to clash.

I honestly thought my friend would be annihilated in that moment, but I doubted his words even registered to Susanos. I had my answer for why she was acting so irrationally and seemingly without thought: love. Love was at the heart of her battering ram-like philosophy and love would be our undoing or Veles'.

It was kind of sweet, really.

Terrifying, but sweet.

Veles, however, was not nearly as invested in her as the reverse. "My dear, it is not me, it's you. Stars have been born, changed color, and exploded in the time it takes me to care about someone. You were never more than a passing fancy, a convenience, and your worth to me is less than the dirt I could pick up in my hand."

"Ouch," I said, grimacing.

Veles wasn't done yet, though. "Godhood? You? You have neither the pedigree nor the temperament to be raised even to the least ranks of my kind. Given near unlimited power and immortality, you have accomplished less than Aaron has in a year."

"Don't bring me into this," I said, frowning.

"You wish to distract me," Susanos said, narrowing her eyes. "You think I am still a besotted young milkmaid living in a hovel like you found me. I have grown more powerful than you could possibly comprehend, so-called creator god. No, this is the hour of your end."

Wow, this really was just about two exes.

"You are just that besotted young milkmaid," Veles said. "Except you are a mummified corpse of her that clothes herself in illusions and artifice. As for the hour of my end? Your delusions are as asinine as your ambitions. I am at the moment of my triumph over not only the gods of Mokosh and Earth but all of the pantheons."

Garland, Maelor, Maria, Alek, and Rachel moved into battle positions. I could tell all of them were ready and willing to fight but this all felt wrong. Also, none of them had heard that this place was about to explode. I didn't want to tell, though.

Was I cold-blooded enough to try to turn this into an involuntary suicide strike? I wasn't. Not just because Alek was my brother-cousin, as stupid as the choices he made, and Rachel was my sorta-daughter, weird incest vibes that she seemed to think were funny. No, it was that it was bad tactics. I had no idea if it would take out Veles and never would unless he decided to let me know in the afterlife.

"Triumph? I see no signs of triumph," Susanos said, glowing brightly with a nimbus of magical power. "I see a monster that relied deeply on the four Elemental Demons to vampirize Mokosh in his place. I see a scavenger and worm who fled with a handful of forces when the tide turned. You are nothing but false bravado concealing a weak assassin and kinslayer. You are spent, Ancient One. Being one of the Old Gods does not make you stronger, simply old."

Veles smiled.

It was not a pretty look. He looked identical to the actor Peter Stormare, and it was the kind of ridiculousness that had allowed me to overlook how terrifying my past year of adventures had been. Except, it no longer worked. Somewhere along the way, it had become just the face of the god of evil.

"Oh, my dear, you did me the favor of assembling all of my enemies in one place," Veles replied. "Better still, you separated the one person who had an infinitesimally small but real chance of defeating me from those who most had his back."

"Die, God of Evil!" Susanos shouted, blasting Veles with a beam formed of the rawest magic. Something that wasn't sorcery formed into fire or ice. It was the kind of primordial energy the universe was formed from.

The beam sailed outward and struck Veles at point blank range. Half of the creator deity's face melted away, exposing a skull that caught fire. It reminded me of Ghost Rider for a brief second before I realized Veles was preparing for his counterattack.

Everyone else in the ground proceeded to strike at Veles even as I conjured a Globe of Invulnerability to hold off the friendly fire. Alek fired his enhanced M-16, magical bullets firing in a burst. Maria shouted a prayer to the long-deceased spirit of Perun to bless her strike with her whip. Maelor pulled out a pair of shadow infused short swords while he used short range teleportation to stab quickly before retreating. Garland swung his blade and green fire shot forth that blasted against Veles. Jon reminded everyone that he'd been a bare-fisted martial artist before he'd been a dragon by combining them into his next attack.

"DRAGON PUNCH!" Jon shouted, glowing with a blue aura before striking at Veles with a blow that would have insta-killed a giant.

Rachel called forth a Meteor Strike that hit Veles like an orbital mass driver. I was very glad of the Globe of Invulnerability because it would have annihilated me as well.

Not cool, Rachel.

Veles laughed like this was funny. "And you, Aaron? What is your assault? Perun cannot protect you anymore."

That was one of the differences between reality and tabletop RPGs. There was no such thing as turn-based combat and whoever was fastest could hit as hard as they could as many times as they could in as short a time as possible. Still, Veles was just letting everyone take their shot. This was all wrong and was either a case of gross overconfidence on his part or he knew something we didn't.

But, dammit, sometimes you had to take your best shot. I dispelled the Globe of Invulnerability around me, took the Sword of Perun, and swung it around. I buried it into the side of Veles and channeled the lightning within me. The divine power of Perun remaining in my bracelets crackled and I realized they were trying to communicate with me. They had one word: Run.

Veles cackled as the rest of his face fell away to become purely a decaying skull, the flames around his face turned blue, white. "I actually felt that, Aaron. It's a pity you ran from power for so long that it killed you."

Susanos intensified her blasting of Veles with her magic, only for Veles to raise his hand. "REFLECT."

The spell that struck us was horrifying as Susanos was hit with all of the flames she'd struck Veles with, Rachel screamed as she caught fire with flaming meteor fragments, Alek was hit by multiple bullets, shadows engulfed Maelor, terrible flaming whip burns struck Maria, Jon flew across the air like he'd been kicked by Bruce Lee, and I felt myself electrocuted.

YOU HAVE TAKEN FIFTY-ONE POINTS OF DAMAGE.

The whole video game nature of magic was fundamentally silly but it was just an extrapolation of how sorcery worked on Mokosh. For Veles, the rules were more like guidelines, and he'd just hit us with a 10th level spell equivalent. Something that took all of our attacks and forced us to experience them.

"Poor fools," Veles said, grabbing Susanos by her throat and draining the energy of the lich into himself. "This was never a fight that could be settled by force of arms. Who did you think you were, marching up to me as if I would choose to fight fair? Tales of heroism and daring deeds are nothing more than the poppy juice of the common man. Lies told to children that make them think they have a chance to fight against the boot that will rest upon their throat forever."

"Curse you, Veles!" Susanos said, spitting bone dust. She was once more the hideously desiccated thing that was her true form. She spoke some sort of spell in a language I didn't understand, and I felt myself suddenly better.

YOU HAVE BEEN HEALED OF FIFTY POINTS OF DAMAGE.

"One cannot fight the ocean with a rainstorm," Veles said. "Everything that you are, Susanos is something that I gave you. I now take back that power and consign you to the pit of oathbreakers with all those other poor whores that were unwise enough to trust me."

"No!" Jon shouted, conjuring a fireball in his hands before shooting it at Veles despite the spell that the creator god had cast. The magic Susanos had worked upon him might have been artificial, but it was no less real. Jon was a man in love and ready to die for a woman who was exploiting him.

Knowing that Jon was going to get himself killed, I called forth every bit of my will to try to cast a spell. "DISPEL MAGIC!"

Much to my surprise, the magic crashed against the spell Veles had woven around him and shattered it. Veles, despite having his face reduced to a burning skull, looked at me in surprise before the others descended upon him. He was struck first with Jon's fireball blast, Susanos' fire, and Garland's strike with his sword. Our group prepared to rally against the god of evil.

That was when things went to hell.

"Alright," Veles said. "Point to you."

Maelor pulled out a bow made of shadows, only for Veles to flash step toward him and shove his fist through the elvish vampire's chest. The god of the Underworld ripped out Maelor's soul, causing the ancient assassin to disintegrate. Maelor's spirit thrashed in Veles' hand before the god let him go, causing his ghost to vanish.

"No!" Maria screamed. "Monster!"

MAELOR HAS DIED.

"Yes," Veles said, pointing a bony finger at her. "Who sends a bunch of undead against the god who created them? RELEASE SOUL."

Maria thrashed back and began vomiting blood, her body developing horrific red veins before she exploded. It was a nightmarish sight, not the least because it meant that Ania and Agata would never get a chance to reunite with her mother.

MARIA HAS DIED.

"Eat modern weaponry, asshole!" Alek shouted, throwing a sticky grenade. The grenade stopped midair and reversed itself, slamming into my cousin before throwing him across the room. I didn't have a chance to react before the explosion signaled his death.

ALEK HAS DIED.

"Ha!" Veles said. "You're right, Aaron, PUSH is incredibly fun."

"Bastard!" I shouted, striking again with Perun's sword.

Veles was promptly impaled by Garland with his sword as the weapon went through his chest and out his back.

"You are not a god," Garland said, coldly. "There is no such thing. You are just a very old and powerful wizard that has delusions of grandeur. Even the afterlife is just a simulation of those we have lost."

"You should have stayed dead, Garland," Veles said. "The only reason you were worshiped as a hero is that people enjoy pretending mediocre men like themselves have a chance of attracting women. RELEASE SOUL!"

Garland's final death was less gruesome than Maria's but no less distressing. The greenish balefire within him escaped from his mouth and eyes as he burned from within. The great hero of the Dark Undermaster Saga had only come back for a short time, but I was helpless to do anything about his end. Like the Wise Man, the forces set against Veles were collapsing in rapid order.

I changed my mind about not being willing to sacrifice myself to destroy Veles. It was increasingly clear we were losing this fight. I wouldn't be able to protect my daughter any more than I would be able to protect my cousin. Keeping Veles here until the place exploded might be the only chance we had to destroy the ancient monster.

"Death has no hold on me, Veles," Susanos said, making elaborate hand gestures as strange glowing sigil patterns appeared in the air. Some of them being elaborate Enochian circles and others collections of runes. All of them formed together into a single symbol. "My soul is hidden away from you, and I know part of your true name. Enough to bind you to this place and keep you here until all of us die. Only I will remain to be reborn."

Veles glowed and struggled as the symbol appeared on his chest. It was hard to see facial expressions on a skeleton and mummy, but it seemed the two of them were locked in an epic contest of wills. Whether or not it would be enough to hold Veles in place long enough for this place to go up was anyone's guess.

"Oh," I said, pausing. "So, you did hear me. Is this the plan we're going with? Right. Thanks for telling us."

"Wait, what?" Jon asked.

"Yeah, I don't think she's that into you," I said, falling back and throwing every single spell I could at Veles.

Rachel grabbed me. "No, Father. Now is not the hour of your death. Be gone from this place and survive. TELEPORT WITHOUT ERROR."

"Hold on, I'm not leaving—"

I didn't get to say anything more because I found myself disappearing from the field and collapsed on the ground a mile or more from the place. I was surrounded by a bunch of abandoned houses in the suburbs. The houses were boarded up and there were warning signs against zombies. Another sign that my world had changed dramatically in the time I'd been away from it.

That was when I saw the mushroom cloud in the distance.

"No," I muttered in horror.

QUEST COMPLETED
SURVIVE 1/1

CHAPTER TWENTY-ONE
ESCAPE FROM CAMP 32

I'd wandered around for an hour after the nuclear (magic?) event. I was in a fugue state over the death of my cousin and possibly my daughter. I had no idea if I was once more exposed to lethal amounts of radiation or whether the mushroom cloud was just a result of a sufficiently large explosion.

At least my Mark of the Champion still worked. Both functioned perfectly but could give me no updates to the status of the other members of my team.

Rachel [???]
Jon [???]
Susanos [???]

REWARD:
80,000 EXP [Defeat Avatar]
17,500 EXP (Sabotage UMCs]

Level 17 to 18
2,000,000/3,000,000

I only cared about two of the names. Unfortunately, it was the reward for "killing" Veles that disturbed me most. Even though

Susanos had prevented him from teleporting away and blowing up an entire field of magical towers in his face, it didn't say that he'd been killed, only defeated. Worse, 80,000 EXP wasn't nearly enough to justify him being finally defeated forever.

Veles was alive.

I could feel it

But what was going on? When even your magical bracelets couldn't tell you what the hell was going on, you didn't have many options. I didn't resist when a pair of FBI agents (I think) grabbed me. They had magical fireballs and I wanted to know what was going on. But that was how I ended up at the black site.

Which I was now fleeing through.

"Okay, that was awesome," Jon said, jogging ahead of me. "I mean, terrifying but awesome. If Michael Bay was directing us, we totally would have had that as the big finale. Will Smith and Martin Lawrence could play us in some race-blind casting. Obviously, I'm Will Smith. Bad boys, bad boys, whatcha gonna do—"

"My cousin died, Jon," I said, not exactly in the mood to make cracks at this time.

"With all due respect to your grief and longstanding personal relationship with the man, Alek was sort of an enormous asshole who killed *a lot* of innocent people," Jon said, looking uncomfortable. "Including Ania and Agata's aunt. Okay, innocent-ish."

I didn't really have a defense for that. "Be that as it may—"

"Maybe we should file him under the Thistle and Nightchilde portion of our allies list. I.e. the people only Aaron and the immediate family will mourn. You, because you're Ranger Jesus, which is distinct from Marvel Jesus who is Deadpool. Did you know they rebooted the Marvel Cinematic Universe while we were away? Henry Cavill is now Captain America."

"Jon..."

"I mean, I'm going to show all the respect to your parents and sister about Alek's death. Don't get me wrong. I like them, especially your sister. Speaking of which, were she and Alek fucking? I just want to be

100% sure because your family has strong Targaryen vibes. What with the divine blood and all."

"Jon!" I inserted. "Why is this place empty? Please answer that so we can change the subject, and I don't have to beat the shit out of you. Because, right now, I'm ready to."

The black site where I'd been dumped was almost completely abandoned. Every workstation we passed had signs of people working there from half-eaten salads to coffee but no actual people. The massive numbers of guards and secret agents I'd expected, though, were missing. We'd encountered a few wights but the one janitor we'd come across took one look at us and ran like hell.

"Still waters before a storm, gotcha," Jon said, sighing. "My bad. I'm trying to cope with this myself."

That was about as honest as I was ever going to get from Jon in all likelihood. "Yeah, well, I am sorry about your, uh, undead dommy mommy."

"Oh, I don't mind that!" Jon said, giving a dismissive wave. "She was mind-controlling me the whole time! It was purely metaphysical. Also, physical."

"Which I suppose distracts from the fact you were fucking a corpse," I replied.

"Says the guy who banged multiple vampires," Jon said.

"Who were still moist and bouncy," I replied. "Whereas the other is just mind control and illusion."

"Does that matter? Are there tiers to the desirability of the undead?"

"I think so, yeah," I said, glad to get back into the pattern of snarking at one another. "Where are we headed."

I almost stopped dead in my tracks when we passed the cafeteria, and I saw it was full of wights. Mindless, horrifying, and fresh ones pounding at the door that had been chained up. It was a scene straight from Dawn of the Dead as there were hundreds of individuals inside. They were also wearing lanyards, suits, lab coats, hospital scrubs, and military uniforms. So, yeah, I now had a pretty good idea as to what happened to the staff at the black site.

Jon didn't stop.

So, neither did I.

"Have I missed something?" I asked.

"Sort of, yeah," Jon said. "Not the complete fall of civilization but certainly something that is probably going to preempt the *Game of Thrones* revival as well as all other television for the next few months."

"They revived *Game of Thrones*?" I asked. "As what?"

Jon didn't get a chance to answer that question, though, because the two of us burst through a door to the parking lot. I immediately heard gunfire and saw that Rachel was standing there, scars on her face, and in a pair of blue jeans with a tank top. She was shooting at several wights and had already put down three.

"Ah, crap," Jon said, pulling out two pistols and throwing himself to the side as everything slowed down around us. Jon proceeded to double tap each zombie in the head before time resumed and he slammed against the concrete walkway down from the door entrance. Veles might be evil but at least his facilities were handicap accessible.

"When the hell did you get bullet time powers?" I asked, looking at Jon.

"Apparently, that's just a thing I can do as an 18th level warrior [monk]," Jon said. "I mean, it turns out there's a huge number of abilities I never got to use because I was too focused on Pwiffle. Oh, btw, Pwiffle is a massive esport now. Not just in Korea. They have television matches and everything these days."

"Uh huh," I said, jumping over Jon's fallen form and heading to Rachel's side.

I gave my erstwhile daughter a big hug. "I am so glad you're alive."

"Enough to let me give you a BJ?" Rachel asked.

I pulled back and lifted my arms. "And you've ruined it. Forever."

"I'm kidding," Rachel said. "Unless you say yes."

"She's kidding," Jon said. "We're dating now!"

I stared between them. "What the hell is wrong with both of you? Also, when the hell did this happen?"

"About a year ago," Jon said. "We were working on ways to break it to you."

"It was time we mostly spent coordinating mind games upon you," Rachel said. "It brought us closer to together."

I stared between them. "I am so happy to see you both, I am going to ignore that is fucking evil. How are you alive?"

"I keep two teleportation spells on me," Rachel said, simply. "Getting you away was the priority and trying to keep Veles imprisoned at the tower site long enough for his avatar to be destroyed was the second. I took Jon away at the last second."

"Like, literally, the last second," Jon said, pausing. "Which is not a good thing to do if you don't want to give a dragon kung fu master a heart attack."

"What happened to Susanos?" I asked, looking around and half expecting her to show up.

"Who cares!" Jon said, waving around his arms as if he was flapping them. "She was mind controlling me to not realize I already had an awesome thing going on with a goddess of love. Seriously, you're not very observant. We've been banging—"

"I will break your face," I replied.

"Wow, this war has taken a toll on you," Jon said, shaking his head. "You're going from Spider-Man to Frank Castle. Ranger War Journal: *I am really mean to Jon and threatening him with violence because he took my incest baby.*"

"You both suck," I said, not missing a beat. Weirdly, it was reassuring to know this whole creepy vibe had been a yearlong prank orchestrated by my supposed best friend. Mind you, that meant he was a psychopath (or just incredibly bored). "Still, the question stands. Where *is* the Witch Queen?"

"Susanos' physical body has been destroyed but she almost certainly brought her soul object with her. Then it becomes a question if she'd had time to hide it some place before the tower field exploded. If she didn't, then she's permanently dead. If she did—"

"We'll see her again," I muttered. "Great."

"Well, she was on our side," Jon said, pausing. "Sort of."

"We were just tools for her revenge plan," I replied. "A not terribly well-conceived revenge plan, I might add. Do we have a car? Because

I'm pretty sure this place is going to be overrun with wights once they break free from the cafeteria."

"Yes," Rachel said, lifting a key fob and clicking it.

A futuristic black Lamborghini that looked like one of the top tier cars in *Cyber Dragons 2080* flickered its lights. Apparently, being a civil servant in the dark world ruled by Veles paid a lot more than it did previously.

"Nice," I said, simply. "What about Veles?"

That was when there was the sound of a door smashing open along with moaning from the inside of the building. The benefit of divine hearing, I supposed. It seemed the wights had broken out and were now spreading through the facility.

"Later," Rachel said. "We've got to get out of here."

I'd expended all my magic trying to take down Veles except for *Mass Undead Slaying*. I took a moment to cast that spell and shot it down through the hall. It went through the death wights like an anime laser blast and annihilated something like ninety of them in a single go. Much to my surprise, it left a glowing blue flame on the ground that the survivors stumbled on and caught fire from before the flames leapt to other wights. In a few seconds, it seemed like they'd all been destroyed.

REWARD:
100,000 EXP (Clear Black Site 31)

Level 17 to 18
2,100,000/3,000,000

Rachel blinked. "Okay, maybe we can spare a few minutes."

"Wow, you got more EXP for wiping out a bunch of mooks than destroying Veles' avatar," Jon said, staring. "That is bullshit."

"You can see those?" I asked.

"Duh, I'm your familiar," Jon said.

Amazing how he can say so much and explain so very little. "Right. Anyway, I'm optimized to slay the undead," I replied, shrugging. "The benefits of min/maxing."

"Yeah, yeah, you have hate crime powers against the living dead," Jon said, shrugging. "It would have been great if you'd had godslaying skills back when we were following Susanos. As much as I hate to admit it, you are the better tactician. I, on the other hand, am more a lover than a strategist."

I rolled my eyes. "Does that mean Veles' avatar was destroyed?"

"No," Rachel said, walking to the Lambo. "He drained something like a hundred thousand of his followers of their life force to sustain himself. That's resulted in panic across Washington DC. Whole swaths of the government and Epic Dungeoneering™ have dropped over before rising from the dead. The illusions covering a lot of them have also failed. Everyone is being advised to stay indoors and wait for reinforcements from the Anti-Undead Task Force."

I stared in horror. "A hundred thousand people?"

"Those who knew what Veles was and sold themselves to him," Rachel said. "These kind of soul pacts can't be made without full knowledge from both participants. Because magic."

"It's okay, Aaron. They were bad, so it was okay to murder them. It's the American way," Jon said, patting me on the shoulder.

I glared. "What does this mean?"

"It means that Veles is weakened," Rachel said. "But not dead. He's going to be extremely pissed off when he recovers."

The Lamborghini's doors rose up in the air.

"Great," I said, walking down to get into the driver's seat. Much to my surprise, I found that its steering wheel was bound and there was a weird computer that had a low level magical feed. "Huh. I have no idea how to drive this."

"You don't," Rachel said. "All the cars in the future are self-driving."

"Ah," I said.

"Don't worry," Rachel said. "None of the demons bound to them are sentient so it's not slavery."

I blinked. "Demons, huh."

"Yep," Rachel said, getting in the backseat. "There's a reason Epic Dungeoneering™'s EVs are the best on the market."

Jon, of course, climbed in the passenger side. "I'm not going to lie, our chances went from shitty to really shitty with what happened."

"I get that," I said, pausing. "I guess I'm going to have to figure out a way to beat a god that doesn't obey any rules."

I stared at the steering wheel for a second then shrugged and snapped my fingers in front of it. Much to my surprise, the vehicle started up and displayed a map of Washington DC's transformed landscape, listing all the various places that were now cordoned off due to zombie infestations. Great, I had started *The Walking Dead*. Or, at least, Veles had and I wasn't someone who'd prepared for it.

That Veles could draw on his followers to keep himself alive was a sign that we were no longer operating on "fair play" RPG rules. I mean, Veles had been cheating from the very beginning, but this was beyond the pale. It meant he would do anything to survive and win our conflict. I'd hoped, on some level, that the original Veles would let us "reset" him the same way the other Old Ones had been, restoring them.

No dice it seemed.

Hehe, dice.

"Well, you can talk to Ania about it," Jon said, entering an address on the computer screen.

"What?" I asked, doing a double take.

CHAPTER TWENTY-TWO
GETTING THE BAND BACK TOGETHER

"Ania is here?" I asked, genuinely surprised.

"Uh, duh," Jon said, sitting in the backseat. "Wasn't that part of your master plan?"

"The assumption I have a master plan seems to be the place where you start being wrong," I said, sighing. "I thought Susanos had a master plan."

I probably should have seen it coming since I'd sent out a message right before I'd left. If I'd been thinking—which I hadn't been—I probably would have realized there was no way that Ania would just let me go off on her own. There was no way that Agata and Bloodstorm would go with a new baby on the way, though. Which was a good thing since I'd already gotten most of my team killed here.

"Yeah, she did," Rachel said, looking out the window as the car took us out into DC's night. "However, her plan was to try to sacrifice all of us to hurt Veles. Victory was incidental to making him pay."

Washington DC looked like a ghost town, and I couldn't help but wonder what everyone was feeling. They'd been dealing with this craziness for the better part of ten years, but it had been under the carefully controlled influence of, well, the god of evil. I'd seen some crooked politicians and celebrities influence people to do things but none of them held a candle to Veles.

"I guess I was just expecting more than just 'beware the wrath of a woman scorned'," I said, shrugging. "It seems a bit disappointing."

I admit, I'd been kind of expecting some devious master plan and cold-blooded ruthlessness instead of just throwing us as meat to the grinder.

"Yeah, you forgot one small detail," Rachel said, sharing her insights. Which I should have been paying attention to from the beginning. After all, she was a goddess of war.

"What's that?" I asked.

"Susanos was—probably still is—evil," Rachel said. "Like, really, *really* evil."

"I didn't forget that," I said, confused.

"Didn't you?" Rachel asked. "Because there's something rather important to remember about dealing with narcissistic sociopaths, especially undead ones—which Susanos definitely qualifies as—they don't care about other people."

"Why must the hot ones always be so evil?" Jon lamented.

Rachel gave him a dirty look. "Specifically, Aaron, this was always going to be about wounded pride and power lust rather than saving the universe."

"Even when the universe is where we keep our stuff," Jon said, making a reference to *The Tick*.

I shrugged, not entirely convinced. "I suppose it still felt a bit beneath them both."

"Not every villain is Magneto or Saruman, Aaron," Jon said. "There's not some tragic glory to them. More often, they're just assholes about windmills because some were obstructing their view of their golf course. Which I just realized is an incredibly outdated reference these days. Probably about as much as 'I am not a crook.'"

I ignored Jon. "I dunno, there just felt like there was something so incredibly *performative* about it. Like the two of them were acting out a scene—"

"For the Netflix adaptation?" Jon asked. "I admit, the thought did occur to me. Let's be honest, except for Agata and Ania, Larry C.C. Weis straight up can't write women. I mean, we can argue about Maria but then he made her a vampire hooker. Which, fair enough, was a twist."

I grimaced. "Yeah, that is not a conversation I'm looking forward to."

"Ania was a public figure at Dragon Keep. Maria had a year to get back in touch with Ania," Rachel said, simply. "Possibly more. Maelor obviously knew where she was the entire time. Instead, Maria spent her entire time working on revenge. First against the late Mad Queen and later against Veles."

"It's like Lady Stoneheart," Jon said, shrugging. "There's no way that final confrontation will end well for Catelyn and the girls."

I sighed. "You do realize that this isn't a book anymore, Jon? Right? Larry is dead. No one is penning this."

"Maybe," Rachel said, surprising me by responding. "The power of narrative was something that the Wise Man worked many powerful magics into the world with. It was why he was so dedicated to the idea of making champions."

I'd heard a lot about this so-called, "gods are made of stories" thing and the power of storytelling. So far, I hadn't seen any evidence it was real. Funny how you could have visible proof about the existence of magic and gods, there were still things that I found to be utterly ridiculous.

Part of the reason was because so many other so-called Chosen Ones had fallen before me. People like Francine and Jon had given their lives to stop Veles only to have their place in the so-called story replaced with someone new. Heroes that turned out to be utterly interchangeable as far as the narrative was concerned. It sickened me. There was no plot armor, no contrivance that made them immune to a meaningless death.

Hell, the entirety of this journey had begun when Garland had unexpectedly died at the hands of his fellows with no one able to resurrect him. Because he had not wanted to be resurrected. Meeting the man had also exposed me to the fact that he was just another person stuck with an impossible task. I wish I'd gotten a chance to know him better but, well, that wasn't going to happen.

"Right," I muttered.

"I see you're skeptical," Rachel said.

"No shit," I replied.

"Prophecies are less like absolutes and more like instructions," Rachel said, looking at me. "Even when you can see the future. The Wise Man saw a probable way to defeat Veles and did his best to try to navigate matters to that conclusion. The problem is that Veles also saw that very possibility and has been throwing obstacles the entire way. But here you are, Aaron. You're alive and working against Veles while his avatar has been severely damaged."

"Honestly, I'm going to rule our first boss fight against Calamity Veles as mid," Jon said, making a *Legend of Zelda* reference. "In fact, I'm going to go so far as to say all of the previous Elemental Demon bosses were much better. What? Veles just shows up at a power plant and kills some of our crew then almost dies in an explosion? Mediocre."

I took a deep breath. "Really not in the mood for joking about that, Jon."

"Alek died nobly," Rachel said. "I believe he atoned for his past sins."

"Nobly or not, he's still dead and I doubt there's anything left of him to resurrect," I said, wishing I'd never allied with Susanos and hoping that she was gone for good. "Why did you decide to ally with Susanos, anyway? You had to have seen this coming."

Rachel paused as if considering how to explain. "That's a complicated question."

"Is it?" I asked. "Because I know you're 90% Zorya Dawnbringer and 10% whatever fake memories that the Wise Man gave you when you were reborn."

"Not fake memories," Rachel said. "Rachel Morning was woven into the timeline by the Fates. I had adoptive parents, friends, and a life before my truth was revealed to me."

"She grew up in the Sky Academy, which is a place for gifted youngsters learning to use their powers for the greater good," Jon said. "Perfect for a YA series."

"Except with more fucking," Rachel said, cheerfully.

"No, that's still accurate," Jon said. "Have you read some of those books lately?"

"You're dodging the question," I said, noting we were leaving the nicer parts of Washington DC, such as they were, and heading into a part that looked significantly worse. It seemed President Veles' reign hadn't been overly concerned about making the lives of the average citizen better.

Rachel took a deep breath. "This incarnation of me is softer and kinder than the previous Zorya. That has its downsides. For one, I came to cherish the people around me in a way that the warrior part of me never could."

"Okay," I said, wondering where she was going with this.

"You ask me why I chose to go with Susanos to fight Veles rather than my true companions," Rachel said, pausing. "Well, I think it is the same reason that you did: I did not want to lose the people I love."

That was when our self-driving vehicle arrived at an incredibly seedy-looking hotel called the Scarlet Lady. It was not just that it looked like it charged by the hour but that you should probably be paid to stay there. It had a red neon sign with a few letters missing and a couple of guys with shotguns standing out front.

"I think I visited this place in *Cyber Dragons 2080*," I muttered, looking around. "Is there any chance that our car will still be here when we get back?"

"You have a very poor opinion of your fellow man," Rachel said, chidingly. "Also, I remind you that this car is stolen in the first place."

I blinked. "Oh, right. Never mind."

"Yeah, we can always steal another one," Jon said, cheerfully. "It's the circle of life, really."

I shook my head. "Jon, how did you become who you are?"

"It's amazing what dying and becoming a bird will do to your sense of propriety," Jon said, pausing. "No, wait, no, I was an asshole well before I died."

Much to my surprise, the car found its own parking spot and shut down on its own. "I feel like we should name her Christine."

"Don't name cars, Aaron," Jon said. "It gives them ideas."

The three of us got out of the car and I struggled to figure out what I was going to say to Ania. There wasn't really a good excuse for what I'd done, and I was prepared to face the music for it. Well, probably. I had no idea how pissed off she was going to be and there really wasn't a measure that could be applied from my past. "It's not you, it's my enemies" was an excuse that only existed in superhero comics.

The interior of the Scarlet Lady hotel wasn't any better than the exterior and I had to wonder just how bad things had gotten in America. I'd been so used to thinking of Mokosh as a fantasy land under the rule of a dark god that I had never given any thought to the idea that Earth might become Mordor.

Either way, the place's floor was covered by a ratty shag carpet with all manner of stains. There was a kiosk that was protected by bullet proof glass, an old cement staircase leading up to the second floor, and an elevator marked OUT OF ORDER. The smell of the place was, uh, incredible in the Death Star trash compactor sense.

There were also people, lots of them, of every variety of race with an oddball sense of mismatched fashion that reminded me a bit of *Fallout*. Almost everyone was armed, and I could see the fear in their eyes. What they were discussing wasn't reassuring either and reminded me just what sort of consequences there were to my actions.

"I heard it was terrorists," a woman in a black leather miniskirt and tank top said. "They destroyed the UMCs."

"What terrorists would want to unleash a bunch of zombies on everyone else?" a blind man in a fedora said. Apparently, the UMCs were supposed to keep the people safe from the undead. How little they knew.

"Who knows what terrorists want?" the woman in the miniskirt said. "I heard everyone in the Epic Dungeoneering™ building died instantly."

"I heard it was every employee of Epic Dungeoneering everywhere," A third man, black and wearing a leather jacket with sunglasses, said. "Like somehow they were all killed instantly and turned into monsters. A bunch of government institutions like the FBI and CIA too. It can't be terrorists. Must be China."

It was weird him leaving off the trademark bothered me. Corporate culture had really done a number on me.

"Did you know this is a designated shelter during outbreaks of necrophagia?" Rachel asked. "I find that fascinating."

"Huh," I said, surprised. "I wonder why they don't use churches."

"Probably because Veles is taxing all the churches in America that haven't switched to worshiping him," Jon said. "Not literally but I doubt you'd find much difference in the doctrines of Supply Side Jesus and the god of evil. The only people that should be bigger than Jesus are the Beatles, dammit."

There was a surprising amount of bitterness in Jon's voice. I hadn't thought him religious in the slightest but there was a genuine offense at what Veles was apparently doing to America's religious community.

"Aaron? Is that you?" an unexpected voice spoke through the crowd who reluctantly parted to reveal the white-haired figure of Pope Joan.

Joan wasn't dressed like the Pope of Mythras or otherwise, though. Instead, she looked like a somewhat ganglier white-haired teenage girl with prominent front teeth. She'd hit a growth spurt since our association and was now dressed in the same sort of Neo-Eighties attire that seemed everywhere. In her case, she had ripped jeans, a t-shirt with a dead unicorn on it, and a jean jacket. She also had a bandana of all things. Seriously, it was like the guy who'd wardrobed *The Warriors* had started dressing everyone.

She wasn't alone, though. Standing beside her was Sparky, also looking slightly older but that was difficult to judge when dealing with shapeshifters. In his case, he looked now like he was Joan's age at about sixteen years old. He was wearing sweatpants and a hoodie with the words Michigan Corvids on it. A sports team that I'd never heard of.

"You both came!" I said, hugging them both. "It's been so long."

"Like a day," Joan said, confused by my public display of affection. "From your perspective at least."

"But like six months for us," Sparky said.

"What?" I asked, confused. "How is that possible if you came here after me?"

Joan shrugged. "Magic?"

Ask a stupid question, get a stupid answer.

"Did you, uh, do the thing?" Sparky asked, making an explosion gesture. "Boom!"

"Let's, uh, talk about that... upstairs?" I asked, not sure if they had a room here or what the situation was.

"Backroom," Joan said, gesturing to the EMPLOYEES ONLY sign over a nearby door.

"This is Ania's place," Sparky said.

I blinked. "I think she could have probably invested better."

"Why? It's got running water, toilets, and electricity," Joan said. "This place is nice. It doesn't even smell of manure. The servants don't even have to live here."

"Huh," I said, acknowledging that one man's trash was another man's treasure. Then again, I probably wouldn't have enjoyed Mokosh nearly as much if not for CLEAN SELF cantrips.

I followed them into the back room, which was a storage room, and I saw people I wasn't expecting waiting for me: Bloodstorm, Agata, Ania, and someone new. She was a blue haired, brown-skinned woman who was 5'10" and dressed in a blue robe with a witch's hat.

Nightbringer.

Damn.

CHAPTER TWENTY-THREE
REUNITED WITH THE PARTY

I took a deep breath and tried to figure out what to say or do in a situation where clearly a lot of crap had gone down that I'd missed. It wasn't hard to figure out what had happened: Zorya Nightbringer had been reborn as Agata and Bloodstorm's daughter. It was just as the gods had claimed would happen. I tried to imagine what that would have been like and despite the fact I was probably the only human being on two planets who could relate, I couldn't. There was a difference to my finding out I had a reincarnated goddess as a daughter somewhere before being informed at the last minute my child was going to be the host for an alien entity.

I'd owed Agata and Bloodstorm a face-to-face confrontation over the ethical and emotional fallout. Maybe I'd even owed them a solution. I mean, yeah, I had no idea what the hell I could have done under the circumstances. I knew, intellectually, that there'd been like maybe five or ten minutes that someone wasn't trying to kill me between when I'd found out their child was going to be possessed (merged with?) and now. But guilt wasn't rational.

"So, hey," I said, looking at everyone. "What's up?'

Smooth, Aaron.

Real, Smooth.

"Aaron, I love you," Bloodstorm said, walking up to me and putting his hand on my shoulder. "But I am going to hit you now."

Given he had the strength of Joe Fixit AKA Gray Hulk, I wasn't sure if that would kill me or not. Ranger I might be, but I was still a squishy wizard that just so happened to not have an utterly shitty constitution score.

"You are not hitting Aaron!" Agata said.

"Thank you," I said, breathing a sigh of relief.

"Because I want to hit him!" Agata said. "With a fireball."

Okay, so they were a little mad.

"No one is hurting Aaron," Ania said. "That's including me, and I have every right to hurt him."

"Yes, you do," I said.

"I was mind controlled," Jon said, raising his hands in surrender. "Aaron, however, was completely in his right mind when he betrayed you."

Rachel dope-slapped him.

"Ow!" Jon said. "Hey, I waited a full three seconds before throwing him under the bus! That's long for me."

Rachel facepalmed.

"I do want to know, though," Ania said, taking a deep breath. "Why?"

I paused. "I figured pointing the Witch Queen at Veles would be better than her being pointed at us. So many people have given their lives to try to destroy the Dark Lord, I was wondering if maybe, just maybe, we could avoid sacrificing any more of the people we care about to bring him down."

"That plan failed miserably," Jon said. "FYI, your dad is dead, Kragen. Your mom is dead, Rose sisters. Oh, and if anyone cares other than Aaron, so is Alek."

I turned to look at Jon. "Are you biologically programmed to be an asshole or was it a learned skill?"

Jon seemed to take the question seriously. "I honestly don't know."

"Poor Alek," Joan said, frowning. "He could have been a great man but kind of sucked at it."

"I liked him," Sparky said. "We had similar names! Alek and Alexi!"

No one else was thinking of Alek, though.

"So, ole Maelor is dead, huh?" Bloodstorm said, frowning. "He deserves a king's funeral. I don't think they give those here on Earth, though."

"Not in America, at least," I muttered. "That might change under the new regime, though. Ania, Agata, I'm sorry, I tried to talk to Maria—"

"Our mother was lost a long time ago, Aaron," Ania said. "I read those shitty books by Larry C.C. Weis. I know what happened to her and that she spent the past twenty years focusing more on her vengeance than she did on recovering her children. We could have been a family again, but she refused to believe it was possible."

"Her family died at Blackwoods Bog," Agata said. "She was a vampire, you were an elvish terrorist, and I was pretending to be the Mad Queen's supporter. The people she left behind were not the people we became."

"Which goes to show she was a shitty mother," Ania said. "What sort of woman abandons those children she gave birth to just because they don't live up to the standards she wanted?"

"A typical one," Rachel said, speaking more as a goddess than a person. "Children are often abandoned in the woods to die when times are lean and far too many are cast out for arbitrary distinctions. I hold you in great esteem because you did not abandon my sister." She was referring to Nightbringer.

"So, yeah, how about that?" I asked, uncomfortable.

"You tried to warn us," Bloodstorm said. "I appreciate that. Which is why I was only going to punch you and not drive an ax into your head."

"Uh, thanks," I said, not sure if I was grateful or not. "The gods did you dirty."

Yeah, I didn't have much to say. There wasn't really a greeting card for "sorry your child was possessed by an evil goddess before being artificially aged to adulthood." Aside from Xena or the X-men, I didn't even know whether there was an equivalent.

"The gods were more merciful than they might have been," Agata said, surprising me. "When Nyx was born, we were transported by Perun's messengers to the World Above. We got to raise her for the next twenty years of her life while no time passed in the real world."

I blinked. "Huh."

That was a lot nicer than I expected of the gods.

"You look good for a woman in her fifties!" Jon said, pointing at her. "Got that Demi Moore thing going."

Rachel swatted him on the shoulder.

"I'm getting a lot of bruising here," Jon said, rubbing his shoulder. "Hit Aaron, he's the one who tortures himself over all this. Seriously, dude, you're going from Ranger Spider-Man to Ranger Daredevil."

"I'm not sure we aged there," Agata said, as if spending a couple of decades in Polish Olympus wasn't the weirdest thing ever. "However, I managed to learn many things about the true nature of magic. Things that will be beneficial in our fight against Veles. Bloodstorm learned a lot about how to fight the darkness within and I'm sure he is grateful for his time there as well."

"I absolutely was not," Bloodstorm said, frowning. "I was going crazy in that place full of air conditioning, instant meals, alcohol that doesn't get you drunk, and everyone preferring talking to fighting. It was like being trapped in fucking *Star Trek*, only it was full of absurdly hot angels."

"Oh, you poor thing," I said, sarcastically. "That sounds terrible."

"I know, right!" Bloodstorm proclaimed.

"We all received blessings while you were... doing your thing," Ania said, still obviously pissed at me but trying to be reasonable. It was a bit like a shark trying to be nice to minnows. Ania was not wired to be reasonable. But I had to admit her efforts were proof positive she loved me.

"Blessings?" I asked, still trying to catch up.

"Of the gods," Ania said, as if it left an unpleasant taste in her mouth. "My biological mother... well, whatever the hell you want to call her, Mokosh, awakened some more of the demigod inside me. Joan received a power-up from Mythras—"

"Please don't call it a power-up," Joan said.

Ania ignored her. "Sparky also got a gift from Svarog as the god of fire."

"I burn things good!" Sparky said. "Even better than before."

"Glad to hear it, kid," Jon said. "So, by going off to join Team Evil, we got screwed out of a bonus. Of course. I swear, these games never treat the antihero paths with any dignity. Be a Paragon and Shepard gets showered with cool shit. Play Renegade Shepard and the galaxy is fucked. That's from *Mass Effect*, y'know."

"I know, Jon," I said, sarcastically. "So, everyone got a boost, huh?"

"Except you three, yeah," Ania said. "Hopefully, that makes you think next time you go off to do something stupid."

"Probably not," I said, admitting the truth. "I am still average WIS at best."

Ania smirked.

My bracelet pinged, right on time.

ANIA ROSE HAS REJOINED THE PARTY
AGATA ROSE HAS REJOINED THE PARTY
KRAGEN BLOODSTORM HAS REJOINED THE PARTY
POPE JOAN HAS REJOINED THE PARTY
ALEXI "SPARKY" POPPY HAS REJOINED THE PARTY
NYX BLOODROSE HAS JOINED THE PARTY

AGATA ROSE IS NOW A CELESTIAL ARCHPRIESTESS [Chosen of Mokosh]
ANIA ROSE IS NOW A HEAVENLY ASSASSIN [Demigoddess]
KRAGEN BLOODSTORM IS NOW A PALADIN OF WRATH
POPE JOAN IS NOW A SAINT OF MYTHRAS [Chosen of Mythras]
ALEXI "SPARKY" POPPY IS NOW A CELESTIAL ARCHDRAGON

"Aaron's choice of actions, ones I endorsed, did have some positive effects," Rachel said, interjecting. "It was not a complete failure."

"Really? Because it looked like a complete failure to me," Jon said. "I also continue to blame Aaron for all of this despite it being Susanos' plan and my taking part in it. Mind control is the absolute best get out of jail card there is. Never mind that I probably would have done the exact same thing without it."

"Veles is severely injured," Rachel said, as if listening to some unseen sound. "You can hear his screams in the æther. We can take advantage of the fact he's had to destroy a substantial chunk of his forces here on Earth to survive."

"Really? Because from my perspective he utterly spanked us," Jon said, looking skeptically at Rachel.

"He could have simply destroyed us outright," Rachel said. "Instead, his desire to show off has turned his omnipotence into a joke. The UMC field was also destroyed. It wasn't the only one, but it was the largest and most powerful. We've effectively turned off the spigot for the flow of magic to him. Despite what you might believe, it was a victory."

"You're right," I said, nodding to her. "I don't believe it's a victory."

Ania looked at me. "Due to the vagaries of time travel, dimensions, and other bullshit, we arrived here before you. It's been about six months of us living in the shadow of President Veles."

I nodded. "Joan mentioned something like that."

"Nyx's presence has kept us secret," Ania said. "Her divine presence or whatever keeps us hidden from Veles."

"How's that work?" I asked.

"I have no idea," Ania said. "It's magic bullshit."

Spoken like someone who wasn't a wizard. Mind you, I 100% agreed. "Fair enough. What have you been doing?"

"Trying to undermine him," Ania said. "We've established ties with the resistance but Americans are not—"

"I really don't want you to finish that sentence," I muttered. "I'm glad to hear not everyone is rolling over for Veles but we need ideas for actually defeating him."

"I have a few," Nyx said, looking at me.

"Oh, hi, nice to meet you," I said, "Uh, Nyx, is it?"

"Yes," Nyx said. "Don't worry, I'm not going to engage in an elaborate head game for over a year to make you think I want to have incestuous sexual relations."

"Oh, thank God," I muttered.

"Wait, that was a head game?" Bloodstorm asked.

Agata swatted his arm like Rachel did Jon's.

"What?" Bloodstorm asked. "Non-elves and ogres are just plain weird."

"You have ideas?" I asked Nyx, glad to finally have an excuse to be off this topic.

"Yes," Nyx said. "We can harness the remaining divine power in your bracelets."

"You mean finally get Aaron to become a god?" Jon asked. "Really, I'm all down for that. I mean, I would have made a better one, but you take what life gives you."

"No," Nyx said, pausing. "Though Aaron could attempt that, I was thinking we could harness the magic of the two remaining Marks of the Champion and create a divine weapon capable of killing Veles."

"Is that possible?" I asked.

"Yes," Nyx said. "With both Rachel and me working together."

"Okay, that's a plan," I said, pausing. I wasn't sure how good a plan it was, but at least it was a plan. "Anything else?"

"Contact Mat Zemalya," Nyx said. "The Goddess of Earth and mother of all its pantheons. She was originally Veles' bride but turned against him. If she is still alive then she might prove to be one of the few gods capable of aiding us against him."

I wasn't so sure about that plan. As every experience with the gods so far had taught me, they had their own agendas that rarely coincided with what you wanted to do. I didn't think they were evil, or even bad guys, but they had the kind of arrogance that kings or CEOs had. Okay, maybe they were bad guys with that comparison, but I liked some of them.

"Well, that's certainly a plan," I said. "I take it you haven't been able to contact her yet?"

"No," Agata said. "I suspect she's only able to be contacted by a fellow deity. Which might be an argument to make the full transition to god. There's no reason not to now that we know Veles isn't playing by Weis' rules."

I would have pointed out that both Rachel and Nyx were full-fledged gods themselves, but I was more interested in any other ideas the youngest member of the group might have. "At this point, I'm for whatever works in bringing down Veles. He must be getting desperate now. What's your last idea, Nyx?"

"We should find Susanos' soul jar and use it to bring her back," Nyx said.

Everyone stared.

Okay, I regret ever asking her for advice.

CHAPTER TWENTY-FOUR
THE TERRIBLE IDEAS KEEP COMING

I blinked. "Excuse me?"

"Recover Susanos' soul jar and proceed to resurrect the Witch—" Nyx started to speak.

"Yeah, I got that part," I said, interrupting her. I'd gotten casual about interrupting gods these days. Blame killing four of them. "It's more the fact that's such a blindingly terrible idea that I'm having difficulty processing it."

"You mean a terrible idea like teaming up with her collection of undead monsters to fight Veles?" Ania asked.

I paused. "Okay, that actually isn't hypocrisy. It's me having learned from my mistakes."

"Do you?" Jon asked. "Because I'm still seeing a lot of allying with objectively terrible people because you think there's good in everyone. I mean, take me for instance."

"It's kinda worked so far!" I lamented, unwittingly insulting everyone here. "I just have limits here."

"I never thought I'd say this," Agata said, taking a deep breath. "But I agree with Aaron."

"Hey!" I snapped.

Agata ignored me. "Susanos already took her shot at Veles and failed miserably."

"I wouldn't say that," Rachel said, rubbing the scars on her face. "Admittedly, I not being a complete failure was entirely because Aaron managed to think of a way to turn it around. Even then, I still took an explosion distinct from but close to a nuke in the face. That hurt!"

"There's no such thing as a bit of nuke, dear," Jon said. "Be proud you took one to the face and it just gave you an ouchie."

"You always know the right thing to say," Rachel said, sighing.

Okay, that was weird.

"You poor thing," Nyx said, taking a condescending tone. "It is a true tragedy for a goddess of love to be less than perfect."

"Yes, Rachel's clearly become unfuckable," Jon said, heavily sarcastic. "It's like ladies who put on a little weight. Oh, wow, you a have bigger ass and set—"

"Shut up, Jon," Rachel said.

"Got it," Jon said, making finger guns to Rachel and showing that he and she might stand the test of time.

"We need all the help we can get," Nyx continued to explain her incredibly reckless plan. "The power balance would be different now. Before, you were directly under her thumb. Now, you would be the one in charge and have all the empowered associates beside you able to rein her in."

"That's assuming she agrees," Rachel said. "Besides, we haven't exactly seen much tactical genius from her. It turned out the world's most powerful sorceress was motivated by little more than petty spite. It blinded her to any possibilities other than the direct assault that got our associates killed."

"Unless," Jon said, pointing at Agata then Rachel. "Hear me out, *unless*, that was her plan all along!"

Everyone stared at Jon, skeptically.

"What?" Jon asked. "It's possible."

I took a deep breath. "I've probably lost the trust of a lot of people here—"

"Don't wallow in self-pity, Aaron," Ania said. "It's deeply unattractive. I haven't seen you in six months and will tear your clothes off right after this meeting."

"Right," I said, doing an immediate course correction. "Well, speaking as the unofficial leader of our merry band of misfits, I think we don't have time to go searching the universe for Susanos' soul jar. That's assuming it even exists and she's not dead-dead."

"Did your Marks of the Champion register her as dying," Rachel asked.

I paused. "No."

"That's pretty good evidence she's still alive. Well, unalive," Rachel said.

I glared at Rachel, not appreciating her backing that argument up. "Thanks, Rachel."

"I'm a helper!" she said, cheerfully.

"We know where her soul jar is," Nyx said, pausing. "Like forging the Marks of the Champion into a weapon to kill Veles, we don't have to go anywhere. All the equipment for resurrecting Susanos is right here."

I blinked. "It is?"

"It is?" Jon added.

Even Rachel looked surprised.

"Yes," Nyx said, pointing at Jon. "Susanos' soul jar has been hidden in Jon."

"Dum, dum, dum!" Bloodstorm chanted before pausing. "Okay, I just said that because I was sick of not contributing anything to the conversation."

Agata patted him on the shoulder. "There, there."

"Huh," Jon said, blinking. "I always knew I had a feminine side. I just assumed she was a lesbian."

Rachel rolled her eyes.

"Yeah, well, you try to keep pace at this snark fest," Jon said. "Not every one of my cracks is going to be a banger."

"That would imply any of them are," Ania replied. "Jon is the soul jar for Susanos?"

"In him at least," Nyx replied. "I can detect it."

"I didn't," Rachel said. "I've been very close to Jon."

"Uh huh," I said.

"Very, very close," Rachel said, suggestively. "If you know what I mean."

"We know," Ania muttered, sarcastically.

"Hint, hint," Rachel said, winking.

"For fuck's sake," Ania muttered. "Could you double check, Rachel?"

"Okay, but I'm not gonna..." Rachel said, trailing off as she grabbed Jon's head and stared at him. "Hmm."

"What do you mean, 'hmm'?" Jon asked, looking very comfortable.

"I mean hmm," Rachel replied. "Okay, yeah, Nyx is right."

"What?" Jon asked, shocked.

"Yeah, you've got her soul in you," Rachel said. "The Mark of the Champion influence is keeping you from being possessed, though."

"Oh, thank you," Jon said, taking a deep breath. "I wasn't really taking the six-month-old twenty-year-old seriously."

"Jon please don't make that weirder," I replied.

"I'm not sure it can be made weirder and I'm dating Rachel," Jon said. "Okay, I may have shot myself in the foot with that one."

"Believe me, spending twenty years away from my sister was difficult," Agata said, speaking in a tone that suggested she wasn't entirely telling the truth. "I have seen wonders you would not believe."

"Attack ships on fire off the shoulder of Orion. I watched C-beams glitter in the dark near the Tannhäuser Gate," I said, making fun of her. "Okay, we'll put it on the list to get Susanos out of Jon. I don't want her possessing him and making him a walking meat puppet at an inconvenient time. Two dragons are better than one, especially when one of those dragons knows kung fu."

"Woah," Jon said, clearly uncomfortable. It seemed to be sinking in just how dangerous this might be. "Wait, did she think I was going to survive the battle with Veles? Is that why she made me a soul jar?"

"She probably had a spell ready to teleport you away if I didn't," Rachel replied. "Either way, we can provide a corpse for her to move her spirit and carry out the ritual to resurrect Susanos."

"Or exorcise him," Joan said, interjecting. "That way we have one less nightmarish evil sorceress in the world and don't have to kill Jon like you're all thinking we should."

I was appalled. "What? No one is thinking about killing Jon!"

Everyone but Rachel, Joan, Jon, and Nyx looked away from me.

"Come on!" I said, upset on my friends' behalf.

"I don't want to kill him but I kind of think he's intruding on my thing as the dragon in the group," Sparky said.

"*Et tu* Sparky?" Jon said, looking at him.

"Don't be cursing at me in no weird Imperial witchcraft language," Sparky said, pointing at Jon. "That's what Joan speaks when she's casting her spells."

"It's Latin and it's what I use for prayers," Joan said, rolling her eyes.

"Exactly!" Sparky said. "Imperial witchcraft language!"

I rubbed my temples and took a second to clear my head. "Okay, this is something I need to think about."

"Just how much time do I have before I become a meat puppet?" Jon asked. "I'd like to know if we're talking days, weeks, months, or if we should pull this thing out of me now. I'm imagining the dinner scene from *Alien* except it's Monica Belluci bursting out of my chest. Which, contrary to what you might think, isn't something I'd be into."

I looked to Nyx. "Uh, any ideas?"

"We have time," Nyx said. "Usually, it takes at least three days for a resurrection to occur with a death lord. Susanos is different, though. That she didn't automatically seize control over his body and consume his soul is a good sign."

"*Nothing* about that sentence was reassuring," Jon said.

I took a deep breath and looked at Ania. "I think we should discuss this in private."

"Before sex or after?" Ania asked.

Yeah, that was an interesting element of my girlfriend. She was very clear about when and how she wanted to be intimate. Apparently, killing was a thing that got her hot and bothered. I'd be terrified if I wasn't so turned on.

"Before," I said, reluctantly.

Ania muttered something unpleasant under her breath. "Fine. But I have a room all set up."

"I'd rather not have our reunion be somewhere that will give us hepatitis," I said, noting this place reminded me of the kind of place the Punisher would fight dirty cops in.

"Cast some cleaning spells then," Ania said. "Besides, we've got some modifications here that I think you'll be impressed by."

I wasn't sure what she meant by that and tried to figure out how Veles hadn't noticed his worst enemies based here. Maybe the fact that the Zoryas were gods really was the great equalizer. Also, disturbingly, there was the possibility that Veles had just left them alone until I was here. Maybe that was just my natural pessimism, but every step forward seemed to be one that came with additional disasters.

"So where can we speak in private?" I asked, uncomfortable with everyone else here despite most of them being literal family to me now.

Or, at least, soon would be.

"Down here," Ania gestured to a doorway that opened to a set of steps. I followed her inside and found that it led to a set of steam tunnels. Except it wasn't just steam piping but a lot of weird electrical wiring and tubes that were channeling energies I could feel from a foot away.

"Huh, interesting," I said.

"Veles has rebuilt most of the city after it was destroyed," Ania replied. "A lot of the upgrades are to make his magitech serviceable here on Earth. I think it's whatever his big plan is. No matter what I may think of Susanos personally, destroying his UMC field was a big blow to his efforts."

"It wasn't guarded," I said, frowning. "That still bothers me."

"The people of Earth think the UMCs are keeping the undead at bay," Ania replied. "The deathrot plague has shown up in many parts of this world. We've been trying to help people with it, but the fact that Veles has intelligent wights working for him makes it difficult. I thought that might be the vector he's going to use to destroy your world but there's a problem with that."

"Which is?" I asked, wondering just how many people of my planet he'd killed while I was off playing hero. It was a stupid thing to feel guilty about because if I'd been here, I certainly wouldn't have been heroically saving the day. No, I would have probably been just another victim.

Or worse.

As an employee of Epic Dungeoneering™, I might have ended up brainwashed or turned into a monster myself. There might have been a time I would have eagerly signed up to learn real magic, regardless of the source. Who knew what kind of contract I would have signed without reading it. Actually, I knew because that was how I'd ended up on Mokosh in the first place.

"If Veles wanted to wipe out your world then he probably could have done it by now," Ania said, taking a deep breath. "No offense but the leaders of this world are some of the stupidest, most selfish, backstabbing pieces of shit I've found outside of the Ledzianan nobility."

"You're Ledzianan nobility," I said, before I could stop myself. I also didn't mention that her impression of my world was probably being influenced by the fact she was in Washington DC. Still, I agreed with her. We were missing something about Veles' overall plan.

"Yes, but my backstabbing is literal," Ania said. "What did you want to talk about?"

I kissed her. "I wanted to say how much I've missed you, how much I hated being apart, and how it was the biggest mistake of my life to go with Susanos."

"And yet you don't want to have sex now," Ania said, pressing up against me.

I sighed. "There are a few other things we have to cover."

"I prefer uncover," Ania said, purring.

I rolled my eyes. "Just bear with me a few more minutes."

Ania sighed. "Fine, tell me why we have to free Susanos and give her a new body."

"What?" I asked, not having intended to do that at all.

"You're you, Aaron," Ania said, pulling away. "No one is beyond redemption. The best way to defeat an enemy is to turn them into a friend. Alliances are better than rivalries. If we all just care enough, the world will become a giant flowerpot."

I blinked. "That doesn't sound like me."

"Really? Because I've been listening to this bullshit for a year," Ania said. "It's fine, I agree with you."

"You do?" I asked.

"Yes," Ania said. "Your plan to take out Veles by turning his bitch whore wife into a weapon against him wasn't terrible. I mean, it was because you weren't the one doing the strategizing. If we can resurrect her, I mean fully alive, then he won't have as much power over her as before. She'll be a tank—that's one of the machines I learned about here—and we can have her help bring down Veles' power. We can also bring her back with a geas by combining all of our magical strength to bind her."

"Uh huh," I said.

"That's what you were going to say, right?" Ania asked.

"No, I was going to say we should destroy her because she got my cousin and Maelor killed," I replied. "Your mother too."

I didn't want to bring up Garland.

"Oh," Ania said, "Well, that works too."

"No, no, you persuaded me," I said. "It's clearly a good idea to recruit Sauron to fight Morgoth. I'm sure she'll appreciate the mercy we showed us and not turn on us like Gollum."

Ania closed her eyes. "I watched the movies. I know what that means."

"We'll make the god-killing blade or whatever Nyx has planned," I said. "I'm sorry your sister lived twenty years without you."

Ania paused. "Me too. She's almost a stranger now. I worry the gods may have done something to her and Bloodstorm. It's just hard to tell what is the distance of time and what is her natural haughtiness. I'm glad I didn't have to live that time without you, though."

I smiled. "That brings me to what I wanted to ask you."

"What?" Ania asked.

I took her hands in mine. "Can we get married now?"

CHAPTER TWENTY-FIVE
MARRIAGE IS A DREAM WITHIN A DREAM

Ania looked up at me with despairing eyes. "You really don't want to get laid tonight, do you?"

"That's only if you assume married people shouldn't have sex," I replied.

"Most people think that," Ania joked, or at least I hoped she was. "You have this weird habit of mixing it with feelings. It sucks all the passion out of it."

I rolled my eyes. "You are a very strange girl, Ania."

"Yeah, I am your Magical Pixie Dream Consort," Ania said. "The Leliana-Arya-Imoen."

"You don't know what any of those words mean, do you?" I asked, presuming she was repeating something she'd heard from Jon. Hell, from me.

"No," Ania said.

"Let's establish you're about as far from Natalie Portman in *Garden State* as possible," I replied. "Though I wouldn't mind seeing her play a Goth murder elf."

Okay, now that was an image in my head.

"Aaron," Ania said, snapping her fingers in front of me.

"Goth murder elf!" I said, suddenly.

Ania snorted. "But why do you want to get married now?"

"Because I almost died," I said, simply. "It kind of puts things in perspective."

"You almost die all the time," Ania said. "I would argue that it is the thing you are best at."

"That's not very reassuring," I said.

"I find it to be incredibly reassuring," Ania said. "Because the emphasis is on the fact that you don't die. You come close to danger very often but always manage to escape from it."

"I think this is one of those things where our language barrier is showing up, translation spell or not," I said.

"You've been speaking Ledzianan to me for the past couple of months," Ania said, pausing. "Well, from your perspective. I hate this variable timeline bullshit. I was alone, without you, Aaron, for six months. I did not sleep around on you."

"Yes, I understand—"

"Six months," Ania said, emphasizing it. "I had a lot of alone time."

"Okay, now I have another image in my head," I said, blinking.

Ania sighed.

"How much alone time?" I asked. "What were you—"

Ania lightly slapped me on my face.

"Right, I'm back," I said.

"Good boy," Ania said. "The question still remains, though."

"What question?" I asked, having genuinely forgotten it thanks to all the things I'd been thinking of.

"Why do you want to get married now? Instead of getting naked and having sex in this steam tunnel?"

"Is it cleaner than the hotel?" I asked.

Ania sighed. "It's closer."

I smiled. "I've always wanted to marry you, Ania. Since the moment I met you."

"Surrounded by dead bodies in my burning hometown?" Ania asked, referring to the circumstances of our meeting. "When I was still disgusted with you for being another imposter Garland?".

I blinked. "Well, maybe not the first moment, but close to it."

"You slept with like five women before we became exclusive," Ania said.

"It was close this time, Ania," I said, taking a deep breath. "You said you wanted to wait until Veles was defeated."

"Yes," Ania said. "Because that has to be the focus of everything."

"But we've come so far," I said, staring at her. "Done so much. I just want—"

"I don't understand the appeal," Ania said, shaking her head. "Marriage has always been just a bunch of words to me."

"It's a promise," I said, pausing. "I don't break my promises."

"Unlike Veles," Ania said.

I paused. "Yeah, unlike him."

"You know he used to be the god who punished oath breakers, right?" Ania asked.

"Yes, I did."

"You should also know that not every promise can be honored," Ania said, pausing. "I've seen every nobleman, every marriage, and every knight break their oaths. Parents who promise to love their children and do the most horrible things. Clergy who break every single—"

"Do you believe I will honor any promise I will make you?" I asked.

Ania sighed. "I believe you will do everything in your power to fulfill any promise you make, as wildly stupid and misconceived as they may be."

"Like killing Veles," I said, frowning.

"Yes," Ania said, pulling away from me. "You don't get it, Aaron, and I don't think you ever will."

"You never thought you'd get this far," I said.

Ania closed her eyes. "No, no I didn't. Hope was not a luxury I ever afforded myself. When I was a member of the Dark Moon elves, I gave up my life to the Nightbringer and ritually buried myself. I became no one."

Wow, Larry C.C. Weis was an enormous plagiarist.

No, dammit, get out of that mindset.

"You're not no one," I said. "You're Ania Rose."

"I know that!" Ania said, looking tormented by the thought that she just couldn't let go of. "But I dedicated myself to this fight knowing it was futile. Hopeless. Garland could never have pulled off what you have, Aaron, and every single champion since him was worse than the last."

"Francine and Jon were... not terrible," I said, pausing. That was damning with faint praise. "Alek... okay, he was awful, but he was misled."

Ania gave a half-smile. "We're almost to the finish line. That was one of the few metaphors from Jon that I understood. We used to have footraces at the Dragon Keep Fair every year. I won them against boys and girls five years older than me. Veles is wounded. His armies are no more. We have divine allies. If you... become a god, we might win."

That was monumental but it was conditional. "If I become a god."

"If you do, we have a small chance," Ania said. "I think that's the way Larry C.C. Weis wrote the story to end. You become Perun and you forget about the mortal girl you left behind."

I stared at her. "I'd rather have you than be a god."

Ania punched me in the shoulder.

"Ow!" I said, putting my hand on my shoulder. "What the fuck?"

"The fact you mean that pisses me off!" Ania said. "This is not about happiness or love!"

"You're wearing Mokosh's catsuit of protection so maybe it is," I said, rubbing the bruise she'd made. "But maybe that's why I want to marry you. So many ifs, ands, and buts. Maybe we'll win. Maybe evil will triumph. But I want to make a promise that I will love you in this life and the next, assuming there is one after Veles gets done with this universe. Call it crazy. I want to believe there's a future but it's all about the present and honoring what I feel for you."

"That is the stupidest thing I've ever heard," Ania said, staring.

I sighed and looked away. "Fine. I'll stop bringing it up. I didn't come here to fight."

Ania sighed and took my hand. She squeezed it tight. "I promise to love you and cherish you too. By the gods, by the kings of old, by the kings of the future, and by my word—as broken as it has been so many times. Fine, we're married."

"What?" I asked.

"We don't get married before priests in Ledziana," Ania said. "Not if you're a peasant. The priesthood of the Old Gods was the nobility imitating people like Mythras and I never liked it. Mokosh's priestesses might bless unions, but they aren't needed for them."

"Huh," I said, wondering where I'd missed that in my sourcebooks.

"But yes, do you love me?" Ania asked.

"Yes, you know I do," I said, very confused.

"Do you swear blah, blah, blah," Ania said.

"Sure," I said, not exactly feeling the ceremony. "Assuming blah blah blah means loving you and cherishing you as my wife"

"Then we're married," Ania said. "I'm a Paladin of Mokosh because Mokosh said so. Even if I don't want to be. So, if you want—"

I kissed her.

"Finally," Ania said, starting to remove my pants.

Yeah, I didn't have much to say after that.

Ania was ferocious. At some time later in our interlude, I heard the door open before quickly closing. Which implied someone walked in. I didn't care. By the time we were done, we were both exhausted. I drifted off to sleep afterward in the warm steam tunnel, satisfied and in love. Unfortunately, what lay beyond sleep wasn't more time with Ania.

It *was* the Oval Office.

Of Hell.

Veles was sitting behind the White House desk, his face twisted into a mass of burns and scar tissue that made him look less like Peter Stormare and more like Freddy Krueger. His skin was bright red, too, as if he'd been flayed down to the muscle. His white suit burned black in several places. There were Secret Service members present but all of them were as dead (or undead) as the security guard at the UMC.

I was naked.

I covered my privates with my hands. "Crap."

"For fuck's sake," Veles said, snapping his fingers.

I was once more covered in the attire of a Dark Undermaster. "I don't need your gifts."

"It's a dream," Veles said. "You don't have to worry about me killing you. This is the one realm where I have no power because it belongs to Mokosh. It's why I tried to have Valentin kill you versus doing it myself the last time we had one of our conferences. He, at least, had the magic to do it."

"You're saying you can't kill me here," I said, skeptically. "Forgive me if I'm not exactly trusting you at your word anymore."

"That's what I said, didn't I? Believe me, if I could, I would," Veles said. "That I am not killing you should indicate that I cannot. As for trusting me at my word, that used to be so important. Before I changed, I would rather have been obliterated body and soul than to break a promise. Now? They sound like empty words to me. In that, I have become more human."

"Because of the Twisted Gods," I said, once more trying to reach Veles.

Veles stared. "You keep bringing them up. What do you hope to accomplish? Do you think I'll come back from my so-called madness? That I'll realize that I have become corrupted by their influence? Repent my wicked ways? Let you strike me down so I could be reborn?"

"I dunno," I said, shrugging. "Maybe. It seemed worthwhile to try."

A lot of people were going to die if this kept on. I was willing to sacrifice justice, assuming such a thing existed, to stop even one more death from happening.

Veles snorted through his singed nostrils. "It is futile. I like what the Twisted Gods' influence has done for me. For years, millennia beyond count, I tempted mortals with the hope that they would resist the lures I placed in front of them. Do you know what I found out? There is no need for me to whisper into the ears of men and women to be their worst selves. They do not even try to be better than their hatred and greed. They find the flimsiest, most ridiculous and insane justifications to say good is evil and evil is good. That, more than anything, is why I will end this universe."

"Will there even be a new universe afterward?" I asked.

"Oh yes," Veles said. "Don't think the Twisted Gods will get that far. Every man, woman, and child will be mine. They won't be humankind as you know them, though. They will each be perfect. Loving, obedient, and happy. Like dogs."

"And you'll be whipping them," I said.

Veles narrowed his eyes. "I hate humans, not dogs. Do you really want to die defending the people that made me their leader? This world is nothing but war, horror, hate-speech, and libel. You? You have hope now. Someone you love. That means you have something to lose. Congratulations on your marriage."

"You know, I think the reason you keep contacting me is because all of this isn't to convince me," I said, crossing my arms. "It's to convince yourself."

"Really?" Veles asked.

"Yeah," I said, shaking my head. "I think there's some part of the original Veles left in you. Don't get me wrong, everything I've heard and seen indicates you were a fucking awful person even before you were infected."

"Enlighten—"

"Infected," I said. "But you were someone who had principles. You loved some people. Even when you hated them."

"Do not speak to me as if you were my brother, nephew," Veles said, his voice becoming dangerous. "He, too, thought—"

"I think you want me to stop you," I said. "That's why you agreed to Larry C.C. Weis' insane quest. That's why you have been dragging your feet the entire time. It's why you keep trying to offer me ways out. You want to lose but can't bring yourself to admit it to the rest of yourself."

Veles stared. "In the words of Ms. Rose, that is the stupidest thing I have ever heard."

"Is it?" I asked. "Either way, we'll be seeing you."

Veles smirked. "One week."

"What?" I asked.

"You have one week until the end of this world and Mokosh," Veles said. "The worlds will collide and a second Big Bang will begin overwriting this universe the way the previous one was overwritten. Oh yes, there was one of those. Me and the other creator gods are its survivors. Maybe we were once creatures like you. But I will emerge more powerful than Triglav ever was. You think I want to lose? No, Aaron. I have been losing for thousands of years. My stupid brother defeating me every year and the Slavs celebrating it as the end of winter. Now I want to win. Why do I spare you? You think because I feel some kinship with you over the tens of thousands of other bastards and bastardspawn he's created? Because I thought it would be fun. Because I never actually believed you were a threat. Because it was more fun to dangle the thread of destiny in front of you like a cat."

"Do you now feel the threat?" I asked, feeling some shred of truth in his words.

Veles smiled. "Say goodbye to Ania for me."

That was when I awoke.

CHAPTER TWENTY-SIX
TAKING A MOMENT TO MOURN

Well, that was a zigzag of emotions.

I was married to Ania, at least in her eyes, and we'd got to spend at least a few hours of comfort in each other's arms. However, Veles knew I was here and had rejected my last attempt at reaching him. I never really hoped for a kind of last-minute *Return of the Jedi* appeal to his morality. Veles was closer to Palpatine than Vader anyway, but I'd still wanted to try.

Now there was no way this was going to end, except for one of us to die. Or possibly both. Veles had said we had a week left until the end of everything and while it made no sense that he would tell me that unless my theory he wanted to lose was right, I believed him. Maybe he was just taunting me with how futile he considered my efforts to oppose him were.

Ania raised her head up, awakened by my movements. "Already awake?"

"Just had a nightmare," I said, which was neither a lie nor the full truth. I'd tell her what happened in time.

"Veles visited you, didn't he?" Ania asked.

Or now it seemed.

"Yeah," I said, taking a deep breath. "He's looked better. Apparently, taking a nuke's worth of force to the face hurt him a lot harder than it hurt Rachel."

"Rachel is Zorya Dawnbringer and the goddess of fire," Ania said. "I'm surprised it hurt her at all."

I blinked. "Huh, so I guess it works like Pokémon."

"I have no idea what that means and really hope I never do," Ania said, shaking her head and pulling back. "In any case, I hope you realize you're not allowed to die now."

"I'm sorry, what?" I asked.

"You forced me to marry you," Ania said, like I'd dragged her kicking and screaming across the aisle. "The least you can do now is promise you're never going to die."

"I'm not sure I can really promise that," I said, blinking.

"Yes, well, that's your problem, isn't it?" Ania asked. "I didn't want to get married until Veles was good and defeated but you insisted —"

"You're going to hold that over my head for the rest of eternity, aren't you?" I asked, already feeling like we were truly married.

"Yes," Ania said, crossing her arms over her breasts. She started to dress then, and I was disappointed. "But I mean it. You must do your very best to stay alive, no heroic sacrifices, and the two of us will be victorious. Everyone else is expendable."

"Uh huh," I said, pausing.

"Not saying I want my sister to die but if we absolutely need someone to sacrifice themselves, you know she's there," Ania said.

I rolled my eyes. "I was hoping you two were getting along better."

"We were then she abandoned me for twenty subjective years," Ania said, now once more dressed like a catsuit-wearing spy despite being from a world that had barely discovered steam power. Seriously, they had been all but ready to undergo their own magical Industrial Revolution when the Twisted Gods had ruined it for everyone.

"I'm sorry," I said, "I'm sure she had a good reason."

"She's the pawn of the gods," Ania said. "My sister would have agreed to having her child possessed if they'd asked. Bloodstorm is too besotted to care about what they've really got planned."

I'd clearly lost the plot here. Watching Ania get dressed had that effect on me. "What do you think the gods have planned?"

"Conquest of this world's faithful!" Ania said, "They're going to use your resurrected ex-girlfriends, one of whom is your daughter now—"

"Can we never mention that again? I just found out the whole incest thing was an elaborate prank on me, which is way more relieving than I thought it would be, and I kind of would like to put it to bed. Permanently."

Ania reached over and kissed me on the cheek. "Sure. I'll just consider this the first of many favors I'll be doing for you with the expectation of you repaying them later."

"You've clearly mastered this marriage thing very quickly," I said, dryly.

"I only have my parents relationship to draw from," Ania said. "A union that can best be described as tense. What with Garland and—"

"Yeah," I said, looking down.

"You're hiding something," Ania said, sharply.

"What? No, I'm not!" I said, in the least convincing manner possible. It was a shame that the Mark of the Champion didn't mark skills, only Feats. I would have put a bunch of points into my Bluff skill.

"What happened, Aaron?" Ania asked, sitting down beside me. "I already know my mother and Maelor were there. This can't be worse. I liked Maelor."

Ouch.

"No love lost in the Rose family, I see," I muttered, uncomfortable with the way the conversation had turned.

Ania stared. "I loved my mother, but she never understood me. I don't know if becoming a vampire changed the person she was or just underlined it. I love my sister and I hope I won't have to kill her because she turns into a giant angelic monster that exists to enslave humanity."

I stared at her. "What now?"

"I've been watching a lot of the painted television shows made in Japan," Ania said. "They have a lot of stories about evil gods made of metal."

I blinked. "I don't think you should watch anime."

"You sure?" Ania asked. "Joan really likes it. So does Sparky."

"Yes," I said, my tone flat. "None of you should be watching anime unless you want to start thinking about souls combining into giant cloned robot moms."

"Ah, I see you have seen the Evangelion," Ania said. "What was that about?"

"I have no idea, and I've had most of my adult life to try to figure it out."

Ania paused. "You were trying to divert my attention, Aaron."

I grimaced. "Not consciously."

"So, spill," Ania said, already sounding more like an Earther.

I regretted I would have to be the one to bring the news to her. "Garland was back to help against Veles. Briefly."

If anything could have killed Ania's giddy mood, that was it. Her expression darkened and there seemed a brief flash of anger. Then her gaze softened as if there was too much sorrow to properly sort through.

"Resurrection or undeath?" Ania asked the kind of question that only made sense in the circles we travelled.

"Undead," I said, unhappily. "Some kind of revenant."

Ania stared down. "Garland hated the undead. It would take a powerful inducement to get him to come back. He didn't even want to be alive after his first death."

"There's apparently a lot going on in the afterlife," I said, pausing. "Some real *God of War* and *Planescape: Torment* bullshit."

I doubted that Ania would get those references, but it was less like an attempt to explain the matter to her and more like me trying to explain it to myself. I hadn't believed in gods or an afterlife until I'd come to Ledziana. Still, it was hard to imagine a war being fought among the dead due to, well, everyone being dead.

"And he's gone," Ania said.

"Yeah," I said. "I didn't get to meet with him for long, but he seemed like a nice guy."

Ania stared at me skeptically. "Really?"

"Well, he said he couldn't have done what I'd done," I said, simply. "He said that he never wanted to be the Chosen One and I was the hero we needed."

"So, he flattered you," Ania said.

I grimaced. "Uh, sort of?"

Ania snorted. "He was right, though."

"He was?" I asked.

Ania put her hand on my shoulder. "Aaron, you have far exceeded my belief that anything could be accomplished against the Old Gods. Mostly because I didn't believe you *could* accomplish anything."

"Ania, you're really shit at this reassuring thing," I said, chuckling.

"Yeah, well, I'm good at the sex part," Ania said.

"This is true," I said.

"Can married couples have sex?" Ania asked, making a joke. "I'm not sure. I thought all children born after marriage were illegitimate. Every husband being with another man's wife. At least that's how it felt in Crossroad."

"I am starting to see why you were so hesitant," I replied.

"I admit to having certain issues with the bonding men and women under Mokosh," Ania said. "The Wiseman wrote all my parents dirty secrets. I loved them both but they were terrible together."

"If it helps, he's both dead and a pathological liar," I replied.

Ania chuckled, which was as rare as hen's teeth (a rural aphorism I picked up). "I wish Garland was fighting at our side, but I hope he finds peace with his second death."

"Me too," I said, frowning.

That was when the metal door to the steam tunnels opened and Agata's voice called down. "We've given you time to do whatever it is you two have been doing—"

"Sex!" Ania shouted. "And sleeping! You know, the thing you as a priestess of love should be encouraging!"

Agata paused. "Any response I would give would probably be blasphemy, Ania! Are you done now?"

"No!" Ania shouted again. "It's also none of your damned business what I do with my husband."

Ah, that word was music to my ears.

Or it would be if she wasn't shouting right by my eardrums.

"Your…what?" Agata called back, sounding shocked. "When did you get married?"

"Just now!" Ania called.

"Can we get closer to her?" I asked.

Ania looked annoyed. "You're spoiling the fun."

Having my own sister and knowing what a personal war it was to possess one, I understood better than most. "It'll be just as fun telling it to her face, if not more so."

Ania smirked. "Aaron, despite everything, I do believe you have a devious side."

I was offended at that since I was certain everything that had happened should have reinforced that I did have a devious side. Either way, I pulled on my clothes, and we walked to the base of the steam tunnel stairs where Agata was already standing.

"How could you?" Agata asked, staring in horror.

"What? Get married?" Ania asked, confused.

"Yes!" Agata asked.

"Okay now I am offended," I said. "You've been married twice."

"Once to Garland," Ania said. "Which is oath breaking. Something that everyone here is guilty of other than Aaron."

"There are oaths and there are oaths," Agata said, putting her hands on her hips indignantly.

"You broke one of the most important ones," Ania said. "Anyway, yes, Aaron and I are married."

"By whom?" Agata asked.

"By us," I replied. "Which Ania said was how it can be done in Ledziana."

"When there's not a priestess of Mokosh around!" Agata said, appalled.

"There was," Ania said. "Sort of me. I think that I'm blessed by her and something, something."

"That does not count!" Agata said, frowning. "I could have prepared a massive wedding feast, guests of honor, and a holy summoning!"

"That's part of why I'm glad we did it this way," Ania replied. "I'm not a holy summoning kind of girl."

Agata balled her fists. "I don't know what's wrong with you two. This should have been a special occasion!"

"It was for me," I said, dryly. I put my arm around Ania's waist and gave her a squeeze. "It's a way to show how much I love her."

Ania frowned. "Yes, which is what marriage means rather than an attempt to control the other partner's finances."

"Your elf is showing," I said, under my breath.

"I admit, they do influence me a great deal," Ania said, looking at me. "However, your parents have shown me that not all marriages have to be miserable alliances driven only by societal pressure and responsibility."

"I can hear you!" Agata said, pointing at me.

"I'm not trying to hide my opinion!" Ania said.

"It is a sacred institution!" Agata said.

"Did you ever sleep with anyone else other than Garland while he was alive?" Ania asked.

"Only my fellow sisters and when he was present!" Agata said.

My eyes widened.

"Stop fantasizing about my sister," Ania said, elbowing me.

"I'm not!" I wondered if everyone was bi in Ledziana or if it was just a party-specific thing. Maybe they also had more flexible rules about what qualified. Hell, maybe Agata was just screwing with me. She did have a sense of humor under all those extremely flattering, sheer, gown-like robes after all.

Agata sighed. "Well, you should come up here and speak with my daughter. Nyx has figured out how to turn your Marks of the Champion into a covering for your blade."

"So we're reforging the Master Sword into a weapon that can kill Ganon, huh?" I asked, smirking.

"You think you're funny, Aaron, but you're not," Agata said. "I can't help but think what might have happened if we'd been the soldiers at your side when you fought Veles."

"More friends would be dead or maybe my cousin would be alive," I said, not exactly interested in hearing any sass from her about my choices.

Agata, perhaps realizing she'd gone too far, lowered her head. "I can't forgive Alek for killing the Great Mother. I can't forgive Susanos because she led my mother to her death. Unlike Ania, I forgave my mother a thousand times over and would have gladly welcomed her back."

Ania stepped forward as if to say something but, unexpectedly, lowered her head.

"But I am sorry for your loss, Aaron," Agata said, taking a deep breath. "This is a war and there is no conflict where the good do not die in vast amounts among the evil. We are called to make sacrifices, and I fear there will be many more made before victory but victory we must have or life itself will cease. There is no other option."

With that, she departed.

"How long do you think she rehearsed that speech?" I asked.

"Probably years in Sky Realm," Ania said, shaking her head. "Do you really think this weapon of Nyx's will win the war?"

I had no idea. "Yes."

"Liar," Ania said, swatting me in the shoulder.

We were so close to victory.

Why did it seem like we were further away than ever?

CHAPTER TWENTY-SEVEN
THE WEAPON TO KILL GODS

"What the hell is this?" I asked, following Ania up the steps and down another hallway into what looked like the Mako reactor from *Final Fantasy VII*. Given we were in a cheap hotel that was packed with refugees, the fact it looked like a football stadium with a nuclear reactor was a little off-putting. It was kind of like *Doctor Who* when the companions always reacted with shock and surprise that the TARDIS' inside was bigger than the outside.

Wow.

I was a nerd.

I mean, I always knew I was, but it was becoming increasingly clear my mind was just strung together pop culture. It made me wonder if I'd lost my sanity some time ago or never had it in the first place. On the other hand, I supposed if I'd taken the right lessons from media then I was probably better off than most.

Yeah, I was coping.

"It's Nyx's laboratory," Ania said. "It's apparently a pocket dimension that she decided to fill up with her nonsense."

"Huh," I said, remembering my brief visit to Sky Realm. "I just made a cute little home in my pocket dimension. I am clearly not using the mod system correctly."

"What?" Ania asked.

Jon was back to raven form and flew onto my shoulder. "If you ask me, it's all pay to win bullshit. Aaron's domain contents probably cost a few hundred bucks in the Sky Realm online shop. It's addictive. I once blew a grand on stuff for *Fallout 76*."

"Thankfully, I've only ever been addicted to Pwiffle cards," I said, pausing. "Man, it's been a while since I played."

The last game of Pwiffle I'd played had been against Veles of all people and I'd managed to play him to a stalemate where he'd forfeited at the end. I'd used it to force him to swear to me that he'd fight a fair fight. What a waste of a wish. Still, it felt like a simpler time when I could just game away most of my problems. That and I had a serious problem with those cards and hated that I wasn't collecting them anymore.

"You know that's had thirteen massive expansions since Veles took over?" Jon asked. "They even have Pwiffle streaming matches on ESPN."

"What?" I asked, my eyes widening with the childish glee of someone who'd just been told Santa Claus was real. "Can we watch—"

Ania swatted at Jon. "Don't feed my husband's addiction."

"I can't help it," Jon said, shrugging. "He does his best work while high as fuck on his vice. It's like Ozzie. Wave some rare cards in front of him and we may have Veles taken out in a few hours."

"I am now offended," I said, looking around. "So, what exactly is the whole magical nuclear reactor for?"

That was when Nyx walked up wearing a lab coat with a white witch's hat and white gloves, which was ridiculous but befitted the goddess' somewhat quirky style. "It's all necessary for gathering enough magical power to create the Spear of Hope."

"The Spear of Hope?" I asked.

"Yeah, I'm not digging the name," Jon said. "We need something more anime sounding. Can we call it the Spear of Ultimate Destiny God Slaying?"

Nyx blinked. "No."

"Are you sure? I am with the bird on this," Ania said. "The Spear of Hope sounds..."

"Cheesy?" I asked.

"Stupid," Ania said.

"It's called that because it's our last hope," Nyx said, annoyed.

"Then you should call it the Spear of Last Hope," I replied. "That at least has some dash."

"Ooo, the Spear of Lost Hope Ultimate God Slayer!" Jon said.

"I actually like that one," I said, nodding.

"It sounds like it was translated from another language," Ania said. "Then translated back again."

Nyx did not appear amused. "I am not going to take this from someone who hasn't even reached 20th level."

"I was 18th before I became a bird," Jon said. "I'm about ready to hit 19th. Aaron is still 17th."

"You also missed out on those weird upgrades," Ania said, "I miss having a Mark of the Champion to keep track of the absurd numbers on which the gods define our value."

"I will never get used to *Dungeons and Dragons* rules being the defining mathematics of the cosmos," I muttered.

"You should," Nyx said. "I was a fantastic Dungeon Master for my family."

"You were a killer DM!" Rachel shouted from a nearby catwalk. "Every player character died horribly in your games."

"That's the way it's supposed to be played!" Nyx shouted back. "It's better than you giving away all the magical items and EXP!"

"My players had fun!" Rachel said. "Which is the most important part!"

"It is not!" Nyx said. "What's important is the DM exerting their authority!"

I paused, looking between them. "Well, I didn't really believe this 'sisters from a different set of parents' thing until now but they certainly act like siblings."

"Siblings? Yes. Gods? No," Ania said. "I like to think the gods have more maturity than being a pair of—"

"Sisters constantly bickering during the literal apocalypse?" Jon asked. "Yes, I can see why you hold the gods to a higher standard than yourself."

Ania flipped Jon off. "Agata and I have complicated feelings for one another. Love and hate."

"Yes, I said you were sisters," Jon said.

Ania snorted.

"So, what is the plan exactly?" I asked. "Assuming there is one and I don't have to come up with one on the fly."

"I thought the plan was the Holy Lance of Ultimate God Slaying Bada Bing Bong Lost Hope," Jon said. "Oh, and it's a +5. No wait, +6."

"How did you even say that without stuttering?" I asked.

"Magic," Jon said, spreading out his wing.

"I meant more what do we do to make the spear?" I spread my hands out. "Do I have to pound a bunch of metal or throw lightning in the machine?"

"This isn't a story, Aaron," Ania said. "I'm sure—"

"I need him to go inside the reactor," Nyx said. "Then we'll use him as the conductor for transforming the Marks of the Champion into the weapon we need. From there, we'll have to take the spear to Veles avatar and, well, stab him in the heart with it. That will result in him having his creator god power drained away to Sky Realm. It will resurrect Perun and we'll all live happily ever after."

We all stared at her.

"Bullshit," I said.

"Agreed," Ania said.

"Yeah, it's not that kind of story," Jon said. "What's the catch?"

Nyx sighed, clearly annoyed at being questioned. "The catch is that it is an incredibly difficult thing to stab a creator deity in the heart when you are mere mortals. He's been hideously wounded by Aaron so it's now just hard rather than impossible."

"Falling into success is the summary of Aaron's life," Jon said. "Somehow turning the stupidest of decisions into victories through the power of dumb luck."

"I'd argue but I'm not sure I disagree," I said. "Well, I suppose that's about as much of a downside as we're going to get."

"We can develop a more coherent plan," Ania said. "We have time."

I grimaced. "Actually, I'm not sure we do."

Ania looked at me. "Aaron..."

"Veles kind of told me he's going to destroy all of reality or at least the Earth section this weekend," I replied, tapping the tips of my fingers together nervously. "I'm pretty sure he's telling the truth."

"Why would he tell you his plans?" Nyx asked, staring at me sideways. She looked uncomfortably like Nightchilde and Agata both.

I almost sarcastically answered that we all couldn't be like Nightchilde and attempt to live our lives by the internet's Evil Overlord's List, but I didn't want to blame Nyx for the sins of her past incarnation. Nightchilde had manipulated me, stomped on my heart, and murdered gods knew how many people. Being an incredibly genre-savvy supervillain hadn't worked out for her any better than Veles' heavily playing into tropes.

"I think he thinks it's more fun that way," I said, not wanting to admit that we were dealing with not just a god but an insane god. "He also thinks it'll be better to lure us out of our holes to fight him."

"I wouldn't describe our base as a hole," Ania said, defensively. "I mean it has running water and electricity. I've barely seen any rats. Roaches? Yes. But no rats. Really, I'd rank this with some of the finer inns I've been in."

"Uh huh," I said. "I suppose flush toilets really are a hard thing to argue with."

"I mean, magic is better," Ania said. "But—"

Nyx cleared her throat. "Well, there is a small danger."

"A small danger," I repeated her words.

"You mean going into a magical nuclear reactor isn't safe?" Jon mocked. "Perish the thought."

"On a scale of one to ten..." I trailed off.

"Five," Nyx admitted.

"So, a fifty percent chance of what... being melted?" I asked. "Horribly irradiated?"

"I actually don't know what would happen if the fusion process became unstable," Nyx said.

"You *don't know*?" I asked, raising my voice.

Nyx grimaced. "Listen, I am very smart! I have studied all your science, and I mean all of it. This is a perfect mixture of it with Sky Realm sorcery."

"With a fifty percent projected failure rate," I said, sarcastically.

"Which is a fifty percent success rate!" Rachel called over from her catwalk. Really, I wondered how she heard us from so far away before remembering, yes, goddess.

"You're really dating Ms. Sunshine here, huh?" I asked.

"Your DNA is responsible for her unbridled optimism," Jon said, looking at me. "I think. I'm not sure gods have DNA. I think they're made of magic and then replicate bodies when they need them."

"We're not risking Aaron on such a stupid plan," Ania said, stepping in front of me. "I never would have agreed to it if I'd known it had such a high chance of failure."

Nyx conjured a clipboard in her hands. "The chances of a catastrophic failure that destroys this city or world are almost infinitesimal. Really, the chance of Aaron dying is about ten percent at most. Mostly, we'll probably just have to drag him out with the Marks of the Champion ruined."

"No," Ania said, growling. "Listen, you may technically be family but—"

"I'll do it," I interrupted.

"Goddammit, Aaron," Ania said, deflating.

"We're running out of time," I said, taking a deep breath. "If Veles is going to destroy my world then we need a magic bullet."

"Spear," Nyx corrected.

"Not helping, Nyx," I said, staring at my wife. "Ania, you're the one who repeatedly insisted that we need to be willing to sacrifice everything in order to defeat him."

"Yeah, but that was before I had something to lose," Ania said, uncomfortable. "Which is your fault, by the way. The whole point of keeping myself emotionally isolated was to keep me from forming these kinds of attachments."

"Have you been reading psychology books?" I asked, confused at her wording.

"I saw the movies with the warrior training puppet and laser swords," Ania said. "The ones started by taxes were my favorites."

Oh poor Ania, forced to watch those films. Admittedly, they'd aged better than I'd expected given that America had apparently ended up electing its own version of Palpatine. "Yeah, but the Jedi being unattached is actually a mistake because—"

"Are you sure you're willing, Uncle Aaron?" Nyx asked. "I ask because you are family."

"Thank you," I said, taking a deep breath. "I am."

"Also because my previous incarnation was also your lover," Nyx said. "So, technically—"

I glared. "Don't you start."

Nyx smiled. "The machine is prepared."

"I'm not comfortable with this, Aaron," Ania said, reaching out to squeeze my hand.

I gave a half-smile. "What's the worst that could happen? I mean, aside from the world being destroyed a few days early."

"Not funny," Ania said.

"It's only a very small chance!" Nyx added.

Really, it was surreal how chipper those two goddesses had become after their reincarnations. Then again, everything about them and their rebirths was surreal. I wasn't sure where I was supposed to draw the line.

I walked up to the large central reactor and saw Joan standing by it, looking uncomfortable. There was a little elevator-sized chamber underneath the reactor and I wondered if I was making a horrific mistake. Unfortunately, for all my supposed super-intelligence, I couldn't figure out a better way to defeat Veles.

We were out of time.

I stepped into the chamber and proceeded to brace myself against the sides of the interior. "I'm ready."

Joan looked in. "I really hope Nyx isn't evil anymore. I really wasn't fond of Nightchilde."

I remembered how she'd used and manipulated Alek. "Yeah, well, I have to trust Agata and Bloodstorm's child."

"You're a good man, Aaron Bartkowski," Joan said. "But I'm not sure a good man is what we need right now."

Neither was I.

The chamber doors closed on me.

Everything turned blue-white.

CHAPTER TWENTY-EIGHT
I AM THE SPEAR

I had made a terrible mistake. I should have been used to that by now given how often it happened. I took great pride in the fact that I'd managed to turn around so many of my mistakes and ride them out. But, you know what they say: Pride goeth before the fall.

There was bound to be an occasion when I found myself in a situation where I couldn't think my way out of events. Indeed, that seemed to keep happening and I was really getting annoyed by it. What was the point of being the world's smartest man (the smartest man on two worlds) if there was no solution for you to find?

I was surrounded by the glowing light of the reactor and blinded like I was inside a tanning bed. Except, the light was the raw substance of magic, and I was being irradiated with it like a chicken in a microwave. It didn't hurt, really, but I could tell that it was blasting my body with the equivalent of 1,000,000 megahertz of sorcerous power. It was situations like this that I had to wonder if raising my low WIS score had not so much made me less prone to stupid mistakes but simply removed my last remaining excuse for doing so.

Either way, I could feel myself penetrated by the massive amount of magic spreading through my body and the Marks of the Champion merging with my flesh. I was trying desperately to mentally form the excess energy into a sword, but it was proving... well, it wasn't working. Let's just leave it at that. Worse, I had no way to get out of the situation."

"PUSH!" I shouted, trying to get out.

SPELLCASTING IS CURRENTLY DISABLED.

Dammit.

"Let me out!" I shouted, struggling with the big metal wheel on the door.

It didn't move.

DOOR IS OPENED FROM THE OTHER SIDE.

"No kidding, really!" I shouted, wondering why my Marks were suddenly so chatty. 'How do I get out then?"

No answer.

I'd had a huge amount of magical knowledge downloaded into my brain but there was no solution among the vast diagrams and philosophical treatise on the nature of the universe. Stephen Hawking and Carl Sagen would have loved to have gotten a look at it, assuming they could get over how much ended up being, "A God did it." However, neither of them would have been able to come up with a solution either.

Because there wasn't one.

There was no way to transform the energy being flooded into my demigod's body into an external weapon that could slay gods. Instead, the energy was designed to overwhelm my existing form until it exploded or changed into something that could channel the energy as well as store it. It was a trap, and I'd fallen for it. I could just hear Ania taunting me about it, "Oh, you thought to trust the child raised in Sky Realm just because she was a blood relative to someone you trusted? My blood relatives are some of the worst people on Mokosh."

Of course, the solution presented itself to me soon after. Maybe just a few seconds before I died but enough that I knew what exactly I'd been trapped into doing. Nyx was still Zorya Nightbringer despite her lack of corruption and that person was similar enough to Nightchilde that she knew it was better to ask forgiveness than permission. Even more so, she'd known me from her previous life and how to press my buttons. There was only one way to survive what was happening to me.

To become a god.

A true god.

To take all of Perun's remaining energy into myself and destroy everything that had been Aaron Bartkowski. Maybe I would still be me. Maybe I would be Perun. I had no idea. It was one of the reasons that I never would have voluntarily become a god. It was too risky to lose what I cherished most: my humanity. My humanity that allowed me to love Ania and show the kind of compassion and empathy that had stupidly led me to this situation in the first place.

WOULD YOU LIKE TO ABSORB DIVINE ESSENCE? Y/N

The marks were gone but I saw the information across my eyes anyway, the interface now integrated into my very soul.

I could have taken the other way out: let myself explode and ruin Nyx's plans, whatever they were. However, a small chance of life is better than no chance at all. "I accept the power of the Marks of the Champion into me. I accept becoming a god."

So, yes.

What happened next was difficult to put into words but pretty much was the final scene from the original *Highlander*. You know, the only good one. I say that with no offense to the anime or Adrian Paul's TV show. I felt myself absorbing all the previous champions' power and each fragment of Perun that they'd been carrying. But it wasn't just Perun's power that I absorbed, but the strength as well as heroism that they'd all brought into the world.

I was Francine and understood how desperate she was to try to do the right thing. How she was always trying to thread the needle between her moral values and the constant cynicism of politics. How she'd loved the Bastard Knight as a friend and brother.

I was Jon who, despite his constant air of being a stupid prankster, had tried to do good things but only trusted himself to do them on a personal level.

I saw the farmers, cobblers, and peasants he'd protected whereas everyone else tried to save kingdoms.

I was also a girl named Becky who had barely begun her championship when she'd been cut down attempting to do the right thing by people who absolutely didn't deserve her sympathy.

I experienced the champions' villainy too.

Arete was a Greek word for greatness and reflected the fact that their heroes could be bona fide assholes at times even if they did amazing deeds. They regularly abandoned people that helped them, murdered people in berserk rages, or got themselves killed by the loved ones they betrayed. There was some of that among the people who had tried to do good.

In a moment, I was Valentin, slaughtering my way across the Southern Kingdoms. A man who served Veles willingly because he had been unleashed by a monster who wanted him to indulge every worst impulse.

In a moment, I was Alek, who was consumed with a need for revenge. He'd pretended to be a hero for the sake of the Dragon Queen that he loved but could never escape the belief he was a monster because of what he'd done in Afghanistan.

In a moment, I was a man named Carver who was far more subdued in his motivations. Being a hero in Mokosh was a chance to do whatever the hell he wanted and indulge in every possible vice with no regards to the consequences.

A decade of various people carrying the torch of Garland the Black Rose had fanned the embers of Perun's essence until they all joined together to form a fire within me. But that wasn't the secret of the Marks of the Champion. No, the secret of the Marks of the Champion was that they contained one more source of divine energy.

The Wise Man himself.

The entire history of the Wiseman could not readily be described but he dwarfed all our lives put together.

I saw the Wiseman travelling with the nomadic peoples that would eventually become both the early Polish and later Ledzianans.

I saw the Wise Man on a mountaintop, meeting Perun for the first time.

I saw him battling endless numbers of evil wizards, corrupt kings, and wicked warlords. Rescuing imperiled damsels and occasionally dudes.

Seriously, Larry C.C. Weis apparently lived like Conan the Barbarian for about a thousand years.

That was when I'd found myself feeling the immense gulf of years that started to weigh upon Larry C.C. Weis. A thing I hadn't expected but soon threatened to overwhelm me.

Larry was old.

Old in a way that humans were never meant to be. Larry (obviously not his original name) felt the loss of friends, lovers, and family repeatedly. The triumph of his successes never seemed to outweigh the regrets of his failures. Ledziana and the various kingdoms always seemed to be caught in an endless cycle of war, peace, and revenge.

I understood in a moment why the Wise Man chose to be a fantasy author. He had seen every possible iteration of humankind's interaction, most of them being disappointing, and had become addicted to the idea of heroism.

True heroism.

It made me realize just why he'd treasured Garland's actions, however misguided and error prone they'd been. For a man who had seen everything, the Knight of Nowhere had continually surprised him, and it was worth sharing with the rest of humanity. Unfortunately, this had also deeply wronged Garland because that fame had attracted envy and hatred from those who found themselves wanting by comparison.

Then he found me.

You were my last desperate hope, Aaron. I didn't believe you would work out, but you did. Be the hero we need. Larry's voice echoed in my mind.

I'm not a hero. I'm just playing one.

That's all anyone can do.

I can't do this. It's too much.

Not for a god. So, either be a good one or we're doomed.

With that, I was consumed by all the magical energy surrounding me and reborn into something else.

YOU HAVE GAINED DIVINITY SCORE: 21
* Automatic success on all attack rolls to non-divine beings.

* Automatic success on all non-divine saving throws.
* Avatar Form Unlocked
* Avatar Level raised to 20th Level [Avatar Maximum]
* All Attributes raised to 30 for Avatar.
* Divine Attributes now Unlocked.
* Epic Levels Now Unlocked.
* Portfolio Mode Now Unlocked
* PORTFOLIOS GAINED: Idealism, Compassion, and Trickery [Bonus: Push]
* ANTI-PORTFOLIOS GAINED: Evil, Cynicism, Wisdom
* Celestial Realm Creator Mode Unlocked [Sky Realm]
* PATRON GOD: Ratkin (Mokosh), Ania Rose (Earth)
* Mana now replaces the expenditure of spell slots [Mana Score: 999+]
* Can cast MIRACLE once per day on Prime Material Plane, Unlimited Times in Realm.
* Can cast PERUN'S DIVINE LIGHTNING BOLT (9th level spell) three times per day.
* PERUN'S SWORD is now changed to AARON'S MERCIFUL BLADE
* PUSH is now HAND OF GOD
* Can grant 9th level spells to priests and answer PRAYER [ACTIVE]
* You are ranked an Intermediate God

Holy crap.

That was so overwhelming that I almost felt like I couldn't look at my stats anymore (and didn't for the time being). This was endgame content level upgrades and the kind of thing that really sort of took the mechanics out of things. Epic Levels had been unlocked? I had a portfolio now? I had an anti-portfolio? What was that? Also, wisdom was my *anti*-portfolio? That was just cheap on the part of whoever was running this.

I was especially curious about whatever Avatar mode meant. Did that mean that I was no longer a person and the thing that was running around in my body was just an extension of something greater? It was the kind of thing that all the gods who had been trying to manipulate me would have come in real handy with about now.

ACHIEVEMENT UNLOCKED: APOTHEOSIS
(A) 50 - Become a full god.
ACHIEVEMENT UNLOCKED: SKYLORD
(A) 50 - Become a god of good.
ACHIEVEMENT UNLOCKED: Nightbringer's Spear
(A) 25 - Follow Nyx's Plan to Defeat Veles

I wondered what would have qualified as a plan to defeat Veles that didn't involve Nyx. It was enough, though, that I already regretted allowing myself to be tricked into this because that level of power couldn't help but change a person irrevocably. I would never be able to go back to being just an ordinary person after this. I mean, I could shoot lightning from my hands and conjure food so maybe ordinary was relative, but I suddenly realized why I'd been so hesitant to make a transition to godhood until this point.

With great power came great responsibility. Goddammit. Yep. There was no escaping Spider-Man here. The simple fact was that I couldn't just be an ordinary person after this. There was no returning to the Shire (or Michigan) after the adventure was done. Maybe not with my hot ninja elf wife. There wasn't even a chance to return to Dragon Keep and sit in it as a common Dark Undermaster. No, I was stuck being a god now.

What was described on the interface was the kind of power that could change the course of nations, alter the nature of human civilization, and start religions. Which, I suppose, was pretty much the definition of godhood. I was now moving from Spider-Man to not even the Mighty Thor but Galactus or Odin here.

NPC quest giver status.

In the words of Jon Snow, "I don't want it."

I could see the future of my life now where I would either end up permanently warping life around whoever I chose to stay with, becoming like the Emperor of Mankind from *Warhammer 40K* (pre-brain death), or I would have to retreat to Sky Realm or some other dimension to avoid utterly smashing everyone's free will. If you ever wondered why the gods didn't solve everyone else's problems, it was a pretty good argument because I could see myself becoming a tyrant out of a desire to do good. A Gandalf the Gray with the One Ring of Sauron situation. What did this mean for me and Ania? I didn't know.

That was when the light faded and I found myself naked on the ground, all my clothes, armor and weapons disintegrated by the light that had been infusing me for the past, well, I didn't know how long I'd been in there. The chamber was now a dirty metal one like an old submarine's interior or maybe an empty vault in *Fallout*. It was larger than I thought and probably about ten or fifteen yards. I wish I'd been warned about losing my stuff and wondered if I could conjure it back or if it was time to get upgraded god gear. There were large spots in my eyes from, you know, where I'd been blasted with so much light— god upgrade or not.

"Perhaps you are putting the cart before the horse, Aaron," a voice spoke in the glowing light around me. "You are thinking of how much you will have to adjust to the life of unlimited power and prestige when you haven't yet beaten Veles. You also haven't contemplated that you might never even face the Dark Lord yourself. You, after all, are only an Intermediate God and there are hundreds of greater gods and pantheon heads who are terrified of him. Ones who might think your power is better spent... elsewhere."

That was when I saw Agata, except it was not Agata. Without getting too sleazy, it looked like a bunch of guys on DV8art.zero had decided to do a *World of Warcraft*-style porn version of her. What if Agata Rose was a murderous succubus with leathery wings, claws, fangs, and clearly some work done despite being perfectly fine in those areas to begin with. Her eyes glowed yellow-green and I could feel a strange power radiating from her that seemed to feed on my aura.

"What the hell happened to you?" I asked, turning around.

"Close enough," Agata asked. "The gods have blessed me, Aaron. I am now ready for my ascension and to be the champion that both worlds need."

She came up to me and kissed me on the lips.

DIVINE ABILITIES NEUTRALIZED

I felt my newly achieved godhood start to drain away from me. Shit.

CHAPTER TWENTY-NINE
THE BETRAYAL

In the words of *Futurama*'s Fry, I never thought I'd die like this but I always kinda wanted to. Okay, no, that's not accurate. Dying at the hand of a beautiful succubus draining my life from me might not be the worst way to die but even if I wanted to avoid the heavy responsibilities ahead, I wasn't suicidal and couldn't even enjoy the salaciousness of it. No, because it was Agata doing it and that ruined even the mildest enjoyment.

If you never repeat it to anyone else and it doesn't end in some popular fantasy novel somewhere, I'll share a secret: I was attracted to Agata. I'd always been more attracted to Ania and would never stand in the way of Agata and Bloodstorm's relationship. However, Ania had dumped Agata's naked form in my bed to nuzzle me back to life after I'd absorbed all the divine energies from Zorya Dawnbringer.

That left an impression.

The real Agata would never have done the thing she was doing to me now, draining me like an *Advanced Dungeons and Dragons* vampire level by level. No, it had to be something the gods of Ledziana had altered her to be able to do. They'd transformed her into a weapon and, worse, an unwilling one.

I should have seen this coming but as the interface had helpfully informed me, I had an anti-portfolio against cynicism. I wanted to believe the best of people and when I didn't, like when I'd scared the shit out of Ivan, it felt unnatural. I wanted to inspire people, not terrify them into submission.

The gods of Mokosh had repeatedly shown themselves to be sketchy as hell. Their love—even Mokosh's—was conditional. Some might individually be decent people, though even that was probably me extending them more credit than they deserved, but their worst qualities were brought out by working in concert. A god might be interested in their worshipers as a shepherd might love their flock— thank you New Testament for that metaphor—but the gods can only look after the system that kept them in power.

It was as I fell to my knees, uncomfortably aroused with Agata's hands in very inappropriate places, that I remembered I should probably be more interested in rescuing myself from certain doom than musing about how I'd been disappointed by the powers that be. I could curse the heavens, or I could try to stop Agata as well as work to release her from the brainwashing they'd clearly put her under.

I managed to use the super strength I'd gained from my upgrade (which was rapidly fading). I forced her from kissing me and managed to speak out, "Agata, don't... stop... please."

Okay, not my most intimidating but I was already on my knees. I was also, uh, distractedly feeling things that my body was resisting. Seriously, there was no dignity at being at full attention while someone was trying to eat your soul.

"You left me!" Agata spoke in a tone that did not sound remotely like her. "You were supposed to take me from this place! Instead, you left me in Sky Realm, and I was forced to serve him!"

I had no idea what the hell she was talking about. However, a strong sense of dread filled me. Her brief rant, however, gave me a second to react. "PUSH!"

I was stripped of my divine abilities that I'd previously been complaining about being too overpowered but, right now, I would have wished for anything to have them back. Especially as Agata was now blessed with a substantial chunk of the abilities I'd just been granted.

Which explained why she moved about an inch backward.

Shit.

Agata laughed. "Haha. Pathetic. I can't imagine what Ania sees in you."

Things started to fall into place. "Who are you?"

This wasn't Agata.

The Agata imposter stared at me with fury in her eyes. "That you have the audacity to say that is enough to warrant your death. You slew my goddess and could have made me your companion but instead I was an embarrassment. A monument to your foul concept of mercy."

"I'm sorry," I said, figuring out who she was. I saw the shattered pieces of the Mark of the Champion on the ground and grabbed a handful, using them to draw blood from my hand. I hope that there was a small fragment of Perun's power still clinging to them.

DIVINE POWER RESTORED (2%)

The Agata imposter stared at me for a second as she saw my body glow with the divine power that she'd removed, albeit at a fraction of its original level. She proceeded to go for my throat like a vampire, which she was.

That was when I impaled her with the Sword of Perun, which had taken every bit of divine energy I'd had to summon. I shoved it through the succubus' chest while staring directly up into her eyes.

A mixture of hatred, fear, and regret passed across her eyes before the light left them. The succubus slumped over on my sword before slowly shifting back into their original form.

Thistle.

"What the hell happened to you?" I asked, wondering how she'd gone from being an angel serving in my supposed kingdom in Sky Realm to an utterly insane monster. "What the fuck am I saying? It was the gods."

"Not the gods but *a* god," Nyx said, behind me. She'd walked through the walls of her reactor, and I was debating stabbing her too. "Mythras."

"Your plan failed," I said, standing up and staring down at Thistle. "It may have also resulted in all of that divine energy being lost."

"It's not lost," Nyx said. "You will regenerate it. It would have only permanently transferred to Thistle upon your death. As for the plan, it was not my plan but Mythras. He took Thistle from you and broke her will. Bent her mind and turned her into a weapon against her patron."

All of this had happened in the skewed timeline of Sky Realm versus us.

I stared at her. "Is that what happened to you?"

"No," Nyx said. "I cooperated for a much simpler reason: he has my mother."

"Did you ever even meet your mother?" I asked.

"Yes," Nyx said. "I was raised by her, but she is a prisoner now on this world. The substitution had to be done on this world where it is beyond the authority of the other gods."

I stared at her. "*Why?*"

Nyx frowned, looking sad. "Mythras thinks you're weak. That you show too much compassion to your enemies and focus too much on forging alliances versus taking the necessary steps to end threats."

I stared at her. "Yeah, because he's been doing so much during all of this."

"Ambition has a way of clouding the judgement of even the divine," Nyx said, looking ashamed in a moment. "Mythras was the god of heroism but did nothing to stop the Divine Bull who the Empire calls Veles and left it to you. Maybe he supported Joan against the Empire's fundamentalists but barely. Perhaps Mythras was warped by the fact so many of his worshipers in the Empire have grown fat on conquest, slavery, and national pride. They no longer recognize sacrifice for others as a concept."

I stared at her. "Or you're just lying, and this was your plan all along."

Nyx smiled and I recognized it as one that had been worn by Nightchilde many times. "You're finally learning, Aaron. I wonder if it would be possible for you to recognize that if you were still infused with your full power as a god, though. There is an immense price to being a god and that is the loss of self-determination. Humans rarely make much use of their gift, but gods are the products of their dreams."

I stared at her. "That's not denying the accusation."

"I am not behind this and want Agata rescued as she is hostage to my good behavior but I also know this development is a threat to our defeat of Veles so I will share you a secret: I was not reborn like Dawnbringer. Your daughter, Rachel."

I stared. "What?"

"She was corrupted by the Twisted Gods' magic just like Veles and had to destroy her old self to regain her freewill," Nyx said. "I had already separated my spirit from my corruption and used poor Prince Cezary, the original, to serve as my vessel."

"Yeah, that didn't work out well," I said, having a cold and unfortunate realization as to how much danger I was in.

"It worked out reasonably well," Nyx replied, sounding exactly like the woman I'd been forced to kill. "You destroyed the Wind Demon and taught me a valuable lesson in humility. But I was not reborn in the same way as Rachel. I remember everything that my previous incarnations experienced."

It said something about the way my brain worked that my reaction was not that I was alone, naked, and possessed only of a half-functioning divine sword to help me next to a possible enemy. No, it meant that she remembered our relationship, and I'd technically slept with the woman who was now my niece. God dammit, reality! I thought we were done with the incest jokes! God, Perun, and Santa Claus!

"Seriously?" Nyx asked, staring at me as if I'd grown a second head.

"What?" I asked.

"I can read your mind," Nyx said.

"I think it's a very reasonable thing to complain about!" I said, staring at her.

"I disagree," Nyx said, facepalming. "What this means is that I am changed but it is by my choice and the human soul, the real child of Agata and Bloodstorm, that has been bonded to me."

"Technically, is it a human soul if Bloodstorm is half-ogre and half-elf?" I asked. "Wouldn't it be a half-human soul and—"

"Aaron!" Nyx said.

"Right."

Nyx sighed. "My free will is heavily impacted by my divinity, but it exists enough to make a choice."

"A choice," I said, skeptically. "Because you just admitted your choice was to stand here and let me get eaten?"

"Yes," Nyx said. "But I also saw you survive. Again. Like you always do."

If I was less than impressed with her praise after doing nothing to help me, I tried not to show it on my face. However, given she could read minds, and I wasn't possessed of any divine protection right now, I wouldn't put money on her not knowing how I really felt.

"Tired of giving second chances?" Nyx asked, skeptically.

"I was tired of giving second chances by the time I offered one to Thistle," I said, pausing. "My ego would like to think that Mythras did break her, but I think it's just as likely she turned against me as soon as she had a better offer."

"Perhaps," Nyx said. "Thistle thought she could seduce you into compliance or at least flatter you into making her a chief angel. Instead, you kept her at arms distance and showed only the mercy that gave her a chance to redeem herself. I am not saying that Mythras did not crush her spirit and remake her but perhaps you are correct that her loyalty was never more than a pretense."

"She was a rebel and never going to be any good," I replied with more bitterness than I expected. "You made her that way, or at least Nightchilde did."

"You could blame the Royal Family of Ledziana for their oppression of elves, the elvish race for refusing to fight back in a way as brutal as humanity, or perhaps, and this is a crazy idea, Thistle herself. In the end, Mythras' plan to give himself the remainder of Perun's power and ascend to creator god status has failed."

"Would he be able to beat Veles if he was a creator god?" I asked.

"No," Nyx asked. "He is the spirit of heroism and there is nothing less heroic than backstabbing an ally in order to gain an advantage against a foe you were afraid to be the underdog to. No one would remember the story of David and Goliath if David was crushed like an insect."

"You'd be surprised,' I said, only half-joking. "The US government made an entire cottage industry about being the underdogs against, well, everyone else."

Mind you, there was a reason James Bond as a lone secret agent was popular versus an entire CIA intelligence apparatus so maybe Nyx had the right idea. The gods kept repeating the fact that they were stories and bound by them, maybe there was something to it, even if it was only because they believed it.

"Let me help you, Aaron," Nyx said. "For the sake of my mother."

"So, you want us to take a break from fighting Veles to go rescue your mother, who may or may not be imprisoned in Heaven, and fight another god?" I asked. "Even though your stupid plan to empower me has actually left me less powerful than I was before?"

"Yes," Nyx said.

I sighed, nodding. "Sure."

Nyx blinked. "Really?"

"I'm not going to abandon Agata," I said, simply. "She's family. I've lost enough family this week."

Nyx blinked.

"Alek," I said, simply. "You know, the guy who was in love with you when he thought you were the Dragon Queen."

"Oh, right," Nyx said. "Him."

Yeah, Nyx wasn't doing a bang-up job convincing me that she was on the level. Thankfully, I didn't need to trust her despite my reputation as the All-Loving Hero™. I wasn't Snow White or Kung Fu Jesus and the fact that I had never brought Thistle into my confidence had been deliberate.

Just because you were willing to give someone a second (or third) chance didn't mean you were willing to let them have the keys to your house. I hated what I'd done to Ivan, blowing his head off and resurrecting him, but I also acknowledged it was probably the only reason he'd been willing to do what I asked of him.

One thing I'd been continually confronted with while trying to save Ledziana and its people was that they didn't trust people who tried to show mercy. They were so used to a kind of Mad Max gone medieval post-apocalypse existence after the Great Darkness and deathrot plague that they equated strength with cruelty. It was survival of the fittest and no one seemed to believe looking after each other was a better strategy than being a lone wolf predator. Which was stupid since all of history said otherwise.

"Then we have a deal," I said, sighing. "Because we're utterly screwed if we can't recover Agata."

"We were utterly screwed before," Nyx said. "Now we're just more so."

"Right," I said, sighing.

"You should put some pants on," Nyx suggested.

"You destroyed my only pair of clothes on this world," I muttered.

Nyx grimaced. "Right. Well, I guess I'll have to make you some new ones."

"I'll try and hope they're not poisoned," I replied.

"No promises," Nyx said, making a joke.

That was when Ania appeared behind her and slit her throat with a long, curved dagger. Blackish-blue ichor poured out of Nyx's injury as a look of stunned shock appeared on her face.

"Death to the Nightbringer!" Ania shouted.

Rachel and Jon were behind her.

Well crap.

CHAPTER THIRTY
THE PRACTICALITY OF MERCY

"Goddammit, Ania!" I said, immediately rushing to Nyx's side and hoping we hadn't engaged in accidental deicide. Okay, it wouldn't be accidental, and it would be the first time we'd killed a god without wanting to (or me wanting to).

"I am very confused," Ania said, holding her bloody knife above Nyx's body. The dagger dripped blue ichor.

"You killed my sister!" Rachel said, staring downward. "Who might have been trying to kill your husband, who is my father. Wait does that make you my moth—"

"Finish that sentence and join Nyx," Ania said, growling.

Rachel made a 'zip it' gesture in front of her lips.

"Oh, what a surprise," Jon muttered, looking down at me. "Aaron is trying to save the irredeemable evil bitch who just so happens to be really hot."

"That is not relevant," I said, trying every healing spell I could and hoping that Thistle hadn't drained me of my regular mortal magic too.

"You can't help her, Aaron," Jon said, looking down. "This is a cutscene, I'm sure. It's like, Aerith is going to die no matter how many healing items you've got."

Rachel slapped him in the shoulder. "Now is not the time for jokes!"

"Who is joking?" Jon asked. "I don't see how this theory is weirder than anything else we've encountered."

Rachel frowned as if she didn't quite have a response to that.

Ania looked down at me then behind me. "Aaron, if you do manage to save her then I'll just kill her again. She betrayed us. She betrayed my sister, her mother...sort of. But it's a case of angelic possession like that god you worship here on Earth that knocks up virgins."

Jon grimaced. "There went our chance to be adapted for television in America."

"Yeah, like that was going to happen with all the incest," Rachel muttered. "Unless it would be on HBO."

"*Of course* it would be HBO," Jon muttered.

"How do you know so much Earth pop culture?" I asked.

Rachel shrugged. "We have great reception in Skyworld."

Ask a stupid question, get a stupid answer.

I closed my eyes. "Why does everyone think that my efforts here are motivated by idealism?"

"Because we know you," Jon said.

My healing magic was struggling against the black magic that was inherent in Ania's dagger. It was making progress, but I wasn't sure if it would be enough to save her before her avatar was destroyed. "I'm doing it because no one has any idea where the hell Agata is except her!"

That seemed to give everyone in the room but me a moment of realization that we were screwed if Nyx died (again).

"Low WIS my ass," I muttered.

Rachel knelt to help me in the healing and, thank whatever gods that weren't working against me, Nyx's neck injury finally healed. Which she let me know by spitting a bunch of blue ichor in my face.

"Yuck," I said, wiping it away with my arm.

"I probably deserved that," Nyx muttered, looking over at Ania.

"You did," Ania said, pausing. "I'd apologize but you just tried to kill my husband and are part of a plot to kidnap my sister so I will stab you again if you do not explain where she is right this second."

"Sister, understand that I one hundred percent agree with her," Rachel said. "You have made a terrible mistake siding with Mythras."

Jon shook his head. "Who possibly could have foreseen that the god of a conquest-hungry empire would actually turn out to be bad?"

"He put his trust in Joan," I said, wondering if there wasn't more to the story or if I was just always trying to find the best in people to the point of abject stupidity.

"Anyone want to be the one who tells her that her boss is a complete bastard?" Jon asked. "Because I don't."

"Because you'd break her heart?" Rachel asked.

"No, because I'm scared to death of Sailor Rome," Jon said. "Remember she did get a massive upgrade, and I didn't."

"Jon is upgraded," Rachel said, pausing. "Well, sort of. He's 19th level now but he doesn't have his divine levels."

"Which is like being Batman when we really needed Superman," Jon said. "I'm not one of those people who believes that Batman could defeat anyone with sufficient preparation. The thing about combat is it usually happens when you don't have preparation so Superman could—"

"Where is Agata?" I asked, looking down at Nyx and wishing I was wearing pants. I was finally in a situation where I could contemplate the fact I wasn't wearing clothing.

"The Mithraeum," a voice spoke from nearby.

I looked up and saw Joan at the door of the chamber. She looked like she'd just had her dog run over and I suspect that probably did summarize how she felt regarding the discovery her god was a bad guy. Assuming she believed us. Shaking a person's faith in their deity wasn't something you could just do with a bit of evidence as well as a speech. This wasn't *Star Trek*.

"The what now?" Jon asked.

"It's a place where people worship Mythras, their version of a church," I replied. "London has one."

Excavated in 1954, the Museum of London had found an underground temple to Mythras—or Mithras as he was spelled in Earth English—that was now underneath the Bloomberg Building. It was like #283 on my list of things to do before I died. Mind you, back when I was a computer programmer, it was #283 of the things I could never afford to do and that was only because #112 was get around to finishing the latest *Fallout 76* update. They'd probably had a few since a decade had passed.

"What, our London?" Jon asked.

"Yes, our London," I said.

"My God, Joan is *British*!" Jon said in faux outrage.

Joan was already turned around and running away, though.

"Dammit," I said, moving to chase after her before Ania grabbed my arm.

"What?" I asked, looking at her.

Ania looked down.

So did I.

"Right," I muttered. "Best to put some pants on first. Can any of you conjure pants?"

"Seriously, dude?" Jon asked, shaking his head. "That's the one spell you didn't bother to learn while overloading your magic list?"

I was about ready to punch Jon but decided against it since there was absolutely no point complaining about a pigeon who took a crap on your car. As much as I loved my best friend, he was basically the Jay to my Silent Bob. His idiocy was part of his charm and if you didn't like it then that was your problem because he was never going to change.

Rachel took me by the hand and said, "I can help you, Aaron. We don't want her falling in love with you and developing confused feelings."

"I look like her father," I said, staring at Rachel."

"Okay, one more incest joke for the road," Rachel said, giving a pained smile. With that, she closed her eyes and a glow covered me.

YOU HAVE ACQUIRED CELESTIAL UNDERMASTER ARMOR (+10)

YOU HAVE ACQUIRED CELESTIAL UNDERMASTER BOOTS OF SPEED (+10)

YOU HAVE ACQUIRED CELESTIAL UNDERMASTER BRACERS OF DEFENSE (+10)

YOU HAVE ACQUIRED CELESTIAL *CLOAK OF THE SKY*

FATHER (+10)

Much to my surprise, I was suddenly covered in an incredibly smooth, soft set of armor that felt more like a pair of silk pajamas than a suit of armor.

"What the hell is this?" I asked, shuffling about and noticing she'd conjured some magic underwear too.

"Celestial armor," Rachel said. "I decided since you did get a boost that you should have access to the epic stuff."

I stared at her. "And you didn't think to *conjure this earlier*? You know, when we were fighting other gods and could have used all of the help we could get."

"Maybe there was a level requirement," Jon said.

"Shut up," Ania said, glaring.

Jon made a locking key gesture in front of his lips because as crazy as he was, there was nothing scarier than my wife.

Rachel stared. "You just have to complain about everything, don't you, Aaron?"

I rolled my eyes and walked past her.

Catching up with Joan proved to be easy enough since she didn't walk away far. Joan was staring at the corner of the magical power plant's wall like she was five, clearly trying to gather herself. I couldn't imagine what was going on in her head right now since I'd never had a religion to lose. I mean, I came close after *Rise of the Skywalker* but that was probably different.

"Uh, hey, Joan," I said, raising a hand sympathetically.

"Is this where they send you out to talk to me because you're the only one who understands the concept of diplomacy?" Joan asked, turning around.

"Yeah, pretty much," I said, taking a deep breath. "I'm pretty sure Bloodstorm is going to freak the hell out once he finds out his wife has been kidnapped."

"Wouldn't you?" Joan asked.

"Yes," I said, dryly. "Mind you, I don't know how I would have reacted to Nyx. Having your child possessed by..."

I trailed off, realizing I knew exactly how that felt.

"Yeah," Joan said. "We are just puppets of the gods and their twisted machinations."

"Some of them are okay," I said.

Joan facepalmed. "Okay doesn't cut it, Aaron. Gods are meant to embody the concepts that humans struggle to live up to. Honor, justice, compassion, and mercy. These things are meant to be absolute, and repeatedly they have shown themselves to be... hypocrites!"

I didn't really have a response for that. My experience with the divine was that they were just extremely powerful people and as capable of good or evil as anyone else. Becoming a demigod hadn't really changed my nature either. Maybe the crucible of my struggles had made me *more* Aaron—more aware of my limits—but they hadn't really changed me from *being* Aaron if that made any sense.

"I'm afraid that I can't give you any answers on this," I replied. "I think that absolutes aren't where you should be looking for good, though."

"Only the Sith—" A voice started to shout from the power plant.

"Shut the hell up, Jon! Now is not the time!" I shouted back.

"Which is an absolute!" Jon shouted back.

"Maybe it's a Jedi paradox!" Rachel called back. "Like Zen Buddhism!"

I took a deep breath. "Rachel is an okay god. But the only reason I haven't killed Nyx or let Ania do it, again, is because we need her. I'm sorry your god sucks but you deserve a better class of deity. Mythras doesn't cut it and I'm sorry."

Joan seemed to ponder that. "You're right, Aaron. He doesn't."

It occurred to me breaking her faith in her god right as we were about to face down Veles was probably not a good idea. Unfortunately, there wasn't really going to be a better time to do this. Mythras had really chosen a good time to stab us in the back (assuming such a thing existed). Not only were we deprived of Agata's abilities as a battle mage as well as healer, but we were about to lose our actual healer too.

"Well, I—" I started to say.

"You do, though," Joan said, pulling off her Mythras medallion and throwing it away before grabbing me in a hug.

YOU HAVE GAINED ONE PC-RANKED FOLLOWER.

I reluctantly patted her on the back. "I don't believe that worshiping me as a god is a good thing, Joan."

"You are preaching peace, love, and a hatred of empires as well as the rich. You have also shown yourself willing to die for humanity," Joan said. "I think that would be a very good basis for a religion."

I grimaced. "It's been done."

"Really?" Joan asked.

"Yeah, by a man named John Lennon," I said. "You should look him up."

Joan stared. "I have no idea what you're referencing but have the feeling that you're making fun of me."

I smirked. "You know me too well. But you realize I can't grant you spells and we're kind of in need of a god now."

Joan frowned. "We're at the end of our rope as is, Aaron Bartowski. Mythras' avatar is on this planet, hiding in his own temple in London or at least the shadow of his Temple that exists in his dimension here. He is almost certainly keeping Agata as a hostage to your good behavior. You need to confront him, no matter the danger."

I sighed. "Yeah, just what I needed, another side quest before the final boss."

"Maybe you will be able to persuade him from the cause of evil and to redeem himself."

"You think?" I asked.

"No," Joan said. "I think you should summon the Witch Queen first and have her help in confronting him."

Yeah, Joan was probably not the pope anymore. "Great idea. I wish I'd thought of it."

"See? That I got as sarcasm," Joan said. "But at the very least she'll be a balance against Nyx. You need to bind her with a geas."

"I don't think I have the magic to do that," I said.

"You should check," Joan said, tapping the top of my forehead.

That was a good idea. I mentally asked to see what my stats were now.

ARAGORN "AARON" BARTKOWSKI

LVL: 20
CLASS: Avatar (Sky Realm)
ALIGNMENT: GRAY (Neutral Good)
AGE: 35
SEX: MALE
RACE: HUMAN (Intermediate God)

STR: 30
AGI: 30
CON: 30
INT: 30
WIS: 30 (10)
COM: 30
CHA: 30

ARMOR CLASS: 50
ATTACK: +30 (+30 to ATTACK, 1d10+40/40 [Undead] DAM, *Sword of Perun*, Lightning, Holy, INT bonus])
HEALTH: 320
DIVINITY: 21
FEAT: Taunt, Sword and Shield, Two Handed Fighting, Tracking, Craft Magical Items/Recharge Magical Items, Leadership
SPECIAL ABILITIES: ARCANE FIRE (1d6+13 INT bonus, Eldritch Damage, x3 Staff of Dragon Kings, Critical Hit Possible), BLOCK (requires shield), LESSER MAGIC (unlimited times per day), COUNTERSPELL, ~~DIVINE ENHANCEMENT [Push]~~
LESSER MAGIC EFFECTS: CLEAN SELF, CREATE FOOD,

246 / C. T. Phipps

CREATE FIRE, CREATE WATER, MINOR ILLUSION, REFRESH, TELEKINESIS (1 Kilo per INT bonus), VENTRILOQUISM, MEND, TORCHLIGHT, SILENT WALK, IDENTIFY MAGICAL OBJECT, LESSER SENDING (Party Only), BLESS, SOOTHE ANIMAL
SPELL LIST (MAX/5/5/5/5/5/4/3/3/2)
[1] ARMOR, CURE, FRIENDSHIP, JUMP, PUSH [S-Rank]
[2] ANIMAL SUMMONING, ENTANGLE, SILENCE, WEB
[3] CURE (II), LESSER CHARM, LIGHTNING BOLT, NEUTRALIZE POISON, SUGGESTION
[4] BANISHMENT, CURE (III), POLYMORPH OTHER, DIVINE BOW, REMOVE CURSE
[5] CURE (IV), DRAGONBREATH, IMPROVED LIGHTNING BOLT, REVIVE, SUNSTRIKE
[6] CHAIN LIGHTNING, GLOBE OF INVULNERABILITY, HEAL, AARON'S INERRANT DIPLOMACY
[7] AARON'S AWESOME BATHHOUSE, RAINBOW BLAST, RESURRECTION,
[8] MASS UNDEAD SLAYING, PLANESHIFT, AARON'S INEXHAUSTIBLE PATIENCE
[9] WISH, AARON'S STUPID SACRIFICE
SPIRIT SUMMONS: STOMPY, ~~THISTLE~~, RUSALKA, ZORYA DAWNBRINGER, ZORYA NIGHTBRINGER, SPARKY, LEGALLY DISTINCT COPY OF ASH FROM *EVIL DEAD*

STATUS EFFECTS:
* -20 penalty to WIS
* +10 Bonus to Attack Oathbreakers, Undead, and Creatures of Darkness
* Teleport to and from Divine Realm at will
* Cloak of the Skyfather allows Flight (250 kph) and Immunity to lightning, wind, and electricity-based effects.
* Automatic Success with Push against being equal or lesser

than Divine Rank
* Divine Abilities [Neutralized]

> Huh.
> Not bad.

CHAPTER THIRTY-ONE
DANGEROUS DEALS

"I think this is a terrible idea," I muttered, frowning at Ania.
Ania looked away.

"To have Aaron say that is enough for me to agree," Jon said, looking at the rest of the party gathered around us. We were now in one of the Scarlet Lady's upstairs hotel rooms and it was dirtier than some stables. If people paid by the hour to stay here, then they were paying too much. The place had red wallpaper, neon light pouring in from the rain-soaked windows, and carpet that probably would look like an impressionist painting under a blacklight.

"Do you agree with doing it because you think Aaron is always wrong or do you agree it's a terrible idea because Aaron is against it?" Rachel asked, sitting on the edge of the bed with grey sheets that had probably once been white.

"Yes," Jon said.

"I'll do anything to get my wife back," Bloodstorm said, looking at me. "I also think we should kill the thing pretending to be my daughter."

"I'm not pretending," Nyx said.

Bloodstorm didn't even look at her. "I also approve of killing Joan."

"What did I do?" Joan asked, offended.

Bloodstorm continued not looking at her. "Your god betrayed us, and I've got him on my list as well."

"I have a new god now!" Joan said, pointing at me.

"I'm notably not a god right now," I said, still uncomfortable with the entire concept.

"Because of her!" Bloodstorm said, pointing between both of us while refusing to meet their gazes. It was kind of fascinating to watch really. "I'm an atheist now."

That was impressive since he was half-god.

"Atheism is like not believing in kings," Ania said. "You can do it philosophically, but it doesn't really mean anything to the people with armies."

"Philosophy classes in Ledziana must be fascinating," I said, thinking of whether a person was an atheist if they knew gods were real. "Anyway, we have to deal with Mythras regardless of whether we believe in him or not."

"We keep adding gods to our hit list," Jon said. "We should recruit Kratos."

"Kratos isn't real," I said, pausing.

"Yeah," Jon said, pausing. "Mind you, he also lost his cool factor when he stopped wrecking worlds and settled down to raise his kid. It's like Ozzy. He was once a rock god but then we saw his reality TV show, and you can't even see the guy who used to bite the heads off bats."

Ania blinked. "Why would you bite the head off a bat?"

"I used to bite the heads off bats," Bloodstorm said. "I mean, you don't want to eat that part of them."

"You are the only person in the world who prefers classic Kratos over the new one," I said, referencing God of War's reboot.

Nyx cleared her throat. "Never in my wildest dreams did I believe I would say this but could you guys be less geeky?"

Sparky punched his fist. "I don't see why Mythras being our enemy is such a big deal."

"You don't?" Joan asked.

"I mean we've already beaten four gods," Sparky said. "It's not hubris to say you can challenge the gods if you have a divine body count."

I grimaced. "We won a lot of those contests by the skin of our teeth."

"Do you know what you call a close victory over the gods, Aaron?" Ania asked.

"What's that?" I asked.

"Victory," Ania said. "That's why we need to do this."

"Aaron's divinity will recover," Rachel said. "He will return to full power as an intermediate level god and that will render the vast majority of our disadvantage against Veles moot. Both Nyx and I are restricted to being lesser gods due to Veles weakening us during our corruption."

"Do we have time for me to recover?" I asked. "Because I'm pretty sure Veles gave us a firm deadline."

"And he's been so truthful to this point," Ania said. "We're, what do you call it, sitting ducks here in the hotel? If Veles was able to reach into your dreams, then I'm certain he either knows where we are or will soon."

I didn't like to think about it and wondered if I was responsible. "I'm not so sure about that since if Veles did know where we were, I would fully expect him to drop a bomb on us. After all, he intends to kill everyone anyway, so it's not like he must worry about poll numbers."

"Man, I would have loved to have seen his campaign," Jon said, shaking his head. "I didn't vote for the other guy, but I have to wonder how you get a literal god of darkness elected. I don't doubt he was but I'm wondering what his campaign promises were."

"Why settle for the lesser evil?" I asked, remembering the old Cthulhu for President meme.

Rachel took a deep breath. "We need the Witch Queen's help."

"I disagree," Jon said. "Having thought long and hard about it, given her team was utterly fucked up and killed, we can do better without her."

"If we can use her to kill Mythras then I'm all for it," Bloodstorm said. "Besides, Aaron is all about allying with evil."

"I am not!" I said. "It happened like, three times."

Everyone in the room stared at me.

"Do I count as evil?" Sparky asked. "I was a bit immature when I was randomly flambéing peasants and knights. I've learned that's wrong. Mostly."

"Good for you," I muttered.

"I'm a knight!" Sparky said, proudly. "Also, why am I constantly being left out of these conversations? It's because Jon is also a dragon and you think you don't need me anymore, isn't it?"

I pinched the bridge of my nose, feeling a migraine coming on. "It's like what everyone else feels when talking to me, isn't it? Listen, the bigger issue of recruiting the Witch Queen isn't that she's ineffective—"

"Really? Because that seems like a pretty big deal," Jon said. "I resent not winning. I have an incredibly high success rate. Also, did you know she brainwashed me?"

"Yes," I said.

"Well, I didn't!" Jon said. "That makes me disinclined to help her!"

"I mean she did get my father killed so I'm all for killing her afterward," Bloodstorm said. "Accent on afterward."

Bloodstorm wasn't handling the revelation of his wife's replacement well. Actually, given the circumstances, he was probably handling it as best as could be expected under the circumstances. Unfortunately, I had no doubt the berserker was going to let loose all his pent-up rage on the first target that he encountered. Indeed, it was a miracle he hadn't gone after Nyx or Joan yet, but I suspected he knew we needed them.

"In any case, we're all agreed that we shouldn't summon Susanos," I said, taking a deep breath.

"No, you're the only person who doesn't think it's a good-bad idea," Ania said. "Well, you and Jon."

"As the leader of this group, what I say should go," Jon replied.

"A good-bad idea?" I asked, ignoring Jon's comment.

"Yes, as opposed to a good-good idea," Ania said. "Which none of us have."

"How would we even go about that?" I asked. "We know where her soul jar is, in Jon."

"Err, about that," Nyx said, pulling out a small platinum amulet. "I made an acquisition of this while you were off consummating your marriage."

"I didn't feel a thing," Jon said. "Which is good because I was expecting a cavity search."

"Never speak again," I said, wishing he wouldn't.

The amulet was a particularly beautiful work of art if you liked Goth jewelry. It had a tiny skull imprinted on it, black roses engraved around it, and two rubies located within the skull's eyes. It was hard to sense the magic within next to Nyx, who positively radiated it, but I sensed a familiar dark force radiating from it.

Susanos.

Great.

I stared at her. "How *did* you find her soul jar?"

"Goddess of secrets," Nyx muttered. "It comes with the territory. It's also why it's impossible to beat Rachel at war games."

"I mean, the honest ones," Rachel said. "A lot of them are just pay to win and designed to make it—"

I raised my hand. "So, if we wanted to, we could destroy her soul jar now and get rid of the Witch Queen forever."

Nyx looked horrified. "That would deprive us of a powerful resource."

"It would also mean that we don't have to deal with Saruman after we deal with Sauron," I replied. "Except Sauron is Morgoth in this case and I'm losing my train of thought."

"Yes, they might take over your hometown and run it like a gang," Ania said. "I thought that was a very strange ending to the books."

"You read *The Lord of the Rings*?" I asked, pathologically incapable of staying on topic. It's how my brain was wired, sorry. It might explain the same about Rachel. As my daughter, she seemed to have inherited a lot of my quirks.

"Interesting post-apocalypse story," Ania said. "The world has been destroyed in numerous wars with their god of evil and now the few survivors await genocide at the hands of the enslaved mutant elves."

I blinked. "I mean, yeah, technically that is the story."

"Their god of good is very weak," Ania said. "Or evil himself."

I grimaced. "I don't think that was Professor Tolkien's plan—"

Nyx lifted the amulet. "With Susanos' help, we can know the weaknesses of Veles and perhaps find out what his ultimate plan is."

"We know what his ultimate plan is," I muttered, annoyed. "He told me. He's going to blow up Mokosh and Earth to become God. I mean, capital G, God."

"What an odd name," Ania muttered.

"Triglav," Rachel said. "The overgod that was the first being in the universe and may predate it several times. Veles was one of the gods split from it to form the creator gods."

"So, I remember," I replied, shaking away Perun's powerful memories. They were just an interpretation of what had happened at the beginning of the universe, but they were still burned into my subconscious.

"I'm with the destroying the amulet thing," Jon said. "Cast it into the fires of Mount Doom, blast it with dragonfire, or whatever else it takes to get rid of it. I was on #TeamSusanos but that was when I was brainwashed. Now I'm totally on #TeamRachel. Which has nothing to do with her cleaning my brain out of all brainwashing and possibly adding her own."

Everyone but Jon looked at Rachel.

"I admit nothing," Rachel said. "Still, I think we're down a sorcerer with Agata's kidnapping. Also, Joan just lost her connection to Mythras and that means she's not going to be able to cast any spells."

"Then what good is she?" Bloodstorm asked.

"She offers moral support," I muttered. "Also, she's against Mythras as well now, Bloodstorm. Cut her some slack."

Bloodstorm grumbled and said something that was so filthy I wasn't sure it was being translated accurately.

"I will regain my power when Aaron's power returns," Joan replied. "I pledge myself to the God of Redemption, Ratkin, and Pushing."

"Is that what you're going with?" Ania asked, skeptically.

"I would have gone with Dumb Plans and Inane References," Bloodstorm said. "No offense."

"None taken. I really am not comfortable with this god thing," I muttered. "It's funny that the ratkin think I'm their messiah but that's really about as far as I'm willing take it."

"The ratkin are disdained by every race in the world and live in utter destitution but you have willingly taken it upon yourself to offer them homes as well as equality," Joan said. "They probably take it very seriously."

I felt a migraine going on. "Does it say something about me that I'm now willing to resurrect the Witch Queen just to end this conversation?"

"Yes, that you're willing to make the right decision," Nyx said. "Also, if worse comes to worse, we can slay the Witch Queen here and harness her energy to jumpstart your godhood's return."

"That plan I like!" Jon said, pointing at her.

"I don't," I said. "Optional boss fights aren't things you want to seek out when you don't have the benefit of resurrection."

I mean, we possibly did but I wasn't taking anything for granted on a world that Veles was so powerful on (especially if it was my own). Still, I was willing to give this a shot if for no other reason that I was running out of ideas just like we were running out of time. I wouldn't have been surprised if Veles told me a deadline that was a few hours ahead of his actual plan's completion, but it was the only information I had so far. Still, hadn't we learned enough from trusting evil? Thistle was *right there.*

"So, what do I need to do to bring her back?" I asked.

"You need to put a sample of your blood on the amulet," Nyx said.

"And I'm already regretting this," I muttered.

"Death lords are not the same sort of creatures that liches are in your board game," Nyx said, referring to *Dungeons and Dragons* that way despite that she damn well knew its actual name. "They cannot come back on their own from death or at least self-regeneration requires centuries. Instead, they need Veles to use a minute portion of his power to accelerate the process."

"A drop of his blood," I said, shaking my head. "Of course. How him."

Nyx nodded. "You may be at a reduced level of power, but your blood is still that of an intermediate god."

"I love how we're measuring godhood," Jon said. "So much dirty joke potential."

"Put it away," Rachel said, jokingly. "Aaron's is bigger."

"Please don't talk that way about your father," I said.

Rachel sighed. "Spoilsport. The incest jokes wouldn't have been funny if you hadn't been going along with them for an entire year."

"I wasn't—"

"Please, Aaron," Bloodstorm said, desperate. "I'll do anything to get Agata back. I was a fool to trust the gods of good. I'll never be anything but a monster to them."

I didn't want to point out I qualified but since technicalities had slowed down our responses by, well, about 900% and that was being conservative.

"Give me the amulet," I said, reaching out.

"You're going to smash it with your divine god hands, aren't you?" Jon said. "Cool twist."

"No," I said, cutting my thumb with a dagger Ania handed me and placing the bloody digit's end on the amulet. "Though that would have been cool."

The amulet started to glow before there was a cackling more akin to an evil witch than lich Monica Belluci. The air turned frigid and I felt an immense power enter the room, easily dwarfing all of us.

"This is gonna suck," I muttered.

CHAPTER THIRTY-TWO
THE BLOODY HAND OF VENGEANCE

The smell was the first thing I noticed and that may seem strange since I had a cackling witch demon here that we were either summoning to destroy or ally with. So, okay, maybe it was the second thing I noticed but I still noticed it. It wasn't the rotting horrible smell of the deathrot wights I remembered from Castle Bloodmoon.

No, it was like incense.

It assaulted the nerves but reminded me that, at least according to the books, the original rites of Veles had corpses stuffed like turkeys. They were hollowed out and filled with incense, herbs, and mistletoe of all things as part of the sacred rights. Sort of a more Eastern European version of mummification. It made you think since Jon had supposedly been with Susanos in the Biblical sense.

Either way, there was a swirl of black smoke that appeared in the air above our heads and descended to the ground before it became a gruesome corpse dressed in the same attire as the Witch Queen before her death.

"In the name of all that is holy by our lord and savior, Bruce Campbell," Jon said.

"Jon please—"

"I quote the holy text of *Army of Darkness*, verse 1:31" Jon said. "And the Lord Chin spoketh, *Honey, you got real ugly*."

Ania took a deep breath. "I forgot Jon might get us all killed here."

"How could you possibly forget?" Rachel asked.

Thankfully, the Witch Queen did not seem to notice Jon's critical commentary on her looks because she was letting forth a primal scream of rage. She tore at her stringy hair, her greenish flesh, and rotted white eyes. Finally, she threw herself on her knees and spit up a disgusting red ooze on the ground.

"Veles!" Susanos said, growling.

"Well, that was dramatic," Rachel said. "Welcome back to the land of the living, Susanos!"

"Yes, what she said but without the welcome," Ania said. "I am already regretting this decision. This is your fault, Aaron, for not convincing me."

I glared at her.

"Shortest honeymoon ever," Jon muttered.

"Oh, please, fighting is their foreplay," Rachel said, clapping her hands together. "So romantic."

I was focused on the monster before us, though. Susanos wasn't attacking us, yet, which was a good sign. However, I wasn't in a very diplomatic mood. Indeed, I could feel my senses projecting a big black skull over her head as if to tell me we were way too under-leveled to take her.

Bloodstorm threw himself to the ground and held his war hammer in front of him. "Witch Queen Susanos, I am Bloodstorm, son of Baba Yaga and Maelor the Black. I pledge my soul to you if you can help me—"

"I do not care, Kragen Bloodstorm," Susanos said, pausing. "Nor do I want anything from you, least of all your soul."

Slowly but surely, Susanos' appearance transformed back into her previous beauty but she was marred by scars. Her eyes also turned completely red with her irises black as coal. The smell of incense hung in the air, though.

I tried to remain calm, wondering why I was afraid as I remembered just how bad things had gone before. "Your plan failed, Queenie."

Okay, maybe that was a little too much in the other direction.

"Yeah, that wasn't just a disaster but a fucking disaster," Jon said. "Seriously, the only reason that Veles took any damage was due to Aaron nuking the place. Mr. Neutral Good ended up salvaging the mission from complete failure to just total failure. The Token Good Teammate who everyone thinks—"

"Silence," Susanos said, her voice echoing around us.

Jon immediately shut up.

Susanos stared at me. "It was a trap."

"No kidding," I said.

"No," Susanos said, very carefully. "You do not understand. I have been a warrior for the cause of Veles for a thousand years. I have ruled nations, directed armies, and explored the heights of other planes. Instead, I was reduced to a quivering shell of a scorned woman that did not have the dignity to confront my betrayer the way I wanted."

I blinked. "You're saying you weren't in your right mind?"

"So many possible responses," Jon muttered. "All of them would get me killed by the women around me."

"Then don't say them," I said. "What happened?"

Susanos stared at her hands. "Veles exploited our bond. Twisted my emotions and insights through our link through the soul gem. He wanted me to be stripped of my higher reasoning and to bring you like lambs to the slaughter."

"Well, it worked," Jon said, frowning. "Garland is dead, again! I barely got to talk to the guy. Couldn't even get the guy's autograph."

I ignored Jon. "What would you have done if you were in your right mind?"

She wasn't attacking us and that was a good thing. However, if Veles really could influence her mind that way then she wasn't going to be the silver bullet we were looking for. Which might be useful now that werewolves were probably a thing on Earth these days (I didn't know for sure but wouldn't be surprised).

Susanos clenched her fists. "Obviously, I would have sided with Veles. You have no chance of victory."

"Well, I guess I owe you a cola," Ania said, looking at me. "Susanos will not be the ally we want her to be."

"You are incorrect, Lady Rose," Susanos said, frowning. "My loyalty to my consort was dictated by the assumption that he wasn't actually affected by the Twisted Gods' magic. Instead, his betrayal here proves that he has lost his mind."

"That and wanting to destroy the universe," I said. "I find that to be worthy of betrayal as well."

Susanos shrugged as if it was irrelevant. "If you know an afterlife is in existence and is under your power then keeping anyone alive is only a matter of whether you want to make more souls. Veles could have been ruler of two worlds and their afterlives. No other god could have stopped him."

Yeah, it seemed Susanos hadn't changed that much. "So, are we going to have to fight now?"

"I cannot," Susanos said.

"That's nice of you!" Sparky said, piping up.

"You can't or you won't?" I asked, knowing that it was a good idea to clarify which.

"Cannot," Nyx spoke for Susanos, surprising me. "Using your blood means that she is no longer linked to Veles. That means he can no longer influence her behavior with his power. She also cannot attack you, Aaron, or work against your interests."

"You might have opened with that," I said, dryly.

"Mind you, if we attack her then she is free to defend herself," Nyx said. "Also, if we ordered her to."

"Why would we do that?" Jon asked. "I mean, if I told her—"

"Don't," Ania interrupted, preventing a possibly disastrous, if humorous, misunderstanding from happening.

Jon looked like he was upset such a disaster had been prevented and crossed his arms petulantly.

"I may not be able to kill you, but I can kill the others," Susanos said, hardening her voice. Which was impressive since it had started at tempered steel. "I can also ignore any command you give. You are not Veles."

"No, I am not," I said, pointing at her. "Who betrayed you whether you were acting like a crazy jealous ex—"

"Of which Aaron has several!" Jon said. "Including one who is now his niece, which is not nearly as horrifying as it sounds."

Susanos stared.

Nyx sighed. "He means me."

"I should hope so!" Susanos said.

Bloodstorm gritted his teeth. "She is not your niece because she is not my daughter. My daughter died and this is the Old God possessing her."

I wasn't really 100% sure that I disagreed with Bloodstorm's estimation of the situation. After all, a newborn (let alone a fetus) was a blank slate that wasn't going to be able to contribute much when a god's lifetime worth of knowledge was downloaded into their brain. However, my horror at the possibility was diluted by the facts that A) I couldn't do anything about it and B) Rachel was nothing like the Zorya Dawnbringer I'd met. Something had changed within her, and I mentally likened it to the Doctor regenerating because my entire life was enjoying science fiction-fantasy until the point I started living it.

"Veles has shown you no loyalty," I said, looking at Susanos. "But now that your mind is clear, you can teach him what a terrible idea that is. This time as the brilliant general you are rather than his embittered ex."

I didn't know how having my charisma and intelligence raised to 30 was going to change my ability to come up with horseshit. Would it make my words more persuasive, or would I think of the kind of things that would be persuasive in the first place? I got my answer a few seconds later when she laughed.

"Is this how desperate you have become, Champion of the Wise Man?" Susanos said. "You actually think you can turn me? Me?"

Oh dear, she thought her loyalty to Veles meant something. I would have to divest her of that. Could I, though? That was the question. Veles was a literal god and that meant, by definition, his followers were part of a literal cult. They usually clung to every single possible excuse for the leader's behavior right up until they couldn't anymore.

"Yes," I replied. "Because, you already recruited us on the basis of taking out Veles and he made it so you would die in the process in a way that humiliated you. Because if what you're saying is true about how he influenced you then he looks at you not as a trusted lieutenant but a degraded concubine."

"Ooo, burn," Rachel said.

I glared at her.

You could have heard a pin drop in the room as Susanos' eyes turned into blazing green balefires, and I saw flames appear around her hands. "HOW DARE YOU."

"I dare a lot," I said, not modulating my voice in the slightest. "Because someone has to. Veles has been allowed to run roughshod over two worlds because everyone but a handful of people are too afraid to stand up to him. Here's the thing, though, those people who have stood up to him are still around. Ania, Bloodstorm, Rachel, Nyx, me, Joan, and Sparky here are all alive. He's here on Earth and not Mokosh, not because he wanted to but because he must be. We drove him off."

"That is a very charitable interpretation of events," Susanos said, clearly skeptical. "I also remind you that it didn't take much to make you fall into a trap. So little that I'd say you walked headfirst into it."

"And I'm still alive," I replied. "Veles also took a nuclear explosion to the face."

"Technically, hyper-magical," Rachel replied. "You've been misusing nuke for awhile now and it's starting to annoy me."

"Shut up, Rachel," I said. "Not the time."

Rachel frowned. "Well excuse me all to hell on proper terminology."

"So, your argument is that I should join your suicidal quest to oppose a creator god because of petty revenge and he has not been successful in stamping you out," Susanos said, her eyes and fists returning to normal.

"No, my argument is you should oppose a creator god because of extremely justified revenge," I replied. "Also, he's already shown that you're not going to be part of his New Universal Order."

"That's a George H.W. Bush quote," Jon said, pausing. "I think. He was the boring king who was replaced by his idiot son. But the idiot son wasn't the biggest idiot—"

I interrupted for the sake of our sanity. "That's assuming there's even going to be a New Universal Order after Veles is done."

"What do you mean?" Susanos asked, sounding intrigued.

It was strange how it was all so clear now, but I supposed that was the benefit of literally being smarter than any other human being on Two Planets. "The Old Gods that Veles created by corrupting his children with the Twisted Gods were all psychotic violent monsters."

"Gee, thanks," Rachel muttered.

"I mean, it was accurate," Nyx said.

"That's because the Twisted Gods are a living wound in reality," Susanos said, defining them as if I hadn't already been dealing with them for a year. "Their very existence is agony because they despise reality as it exists. They have no ambitions other than to tear down what is in existence and return to nothingness."

"Exactly," I said, surprising her. "Veles has resisted the transformation better than just about everyone else but it's clearly gotten into his head. It got him to kill his brother, to try to kill everyone in the world, and now planning to blow up the universe. How long do you think it'll be until he starts unmaking souls and destroying the afterlife as well as the physical world? The Twisted Gods won't be satisfied until there's nothing but oblivion."

I had no idea if that was the case as I hadn't talked to any Twisted Gods. Indeed, I wasn't sure they existed as a separate group of individuals or were more like a disease that just so happened to affect divinities. I was reluctant to believe anyone was pure evil but it was hard not to apply that moniker to someone or something that wanted to destroy everything to the last atom. Maybe they didn't have that as a motivation? Well, at least two of my companions were ex-corrupted so they would know at least.

"You make a compelling point," Susanos said. "However, that just encourages me to believe that curing Veles is the best course of action."

"I'm fine with that," I said, a little too quickly.

"Godsdammit, Aaron!" Ania said.

Everyone was looking at me like I'd said something amazingly stupid. Which, fair enough, maybe I had.

Being neutral good sucked some days.

"But we need to kill another god first," I said, simply.

Susanos stared. "Who?"

"Mythras," I said, simply. "He has Agata, and we need to get her back by any means necessary."

Joan looked away. "He has to be stopped. No matter what the cost. He's not the god I thought I was."

"Boo, frigging hoo," Bloodstorm grumbled, having clearly turned against most of the party. I didn't blame him. I would have gone absolutely ape shit if something happened to Ania.

I still might.

Susanos didn't respond for a long moment. "You want me to kill Mythras? Why didn't you say so? Consider us in an alliance."

Why didn't this feel like a triumph?

CHAPTER THIRTY-THREE
GOING TO KILL ANOTHER GOD

"So, where the hell did you get a jet?" I asked, looking over at Nyx as I sat in the co-pilot's seat.

We were traveling in what effectively felt like a vehicle designed more for comic book superheroes than anything built by military contractors. It had required us sneaking away from the hotel and heading to an airport, which had gone remarkably smoothly. In a warehouse there had been what looked like the Quinjet.

There was ample room in the back for everyone else to sit down as well as a small cargo area in the back where we'd loaded up our weapons plus a decent set of magical supplies ranging from potions to crafting materials. It was a combination of RPG consumables, Special Ops gear, and the proverbial kitchen sink approach to adventuring.

"I'm the goddess of magic, I conjured it," Nyx said, shrugging as she piloted the plane. She was wearing a black leather jumpsuit, the uniform everyone had changed into that, supposedly, would keep us from being sensed by Veles or Mythras. At least according to Susanos, who'd enchanted them.

"You really liked those Nineties X-men movies, didn't you?" Jon said, looking down at his jumpsuit. "Personally, I prefer yellow spandex."

"Yeah, like you're Wolverine," I muttered.

"Then who is?" Jon asked.

"Ania obviously," I replied.

Ania grunted.

"Ooo, you're right," Rachel said, looking at her.

I had to wonder where Rachel had seen so much pop culture and wondered if it was a result of my DNA somehow transmitting it to her brain like a racial memory. Then I realized that was idiotic and I should stop questioning how gods knew things even though I was one now.

"Could we keep focused on rescuing my wife?" Bloodstorm asked, sitting in the back sullen and clenching his fists. "I'm struggling enough as is."

"We'll find her," I said, giving false reassurance. Truth be told, I had no idea what condition we'd find Agata in. Mythras had who knows how long of a time to warp her mind or do gods knows what to her to make his assassin.

A dark part of my mind, one that I didn't want to contemplate, also wondered if Agata might have been a willing participant in this. That was unlikely. Agata was a flawed but good person in the books, but I also knew that desperation could drive people to awful things. Particularly during war. With two worlds at stake, could anyone blame Agata if she believed that I wasn't the guy who could save everything?

I dismissed that thought, though. Not just because I believed Agata would never betray her family or our party that way, but also because she didn't worship the god Mythras. He had covertly supported the Empire trying to replace the Old Gods of Ledziana and the atrocities they'd committed were beyond count. In simple terms, I had too much respect for Agata to think that she would work with someone like Mythras.

Except, her goddess works with Mythras, Susanos' voice spoke in my mind. *So were you until he betrayed you.*

Great, telepathy, I replied. *That's not invasive.*

I am attempting to gauge the minds of everyone in this group now that you have removed Veles' influence from my mind, Susanos said. *Things are much clearer now. I also respect you all much more than I did before.*

And what did you think before? I asked, mentally.

I thought you were disposable cannon fodder for my vengeance, Susanos said. *I'm curious. Do you really think Veles is self-sabotaging? Such an intriguing insight. I wonder if it's not motivated by your attempt to believe even your archenemy has redeeming qualities.*

I worked in Corporate America, I replied. *I don't believe everyone has redeeming qualities.*

Or so you claim, Susanos said. *I note that I think others are more inclined to see themselves in you than pay attention to your reality.*

This is a head game, isn't it? I asked.

In the context that I am going to subtly try to manipulate you by approaching you secretly, yes, Susanos admitted. surprising me. *But allow me to flatter you in a way I think you will appreciate. You are not actually that idealistic.*

This shouldn't have worked in getting my attention, but it did. *Oh?*

Yes, I believe what no one acknowledges is not that you were motivated by a desire to do good and redeem souls but that you have been extremely pragmatic, Susanos said. *That you are motivated by mathematics.*

Mathematics, I thought back, knowing she had me and hated it.

People concentrated on my low WIS score and maybe that was related to my idealism, but they also neglected the fact that I kept putting my points into INT to max it out. Why? Because I wanted to be acknowledged as absurdly smart. CHR might have been more useful or maybe even STR. However, I'd fallen prey to the nerd fantasy that was up there with the hot Goth girl and being paid to make video games: being acknowledged as the smartest guy in the room. Something that was already not true because Susanos had a few thousand years on me as an all-powerful wizard queen.

Yes, mathematics, Susanos said. *You checked the numbers of Veles war against Mokosh and proceeded to determine victory was impossible. So, you set about waging a game of diplomacy rather than outright conflict. This provided you with the allies you required to be able to achieve results the other champions didn't.*

It didn't always work, I replied.

No, nor is it necessary working with me, Susanos said. *Going against Mythras benefits us both. Mythras plans on fighting Veles and his defeat are something I can argue is serving the Dark Lord's purpose. Especially if it becomes necessary to serve you up to him after we defeat the Sun King.*

You aren't really persuading me that working with you was a good idea, I replied.

Aren't I? Mathematics should then, Susanos said. *Ours is an alliance of convenience. You are not trying to redeem me. You are trying to use me. Our association is proof that you are more pragmatic than they perceive you to be.*

Flattery will only get you so far, I thought.

Perhaps, Susanos said in a way I didn't entirely like. *But your argument isn't without merit either.*

Which one? I asked. *I argue a lot.*

I had a pretty good idea, though.

You have presented an argument that Veles is not in his right mind and will destroy himself as well as his followers, Susanos replied. *Worse, that he is himself aware of this and undermining his own efforts.*

How is that worse? I asked, trying to figure out what could motivate that kind of blind devotion.

You are American, Susanos said in a way that was insulting but also so nonchalant that it was somehow polite. *You are used to the delusion that most human beings crave self-determination and would choose that option if given a viable alternative. In truth, most human beings crave fulfillment through service. To be elevated by their devotion to a specific concept, god, or country. I wish to be ruler of the world and a goddess worshipped by billions, but as a reward for my loyalty.*

I'd have thought you'd want to be the Sith Master and not the apprentice, I muttered.

Veles would have to have been a very foolish dark lord to fill his inner circle with followers who wanted to overthrow him, Susanos replied. *Emperor Palpatine seems to have been quite a foolish sorcerer to deliberately goad individuals into striking him down.*

He was trying to corrupt Luke to the Dark Side, I thought, noting that bit from *Return of the Jedi* had never made much sense to me either.

What is the dark lord who gains a soul but loses the world? Susanos said, mocking that passage of the Bible. She was clearly familiar with Earth and its culture.

So, your plan is to kill Mythras with us and then betray us to Veles unless you can figure out a way to heal Veles' mind. Which won't make him good, but you hope will just content him with universal domination versus killing everything? However, if you can't heal his mind, you'll still betray us to him because you'd prefer to risk him destroying everything than actually opposing him.

Yes, Susanos said. *Which is another sign that you are pragmatic versus idealistic. An ally today who might be an enemy tomorrow.*

Or you're just screwing with me by suggesting that since you claim to be untrustworthy, you're trustworthy, I replied. *I saw the first season of* Game of Thrones. *It may be derivative of the Dark Undermaster books, but I got the lesson: when someone tells you they are, believe them.*

"We're almost to the Mythraeum," Nyx said. "Technically, I suppose it's the Mithraeum here on Earth."

"You're pronouncing it exactly the same," Jon said.

"No, I first used a Y instead of an I," Nyx said. "Completely different."

"Uh huh," I said. "We're not going to be shot down approaching London, are we?"

"The United Kingdom has been taken over by a fascist paramilitary government," Rachel said. "Veles' influence is strong everywhere, not just the United States. The worst of humanity has come to power in much of the globe. The rich get richer, the poor get poorer, and freedom is a lie meant to preserve the masses' compliance."

"How could you tell any difference?" Jon asked.

"There's magic now!" Rachel said, cheerfully.

Ania looked at Bloodstorm sympathetically, which was not an expression I was accustomed to from her. "My sister is down there. Your wife. The mother of your—"

"Don't call her that," Bloodstorm said, simply. "No matter what happens, Nyx will never be our child."

Ouch.

Ania didn't say anything else.

I didn't have words of comfort for my friend. Still, I tried. "Have hope, friend."

"Vengeance is all that I have left," Bloodstorm said. "I can't bring myself to hope through all of this."

Joan looked up. "You need to be prepared, Aaron. Mythras keeps his own extra-dimensional space in the temple here."

"Yeah, I wasn't thinking he was going to be based in a London Museum," I said, unsure just how prepared we were for this latest place. Would we be fighting angels like we were in a dungeon or would it have a bunch of guys with machine guns? Or both? How powerful would Mythras be in a place dedicated to him? The other Old Gods had been empowered by the Earthmother's temples, and we'd barely won against any of them.

That was when there were several alarms and noises that spread across the dashboard. It was the kind of thing that you'd only see in a movie but that was part of the nature of gods. They didn't do anything by halves and if they were going to make a super-jet, they were damn well going to make one with all the bells and whistles.

"That's not good, I take it?" I asked.

"No," Nyx said. "This plane is rigged against all mundane defenses."

"And this isn't mundane?" I asked.

"No," Nyx said. "Not in the slightest. Are you okay with bailing?"

"No, not in the slightest," I replied.

"Too bad," Nyx said, pushing a red button.

"Score!" Sparky said in the back.

"I am a dragon but object to—" Jon started to make a crack.

Instead, the roof of our jet flew open and there was a massive crack boom noise as the seats all flew into the air at once before breaking up into multiple parachutes. The plane continued onward over the London Eye (visible from our position) and red streaks sailing past us after it. The plane proceeded to explode and I grimaced, hoping that a bunch of innocent Londoners weren't about to be hit by shrapnel.

But I wasn't holding out a lot of hope.

"Okay, who the hell just blew us up?" I shouted, as we descended. It said something about how much I had been changed by my experiences in the Southern Kingdoms that I was more afraid of being shot in the air than I was of the actual fall. I'd fallen enough from great heights that it wasn't disturbing. At least until I noticed my parachute was on fire.

"Shit, shit, shit," I said, suddenly falling towards the city below. "Not good!"

The other members of the team were suffering their own troubles with flaming parachutes and descent toward the ground below. That made me wonder if I should cast FEATHER FALL before I realized that would just make me a target for whoever, or whatever, was assaulting us. Instead, I came up with my own solution.

"STOMPY, COME!" I shouted at the top of my lungs.

I half-expected the horse not to appear because everything that could have gone wrong these past few weeks had. Murphy's Law was in strict enforcement around me these days. Instead, my demonic steed appeared with a brilliant flash of light, spreading out a pair of fiery black leathery wings and spreading shadow behind him in fascinating contrast. I managed to grab a hold of Stompy's mane and stabilize my fall.

"So, you're a god now but you don't have any god powers right now?" Stompy asked, his voice something that I heard in my mind as much as my ears.

"Yeah!" I shouted.

"Also, is that Susanos?" Stompy asked.

"Yes," I admitted.

"This is a trap," Stompy said, bringing me down to the Mithraeum as I saw Jon and Sparky scooping up the rest of the group.

"No, no, she just wants me to kill Mythras!" I said, realizing how stupid that sounded. "Yeah, it's a trap,"

"I'm sure you have a reason that involves either a hot lady or trying to reach out to someone irredeemably evil," Stompy said. "It worked for me! The latter part."

"It's mathematics!" I shouted, paraphrasing Susanos.

"I have no idea what that means!"

Stompy dropped me in the middle of a garden at the foot of the skyscraper that had been constructed over the Mithraeum. The building read BULLSLAYER PMC in big neon letters, which was probably the worst name for a military contractor I could think of. The gardens were immaculately maintained with sidewalks between beds of flowers and hedge sculptures of soldiers.

I could sense the power humming beneath the garden, hidden away from the rest of the world, which was every bit as powerful as Veles in some ways. It was self-righteous, brilliant but colorless, and full of a perfect order that didn't allow the slightest deviation. I understood Mythras in that moment and that he probably had never left Earth unlike most other gods. He'd simply changed his name and embodied religion that did not have any humility.

Only control.

"You should not have come here, Aaron," a familiar voice spoke. "All you had to do was give up your divinity and Veles could have been destroyed. You don't even want to be a god."

A single figure was walking down the sidewalk I was standing on. A golden dome appeared above us, and the rest of my party were sliding down the sides. The figure was Agata but dressed in a glowing golden dress with a crown of sunlight that made her look like a woman wearing a spotlight. In her right hand, rather than a staff, she had a flaming sword made of light.

"Agata?" I asked.

"No," Agata said. "Not just Agata."

Mythras.

CHAPTER THIRTY-FOUR
FUNERAL FOR A FRIEND

"Mythras," I whispered, shaking my head. "Not Agata."

"We are both," Agata-Mythras said simultaneously.

I climbed on Stompy's back, staring at her. "I thought Mythras was a man."

Fun fact, I wasn't quoting *Ghostbusters*, I was just genuinely confused by this. Call me crazy that I was focusing on this rather than Agata currently being used as Mythras' meat puppet and they'd cut me off from the others but, well, I was curious.

"Oh, poor Aaron," Agata-Mythras said, smiling with the light all around her not reaching her eyes. "You do not understand so much and your little time left on this physical plane will prevent you from learning more. Gods are defined by their avatars as much as their raw pure essence. I have one on Mokosh, but I needed one here. If you ever had become a truly powerful force of nature, you would have your own incarnation and potentially many more. That is the origin of hundreds of gods as their incarnations take on lives of their own. Here on Earth, I was simply waiting for the right vessel to be sent by my kin on Mokosh."

I wasn't eager to start a fight with no backup but there was no way I was going to leave her either. It seemed we were no longer operating on *Dungeons and Dragons* logic for how we fought one another. No, the enemy was perfectly willing to cheat. Now it was time to return the favor.

"Are you here to lecture me or kill me?" I asked. "Because you've already tried the latter and failed."

Agata-Mythras laughed contemptuously. "Thistle exceeded her orders, Aaron. You were never supposed to be killed, only stripped of power that you were never meant to possess in the first place."

"You'll forgive me if I don't take your word for it," I said, staring at the woman that presently hosted a monster. "What with you lying and manipulating me this entire time."

"Oh, boo hoo," Agata-Mythras made a childish crying face with her fists up beside her eyes. "Do you wish to know what the secret of godhood is? Controlling the minds of lesser beings. You could never have been a god if you couldn't keep the loyalty of such a pathetic being as Thistle. Someone who served as the executioner of the Nightbringer before running to me when you refused to make her yours."

I narrowed my eyes, not interested in having a dialogue for perhaps the first time in this insane conflict. "I couldn't care less about who is god of who or what. I came here for Agata. Give her back."

"No," Agata-Mythras said. "Do you really think this is the right time to try to challenge the gods? You've already exhausted all your divine power. I could strike you down right now and this would be the end of it."

"I sincerely doubt that," I said, not really hoping to test it. "But you were the one to pick this fight, not me. What the hell did you think would happen if you stole my sister-in-law and used her like a suit?"

Agata-Mythras stared at me. "I thought you would put the lives of billions of sapients as well as the future of the cosmos over your own selfish personal ties. Sacrifices have to be made for the greater good."

"Funny, how it's always other people who have to make the sacrifices," I said, staring at him. "You've sat out this entire war and let Veles run roughshod over not one but two planets and are only coming in to 'fix' everything when it will leave you the top god in the aftermath. It's the biggest proof I have that all this 'gods are actually the stories of their followers' thing is bullshit because whatever the fuck this is, it's not heroic, God of Heroism."

I wondered if Mythras was infected with the Twisted Gods' influence. It seemed like an easy answer, though. Too easy. "The Devil made me do it" was the kind of dismissal of motivation and rationale that just didn't work when you were already fighting a guy who might as well be Satan.

That thought didn't last long as I saw that Agata-Mythras was shaking with rage. The light radiating off her turned an eerie shade of red even as I saw the flames around her sword turn orange. Apparently, my off-hand comment about Mythras had infuriated the deity beyond measure and they looked ready to fight.

Which, fine, I doubted we were going to be walking out here hand in hand.

"You have no idea what struggles have been made to keep the world alive," Agata-Mythras said, hissing. "When Perun was defeated, the world of Mokosh was on the brink of annihilation from the Twisted Gods as well as its shattered infrastructure. The Wise Man forced Veles into his games, but it fell to me to unite the—"

"No," I replied.

"Excuse me?" Agata-Mythras asked.

"We're not doing this," I said. "I don't care about your justifications for why you've sat out this war, ignored your church becoming an incredibly large bunch of assholes, and betrayed my group when the entire universe was at stake."

"I didn't betray your group," Agata-Mythras said. "I am the only—"

"Just give Agata back and we'll call it square," I said, betraying Susanos before she could betray me.

"Agata isn't here anymore," Agata-Mythras said, her (his?) eyes glowing a deep red. "Agata voluntarily surrendered herself to be my host when I said the alternative was leaving the fate of everyone in your bumbling hands. My gloriousness has burned away everything that was human within her."

I stared. "I don't believe you."

"Which part?" Stompy asked.

I did believe it, though, because I was terrified that we'd been running on good luck for most of this struggle. We'd managed to come to the edge of the finish line, even though no one expected us to even make it through the first lap.

I'd wanted to have faith we would all get through this alive, but I'd never truly believed it.

Truth be told, I'd expected failure at every step of the way and been constantly surprised by the level of success that we'd achieved. The idea that we'd come so far, though, only for Ania's sister and Bloodstorm's wife to be cast out by this hubristic *thing* was infuriating, though. Agata was worth more than a hundred of him.

A thousand.

A million.

"Your own pontiff rejected you," I said, hissing. "She saw what a petty, vile, weak little man you were in a crown of gold. I believe you when you say that Agata is gone. God help me—any god worth his salt other than you—but if I'm not going to see her again then I'm sure as shit not going to let you walk away from this alive."

"I could have let you and your merry band of idiots survive if you'd passed on your power," Mythras said. "My messengers are even now tearing them to shreds so they might serve an actual purpose in their lives. Now—"

"I WISH for you to suffer pain," I said, spitting it out as a curse.

A black shadow fueled by every bit of fury and hatred in my soul shot out from the tip of my sword, blasting against the brilliant light of the god before me. That I might have hurt Agata in the process didn't even register because I was so angry. Ironically, Mythras might have put themselves in more danger by giving me no reason to hold back.

"DIVINE RETRIBUTION!" Agata-Mythras shouted instead, their glow dissolved around them but their eyes were still two flaming balls of hate.

"GLOBE OF INVULNERABILITY!" I shouted, wondering if we were just going to stand here exchanging spells.

A blast of light struck me and my shield with enough force to send me flying off Stompy and smashing against the back of the globe, and

I didn't think I was going to be able to do that. I felt like I'd been hit with a truck and thrown through a plate glass window.

YOU HAVE RECEIVED 120 DAMAGE

"I am as far above you, Aaron, as you are above the rats who worship you. DIVINE BOLT!" Agata-Mythras shouted, conjuring a staff that they spun like a baton before shooting another blast at me that I felt was going to hit me with the heat of the sun.

I thought, AARON'S INEXHAUSTIBLE PATIENCE, without saying the words but that was apparently enough since the sun blast paused in mid-air and it was like I'd hit the pause button.

Taking advantage of the moment, I got the hell out of the way and time resumed a few seconds later. The DIVINE BOLT spell proceeded to strike against Mythras' dome and caused cracks to appear on its side.

"I know you're still in there, Agata!" I shouted, trying to figure out what I could possibly throw at Mythras that would hurt him. "IMPROVED LIGHTNING BOLT!"

Agata-Mythras swatted the bolt away like she was knocking away a fly. "You're talking to a dead woman, Aaron! You only beat the Dawnbringer because she let you kill her! I will torture your power from you! Break you and force you to comply!"

Stompy took advantage of that to charge and smacked Agata-Mythras in the face with his hooves, growing as an alicorn appeared on top of his head. A black bolt of lightning came down from the sky and struck the god, sending them to their knee.

"Stompy, no!" I shouted, pulling out the Sword of Perun and charging at the deity before they retaliated.

I was too late.

Agata-Mythras struck out with their free hand and tore into Stompy's chest as the demonsteed reared back, causing him to burn away from the inside. I reassured myself that it just meant Stompy was banished but I wasn't sure. After all, if anyone could kill a demon forever, it would be a god.

So, I stuck, struck, and struck again. I used every single lesson I'd learned from Zorya Dawnbringer to attack and dodge Agata-Mythras' blows while making ones of my own. It was the best I'd ever fought. All my speed, strength, and tactical insights had been supercharged.

Not a single bit of it mattered.

Agata-Mythras blocked every single one of my blows and delivered devastating counterattacks. Even when I managed to block all of them, they still inflicted intense pain that drained me of my ability to fight back.

YOU HAVE RECEIVED 30 DAMAGE
YOU HAVE RECEIVED 35 DAMAGE
YOU HAVE RECEIVED 35 DAMAGE
YOU HAVE RECEIVED 40 DAMAGE

I was reduced to 90 HIT POINTS, and I wasn't going to be able to take much more if I continued to get my ass kicked here. Unfortunately, I felt my guard shatter with the next blow of Agata-Mythras before they cast PUSH and sent me flying into the air against the dome again.

YOU HAVE RECEIVED 73 DAMAGE.

"HEAL," I said, putting my hand over my heart.

YOU HAVE HEALED 303 HIT POINTS.

I shakily stood up, lifting my sword and ready to fight some more.

"You are only delaying the inevitable, Aaron," Agata-Mythras said, moving toward me. "I would have thought killing you with your own signature spell would be an appropriate end. Instead, I'm just going to beat the life out of you."

"Bloodstorm is fighting desperately for you," I said, moving into a defensive position. "So is your child."

"THAT THING IS NOT MY CHILD!" Agata-Mythras screamed with a voice that was my first sign that she was still in there. "METEOR SWARM!"

"COUNTERSPELL!" I said, shouting up to the sky as the air above us swirled with giant balls of rock and fire, a tornado of magic. I had to pour every fiber of my being into it to try and disrupt the magic being cast around me. Mythras had been learning sorcery when the Empire of Xerxes was a new idea and all I had to go against him was what had been downloaded into my brain. His spell was super-charged with all of the power of a god behind it and would probably strike me with enough force to obliterate this avatar.

Much to my shock, the spell dissipated.

Agata-Mythras had let it fail.

"What the..." I trailed off, confused.

The dome around us shattered and the sky began raining dead messengers. The winged beings were featureless male figures like Academy Award statues, but all of them were covered in horrible injuries ranging from their guts hanging out to burns all over their fleshy frames. There were at least thirty or forty dead, and I had to wonder what the hell had happened.

"Mythras!" Bloodstorm said, landing in front of me. He was crackling with electricity like the Mighty Thor and holding up a maul that dripped in blood. "Give me back my wife!"

Ania landed behind Agata-Mythras, her curved swords in attack formation.

Above us, I could see blasts of flame from dragons as more messengers were being culled from Mythras' forces. Joan and Susanos were riding on the back of Sparky and Jon, blasting away with powerful magic. It seemed Joan had gotten her abilities back.

No sign of the twin goddesses.

Agata-Mythras looked puzzled, as if they hadn't anticipated this development. "You brought Susanos back from the dead."

"Yeah," I said.

"That is amazingly stupid," Agata-Mythras said. "Even for you."

"Give us back Agata," I said, feeling a lot more confident. "You can still walk away from this."

Whatever answer Agata-Mythras might give was drowned out by Bloodstorm's screaming as he charged with his maul. He was either ignoring that his foe was inside his wife or no longer caring because there was no way to save her from his perspective.

Before I could react, Bloodstorm struck her in the chest and face with his maul as he crackled with supernatural energy. The blows seemed to do far more damage than I was capable of and he managed to hit her a third time before Agata-Mythras grabbed him by the neck.

"No!" I said, trying to think of a spell in time, only for my mind to freeze at the worst possible moment.

There was a sickening crack and Bloodstorm fell limp before falling at the god's feet. The fire left Agata-Mythras' eyes and for a single moment she was herself again. A mixture of hope and horror passed across my face.

Right before she was impaled by a teary-eyed Ania from behind.

"I'm sorry," Ania whispered.

"GOD SLAIN."

CHAPTER THIRTY-FIVE
THIS TIME, EVERYONE LIVES (I HOPE)

ACHIEVEMENT UNLOCKED: With Friends Like These

(A) - 50 - Defeat Mythras, God of Light

YOU HAVE RECEIVED 2,000,000 EXP

YOU HAVE RECEIVED CONTROLLING INTEREST IN BULLSLAYER PMC

YOU HAVE RECEIVED $1,000,000,000

YOU HAVE RECEIVED DIVINE RAIMENT (AGATA ONLY)

YOU HAVE RECEIVED STAFF OF THE SUN GOD (AGATA ONLY)

YOU HAVE RECEIVED GREATER DIVINITY SHARD (AGATA ONLY)

YOU HAVE RECEIVED—

"Not fucking now!" I shouted, growling at the obnoxious banner that appeared in front of my vision.

Agata, despite the death of Mythras inside her, was still clinging to life when I reached her side. Ania was cradling her sister and trying to keep her from bleeding out, even though that was undoubtedly futile.

"I'm sorry," Ania said, looking down at her sister. "I should never have become involved in this quest. If I could have lived a peaceful life with you and father, I would have."

"Liar," Agata said. She looked up at her sister and placed her right hand against Ania's cheek, smearing blood on it. "You were always meant to be a warrior regardless—no, because—of your sex. I do not blame you for what... what you did."

"Why?" Ania asked.

I cursed myself for using my HEAL spell already and tried to figure out how to chain every healing spell I could together. Bloodstorm's corpse was nearby, and I wanted to go to his side as well, but Agata took precedence. Don't ask me why.

She just did.

I poured every single healing spell into her that I could and it was like each of them was absorbed. They were sucked into a terrifying void inside her that seemed to occupy the space where Mythras' soul had once existed.

"I chose this," Agata cursed herself, looking up at the sky. "I wanted to be... the hero. To be the one who changed the world. I thought I wanted... to... love the hero. To be with Garland. Then with Bloodstorm. Also, your husband."

"What?" Ania asked, her tone suddenly changing.

"But it was a cover," Agata said. "Mythras made me betray my goddess... again. The chance to be the goddess of light for this world. I'm..."

I put my hands on Agata and tried to reach down past the source of the magic that I'd had downloaded to my brain, trying to touch something raw and powerful beneath. If the magic I'd learned from the Mark of the Champion was a faucet, then surely there was a reservoir or source of magic that could be harnessed.

Godhood.

"RESURRECTION!" I shouted, tears in my eyes. "RESURRECTION!"

"You don't have to actually shout..." Ania trailed off.

"RESURRECTION!" I cried out to the heavens.

Ania looked at me. "Not even you are able to overcome the power of this story, Aaron. Tragedy follows the road of the so-called hero, and we can't save everyone. We can't even save—"

Agata came alive and proceeded to vomit on her sister.

Ania stared.

Agata coughed heavily.

Ania hugged her sister tightly. "I'd thank the gods but I'm only thanking one now."

"Ugh, take a bath, first!" Agata said, disgusted.

"It's your vomit!" Ania said, pulling away.

"That doesn't matter!" Agata said, casting a series of cantrips rapidly to clean herself off before turning to me. "Aaron, what have you done?"

I wasn't paying attention to her, though, and focused instead on Bloodstorm. Crawling over to him, I immediately tried to bring him back too. "Please work, please work, please work. RAISE DEAD!"

"Does he know he doesn't have to shout the spell's name?" Agata asked. "He's not doing the spell incantations or gestures anyway."

"Just let him have this," Ania said, looking down. "Also, can you do a cantrip for me too?"

Agata seemed to debate it before waving her hand and cleaning off her armor. "Fine. But only because you stabbed me."

"Sisters," I muttered, hoping that I could perform two miracles in one day. "RAISE DEAD, DAMMIT!"

Bloodstorm vomited in my face.

"Okay, is this just a thing that corpses do when they come back?" I asked, looking at Ania. "Because no one told me this."

"They also shit themselves," Ania said, not missing a beat. "It happens when you die. Seriously, it happens at every hanging."

"I absolutely deny that happened," Agata said, making several cleaning cantrips with her offhand as if she didn't want us to notice. "Also, magic."

"Ugh," Bloodstorm asked. "I absolutely shit myself."

I could smell it. "Yeah, yeah you did."

Bloodstorm looked at Agata then me. "Before I perform my next action, I need to know whether you brought Agata back or have decided we should be allied with the monster who killed her."

"The former," I replied, wiping the vomit off my face. "Definitely the former."

"Because you have a history," Bloodstorm said. "A rather unfortunate one."

"Do you want me to kill you again?" I asked. "I can if you like. RAISE DEAD only brings you back with one hit point. At least in this system, I read the spell description. It's like how AARON'S STUPID SACRIFICE kills me but unleashes everything in my soul. Why would you even make that spell?"

Bloodstorm ignored me and slowly climbed to his feet. "Agata, I need to hold you—"

"Let me do some more cleaning cantrips," Agata said, raising her hand.

Bloodstorm didn't wait and embraced her. Tears were in his eyes. "Thank you, Aaron. You truly are a god."

I wasn't so sure about that, especially as I could tell something was wrong. Jon, Susanos, Joan, and Sparky were still not down here. Neither were Rachel and Nyx. I would have known if they were dead, the Mark of the Champion would have told me. Or would it have? It didn't tell me when Bloodstorm and Agata died. My so-called divine guide was no longer perfect, possibly because the Wise Man was dead and Perun was rebirthing himself elsewhere.

"Aaron, you've screwed up," Agata said, pulling away from Bloodstorm or trying to. It was a bit like trying to pull away from a pair of steel beams wrapped around you.

"You'll have to be more specific," I said, wondering if I should go looking for our missing team members. "I screw up a lot."

To quote Star Wars (I know, what a shock), I had a bad feeling about this.

"Mythras isn't dead," Agata said. "I can still feel him inside me."

"I'm not happy about him putting himself inside you," Bloodstorm said, still holding her.

Agata glared.

"I mean we have ground rules about Aaron or Jon—" Bloodstorm started to say.

I had a headache. "Mythras is dead, Agata. The Mark of the Champion said so, or at least its interface did."

"He's not conscious," Agata said, looking like she was struggling to define what she was describing. "The spirit that animated him on this world is dead, or at least lacking a will behind it. He doesn't have enough worshipers on this world to pull himself from the throes of death. But all that energy he's spent centuries accumulating is still here."

Agata looked down at her dress, damaged because I'd hit her multiple times with magic, specifically at the area above her heart.

Bloodstorm and Ania looked confused.

I was more contemplative. "Isn't this... a good thing?"

Agata did a double take. "What?"

"How the fuck could this be a *good thing*?" Bloodstorm asked as if I'd said Veles eating Earth was an idea with potential. Actually, no, if it helped Mokosh's people, Bloodstorm would probably be down with that. He'd miss television, though.

I tried to figure out how to phrase my thought delicately. However, I had a 30 INT right now and was seeing the implications a lot clearer than anyone else was right now. "Well, you have Mythras' energy inside you, without Mythras to control it, but doesn't that make you a god?"

Everyone stared at me.

Then each other.

"Is that how it works?" Bloodstorm asked, looking at Agata.

"I don't know," Agata said. "I don't have any of his species' abilities, but I was ascended to celestial status when we were in Sky Realm. That's what allows me to hold the power within me... albeit, just barely. I can maybe channel it but it'd be raw and untamed. Maybe? I don't know."

"What do you think, Ania?" Bloodstorm asked.

"We need to kill Susanos, now," Ania said, surprising me.

"What?" I asked, doing a double take.

"Our alliance was only until she killed Mythras, which has happened," Ania said, pausing. "Sort of."

I blinked. "I agree."

"You do?" Ania asked, seemingly surprised.

I was surprised that I did. "Something is very wrong, and I don't want to take chances."

"She helped a lot outside the dome," Bloodstorm said. "London is going to have to explain why there are about a dozen dead dragons and hundreds of messengers falling on the city. That's not including all the exploded jets."

I grimaced. I was probably not going to be able to take a UK vacation after this. "I'm certain B. Her loyalty is to Veles even when he does treat her like shit."

"Well, that's not very nice," Susanos said, descending from the sky in dragon form. She'd assumed a Maleficent-esque purple dragon form that was also obviously undead. She had a burning skull with green flames, holes across her body leaking magical energy, and a hideous mummified texture to her scales. There was still a regal grace to the monster, particularly since purple wasn't usually a color to inspire fear in the hearts of men, but it was more *Magic: The Gathering* than heavy metal album cover. Mind you, if she could become a dragon, I don't know why she was riding one earlier but I suppose more dragons=better.

Unfortunately, it wasn't the monster itself that was terrifying. No, it was the fact she had another dragon in her claws that she was carrying like a falcon holding a starling. I couldn't tell if Jon was dead or alive because the once-magnificent dragon monk (don't ever tell him I called him that) was hanging limp from her grip.

"Yeah, who possibly could have seen this coming," Ania muttered sarcastically, looking up.

"I always thought Saruman would try to take down Sauron if he'd gotten the One Ring," I replied. "What can I say?"

That was when Susanos hurled Jon's body at us like a baseball, Agata conjuring a Globe of Invulnerability around us that knocked Jon's body away before it crushed us under its several tons of mass.

Susanos proceeded to resume her Witch Queen form in front of us, glowing with a miasma of evil magic that I was just about sick of seeing these days.

That was when I saw Agata at Jon's side, having perhaps foolishly dropped the globe to go to John's side and start using her own magic to heal him. Jon reverted to his human form and he'd looked like he'd had the shit beaten out of him. Perhaps literally as Bloodstorm and Ania had declared happened when you died.

"You see, this is why you don't recruit evil party members," Jon said, coughing before spitting some bloody phlegm on the ground. "Except hot ones."

"How are you still alive?" Ania asked, confused.

"Ring of regeneration," Jon muttered. "Did you know if you don't take it off, you can't die unless the damage is fire or acid? First edition rules!"

I'd have argued that interpretation of the rules, but I was clearly in the wrong. I was also glad that Jon's penchant for survival had worked in our favor for once.

"He was dead," Agata said. "Aaron is not the only one with spells to bring back the fallen."

"Alas, you have used them up," Susanos said. "I have already informed my master of your presence here."

"Yeah, saw this coming," I said, wondering if Veles would send his minions or launch nukes at the UK. "Thanks for the heads up. Where are the others?"

"Joan and Sparky fled," Susanos said. "As for your goddess child-brides, they have also taken the better part of valor."

That didn't sound like them, especially since I would have given those four even odds of fighting the Witch Queen. She was an endgame boss in the *Dark Undermaster* games but entirely optional in *Dark Undermaster 3*. Someone even did a YouTube video where she could be beaten by fifty hellhounds.

I grimaced. "They are not my... I don't care. Veles won't reward you for this. You know he's gone insane."

"Perhaps," Susanos said, looking oddly contemplative. "But healing him as an ally strikes me as significantly easier than trying to do so as his enemy. Once Veles is the supreme god of this universe, we can start rebuilding reality together."

"Forget it, Aaron," Jon said, crawling to his feet. "You can't reason with crazy. You also shouldn't put your dick in it."

"Or in corpses," Ania said.

"Both you and your husband have fucked Bloodstorm's vampire sister," Agata said, dryly.

Bloodstorm shrugged. "I give even odds they'll be doing it together after this. Aaron's monogamy won't last that long, I'm sure, if his wife is into it."

"Can I get in on that wager?" Ania asked.

Susanos glared, trembling with rage. Apparently, she wasn't used to the kind of banter you'd find in your typical Marvel movie. "I am looking forward to this."

"Nyx cursed your soul jar," I pointed out. "You can't harm me."

"I promised Lord Veles I would keep you alive, Aaron Bartkowski. However, I never said anything about your associates." Susanos began making elaborate gestures with her fingers before everything went white.

I was blinded and couldn't see what was happening.

Susanos screamed.

ELDER ENEMY SLAIN

I felt... different.
Stronger.
What was happening?

YOU HAVE REGAINED THIRTY DIVINITY POINTS

CHAPTER THIRTY-SIX
DIVINE VISIONS

Getting my batteries recharged as a god was not too dissimilar to my rapid ascension to being one in the first place. What did it feel like? Well, I suppose the closest approximation I could make was having a fire hose of cosmic energy blasting down my throat. It was like drowning in information about the secrets of the universe and while that might have some appeal as a computer programmer, it also sucked because drowning was bad.

Bad but enlightening.

Svarog stood at the edge of the universe, hammering away on the Anvil of Creation and creating cosmic star dust with the sparks. Svarog was exactly as I'd remembered from our conversation at the tent but several million miles tall, which worked because I was several million miles tall as well. Specifically, I was Perun and experiencing his memories again. Svarog was forging a planetary ring around a gas giant.

"Sup?" I asked, speaking in an ancient pre-human language that was being translated by my brain to modern English.

"I am attempting to deal with slag," Svarog said, looking unhappy.

"Slag?" I asked.

"It is the waste material leftover after forging," Svarog said.

I rolled my eyes. "No kidding. It's not like I picked that up in the BILLIONS of years we've been in existence."

"Then why ask?" Svarog said, frowning. "Truth be told, I'm not satisfied with some of my earlier efforts."

Time was such a strange thing. Sometimes I regretted creating it. It made everything seem so long.

"Earlier efforts?" I asked. "What do you mean? We've got way more galaxies than we could ever know what to do with. Frankly, I don't know why you kept churning them out—"

"I think the Slag is dangerous," Svarog said, making me realize he meant the term with a capital S. It was a name.

We'd already created most pantheon heads by that point—those who would become known as the Old Gods—and we were far from alone these days. But they had proven the rule that family needed to be kept to funerals, marriages, and holidays. We were planning on creating sentient life on a smaller scale—it would take a long time to fill up all those galaxies after all—but that wasn't what Svarog was referring to.

"You mean the creatures you created before the First Movement," I said, uncomfortable. "The Twisted Gods."

The First Movement was the beginning of the universe as other beings would have known it. Even before it had happened, the three of us had started to develop our own individual personalities. Svarog the Creator, me as the Preserver, and Veles as the Destroyer. Three faces of one being that would gradually drift further apart before we'd combined our powers one last time to make the universe. Before? Before Svarog had tried to create on his own. The results had been disastrous...

"Do not call them that," Svarog said. "I do not like being reminded of our failure. It was only by spreading out our power into the First Movement that we were able to make it work. A piece of the divine in every atom that adds together and grows. The Slag is irredeemably flawed."

I was uncomfortable with Svarog's attitude as I'd seen the flawed creations he'd banished beyond the reaches of space. Their lives were a miserable torment, and they regarded our reality with jealous eyes, unable to make a place in it due to lacking inner light. Destroying them would have been a mercy but Svarog had not instilled mortality into them. They were eternal like we were. Working together, we might have been able to instill mortality into them, but our brother Veles was fascinated with the failed entities.

"Why do you think they're dangerous?" I asked. "They're old things sleeping in the void beyond."

"They have shaped that void into nightmare," Svarog said. "They themselves cannot create, but they can corrupt and pervert. They crave the divine power inherent to this universe in everything just as much as they hate it. I believe they have been siphoning away portions of our creation and will attack soon."

That seemed ridiculous.

But I had never known my brother to exaggerate. "I will gather our forces. Let the War of the Heavens begin."

The memories that followed were of the conflict that inspired the overthrow of Cronos, the war between the Aesir and Vanir, the battle between Apep and Ra, plus gods knew (literally) how many other divine conflicts. The thing was that the conflicts never actually ended. The Twisted Gods corrupted other divinities to their ways and turned them against their fellows only to be beaten down then imprisoned in various underworlds. Then they'd break out and do it again. It was an eternal and terrifying conflict that repeated an unimaginable number of times.

That was when people started to look for a permanent solution.

One of them being the Mother Goddess of Earth.

Mat Zemalya

"I know you feel betrayed, Veles," Mat Zemalya said.

The Mother Goddess of Earth was kind of an interesting contrast to Mokosh. Mokosh was blonde, buxom, and exuberant. Mat Zemalya, by contrast, was pale, dark, and, okay, still buxom. It's a mother thing I'm sure. If Mokosh was Britney Spears, then Mat Zemalya was Angelina Jolie in a V-neck dress.

Maybe this was my mind filling in the blanks because I was interpreting beings that were so far beyond human comprehension that I might as well be watching the Muppets do a re-enactment of their actions. Okay, that was my mind going to a weird place even for me.

"That is a response to being betrayed, yes," Veles said, walking up to her. "I know our marriage hasn't been the best—"

"You're still upset about my birthing Thor."

"No I'm not," Veles said, looking to one side in a suspicious manner.

Mat Zemalya was referring to the somewhat obscure fact that Thor's mother was Jord or the Earthmother in mythology, at least if you were a Marvel comics fan, rather than Odin's wife.

"No," Veles said. "We've all had our children by other relationships."

"That has rarely stopped male gods in the past," Mat Zemalya said. "The Olympians drove half of their women to celibacy."

Veles gave a dismissive wave. "You will not distract me from confronting you about this insane plan."

"Is it insane?" she asked. "Because we have been fighting the Twisted Gods for millennia."

"Yes, because they need to be fought," Veles said. "I tried to make peace with them. To give them purpose. Instead, they became as the demons to a thousand mythologies. Horrors that humans instinctively revile."

"And why is that?" Mat Zemalya asked. "Because humans are made in our image."

Veles questioned that similarity as he had a somewhat lower regard for humans and other races like them. It was why he'd experimented with his monsters as much as he had. "It is because they are the enemies of reality. They exist in their prison, coveting the light of the divine and seeking to warp everything they touch."

"Now you sound like your brother," Mat Zemalya said.

"Hey!" I said, revealing that Perun was there as well. He was just unusually silent.

"Experimenting with their power is dangerous," Veles said, ignoring his brother's discomfort. It was strange to see them on friendly terms as even before Veles had been corrupted, the two spent a month every year fighting like Tom and Jerry.

"I am not experimenting," Mat Zemalya said. "I wish to redeem them."

Veles and I exchanged a glance.

"You've got to be fucking kidding me," I said.

"What he said but more polite," Veles said. "You can't redeem creatures that don't have free will. They are defined by their natures. Which is part of why they hate us and everything."

"But what if we changed their natures?" Mat Zemalya said. *"What if we gave them free will?"*

"I'm listening," Veles said. *"Can we really?"*

"Yes."

That seemed like a terrible idea.

And it was.

Mat Zemalya underestimated the amount of corrosive power that the Twisted Gods could bring to bear. She had ended up becoming the most powerful goddess corrupted by the Twisted Gods and it had resulted in a war that had devastated much of Earth's pantheons. That had led to the collapse of magic on Earth and draining of all its reserves.

It provided additional context to the corruption of Veles and how Earth had become one of the few planets in the universe that didn't have magic. Since I was inhabiting Perun's memories, I knew Mokosh and Earth weren't alone among intelligent species-filled worlds. Indeed, there were ten thousand alone in the Milky Way Galaxy. I would have been overwhelmed by that, but it was a small number if you measured things in absolute terms.

Maybe I'd visit some if I managed to survive this.

Unlikely as that may be.

The deluge of information pouring into my head wasn't entirely done, though. There was one more vision that was penetrating my skull despite everything. It was unrelated to the gods, at least the upper tier ones like Perun and Veles, but something very personal to me. It was how I managed to become the unlikely bearer of the torch that was standing between two worlds and the god of evil.

"No," the voice spoke.

This one was from a very familiar looking man who strongly resembled — if not identical to—me. Unlike the previous two visions, it didn't take place in a surreal space between dimensions, but on the very recognizable rooftop of Dragon Keep. The figure was dressed as a Dark Undermaster with his attire sodden with stains from stab wounds.

Standing next to him was the Wise Man. They were overlooking the village that had yet to be updated by my "improvements" but not having suffered a dozen or more attacks by Veles' forces. Larry C.C. Weis was wearing a pair of modern mass-market produced glasses that contrasted a brown robe that made him look halfway between Obi Wan Kenobi and a monk.

"What do you mean, 'no'?" Larry asked.

"It's a pretty easy word to understand," Garland said. "No. I am not doing it."

"I'm familiar with how these stories go, Garland," Larry said. "Can we skip the Campbellian refusal of the call and just get to you saving the world? We're already in a bad position and it's only going to get worse."

"I don't know what that means and I don't care," Garland said. "This isn't me playing a game or telling you something that I'm going to change my mind on. It's not even that I don't want to do what you want me to do, though I don't. It's that I cannot."

Larry frowned. "You're being stubborn, Garland."

Garland laughed. It was a bitter jackass-like bray. "Stubborn, clearly that's what I'm being. You want me to go on an elaborate quest across the Southern Kingdoms, slay multiple gods, and then the Dark Lord himself. This after resurrecting me from being stabbed to death by my own brothers. All because I thought maybe we should be slightly less discriminating against nonhumans when trying to fight off the hordes of undead."

Larry shrugged and held out his hands. "Well, yes, that's the story. Stories have power, Garland, I've told you this. They're the way the gods are shaped."

Garland looked defeated. "That may be true but it's not my story."

"It absolutely is your story," Larry said, looking furious. "I know because I'm writing it!"

"Yes, it is your story, Laurentis," Garland said, using one of the Wise Man's older aliases that I somehow knew about. "Not mine. When you set out to write this story, you never bothered to see if the man to play your lead wanted the role. No, wait, you never cared. But, as I said, it is not a question of want but capability. Like hiring a soprano to sing tenor, I don't have the range."

Larry frowned. "Garland, you've done things no other man can. When you return from the dead—"

"I am not a leader," Garland said, simply. "I'm terrible at it."

Larry paused.

"I'm an antisocial monster hunter who hates every single hypocrisy that underpins our society," Garland said. "I fight for the poor, but I love the Queen of Ledziana. I'm an atheist—"

"How are you an atheist when you've met gods?" Larry asked.

"It's because I've met gods that I'm an atheist," Garland muttered. "None of you have really covered yourselves in glory upon introducing yourselves."

Larry frowned.

"But I have close friends within the Sisters of Mokosh," Garland said. "I could list all the various people I have ties to but none of them will follow me because I can't inspire them. I can't keep my contempt to myself. You need someone from outside the old feuds and struggles to bring the people together against Veles. Everyone here has too many prejudices and old wounds to bind them."

"That's true but that's not enough to disqualify you," Larry said, looking like he was listening to Garland's objections.

"No, the part that should disqualify me is the fact that I am spent," Garland said. "I died here at the hands of people I've trusted, but I was already on my last legs. I had nightmares every night from all the monsters I've slain and the people I've failed to protect. I've seen war up close and it has sapped the will to fight another one. You ask me why I can't be your champion, it's because I struggled to get out of bed this morning. War defeats us all, Larry. You'd know if you were ever anything but a general."

Larry lowered his gaze. "You have no idea how much war I have experienced, Garland, but I understand what you mean. I have forgotten how few people have the stomach for immortality. For long life even."

"I don't," Garland said, simply. "I am done. Send me off to whatever lies after."

"There are people who still love you," Larry asked. "The Dragon Queen. Ania. Agata."

"They should love someone else," Garland said. "Then I can't disappoint them all again."

Larry had nothing to respond with. He simply waved his hand, causing Garland's body to once more return to death.

I fell to my knees in the present and tried to figure out the meaning of the visions, if any meaning there was at all. After my eyes cleared of the hallucinations, I saw Ania and Agata by my side with Bloodstorm defensively holding his maul over me. Where Susanos was once standing, there was now only a pile of ash.

"Okay, what the hell did I miss?" I asked, standing up and shaking my head. "I feel... weird."

"How weird?" Jon asked, settling down on my shoulder in raven form.

"Like I've been struck down and become more powerful than you could possibly imagine," I said, looking at my hands. "I mean, for real, not just becoming a ghost and giving vague hints to farm boys across the galaxy."

"Does seeing the movies he quotes help any?" Agata asked Ania.

"No," Ania said. "No, it does not."

That was when Joan, Rachel, Sparky, and Nyx all appeared at once. They'd been invisible the entire time or perhaps in another dimension. Either way, they weren't there one moment and they were there the next.

"We decided to prepare for Susanos' sudden but inevitable betrayal," Joan said, pausing. "Which is from a movie."

"Show," I said.

"Both," Ania said, causing me to do a double take.

Joan rolled her eyes. "The whole point was that we'd sacrifice her as part of a spell to recharge your divinity when she turned against us."

I blinked. "You did what?"

"It worked, didn't it?" Rachel said, crossing her arms.

Nyx lifted Susanos' soul jar amulet and crushed it, causing it to fall to pieces. "Ashes to ashes, dust to dust."

"If you don't take it out and use it, it's going to rust," Jon said. "So, we've got a total victory without any losses. Whoo hoo!"

"Except one of the gods of good is dead," Joan said. "Shitty as that god may have been."

"Agata may be a replacement!" Jon said. "Worship her, foolish mortals!"

Agata smirked before looking serious. "How did you regain your power, Joan?"

"The goddesses gave me a bit of their power," Joan said. "At least until I could once more be Aaron's champion."

I opened my mouth to make a joke before I saw Veles standing behind them.

Shit.

CHAPTER THIRTY-SEVEN
TWO-MEN ENTER. ONE MAN LEAVES

"Hey, Veles," I said, looking at him and wondering whether an unexpected GAME OVER was about to happen.

Veles was once more dressed in his black robes but was otherwise exactly as he'd appeared in my dream. He'd been scorched across his face and body by the UMC and hadn't shown any sign of recovery. His expression was stern but there was also the slightest gleam of madness in his eyes, as if I'd managed to hurt him in a way that he still didn't believe was possible.

"Hello, Aaron," Veles said, his eyes focused on me with an intense glare.

"Fuck, it's Freddy Krueger!" Jon shouted, pointing with his right wing.

Everyone reacted to the arrival of the god of evil by freezing up in shock and horror—even the goddesses—except for Ania. Ania pulled out her knives and threw them at Veles with the kind of choreographed efficiency you only see in a movie.

The knives stopped in mid-air before falling to the ground.

"I'm going to be honest, Aaron, this is not only farther than I ever expected you to make but too far to blame anyone but myself," Veles said, not moving any further. "I thought I was taking advantage of the Wise Man's idiocy when I agreed to play his game, but you've chased me as far as Perun ever did. I'd say it's almost a pity that you have to die here but this was always meant to be busy work for the Wiseman's champions."

I took a deep breath and remained calm despite the fact we'd already exhausted ourselves fighting Mythras. Which was almost certainly what Veles had planned from the very beginning. "I think you don't want to win under these circumstances, Veles. I think you've been self-sabotaging yourself the entire way through."

"You do?" Jon asked, looking at me. "Because I think that's a really stupid idea."

"I prefer deeply optimistic."

"I agree with your bird," Veles said. "You're underestimating yourself, really. I admit I didn't take you seriously at first. I had better things to do than deal with you directly and I was gaining power from each failed attempt to set me down, but you've eliminated almost all my lieutenants. You also blew up a UMC in my face, which is actually far worse than having a nuke exploded in your face."

"You tried to blow us up with a nuke as well," Ania replied.

"And you survived that," Veles said, slowly clapping like he was at a golf tournament. "No, Aaron, I fully intended to kill all of you before Chernabog was sent back to the shadows. You're just like a fly that is nearly impossible to hit. Eventually, though, you stopped moving."

Everyone moved across the remains of the Mithraeum to stand beside me. I could hear thunder in the sky as Veles' power poured over the entire British Isles. Becoming a god again, I could sense the avatar was gathering his power now for a full-on assault. A part of me was tempted to attack directly but I was still hoping to reach some part of my foe before we clashed—mostly because our only other option was flight. We were not ready to fight another deity.

"Your approval fills me with shame," I said, simply. "I thought it wasn't going to be until the weekend that you made your big move."

"Oh shock," Veles said, putting his hand over his heart. "I lied. All I needed was for you to dispose of Mythras."

"Mythras wasn't going to do shit!" Joan said, snarling.

Veles laughed. "Ah, poor little pontifex maximus. The last of the true believers in Mythras the Hero God, and I wasted all that time planning for Radu to torture you into losing your faith. No, instead, all it took was Aaron being a better god."

That made me uncomfortable. Unlike virtually everyone else I'd fought with a rare few exceptions, I hadn't hated Mythras. I'd been pissed at him because of the whole kidnapping thing but it felt like a waste to kill him. Maybe I just didn't like the idea that it pleased Veles. That was always a bad sign.

"Mythras was meant to be a protector but—" Joan started to speak.

Veles laughed again. "Oh, how uncomfortable you make the Protector of Earth and Mokosh with your words. He has no desire to be a god and so many mortals will confuse that with humility. No, dear, fear was my weapon against Mythras and I could not have asked for a better use of it. I planted the seeds inside him long ago that he would not be strong enough to face me should we ever do battle and that he needed to preserve his strength for the confrontation."

Joan stared at him as if the implications were sinking in. "You're lying."

"Not about this," Veles said, which was exactly what a liar would say in this situation. "Seeing the fall of Perun and the bitter end of civilization, Mythras was all too easy to manipulate. I crawled into his mind and made it so that he needed an empire strong enough to protect the whole world and so many, many more worshipers so that when we confronted one another, it would be as equals. I undermined his confidence and strength of purpose by forcing him on the defensive. Ironically, had he immediately gone to battle with me when I'd barely triumphed over my brother then he might have won and become eternally known as the Southern Kingdom's god. Now you have laid him low and his power is lost forever."

I shielded my mind and everyone else's from Veles reading them. I'd never shown the ability to do that before, but it came as easily breathing now. I had a lot of new abilities as a god—if such a title was really deserved by anyone—and was using them instinctually. Either way, I didn't want Veles reading their minds and finding out about Agata's recent power-up.

You don't have to worry about that, an indistinct voice spoke in my mind. *The gods upgraded them all, so Veles cannot read their minds or predict their movements in the future.*

Who the hell are you? I asked, wondering what ridiculous plot twist this was now.

Who do you think? The voice asked as if offended.

I have no idea, I said. *Perun, the Wise Man, Mokosh, Kitty Pryde.*

I am not Kitty Pryde, the voice said, which I took as distinctly feminine. *Whoever that is. Just keep Veles talking. I have an idea. Something that I hope is just stupid enough to work like all the rest of your plans.*

I decided the voice was Agata's but that wasn't very reassuring. *You know stupid plans should be avoided, right? I know the low WIS thing is appealing but just because it's too dumb for the enemy to see it coming—*

Keep talking! Agata mentally snarled.

Right, I replied, following her lead.

"So, it really was a trap," I replied, looking at Veles. "Just not for me. After keeping Mythras on the bench the entire time, you sent me and my people to kill him. If we succeeded, then you lost a divine enemy who was waiting right up until the last second to take you out. Presumably after he absorbed all of my divine energy. If he killed us then he eliminated someone who you claimed had managed to wipe out most of your army."

"What have I done?" Joan asked, covering her face as she began to cry. Clearly, she thought Mythras doing all of this as a convoluted plan to take down Veles was a lot more of an extenuating circumstance than I believed it to be. I still thought it was incredibly stupid of Mythras, and he'd apparently never thought we could just team up to fight Veles.

"I wouldn't say most," Veles said, dryly. "Your world is full of people willing and eager to sell their souls for money or power. People who will twist their minds into knots that I'm God or they're somehow justified in siding with me according to their belief structures. It's what you get when you don't strike down your followers with plagues or lightning once they stray. The god of the Israelites became soft—"

I cut him off. "Says the guy who took over the world with a video game company. By the way, I quit. Epic Dungeoneering™ has been going downhill for years and I think I'm going to design indie games from now on."

"Yeah, that's not a great badass boast," Jon said.

"I'm not good at improvising," I said.

"I think that's literally the only thing you *are* good at," Jon said. "Let me take over the speech. Hey, Veles, you forgot one thing!"

"Which is, Ghostbird?" Veles asked.

"This is the ultimate showdown! Of ultimate destiny! The last boss arena! King Koopa's castle! Ganon's skull room in Death Mountain's dungeon! Dracula's throne room! Aaron may be needlessly polite, ridiculously devoted to redeeming hot ladies, kind of a dork—okay massively a dork—and a guy you wouldn't want to manage a Starbucks—"

I facepalmed. "Jon, really—"

"But he's got a pair of goddesses, some hot fantasy ladies he used to wank to when he was reading the books, and a demigod berserker! Oh, and if it wasn't obvious, a pair of dragons! A really cool one and a kind of derpy one!"

"You shouldn't be so hard on yourself," Sparky said to Jon. "You could be cool someday."

Joan smirked, which was the first sign of amusement she'd displayed this entire encounter. It quickly faded. "They also have my support, Veles! I will not betray Aaron the way I betrayed Mythras."

"The word of oathbreakers is valueless," Veles proclaimed. "You are damned to my realm like all others. I will take an eternity to break you down to your basest thoughts and you will beg for oblivion before I am done. Thankfully, I will be—"

Ania interrupted him. "Are you here to fight Veles or yammer?"

Ania's voice wasn't as confident as it usually was. A part of me wondered if that was because she'd been dedicated to in dying in battle against the god of evil for the past decade but now, she had something to live for and that gave her something to lose. I quickly discarded that thought, though. It was equally probable she just recognized we were utterly screwed after having spent all our strength fighting Mythras.

"I am prepared to fight if you are, Daughter of the Rose," Veles said. "Though I wouldn't call it fighting. More extermination of an insect."

No, I'm not ready yet! Agata shouted in my head.

I rubbed my temples. "Actually, we can't fight yet."

"I'm sorry, what?" Veles asked, surprised.

"This is one of those story things that keep being brought up," I said, looking at Veles. "You know how the gods draw their power from the tales told about them? Well, now is the only time that it is possible for you to tell us what your plan is."

Veles stared. "Aaron, I made that up."

"What," I said, blinking.

"Gods can certainly feed on the love and adoration of worshipers," Veles said, as if he was a school lecturer. "But the whole bit about us being constrained by our stories? Yeah, I made that up and convinced plenty of other deities that it was true. One of the benefits of being one of the creator deities. No, it's absolutely not true. It was a perfect way to manipulate all my opposition into following rules that I knew how to counteract. Really, you've been thriving primarily by breaking the rules that the Wiseman thought I would be forced to follow"

"You fiend!" Jon said, flapping his wings. "That is also really clever."

Ania looked furious at me for delaying her attack.

I waved to her, as if to say, "trust me."

Veles chuckled, having seen it. "You still think there's a chance of winning this. The world as you know it will soon be overwhelmed with the deathrot plague while I bring Mat Zemalya back from the realm where she was banished. Both worlds will be—"

"Want to play a game of Pwiffle?" I asked.

"What?" Veles asked.

"You know, for the fate of the world!" I said.

Everyone in my party looked at me like I was crazy, which was understandable.

Got it, Agata said. She lifted her staff and aimed it at me. "Take everything, Aaron!"

With that, all of Mythras' energy poured into me.

I screamed.

But in rapture.

No visions this time.

Only power.

YOU ARE NOW A GREATER GOD.

Veles stared then blinked once. "Huh, I did not see that coming."

I charged at him and the two of us fell into hyperdimensional space.

CHAPTER THIRTY-EIGHT
BOSS FIGHT TIME

Describing hyperdimensional space to you would probably be an exercise in futility because I barely understood it with an INT 30. I hadn't learned about it, but the information had been imprinted on my brain. Basically, much of my skill and knowledge was a hand-me-down from Perun and now Mythras.

It would have been nice to have more than a few seconds to practice what had been unceremoniously uploaded into my brain. However, I was in full "I know kung fu" mode from *The Matrix*. Actually, let's go full on enlightenment mode and not dial it back for the sequels where all he got was the ability to fly.

Sorry for the digression.

Anyway, I was pounding Veles in the face a hundred blows per second as the two of us fell through a starry expanse that took us to the space between realities. I was operating on instinct more than anything else and that was a good thing since the kind of power I was throwing around would have levelled London if not flattened the Northern Hemisphere. If I'd stopped to think about what I was doing, I would have perhaps hesitated to throw hands that could charitably be called Fat Man and Little Boy levels of power. This wasn't just Veles avatar, but it was all the stolen power that he'd summoned to fight me with versus all the power I was. Goku, the Silver Surfer, and Superman would all be proud.

Pure muscle memory could only get you so far, though, when they weren't your memories of punching to start with. Veles seemed genuinely stunned by my attacks for the first few seconds of our fight and I took advantage of that to try to inflict every bit of damage I could before his superior experience turned itself on me.

"Enough!" Veles screamed, swinging his staff around and blasting me in the face with black lightning. It would have destroyed me even as a lesser god, but I somehow brought up a shield that deflected most of it.

I took a moment to take in our surroundings. It looked like an art student had dropped acid and topped it off with PCP (not that I knew what any of those things were like). The two of us were now floating in a vast space of reds, blacks, and whites that had free-floating rocks throughout it. There was no air, heat, or gravity but it was a place where thought was more important than physics. This was probably why we were able to communicate with each other. It was completely removed from how "normal" humans interacted.

I lifted my sword. "You really shouldn't have given me time to talk, Veles."

"Believe me, I know," Veles said. "But I needed to make sure you didn't escape."

"I'm not escaping," I said. "I don't have to win this fight. I just have to make sure you lose."

It was less a boast than an acknowledgement of inevitability. I'd managed to run the gauntlet of vampires, demons, goblins, and evil gods up until this point. No one had thought I would get this far—least of all me—but here was the finish line and I had no real faith that I'd be coming back from this. That didn't matter, though. Ania, Agata, Bloodstorm, Joan, Jon, and the others were elsewhere and if I could save them by making sure Veles didn't come back from wherever this was then that would be enough.

Veles narrowed my eyes. "There it is."

"What?" I asked.

"Why I couldn't figure out your angle." Veles said, shaking his head. "The others were tempted by the power, fame, and worship. You just kept pushing forward with the thoughts of a mortal and ignoring the long-term benefits. That's what separated you from Garland and the other champions. You were always willing to risk it all to win."

"Thanks," I said, waiting for an opening.

"It means you think like a peasant!" Veles shouted, unleashing a storm of raw magic that ripped through our shared space like it was tearing paper.

Unfortunately for Veles, this strategy did not work out well for him. Rather than trying to block or dodge his attack, I proceeded to focus on redirecting the assaults. Veles found himself being rained on by his own blasts, which he frantically struggled to dispel. Apparently, he hadn't thought that his own magic could be turned against him.

What followed was a rhythm that combined every single move I'd learned from my training under Zorya Dawnbringer with the things I'd received from Perun as well as Mythras' downloads. I even substituted some Jedi tricks and things from comic books along the way. Why? Because this was a realm of imagination and things that took Veles off guard would hopefully be smarter than pure strategy.

I fought in a way that might best have been termed aggressively defensive. ("Rope-a-dope" as my father would call it.) My goal was to draw out as much of Veles' power as humanly possible while trying to turn it against him whenever possible. Whether or not it should have been possible to hit him with his own magic didn't matter because we were in an area where raw imagination was the determining factor. I was a game designer and had a lot of imagination. Even more importantly, I had the will to know that my friends were counting on me.

"Oh please!" Veles said, pulling back and conjuring his own sword of shadow. "Your strength is your *friends*?"

I was almost immediately struck in the shoulder, causing me to feel unimaginable pain. My aggressive defensiveness was reduced to pure defensiveness in an instant.

"Fuck," I grunted, blocking the next blow with the Sword of Perun.

"The collected wisdom of countless sages, philosophers, and gods lie within you but your biggest motivation comes from a Saturday morning cartoon?" Veles taunted, continuing his attacks that moved so fast I could barely keep up. Somehow, I was holding them back, but I felt myself getting weaker with each blow as he drained away my strength.

"They don't even have those anymore! What do you fight for, Veles?" I asked, gritting my teeth and remembering Alek and Francine along with all the other people I'd lost. "You're the goddamn god of evil! By choice! Even before the Twisted Gods fucked up your brain beyond all repair! Your own people, your own creations, hate you! The only people who ever gave a shit about you were your brother and Susanos! Both of whom you killed! You're a miserable piece of shit and I am sorry that I tried to reach out to you!"

It wasn't exactly the Saint Crispin's Day speech in terms of oratory but it reflected how I felt. I'd tried very hard to be the good guy, to reject the kind of cynical hopeless nihilism on which Larry C.C. Weis had made his reputation. It had been cool when I was a teenager, but I was now well and truly sick of grimdark.

"Ah, there it is!" Veles said, growling. "Finally! That smug arrogance that so defined your ancestor, nephew! The self-righteous sense of superiority that would rather be good than successful! Do you know why people hate me, Aaron? They hate me because they love to hate! To have someone to blame for their problems be it the Serpent in the Garden or enemies to torment! Hate is an emotion every bit as primal as love, but what they don't teach is how good it feels! How addictive! Why did I let myself become the god of evil, Aaron? Because someone needed to be! Man cannot be good unless he has a thing to contrast it to!"

Veles surprised me as I realized he wasn't just faking his outrage. I'd genuinely pissed him off and that gave me a moment to strike. "Good doesn't need evil to thrive, Veles. Love doesn't need hate to define it. Hate needs love to define it. Evil needs something to persecute. You're the god of something *unnecessary*."

I took my opening and struck with divine force that combined the evil-destroying light of Mythras, the lighting of Perun, and some tiny little part of me that had become a god people believed in. I thought I might be able to destroy him, which was foolish because Veles was older than the universe—or at least he was made from a being that was—and he had been gathering power on two worlds for years.

But I hit him.

Hard.

The Sword of Perun buried itself into Veles wrist as he brought it up to protect himself from being struck in the face. The sword severed through it, striking him in the side of the cheek before drawing forth blood made of the Stygian abyss. Veles reared back and stared at the stump where his hand used to be as the limb burned away into nothingness. It was a look that told me he didn't quite believe I'd managed to harm him.

I made my own mistake then and didn't keep attacking like a wild animal. I forgot the key to winning a battle is will more than anything else—to want to kill your opponent more than anything else. So, it was a huge-ass error as I tried one last time to reach the man I thought might be behind the monster. "It's not too late, Veles."

Did I say mistake?

I should have said fatal error.

If I'd pissed off Veles earlier and gotten him to attack me recklessly, I'd caused him to go apeshit with this. "How dare you? How DARE you! I have lived eons beyond the brief flickering mayfly existence that you claim to be a life! You lecture me on being too late! This universe was a mistake from the very beginning and it requires a mind vast enough to know what is required to fix that!"

Veles transformed before my eyes into his true form, at least as much as anything like him could be said to have one. It was the original dragon, the long serpent with the bull's head that had implanted into every culture that viewed snakes or bulls as evil. Indeed, the places where they were symbols of wisdom probably came from Veles as well. He'd once been so much more than the thing he'd become.

The respective differences in our sizes didn't matter even though Veles was like a skyscraper compared to my King Kong. Everything here was more about perspective than it was reality and Veles wanted me to know just how much larger he was in every conceivable way.

"You're not fixing anything!" I shouted, gathering every bit of what power I'd been given to try to hold off the inevitable assault that was coming. Veles was a conservative god by nature, probably the only reason he'd not just overwhelmed everyone directly, but I'd convinced him to finally cut loose.

Yay me.

"You wouldn't know!" Veles shouted, smoke pouring from his mouth. "Because I am not inclined to tell Weis' hand puppet my plans!"

The flames that poured out of Veles mouth were a veritable sun's worth of wrath and it took every single bit of my power to push it back. At least at the start before I realized Veles was so furious he'd forgotten that Mythras was a sun god and I started absorbing the flames into myself. The sun-infused blast allowed me to get another deep strike into the god of evil, and he yowled in agony.

So, he just hit me in the face with his tail.

Again.

And again.

I found myself wrapped up like a rodent in a python's coils as Veles squeezed. I projected out Perun's lighting to shock Veles enough to loosen his grip but by that point I'd already felt bones breaking. Veles struck down and bit me hard with fangs injecting a kind of mystical venom. Unfortunately, for him, that gave me a chance to stab him in the roof of his mouth, covering me in more of his abyssal blood.

It burned like acid.

My knees weakened.

The Sword of Perun was half-melted down the blade.

Shit.

YOU HAVE BEEN DIVINE POISONED
YOU HAVE RECEIVED 21,881 SOUL DAMAGE

Damn, that must have been bad. The interface hadn't even been reporting the previous injuries. Then again, I suspected it hadn't really been designed to deal with figures this high. Just my luck to reach the buggy portion of the game at the climax. Technically, we'd clipped out of the boss arena for the final battle.

Veles pulled back. "That took a third of my strength, but Perun's strength cannot help you anymore. This was always a suicide mission, Aaron. You were never meant to be anything more than a dead mouse on a string before the housecat. A way for the gods to divert my attention while they debated endlessly about what to do. Trying to strike me down with my own power was clever and none of the other gods would have thought of it. They were too selfish, too arrogant, and too in love with their own power to risk it for others. You may be a peasant god, Aaron, but I give you a salutation before you die: I will remember you when I've forgotten the rest of the universe."

I was feeling cold now.

Weak.

YOU HAVE RECEIVED 37,281 SOUL DAMAGE

That was when it all hit me.

I laughed.

Hard.

Veles, who was pulling back for a killing strike, stopped. "What is it? You have that look in your eye."

"Just hit a natural 20 on my WIS score," I said, looking up. "While you clearly hit a natural 1. If I was sent here to distract you then what am I distracting you from?"

Veles only took a second to understand before lightning, fire, and blades started raining down on his head. Descending from above us were the rest of my party. They weren't the way I remembered them, though. Ania, Agata, Bloodstorm, the Zoryas, Jon, Sparky, and Joan were all glowing with the light of the divine.

They were all greater gods now.

It was, at least on paper, a brilliant plan and I had to give the gods credit. They might have been a bunch of manipulative assholes unwilling to get their hands dirty, but they'd managed to do *something* in the end. They'd lured Veles into confronting me, probably sacrificing Mythras in the process, before getting me to push Veles into a place beyond time and space. A place where Veles wouldn't be able to see the future and counteract their movements the way all those who saw the future could counteract one another.

It wasn't somewhere they would attack Veles directly. No, that was still too dangerous, and gods forbid immortals endanger themselves. But what if all of them passed the hat around and gave up just a little of their divine energy? Mokosh, Baba Yaga, Odin, and the small gods of Earth all doing enough to make a half-dozen gods that could attack Veles after I'd worn him down.

Nyx and Rachel would be down for it.

They were gods of war.

The others were ready to sacrifice themselves from the beginning.

Well, not Jon but he'd already died once.

Veles seemed to realize he'd been played, but there was nowhere to go. Still, even as I was dying, I could tell this wasn't going to be a fight my friends would survive. They might triumph in the end or maybe Veles would, but this was all to make sure he was so weakened that the senior gods could undo all of his efforts up to this point. They'd take advantage of how long it took for Veles to recover to make their own moves. It was a genius plan if you didn't mind sacrificing a bunch of pawns and maybe a rook or two.

I didn't play chess, though.

YOU HAVE RECEIVED 18,000 SOUL DAMAGE

I didn't know how much I had left so I decided to make my last stand and try to save my friends. "AARON'S STUPID SACRIFICE!"

I hadn't read the spell's description for but I'd been thinking about something like it unconsciously since I'd started becoming a god. What would you sacrifice? How much? How far would you go to save everyone you loved? What was the reason the other gods had failed to rein Veles in? Well, I knew the answer to that and so did the Interface, so they'd created a spell for me to show it.

I jabbed the broken fragment of the Sword of Perun into Veles and proceeded to burn every bit of the divine energy left inside of my body up.

Mythras'.

Perun's.

My own.

It consumed both Veles and me in a blaze of light that stretched out in every direction.

Veles' last expression was one of complete shock.

And admiration.

"CREATOR GOD SLAIN."

Another more disturbing thing followed in the same voice.

"YOU HAVE DIED."

CHAPTER THIRTY-NINE
CUE CREDITS

The first indication I wasn't dead-dead— if such a thing existed for gods—was the sound of Sabaton's "Forty-to-One." It was a power metal song about how some Polish warriors fought off a shit-ton of Nazis and my cousin loved it. I loved hearing about people killing Nazis as much anyone who wasn't one, but it hurt my head.

"Urgh," I muttered, slightly moving my head and noting that the music was coming from a television set that was presently displaying credits next to CGI scenes from *Dark Undermaster III*. A PlayStation X— a game console I had never seen before—was hooked up to the TV with its controller in front of me. "You've got to be kidding me."

I was in Larry's living room.

It was mostly like what I'd seen of the place when I'd visited it for a few minutes before my kidnapping to Ledziana. The exception was that someone had held a party, and not the classy kind either. There were Cheetos, beer cans, and the occasionally discarded piece of underwear scattered around.

I was wearing a t-shirt and jeans with my hair having grown out long like I was a hippie. I also had a beard, which was a bit of a surprise. I briefly considered trying to cast some magic but didn't want to try conjuring the eldritch forces of reality with a monster headache.

"Ah, Aragorn, you're awake," Larry C.C. Weis' voice echoed through the room with my headache responding accordingly. "Odin had even money you wouldn't awaken until after true love's kiss or the sun exploded."

"How long?" I asked.

"Not really a question here," Larry said, dressed in black slacks and a blue button-down shirt with his trademark beret. "This is my domain, however, small and as much part of Skyworld as it is Earth. Suffice to say, you missed the party celebrating your victory over Veles but not the next election. They're giving democracy a try again after enjoying the wonders of a god king dictator. I give it a week before they're already propping up replacements: Vote Horus vs. Cthulhu."

"I'm in America?" I asked, unsurprised to find Larry alive. Death seemed like a revolving door when it involved the gods.

"Close enough," Larry said, sitting across from me on the coffee table with a McDonalds bag in his hands. "The Carpenter kid brought you some loaves and fishes. I'm going to be honest, that's about all you can expect in terms of gratitude but it's more than anyone else brought."

I grabbed the bag, suddenly ravenously hungry. "I'll take it."

The insides were Filet-O-Fish and fries. Thankfully, still hot. There was also a second bag with a large iced tea in it.

I ate like eight meals worth.

The contents multiplied with my hunger.

Cute.

"You probably have some questions," Larry said.

"No shit," I said, my head finally clearing. "Like why am I not dead and why are you not dead?"

"Rather than quote Billy Crystal in *The Princess Bride*," Larry said, "I'd prefer that we just skip ahead to the reality that death for the divine is not quite the binary condition it is for mortals. You've already observed how hard it is to keep a god down permanently and without Veles to *keep* us dead, resurrection was guaranteed."

I remembered executing Ivan and resurrecting him immediately thereafter. That was one of those things that was so out of character that it kind of became a defining part of your character, like Batman using a gun when everyone knew Batman didn't kill.

"So, I'm alive again," I said, wondering what the catch was. I was also speculating about what this meant for Veles.

"Yes and no," Larry said. "You still burned like a candle from both ends. The gods were happy to have you win but were thinking you'd sacrifice yourself alongside the rest of your friends, not do it after absorbing Mythras' power and after hitting Veles with his own UMC tower. Which in laymen's terms, means they weren't prepared for a pantheon of greater gods and you at the center. They'd really been hoping for a couple of badly injured survivors and martyrs that they could nurse back to health off in a corner somewhere for the next few thousand years."

"They're upset I won?" I asked, slurping the bottom of my tea with my straw. It magically refilled after I was done.

"More like they're upset you won so handily," Larry replied. "They were already dividing up all the worshipers they planned to show themselves to now that magic has returned to Earth. Now you're inconveniently the Hero of Two Worlds and drowning in worshipers. Believe me, everyone in the universe who had the slightest bit of magical sensitivity was watching the title fight. It was 'The Gods are Back, Baby' pay-per-view event."

"I don't want worshipers," I said, exhausted by the whole thing.

"See?" Larry said, pointing at me. "That's the attitude the gods hate. It makes them feel like you're too cool for them and that's why you are."

I rubbed the bridge of my nose. "How are the others in my group? Can I see them?"

"Sure," Larry said. "They're currently mourning your death. Time works a bit differently here if you remember. Mokosh and Perun are going to clue them in if you don't want to, though."

"How is Perun?" I asked. "Back from the dead officially?"

"Recovering," Larry said. "You weakened Veles enough that he could finally return. He and Mokosh have been helping from the beginning, though. Through the marks or the invisible hand of the Earthmother. I'm inclined to think the reason that Mythras was taken down but not Agata when Ania stabbed them was their doing. All gods are bastards but not all of them are complete bastards, Aaron."

"Well, they can keep it," I said, in my breath.

"What?" Larry asked. "Keep what?"

"All of it," I said, taking a deep breath. "The worshipers, the church, the supernatural power, and the—"

"Valkyries?" Larry suggested. "I'm quite fond of the Valkyries."

"I'm married," I said.

"Ania would probably be fond of them," Larry said.

I glared. "Also, Valkyries are Norse, not Slavic!"

Larry gave a dismissive wave while making a noise like a tire losing air. "Pshaw. Eventually, every culture becomes a casserole of other cultures. Either way, Aaron, you don't know what you're talking about. Once you become a god, it's not a simple matter of turning in your resignation papers. Do you think you can just retire to the wilderness and be left alone?"

"I'd love that, yes," I said.

"You'd go insane without wireless internet," Larry said. "Frankly, I think the only reason you lasted a year in Ledziana is because you still had the Mark of the Champion's interface."

"Seriously," I said, shaking my head. "I don't want it. Perun can make an Aaron-shaped avatar or an office of 'everyone can go fuck right off.' I am *done*."

Larry looked over his shoulder, guiltily.

I narrowed my eyes. "What is it?"

"It's nothing," Larry said, patting me on the shoulder. "You should work on getting your strength back up."

"I died," I said, staring at him. "I beat Veles! What more do you want?"

Jon walked into the room in human form wearing a Wednesday Addams t-shirt and carrying a pitcher of beer with a straw in it. "You know, that's exactly what I told him when I died for the first time. You know what happened? I got turned into a bird who couldn't masturbate."

"You could masturbate, you just didn't know how," Larry said, as if this was the most normal conversation topic in the world.

"I wasn't going to ask for instructions!" Jon complained, putting his pitcher down. "So, when is Aaron going to be turned into a raven?"

"What?" I asked.

"Listen, man, we all went through it!" Jon said, waving up his arms like wings. "You die, you become a bird. Don't worry, maybe some kind soul will eventually teach you shapeshifting or how to masturbate."

"He's not becoming a raven, Jon," Larry said, sighing. "We're past that point. I only reincarnated you as one because I felt we needed to pass on the knowledge being lost between champions."

I was starting to wonder if it wouldn't have been better to have stayed dead. "Guys—"

"Not becoming a raven?" Jon asked, continuing to wave up and down his arms. "I see what this is! This is discrimination! It's because I'm black, isn't it? At least when I'm a raven."

Both Larry and I stared at Jon.

"I'd like to see you try that line in front of Bloodstorm," I said, sighing. "What I'm saying is, Larry, is that I did everything that needed to be done."

The credits on the television set ended and returned to the title screen.

ACHIEVEMENT UNLOCKED: GRAND UNDERMASTER (100) - Complete the main campaign on any difficulty

"Main campaign?" I asked, looking at Larry. "Are you implying there's DLC?"

"Like I said..." Larry trailed off.

"Woo hoo!" Jon said, raising his fists in the air. "USA! USA!"

"We literally killed the president of the United States," I said. "Mind you, he was a Dark Lord and not even American, but I think that precludes us from winning any awards for patriotism."

"Depends on what period of national history it is," Larry said. "There's plenty of people who would have given you a reward for knocking off Andrew Johnson. Particularly after he pardoned all the Confederates."

I didn't decide to answer that and instead cupped my face in my hands. "I'm *dead*. You can't be serious."

If it sounds like I was whining, it was because I was. It was difficult to put into words just how much emotional whiplash one suffered when one prepared to die, carried out the deed that should have killed you, and then one managed to survive. I'd managed to keep it together this entire time and felt I was long overdue for a breakdown.

"Yeah, not quite," Larry said. "The reward for a job well done is to be given more work. Even if you managed to beat Veles, there's always another struggle to fight. Demon kings, undead lords, tyrants, and more. In this case, this is a particularly nasty one."

"I refuse," I said. "I invoke the Garland exemption."

Larry sighed. "That is your option."

There was long pause.

"But—" I said, knowing this was going to end badly.

"But if you do turn this down then people will suffer," Larry said. "Maybe we could pull ourselves together and get this done. There are other heroes, Aaron. You are living proof that no one is irreplaceable, but you aren't Garland."

"Yeah, Garland is off banging his Dragon Queen in the Underworld," Jon said. "By contrast, you are once more in the living room of a guy who has an incest fetish."

"I do not have an incest fetish," Larry said.

"Oh, really?" Jon said. "Because I've read the books and all the sex Garland had with his sisters. Oh, and the sick shit you had planned for Rachel and Aaron. Hell, don't think I didn't see what you had planned for Agata and Nyx. The chicken and egg—"

"I will pay you to tell me what you want me to do," I said, turning to Larry. "Just to end this conversation."

"I would pay me too," Larry said, shaking his head. "Unfortunately, there's something even worse than Jon awaiting this particular favor we need done."

"We?" I asked.

"The gods," Larry said.

"Fuck the—" I started to say.

Larry raised his hands. "That includes your friends, for as long as they remain. I know they would gladly sacrifice all the power they've achieved for you but for now, you have the role of trying to save the Two Worlds from the crisis that Veles created. Unfortunately, there remains one final thing to do before you can even think of resting."

"Okay, now you're scaring me," I said, wondering why Larry was beating around the bush.

"Say you're not afraid," Jon said.

"I just said—" I started to reply.

"Come on!" Jon said.

I sighed. "I'm not afraid."

"You will be," Jon said, doing the Yoda voice. "You will be."

Larry took a deep breath. "You successfully stopped Veles plan to destroy the two worlds and elevate himself to overgod status again. The Twisted Gods' influence was burned out of a creator god and their plan through him was thwarted. There are none of the other gods left with any of their taint left in them."

"Which means we won," I said, really hoping I wasn't misreading things.

"It means that there's no one at the steering wheel," Larry said, shaking his head. "Which isn't the same as the ship not being about to wreck against the shoreline."

"Ledziana, like Poland, is a landlocked nation," I said. "Why are you using a sailing metaphor?"

Larry snapped his fingers in front of my eyes. "Focus, Aaron."

"I'm not the one ducking an explanation," I said, now more annoyed than scared. Which was perhaps deliberate. I was more inclined to go along with whatever asinine scheme the Wise Man had cooking since, well, I was no longer dead and that meant there was a chance of reuniting with Ania.

Ania.

I wondered what she thought of this. She was a goddess now and Veles was dead. Did that mean we could finally be together? Where would we live? This world? Mokosh? Sky Realm? Burbank? Maybe godhood would change her, and she'd want to go hunting demons with Artemis.

But I had hope now.

Maybe I shouldn't have.

"Well, what I mean is that all of the plots that Veles set in motion don't necessarily stop because he's no longer directing them," Larry said. "His cult is trying to finish the ritual and, well, they might succeed. Which won't make Veles an overgod or end the multiverse but could blow up the Two Worlds."

I blinked. "Uh huh."

"I admit, I didn't think that was possible," Larry said.

"No," I said, dryly. "Because that's a pretty big oversight."

"Yes," Jon said. "Larry should be very ashamed of himself. Mind you, now that he's alive again, he better finish the damn books!"

Larry glared at him. "They'll be done when they're good and ready!"

"Like hell!" Jon said. "You have an obligation to finish them before you're dead-dead."

"I already died!" Larry said.

"How do we stop it?" I asked, trying to figure out what sort of rules bound gods after their avatars were destroyed.

"We need his help," Jon said.

"Whose?" I asked, confused.

That was when Veles walked in.

Goddammit.

CHAPTER FORTY
OFF TO THE SHIRE

Veles no longer looked like a burn victim and had changed out of his robes to something that resembled them in the most off-putting way possible: a hoodie and sweats. He looked like he had just come from the kitchen, really. He was still Peter Stormare, but less the actor version and more like you'd caught him going to a Starbucks.

"You have got to be kidding me," I said, looking at Veles. "How?"

"You of all people should know immortal means immortal," Veles said. "The fact you're standing here should be evidence enough of that."

"No, I mean, shouldn't you be trapped in a black hole or imprisoned at the bottom of the Underworld?" I asked. "They locked up the Fenris Wolf, Kronos, and Morgoth until the end of time. Why can't they do the same to you?"

"Believe me, I was just as upset as you," Jon said.

"Were you?" I asked.

"Eh, not really," Jon said. "At this point, I'm pretty used to the complete unfairness of the universe. Like, for instance, you don't have to spend any time as a raven!"

"You learned to love it," Larry said.

"I learned to tolerate it!" Jon said. "Which is an entirely different beast."

"The punishments for deities found to be guilty of crimes against reality are determined by their pantheon heads," Veles said. "Might may not make right but it determines justice. In this case, Perun ordered me to make atonement."

"And Svarog?"

"Was annoyed to have done anything other than work on expanding the universe," Veles said. "Both of them were of the mind that I wasn't in my right mind and thus there were extenuating circumstances."

"Uh huh," I said, staring. "That is the biggest bullshit I have heard since Darth Vader got directly into Jedi Heaven."

"This from the god of redemption," Veles said, dryly. "Congratulations, Aaron, you have successfully committed your first divine hypocrisy. I'd suggest we throw you a party but you already missed your first one."

"I don't want to be god of anything," I said, looking at him.

Veles looked at Larry. "Did you explain that's not really an option?"

Larry shrugged. "Aaron's low wisdom allowed him to literally save reality, so I'm guessing that it would be pointless. In any case, we discussed this."

"No," Veles said, referring to something I had no idea about.

"Reality is at stake!" Larry said.

Veles closed his eyes. "It's always at stake. Fine. Aaron, I apologize for trying to kill you and everyone else you love. You successfully beat me, even though I think it was closer to a tie and—"

"You're apologizing?" I asked. "You think that's going to cut it?"

"See? This is what I have to deal with." Veles looked at Larry helplessly then back at me. "You don't understand, Aaron. When I say your victory determines justice, I mean that in a way you can't understand. It doesn't matter what I believe to be wrong or right since you won. Won-ish. Now you're the person who gets to determine that. If you do want to banish me, that's fine. The Underworld is where I love. If I have to spend the next few hundred millennia cleaning up this mess, that's also fine. I promised I would abide by the rules that Larry set forth and later double promised. I am as bound by the oaths I made as possessed as I am before or after."

"Except you broke your oaths constantly," I said, still wondering why I was talking to King Koopa.

Veles' face made the most imperceptible of twitches, which was a furious scream equivalent for most people. "That is both the allure and curse of the Twisted Gods' influence. Gods are incapable of breaking their oaths and their decisions are set in rock infinitely harder than stone. It is only by the Twisted Gods' influence that they can indulge in what human beings judge to be free will."

"And how do you feel about it?" I asked.

"I think I regret breaking my word," Veles said, staring. "It was a source of pride and a reputation as honorable takes an eternity to earn but only a few short decades to destroy. It also undermines the nature of what one is a god of. It will be generations before the Underworld is set right."

"So, it's like *Dogma*," Jon said. "You undo everything by proving a god wrong."

"Sure, Jon," Veles said. "It's exactly like *Dogma*."

Larry had been uncharacteristically silent during all of this. "The important thing is resolving this because it ends up eradicating everything and rendering all of our efforts moot. Are you willing to make atonement or not, Dark One?"

"Aaron beat me so I am bound to do what he says," Veles said. "What sort of person would I be if I preached might makes justice and then did not follow through on it?"

"Like virtually every single person who preaches it?" I asked, confused. "The whole point is it only is a philosophy you follow when you're the strong one. It's an excuse for assholes."

Veles looked annoyed. "You do not understand the intricacies."

"Except I won so clearly I'm right about there not being any intricacies," I said. "Just saying that maybe you got used to being the top dog."

Veles seemed like he was debating blasting me with force lightning like Emperor Palpatine. "You are not making this easy, Aaron."

"Is there any reason I should?" I asked. "It's your cult that is threatening the world, so why don't you just tell me what I need to do and I'll go wrap this up."

"It'll be like the Scouring of the Shire except probably a lot easier since we're sending Thor, the Hulk, Phoenix, and a bunch of other A-listers to beat up Hydra goons," Jon said. "Assuming Veles doesn't show up, then it's adding Thanos to the mix."

"I'm more of a DC man," Veles said, sighing. "The issue is not my cult."

"On that we disagree," Larry said.

"The cultists I recruited on Earth are venal human beings that were willing to betray their gods, ancestors, and nation with the slightest promise of money," Veles said.

"So, [Insert your political party of choice]," Jon said, making the joke I was thinking.

Veles didn't respond to that, but I got the sense the god of evil agreed with the sentiment. "There are a few of them I taught parlor tricks once I brought magic back to Earth—"

"Speaking of which, is that going to stay?" I asked. "We started with a cyberpunk dystopia as our immediate future and now I'm wondering if it's full *Shadowrun*."

"More *Cyber Dragons*," Jon corrected.

I rolled my eyes. "I do want to know if Earth is going to have to deal with gods and monsters forever."

"Probably," Veles said. "At least until they burn through all of the sorcery like they did before in another thousand years. Earthlings are not known for their ability to manage resources. Still, that's not going to be a problem if the planet is destroyed in the next forty-eight hours."

Okay, that shut me up. Mostly. "Go on."

"What I am getting at is this is not a collection of geniuses. Even the least of my death lords was as far above these fools as I was above you," Veles said, making a sour face. "There was a reason I was directly coordinating things as the supreme leader of your country—"

"You're a control freak?" I asked, not afraid of Veles anymore even if he was probably regaining his power much faster than I was.

Larry chuckled.

"Because I didn't trust them with phenomenal cosmic power far beyond their comprehension," Veles said.

"Except, they somehow have access to it anyway," I said,

Veles narrowed his eyes. "Yes, because I wasn't expecting to be beaten by a god barely out of infancy."

"I'm not a god," I said. "I just have divine powers."

"And worshipers," Jon said. "Mostly rat people, at least until the movie comes out."

I cleared my throat, no longer interested in continuing this conversation. "What do you need me to do? Surely, it can't be that difficult to smite all of them."

I wasn't a fan of summary executions, but this was war and they hadn't surrendered. Plus, you know, the whole threatening the entire fabric of reality thing.

"I'm afraid it's not that simple," Larry said.

I sighed. "It never is."

"The cultists are attempting to..." Veles trailed off.

I raised an eyebrow, curious at what could get Veles to not finish a sentence. "What?"

"Trade up on their deities," Veles said, finally.

Jon burst out laughing.

Veles narrowed his eyes menacingly. A wave of dark energy, purified of the Twisted Gods, but still terrifying washed over us.

"Meep." Jon turned back into a raven and flew behind the couch armrest beside me.

"You're a goddamn dragon," I replied, annoyed.

"Shhh, he can't see us if we don't move," Jon said.

I rolled my eyes. "Your cult has decided since you've died, they're going to worship another deity for ultimate power?"

"Yes," Veles said.

"It's usually how it works," Larry replied. "Contests among the gods are among the easiest way to determine who a worshiper is drawn to."

I'd have asked about free will, but I had the impression that would go over like a lead balloon in this crowd. "What deity are they worshiping instead?"

"Mat Zemalya," Veles said, as if there would be a clap of thunder accompanying her name. There wasn't, thankfully. I'd had enough of cheap theatrics to last a lifetime.

"And?" Jon said, popping his head up from behind. "Isn't she just Earth's mother like Mokosh is, well, Mokosh?"

"Not quite," I muttered. "She's been corrupted by the Twisted Gods, hasn't she?"

"Beyond that," Veles said. "My former bride attempted to redeem the Twisted Gods."

"Well, that's stupid," Jon replied, peering his head from behind the couch.

"It almost worked," Larry said, dryly. "Unfortunately, even a greater goddess like Mat Zemalya was not possessed of enough oomph to rewrite reality to incorporate the Twisted Gods. She ended up absorbing far more of their essence than someone corrupted by their power could normally."

"Which means..." I trailed off this time instead.

"She's far more like the demons I turned mine and Perun's children with Mokosh into than me," I replied. "Except a thousand times more powerful."

I frowned. "Somehow this is not sounding like the cake walk you described,"

"Please, you're Slavic now, Aaron," Jon said. "Describe it as a beer run."

I took my iced tea and sipped it. "Didn't you try to destroy her and reboot her like, well, everyone else did."

"That didn't work," Veles said, sighing. "She's tied to the fundamentals of the Twisted Gods and the primal chaos now."

"I'll pretend that means something" I replied.

"I didn't have the power to fix her," Veles said, simply. "Which is part of the reason I started experimenting with the Twisted Gods' power."

Ah, that was almost sweet. "You spent this entire time trying to meddle with forces dangerous even to the gods for the sake of love."

Veles just stared.

I slurped on my straw some more.

Veles sighed. "In any case, Aaron, I don't want you and your associates to fight Mat Zemalya. At that point, it would be about as dangerous as the two of us fighting in your world and would leave your world destroyed. Which might be preferable to Mat harnessing her former home and turning into a living hellscape. Believe me, there are worse things than death."

I didn't make a crack about waking up with a hangover before a McDonalds brunch. "So, the goal is to deal with the cult before they summon the Earthmother of my world and to proceed with your plan."

"Essentially," Veles replied.

"Yeah, this is definitely DLC," Jon said. "Lots of reused assets, a rehash of the main game's plot, and probably half the main game's initial cost for a tenth of the game's content."

"Be grateful that it's not horse armor," I said.

"Ania's Black Widow bodysuit was definitely paid cosmetics," Jon said.

"I'd ask if you two could take anything seriously but that would sound disingenuous," Veles replied, conjuring himself a Burger King whopper. He proceeded to start chowing down. Somehow that seemed appropriate.

"Why us?" I asked.

"Excuse me?" Larry asked. "I thought you would be eager to get a chance to go back out and fight the good fight."

"Given I just explained how much I didn't want to, I don't know why you'd feel that way," I said.

"I just assumed you were doing the Hero's Journey rejection of the call thing," Larry said, shrugging. "George Lucas and all that."

I decided to ignore this rabbit hole for once. "I mean, why us. You're defeated, Veles. If these guys are just a bunch of nasty ass Cthulhu cultists—"

"Ex-Veles," Veles said.

"Exactly," I said, no longer afraid of the god of evil. "Shouldn't this be something that any of them could send a group of adventurers to deal with? 1ˢᵗ level ones. The kind of people who should be slaying kobolds?"

"Kobolds worship you now," Weis said. "You shouldn't say things like that."

Great, I was the Lord of the Tiny and First Leveled. "My point stands."

"Power," Veles said, simply.

"Power," I said, waiting for more answers.

"You destroyed one of the UMC but there are more," Larry explained. "The other gods don't realize it yet or they're making their moves quietly, but the UMCs had enough power to transform Veles from a creator deity to an overgod."

"They could also restore me or Perun to our full power even at three quarters power," Veles said. "I want you to be the one who shuts down this lunacy because I know—"

"I won't seize it for myself?" I asked, suspicious of Veles playing an angel here. Because my WIS wasn't that low.

"No, because it would be yours if you did seize it," Veles said, between chewing. "Keep it, give it to my brother, or sit on it. It is yours by right of conquest."

"Necromonger rules," Jon said. "See? I called it."

"Some of them brought lunch," I said, shaking the McDonalds bag. "Alright. I'll do it."

Larry breathed a sigh of relief. I hadn't realized until this moment that he'd been lying about thinking I was just kidding about refusing.

Wow, that was a sentence.

Veles finished his meal and conjured a stein of beer before draining it in one go. Sadly, Burger King didn't serve beer. "There's one more thing you need to know, Aaron."

"Which is?"

"The gods operate on several immutable laws," Veles said. "Human-derived gods may be able to violate them with the Twisted

Gods' taint but they remain intact for most. These are violating what their portfolio may be, oaths, and one more principle—"

"Which is?"

"That debt must be repaid," Veles said. "All the gods owe you now. Including me and my brothers. This is partially why they are unhappy that your companions managed to survive, and you haven't taken millennia to regenerate. It is a powerful bargaining chip."

I stared at him. "What are you implying?"

Veles looked at the door. "Nothing that you would understand. It's like explaining chess to a dog."

"Woof," I said, getting up. "Take me to Ania."

Chapter Forty-One
The Final Showdown Begins

"She's right out this door," Larry said, gesturing to his front door. I could see the flocks of ravens in his trees through the windows on its sides. I'd have to talk to him about turning them all back into people, assuming they still wanted to be, but my priority was to get the hell out of here. I never thought I'd say it but I didn't want to spend another minute with my favorite author. Not now. Not a hundred years from now.

"Good," I said, walking toward the door. "I'll see you after this is all over and I'm less pissed off. Maybe after humans discover faster-than-light travel."

Larry stopped me before I headed out his door, placing his hand on my shoulder. "There's something else you need to know before you go, Aaron."

"Which is?" I asked, reluctantly stopping.

I felt like everyone had talked a great deal but said very little. It was like I'd been transported back to Epic Dungeoneering™'s weekly management seminars by Barbara Wojciechowski. God, I hadn't thought about those hand puppets in months, and they still gave me the creeps. The only thing worse was Louis Tolliver's cold disdain for all human emotion.

"There's another reason we need Veles," Larry said, distracting me from my reminiscing.

I stared, waiting for an answer before I realized he expected me to respond first. "Which is?"

"You won't be able to stay long even with his help," Larry said, pausing. "Your time in the world of mortals is done."

That took a second to register. "You're going to have to be a little clearer on that, Larry."

Larry frowned, looking down. "You had a mortal body that could carry your divine essence, but it was killed in destroying Veles."

"Yeah," I said, feeling a sense of panic rising.

"Even if you hadn't lost it fighting Veles, the level of divine energy you'd had would have gradually burned it away anyway," Larry said, pausing. "Probably in a few years as a lesser god. With both Mythras and Perun's power? Well, I'm surprised it lasted the entirety of your fight."

I blinked, processing that revelation. "So, I'm dead. For good."

Wow, I hadn't seen that coming.

I probably should have.

I noticed Veles and Jon standing behind me, Jon having transformed back into a raven and sitting on top of Larry's easy chair.

"You're not only merely dead but really most sincerely dead?" Jon asked, not sounding like he was mocking me but struggling with the idea himself. Then again, of all my friends, I supposed Jon could sympathize with a traumatic post-mortem transformation the best.

Then Jon took a crap on Larry's leather easy chair.

"Goddammit!" Larry shouted.

"I have one sphincter in this form! I can't hold it!" Jon said. "You should know this as a bird keeper!"

"Then stay in human form indoors!" Larry growled, heading to the kitchen.

Veles looked at me with his head to one side, almost sympathetic. "Sacrifices are sadly impossible without actual sacrifice. Mind you, I'm not so sure what you are complaining about. Death has presumably lost a great deal of mystery now that you know you'll be going to Sky Realm and having your own kingdom there. Ania and your associates also sacrificed their mortality to be with you."

"They sacrificed it to beat you," I said, looking at him.

"Details," Veles said, shrugging.

"But to explain it to you, I'm never going to see my parents or sister or nephew again. None of them worship me. I'm never going to be able to live a normal life, whatever family or life I have from this point will be as far removed from what I wanted as anything I could imagine," I said, frowning. "No children, no retirement, no growing old and passing on. You've never been human, and you can't appreciate that."

"No, I can't," Veles said. "Boo frigging hoo."

"Yeah, I'm going to be honest, I think you lucked out," Jon said. "My grandfather forgot who he was, lost control over his bowels (no pun intended there), and died miserable in a home. Maybe they can arrange a day trip for your parents as well. After all, the guy who runs the Underworld owes you."

Veles glared at Jon.

Larry returned with some paper towels and a bottle of cleaning fluid. He started cleaning up under Jon and waved him away. "The more practical matter is that as a mostly exhausted god, you need someone else's help to manifest yourself even for a few hours. That's on Veles."

I looked at him. "You can already project an avatar?"

It seemed like defeating him hadn't done much at all. Well, aside from literally knocking some sense into him—and I meant literally as it should actually be used rather than just for emphasis. That always bugged me.

Veles shrugged. "I am of a different kind than other gods, Aaron. Now that I'm no longer suppressing my brother's resurrection, both of us are returning to full power rapidly. Far quicker than you will recover without help."

Great, Veles literally was saying he was built differently. That was depressing. "So, you're going to loan me some of your power so I can spend a few more hours on Earth saving it from the apocalypse."

"Yes," Veles said, looking annoyed at the front door. "Why?"

"Just curious why Perun isn't helping," I said, frowning. "Kind of was expecting him to be a bit more—"

"Grateful?" Veles asked.

"Helpful," I said.

"He thinks of you as an avatar of himself," Veles said. "After all, it was his divine energy that empowered you. All heroes are ultimately shades of the single greater heroic godhead. Joseph Campbell, Moorcock's Eternal Champion, and so on."

I stared at him. "That is bullshit."

"I know, isn't it?" Veles said, chuckling. "But he thinks it's better for me to do the job. Take heed, you may end up like Mythras and eclipsing him in popularity. Poor Dahzbog ended up becoming a shadow of both, though. Gods are rarely what mortals think they are."

Dahzbog was the Slavic sun god who had apparently merged with Mythras.

"Like Thor," Jon said. "Marvel comics made him look and act like Perun, but the real deal is a dumbass."

There was a thunderclap in the distance.

"Sorry!" Jon said, covering his head with his wings. "Thor is life!"

Veles took a deep breath as if he was swallowing something unpleasant. "My brother will show up if you actually need his help, nephew."

"I really hate you calling me that," I muttered. "I wish you'd stop."

"Yes, well, we can't have everything," Veles said, putting to lie the favor business. If he was telling the truth—which was a big if—it was a favor to be repaid on his terms. "Like it or not, we are family and stuck with each other for all eternity."

"Like *Hades*," Jon said. "The video game series not the Greek god."

"He's not so bad," Veles said. "Probably the second-best run part of my domain."

"How does Lucifer do?" I asked.

"He's maximum security, not running the place," Veles said. "That's Samael. Though plenty of people confuse the two since they were both married to Lilith."

I made a mental note not to believe anything Veles said from this point on. "So, I'm dead, stuck in the afterlife, and still have to save the world."

334 / C. T. Phipps

"Pretty much," Larry said, finishing cleaning his chair and throwing away the dirty paper towels. "I also point out that we're running out of time while you're adjusting to this. Even with time moving differently in my house, we're not exactly in a great position."

"I'm not the one dropping a hundred bombshells every second!" I snapped, taking a moment to rub my temples. "Can I speak with my friends now?"

"Never ask permission, Aaron," Veles said. "You're a god. You make the rules now."

Great, Palpatine-Sauron was my mentor.

Veles snapped his fingers, and I found myself once more in the Mithraeum's gardens. The rest of my group were gathered around, crying and reassuring one another. No one initially noticed me, which I assumed was due to the magic in the area and because the law of narrative casualty said it would be funnier this way.

"I can't believe he's gone," Bloodstorm muttered, looking down. "I said some awful things to him before he died."

"He was a great hero," Agata said, looking to the sky. "A man who could unite the Southern Kingdoms and stand against the darkness."

"He's not dead," Ania said, looking past them at me.

I waved.

"I know, he will live on in our hearts," Agata said, putting her hand on her sister's shoulders. "The divine power we wield will someday allow us to meet him again."

"No, I mean he's right behind you," Ania said, forcing her way past her sister.

"Aaron!" Joan ran past her and grabbed me first into a hug.

I hugged her back.

Sparky gave me a pair of thumbs up. "I knew you'd win this!"

Bloodstorm turned around and stared as if he couldn't believe it. His expression then turned dark. Bloodstorm lifted his maul up, threatening. "How do we know this isn't a trick of Veles."

"I could make a *Star Wars* quote," I said, patting Joan on the back. "Or I could explain how things should be better but are actually worse."

"It's you," Bloodstorm said, lowering his weapon. "How are you alive?"

"I'm not," I said, calmly. "Also, godhood turns out to come with a pretty big caveat. It's going to kill everyone here within a few years. Immortality is awesome, but you have to be dead to get it."

That seemed to shock everyone but Ania.

"I don't care as long as I can be with you," Ania said, smiling. It looked like she'd forgotten how and was deeply unsettling.

"Speak for yourself," Agata said, looking at her sister. "I like living."

"It gets worse," I said, unsure how to bring up the whole Veles and Mat Zemalya thing.

That was when Jon the raven popped back into existence, hovering above us. "I'm back bitches!"

"Were you gone?" Ania asked, looking up. "I didn't notice."

"I did," Agata said, looking up at the bird. "I noticed the distinct lack of idiocy and bird shit."

Neither Rachel nor Nyx had spoken since I'd appeared, the sister deities looking stunned at my arrival. Both had probably been under the impression I was meant to die during all this and not regenerate for a few centuries at the least. I didn't blame them as they were both gods of war and using me had been the right call. I was still pissed, though, because I hated being used. Which was an elaborate way of saying I was mad now but would probably forgive them. I really needed to work on carrying grudges more since that seemed to be a requirement when you were a deity.

Jon flew over to Rachel and resumed his human form. "Hey, good news! It turns out that being a god is more like *Hades I* and *II* than actual fantasy novels. You can be killed over and over again, but the big problem is being stuck in the afterlife."

"We know," Rachel said, annoyed. "It's kind of our thing."

"Oh right," Jon said. "Good news everyone! Aaron has made a deal with evil again."

A collective groan went through the group.

"That is not my thing," I muttered.

"It's totally your thing," Joan said. "Totally is a word they use for emphasis on this world."

"If you were a Nineties Valley girl," I said, pressing my fingertips together. "Okay, good news everyone, Veles is beaten! Bad news everyone, we kind of have to save the world again."

"Just tell us we don't have to ally with Veles," Ania said, staring at me.

"Oh, look at that!" I said, pointing behind her. "Godzilla fighting the Mighty Thor!"

No one looked.

Jon, however, said, "It's actually entirely possible for that to be happening behind me but I'm more interested in you trying to explain this one."

"Veles defeat has cleansed him of the taint of the Twisted Gods," I replied. "He also owes me and is going to help us stop Mat Zemalya, the Mother Goddess of Earth from destroying the universe just like he planned to do."

"Okay," Ania said.

"Okay?" Bloodstorm asked, looking between us as if we'd both gone mad. Which was probably the appropriate reaction as I wouldn't have trusted me in this scenario. "Are you serious?"

Ania stared at him as if he'd asked if water was wet. After all, Ania was famously known for her sense of humor. "Aaron is the god of compassion."

"I didn't agree to that," I said, raising a finger in objection. Not my middle one for once. "It was assigned to me."

"And Push," Agata said.

"Yes," Ania replied. "I can sense the truth in his words."

"Maybe he's also corrupted by the Twisted Gods," Bloodstorm said.

"No, then they'd sound more sensible," Rachel replied. "I can't sense the taint of the Twisted Gods on them."

"Ha," Jon said. "You said taint."

Rachel swatted him. "We've come this far, it's good to trust him one final time."

"Really, only one final time?" I asked, annoyed.

Nyx chuckled. "If anyone can tame Veles one final time, it is you."

Wow, I really hope Veles didn't hear that.

"Well screw that," Bloodstorm said, lifting his maul. "If I ever see Veles again, I'm going to slay him again."

"Boo," Veles said, appearing behind Bloodstorm.

Bloodstorm howled and spun around before whaling on Veles with his hammer, striking him hard repeatedly.

Veles didn't even react.

None of the others joined in either.

It went on for close to a minute before Bloodstorm stopped, the divinely empowered warrior more frustrated than angry now.

"How?" Bloodstorm finally asked.

"Because I'm not actually here," Veles said, flickering like he was a light switch. "I'm empowering Aaron's avatar to exist for the next, oh, forty or so minutes."

"That short, huh?" I asked.

Veles shrugged. "Tick tock, Aaron. I can see the future and know how this will probably end but you continually surprise me. Don't this time."

With that, Veles vanished.

"Well, that was ominous," I muttered. "Mind you, it would have been nice to find out where the end of the world is supposed to be happening so we can stop it."

"Where else?" Jon asked. "Epic Dungeoneering™ HQ in Poland."

I stared. "Son of a bitch."

I really hoped this wasn't going to be like Kefka's Tower and just one long slog of fighting everyone we'd fought until this point across multiple levels.

Yeah, I was going to be that, wasn't it?

CHAPTER FORTY-TWO
HANDS IN MERCY NOT HATE

It wasn't.

In fact, our assault was not remotely worthy of being called that. Nyx teleported us all to the Epic Dungeoneering Tower in Krakow, Poland. It was identical to the one in Washington DC and loomed as the largest building in the city like Sauron's Eye over Bara-Dur. It was illuminated by the many lights of the city and had swirling red clouds gathered over a damaged top floor.

What followed consisted of us entering through the front lobby and getting into an elevator as everyone ran like hell at our sight. Seriously, security guards threw down their guns, secretaries hid under desks, and junior executives just panicked at our arrival like it was the end of the world.

Which it was but not from our doing.

We all managed to get to the elevators leading upwards with no difficulty. It was a tight fit for everyone, but Sparky resumed his baby dragon form, Jon his raven form, and the rest stood shoulder-to-shoulder. Honestly, it was almost comical the way we were a collection of divine beings that were just headed upstairs in the most normal way possible.

Twenty-Nine minutes left, Veles said in my mind. *Make use of that time while you can.*

I don't want to just blow the place up, I replied. *There are people here.*

Some, Veles said. *I drained most of them dry to survive you blowing up the UMC in my face.*

I grimaced. *That's on you.*

Keep telling yourself that, Veles replied.

I hit the button for the top floor with my fist, and we started to move upward to either doom or triumph.

Possibly both.

Twenty-eight minutes left, Veles said.

I don't need running commentary, I replied.

You're here on my dime, Aaron, Veles said. *Allow me my small revenge.*

The only person who deserves revenge is me, I replied. *You killed my cousin.*

Alek is already dining with the Dragon Queen, Veles said. *Mind you, it's a bit awkward between her and Garland. That's common in the afterlife for those who have remarried after widowing. Either way, he will be treated as one of the Great Heroes. If that comforts you.*

It did. Somewhat. *I'm going to confirm that later.*

Twenty-seven minutes, Veles said, continuing to taunt me.

"Okay, on a scale of 1-10, I'm giving this a zero," Jon said, sitting on top of my shoulder. "I was expecting the lobby scene from *The Matrix* and we got the lobby scene from..."

"Yes?" I asked.

"Give me a second," Jon said, pausing. "Some very boring movie with a lobby in it that doesn't have everyone murdered."

"*Home Alone 2?*" I suggested.

"You're not helping, Aaron," Jon said.

The elevator doors opened to reveal the top floor of the Epic Dungeoneering™ building had been blown away, revealing the night sky of Krakow. The ominous red clouds spun in a vortex over the building. A group of a dozen-robed cultists were chanting around a pentacle on the floor. A glowing red beam shot forth from the pentacle into the sky above, signaling things were about to go hard.

Except, well, they didn't.

Veles had perhaps overstated the threat. The cultists were doing real magic, but their robes were all Halloween costumes and their reaction to my arrival was to immediately run for the staircases nearby. A few threw themselves down to surrender but those were trampled by others fleeing. I think I saw Louis Tolliver and Barbara Wojciechowski among the cultists, which made me want to cast a PUSH spell to knock them all off the sixty-six-story skyscraper. I didn't, though, because I was more concerned about stopping the apocalypse.

Walking through the cultists without a care in the world, I entered the pentacle they were using to summon Mat Zemalya and her armies of evil from the void. It was being done with the collected power of the UMCs and I felt myself infused with the energy of Earth's countless intersecting ley lines.

DIVINE POWER RESTORED TO MAXIMUM

It was a heady feeling and if I'd been feeling destructive, I could have channeled that power into an energy blast to destroy the goddess' avatar that was even now coming at us like a snake from its hole. I could see a glowing red orb forming in the sky and knew the Twisted Gods' queen was about to arrive in this world. We might have been able to defeat her, but it would have left most of Europe devastated.

If not the world.

Instead, I decided to do something much simpler and pulled the plug on the feed. I just drained it all into myself and scattered the pentagram's lines in every direction. The summoning ritual ceased, and Mat Zemalya's form was caught between dimensions. The sky was blood red and I could feel her presence all around us but it was no danger to us or the world.

"Well, that was anticlimactic," Ania said, cleaning off her blade. I turned and saw Barbara and Louis on the ground dead alongside several other cultists. Ania hadn't been as inclined to ignore their "threat" as I was. I think it said everything that I had the world's smallest violin playing for my dead boss. Still, my focus remained on the god trapped above us, the spirit of Earth that had been driven from her world and perhaps accelerated humanity's destruction of the environment.

"Well, this is awkward," I said, staring up at the giant glowing orb in the sky as it crackled with impotent fury. "Do we just leave her like this?"

Eleven minutes left, Veles said.

We stopped the summoning, I replied. *I think.*

Seems like something you should work on making permanent while you can, Veles said.

He had a point.

"So, what now?" Ania asked, looking up. "Is she stuck like a cork in a bottle? Do we have to evacuate your version of Ledziana to keep people from worshiping it? Can we send her back through?"

There was thunder, cracks of lightning, and flashes of light from the glowing red orb. Clearly, Mat Zemalya could hear us and was raging with impotent fury at her situation. Insane like the other Old Gods, there was no chance we could heal her by killing her according to Veles. That meant we would just have to keep her imprisoned forever.

That didn't sit right with me.

Ten minutes left, Veles said.

"Ania, do you trust me?" I asked.

"That is an incredibly stupid question, Aaron," Ania said, frowning. "But how stupid are you about to be? Like forgiving your rapist stupid or working with Veles stupid?"

"Very," I replied. "Possibly the stupidest I've ever been."

Ania took my hand and squeezed it. "Then be stupid."

I squeezed it back then shouted up to the sky. "Perun! Svarog! Veles! Three Faces of Triglav! I call upon thee for an audience! Staff meeting! Whatever the hell you guys call a divine powwow."

"Can you say powwow?" Jon asked.

"Shut it," I said.

Much to my surprise, three glowing figures appeared in front of me over the edge of the skyscraper. They gradually became avatars of the three creator gods that I'd been receiving visions of this entire time. Perun seemed brighter and healthier while Svarog mostly looked tired. Veles, of course, looked like he had a half-hour ago.

Agata got on her knees. "Milords!"

Joan stared in awe.

"You're all gods now too," Bloodstorm reminded her. "I don't think we have to kneel. Not that I did when I visited Baba Yaga, my dear old mum. I just didn't give her sass because she'd have eaten me if I had."

"Sup, bitches!" Perun said, giving the peace sign.

"You have stopped Mat Zemalya's return," Svarog said, looking up. "Do you request our help sending her back to the void?"

If Mat Zemalya was pissed off before, she was now a hundred times worse as the sky turned red as far as the eye could see. Which, given we were gods, meant she was probably visible as an aurora borealis covering most of Eastern Europe. That was all she could do, though. We had stopped her with a minimal amount of effort.

"Not quite," I said, pausing. "I saw a vision of how the Twisted Gods came to be. How the Twisted Gods were your creations from before you shared your divine essence or whatever with them."

"Or whatever," Svarog said, annoyed at my colloquialism.

Perun shrugged. "It's a good enough name for it as anything."

"It's really not," Veles muttered. "Go on, Aaron. You have nine minutes remaining."

"I also saw that Mat Zemalya believed that the constant battle against the Twisted Gods was doomed," I replied. "That they'd just keep stealing souls and wrecking the universe until it was nothing but a ruin."

"The war against them is eternal but we rebuild what is destroyed," Svarog said, sounding less triumphant and more resigned. "The price for our children and their children to live is that there must be eternal conflict."

"Yeah, it blows," Perun said.

Veles just grunted.

"Mat Zemalya was like you in that she was too compassionate for our enemy," Svarog replied. "The Slag of the pre-universe is corrupt and horrible. It consumed her as it has many other gods before them. She was not strong enough to repair them. She could not relieve their suffering."

This is where I decided to take my big swing. "But it was possible, yes?"

"Oh gods," Ania muttered, pinching the bridge of her nose.

Veles burst out laughing.

Perun joined in.

The red orb's pulsating grew less violent and the noises it made grew silent. Somehow that was worse.

"You mean remaking Mat Zemalya?" Svarog asked.

"I mean everything," I replied. "You call them Slag but they're only the way they are because they were abandoned and left without divine energy like all beings. What if you could remake them all into part of the universe?"

Was it stupid? I don't know. Maybe. However, it seemed to me that fighting this war for all eternity was equally stupid. The big thing standing in its way was the fact that no one really had enough juice to pull it off except for the creator gods and they'd been divided for the past, oh, eternity. Like Veles said — which was a phrase that rarely went anywhere good — all the gods owed me a favor.

"You would risk infection of everyone?" Svarog asked. "Look what happened to our brother Veles."

"That was one time!" Veles snapped.

Both Perun and Svarog glared at him.

Veles looked away, muttering to himself.

Yeah, the gods were a trio of brothers.

"You know the proper handling of the Twisted Gods' essence better than anyone, brother," Perun said to Svarog. "Also, Veles and Mat Zemalya tried to do this on their own. Together we can watch each other's back and purge any taint that might emerge. It would be a massive undertaking, but the Twisted Ones themselves have changed. Those touched by the divine are not as they were in the beginning."

"No, they're worse," Svarog said. "Evil as we know it is a result of the pure and good being corrupted by the presence of the Twisted Ones."

"Oh bullshit," Veles said, his face briefly taking on a bull aspect. "Evil exists with or without the Twisted Gods. I should now."

Svarog lowered his head in defeat. "You do not know what you ask, Aaron, God of Compassion."

"On the contrary, I think he knows exactly what he's asking," Perun said, looking at Svarog. "Mostly because he asked for it."

"He really is annoyingly good," Veles said, shaking his head. "I saw in the future that he'd do this but I didn't believe it."

"I didn't see it coming," Svarog said. "I must have been blinded by the sheer insanity of it."

"Can you do it or not?" I asked, gesturing to the pentacle on the ground and the near-infinite power.

"We'd have to become Triglav again," Svarog said, shaking his head. "Even with the entirety of the power that Veles has gathered, it would not be enough to fully bring us back to our former level of power. We'd need the help of the other gods, Young and Old. What you are describing is an undertaking as great as the Big Bang and will occupy our efforts for millions of years, billions even. That's assuming most of the Twisted Gods agree. The rest we would have to subdue."

There was another thunderclap.

Agreement, I believed.

Then again, we kind of had their champion in a bind.

"Maybe you can get the help of the ones that are willing to be remade." I looked toward the sky again. "According to Veles, just about everyone owes me a favor. What if I cashed them all in now? Lend you the power to fix Mat Zemalya and remake the Twisted Gods into something that belongs in this universe?"

There was a rumbling.

Svarog lowered his head and stared at us. "Almost enough."

"Almost," I said, pausing. "But not quite enough."

"We'd need all of your divine energy," Perun said, staring down at us. "Not just you, Aaron, but your party as well. They've been blessed with the power of greater gods, but we'd need every last drop. Even then, it'd take eons. You'd be sacrificing your immortality in this life and position."

"I never wanted any of that," I said.

"I did!" Jon said. "I'll still give it up, but I absolutely did."

"We were born gods," Nyx said. "But we would make that sacrifice too."

"Your power would return in time," Svarog said. "But not the ascended humans, dragons, and elf-ogre."

"Do it," Bloodstorm said, averting his gaze. "My father described the Great Darknesses. If we can prevent them from ever happening again, I would consider it worthwhile."

Agata exchanged glances with her sister.

"Aaron is our family as much as Garland ever was," Agata spoke. "We would sacrifice godhood and more for him."

Bloodstorm frowned. "Aaron, seriously, stop showing me up."

I shrugged in a "what can I do?" way.

Ania raised her swords to the air. "You don't need me to say my answer."

Joan and Sparky just stood resolute.

"Very well," Svarog said, looking at Veles. "Was this your plan all along?"

"Not in the slightest," Veles replied, shaking his head. "In no way could I have come up with something this stupid."

"Very well," Svarog said. "Are you sure you are prepared for this?"

"I am sure of nothing but certain," I said. "If I really am a god, even just for a few more minutes, I'd rather spend it in service of the universe than ruling over it."

"That is the dumbest thing I have ever heard in my life," Veles said.

Svarog and Perun exchanged knowing glances, though.

There was a clap of thunder as the red sky glowed. Mat Zemalya approved.

"Then so be it," Svarog said. "Let us heal the world, small gods."

What followed was a moment of profound cosmic insight as I felt the three creator gods join to become Triglav again and link itself to us. I got confirmation that we were part of a much vaster multiverse with beings called Primals above, even the overgods, alternate universes with many different Earths, and even different versions of myself that included a supervillain and weredeer. The moment of clarity passed through with a heavy rain starting to pour down.

The creator gods—indeed, Triglav itself—were gone along with the sense of the other deities that had just returned to Earth in all their glory. The sky was black instead of red, with no sign of angry mother goddesses. The gods were still around, I felt, but would be preoccupied as they had been for the past millennia. Only this time they would be putting their efforts to remake the Twisted Gods and soothe their fury. All it cost me was being a master of the universe.

But I had He-Man figures for that.

YOU ARE NOW DIVINE RANK ZERO.
ACHIEVEMENT UNLOCKED - TRUE ENDING "A Mortal's Life"
(A) 50 - Complete the DLC to Unlock One of the Three Secret Endings

With that, I felt the Interface vanish from my mind along with all remaining trace of Perun and Mythras' power.

I was me again.

Plain, ordinary Aragon Bartkowski.

Everyone else had magic and maybe I did too but it was mortal magic and probably just enough to live in this brave new world.

I was okay with that.

Veles' time-limit passed, and I was still here too, which answered other questions I had left unvoiced.

"I guess we're all human again," I muttered.

"Speak for yourself, flat ear," Bloodstorm said, before laughing and slapping me across the back. I almost fell off the side before he pulled me back. Still, I could feel his palpable relief. Bloodstorm wasn't made to be a god any more than I was.

Agata seemed wistful but laid her head on Bloodstorm's arm. "Thank you, Aaron. You have given the universe a great gift. Whatever horrors which exist from this day forward will be entirely ours."

I wasn't sure that was such a great gift but at least Nazis wouldn't be gaining superpowers anymore. Neither would gods and goddesses go off the deep end at the slightest provocation. Nope, they'd just go off the deep end for the perfectly normal reason that they were just like their creations. Thankfully, Earth and Mokosh would have a reprieve from that for the next couple of hundred years. After that? Well, that wasn't my problem.

Hopefully.

"Goodbye godhood," Jon muttered. "I would be disappointed in this but I'm still with an incredibly hot geek former goddess."

Rachel patted him on the head. "We'll return to Sky Realm after these bodies die. I think I'll try getting fat."

Jon stared in horror.

Nyx chuckled.

Sparky breathed gouts of flame before turning into a full dragon. "I think I'm going to like exploring your world, Ser Aaron."

I gave him a thumbs up.

"I'm still going to worship you," Joan said, looking at me. "I've already started writing your codex."

"Don't even joke about that," I muttered.

Ania kissed me passionately on the top of the skyscraper, the sun rising in the distance. Okay, no, because it was still the middle of the night in this part of Eastern Europe, but you got the gist. Strangely, as this all happened, I realized one more truth: there was no way in hell that fans of the Undermaster books were going to accept this as an ending.

Oh well. We still had the first few volumes.

Maybe I'd try *Wheel of Time* next.

LEXICON

Alignment: A sign of whether you are allied with White, Grey, or Black magical forces. Contrary to expectation, these don't precisely line to Good/Neutral/Evil. White is inherently lawful and self-righteous while Black is chaotic as well as vengeful. Grey is prone to empathy and balance.

Bald Mountain: The headquarters of Veles and where his grand temple is located. It is the pilgrimage site of all evil witches once per year on the Fall Equinox. It is also where the Scholomance is located. Bald Mountain is in the Death Mountains and protected by a magical barrier that no one of good heart can pierce.

Belobog: Chernabog's brother and the god of good fortune. He was corrupted by Veles and is now the guardian of the Elemental Temple of Water. Basically, he's Cthulhu.

The Black Rose: The nickname of the legendary Dark Undermaster, Garland of Nowhere.

Creator God: Also known as elder gods, they are deities who date back to the earliest period of the universe.

Crossroad: The long-suffering village built around Dragon Keep. It is a farming community that is on the verge of becoming a small city if it can just avoid being invaded by the undead.

Cyber Dragons 2080: A non-fantasy game produced by Epic Dungeoneering™. It was a bug-ridden mess set in a post-apocalypse cyberpunk future.

Dark Undermasters: An organization of monster hunters and knights established by Triglav and Mokosh during the Great Darkness to battle the Chaos Gods in 900 AD. They have a writ from the Ledzianan king allowing them to use dark magic and whatever means necessary to protect humanity.

The Dark Undermaster Saga: The incredibly successful fantasy franchise by Larry C.C. Weiss. It has sold over a hundred million copies and been adapted across multiple mediums. It is generally viewed as painfully derivative of other popular franchises, even though it was technically written first.

The Dark Undermaster (**Games**): A series of three games that adapt the first three books of the Dark Undermaster Saga: *A Court of Devils*, *Dead Gods*, and *Princes of Sorrow*. The fourth book, *Lords of Dragon Keep*, has been delayed for almost ten years. This has infuriated the video game developers.

The Dark Undermaster (**Series**): A five season television series on the FANT channel that heavily involved nudity, sex, and adding more grimdark. It is wildly considered to have gone down in quality once they passed Weis' books.

Dahzbog: The god of gifts, the sun, and heroism. Dahzbog is the son of Triglav or Svarog (technically both) as well as one of the most important gods in the pantheon. His worship declined in Ledziana when Perun did far more in the battle against the Twisted Gods. At some point, he either merged with, replaced, or always was the Mythras of the Holy Mythras empire.

Death Lords: Totally not liches.

Death Mountains: A massive barrier between Ledziana and the Turqish Wastes brought about via a death battle between Perun and Veles in the late 1980s. It is populated by the undead, goblins, and cultists now.

Deathrot: A horrifying mystical fungus created by the Twisted Ones that turns people into aggressive, sadistic (but intelligent) wights.

Divine Rank: A measure of one's divine power as calculated by the Interface.

Dragon Keep: An ancient castle established by the Rose family back when they were a legendary clan of dragon tamers. After their betrayal by the Mad Queen and Poppy family, it was given to the Dark Undermasters to be their new headquarters.

Dwarves: One of the five great races of Mokosh. They are the children of Svarog and live underground. Oddly, they're more stout than short. The ones who live on the surface primarily handle banking and financial jobs in addition to skilled labor.

Eldritch Ring: Another video game produced by Epic Dungeoneering™ that is a Soulslike. It incorporates some of the crazier elements of Weis' mythology played down by the books. The goal of the game is to kill Veles and ascend to become Perun's replacement.

The Empire: Also known as the Eastern Empire and Holy Mythran Empire, it was settled by the so-called "Lost Legion" of Rome in 120 AD. It has a senate, emperor, and established religion ruled by the Holy Father. The Empire has entered a conservative period with women's rights and religious freedoms being severely curtailed as it seeks to expand eastward. Its symbol is the bull, and its god is Mythras.

Elves: One of the five great races. Elves have eternal youth until they reach 120 and promptly drop dead. They are the Children of Mokosh and live anarchic, nature-loving lives with communal romances as well as hedonistic behavior. They are also all ruthless killers.

Elemental Temples: Four temples devoted to Mokosh that channel immense amounts of magical might into the natural world and keep it in balance. They also allow magical creatures to live and sorcery to function. They are all considered Grand Temples of Mokosh.

Epic Dungeoneering™: The world's largest video game manufacturer despite its relative lack of product due to buying up many smaller studios with their seemingly unlimited amounts of money. They also have a surprising number of deals with arms manufacturers, lumbering, and other satellite companies.

The First Movement: The Big Bang as triggered by the gods.

Garland of Nowhere: AKA The Black Rose. The bastard son of Perun and Lilandra Rose, born shortly before the god's death. He was a legendary swordsman, womanizer, gambler, and sorcerer who achieved countless great deeds as a Dark Undermaster. Unfortunately, these caused him to suffer severe untreated PTSD and when he was betrayed by his fellow Undermasters, he opted against resurrection.

Goblins: A tribal race of green- and olive-skinned humanoids. Contrary to their reputation as ruthless monsters, they are quite honorable, clannish, and serve Veles only because he is their creator.

Gods: A race of beings that came from the Primordial Chaos and brought order to the universe. Many of those worshiped on Earth are real, but not all, and a lot of what people know about them is nonsense.

They can draw on faith and prayers for sustenance, but it is not the sole source of their power.

Grand Temple: The highest temple that any god has and the base of their religion. The Elemental Temples of Mokosh have been occupied by the Old Gods.

Grand Temple of Water: The Grand Temple of Mokosh built under Lake Śniardwy.

Great Darkness(es): The wars against the Twisted. The last one was the supernatural invasion of Mokosh in 1939 by a Waffen-SS battalion after the Twisted Gods were freed by the Black Sun cult. (Lt) Colonel Helmuth Krieger recruited a rebellious Empire general and unleashed the Scarlet Death to aid his efforts. Perun and Veles put aside their animosity to fight it back. The Great Darkness on Mokosh and events on Earth caused Veles to believe all life had to be purged (so it could be ruled post-mortem by him safely).

Greater God: The most powerful gods in most pantheons and weaker than creator gods.

Lake Śniardwy: The largest lake in Ledziana. It is the secret home of the Grand Temple of Water.

Ledziana: The former nation compromising all the Southern Kingdoms and "Fantasy Poland." It has been divided since the death of the old king and is presently caught in the middle of a civil war, invasion by the Empire, and uprising of the dead.

Lesser God: The most common form of god and usually subordinate to Greater Gods.

Mark of the Champion: Magical bracelets made from river gold infused with the essence of Perun. The Wise Man was able to manufacture fifteen of them in total. For whatever bizarre reason, they primarily give a person abilities equivalent to *Dungeons & Dragons*-esque leveling. This includes rapid advancement in personal power and durability.

Mat Zemalya: Both the planet Earth and its mother goddess. She is the twin of Mokosh and the two are linked via Ledziana. Reckless abuse by her many children gods resulted in magic becoming scarce and most being either killed or forced into slumber. She appears as a seven-headed dragon and is the "mean Gaia" of Greek and Babylonian mythology.

Mokosh: The sister planet and goddess to Earth where magic remains abundant. It has so far only shown to have one continent. It is far less technologically advanced than Earth but more advanced in science (via magic) than it appears.

Mythras: Sun God of the mostly monotheistic faith of the Empire. He is a warrior and protector of the innocent. In practice, his church has fallen into corruption with heavy elements of misogyny and racism against nonhumans. Mythras, himself, has largely abandoned the religion and only patronizes good-hearted warriors. He is a jealous god, though.

Odin: The ruler of the Rus Kingdom's pantheon. You probably have heard of him.

Overgod: The most powerful form of divinity that is able to create or destroy universes. There is usually only one or two in a reality.

Perun: The sky god of the Ledzianan pantheon, creator of humanity, and god of good. He is the protector of mankind and very, very dead. Looks a great deal like Dolph Lundgren's He-Man and has the personality of Marvel's Thor except hornier. He expended most of his power destroying the Twisted summoned by Nazis from Earth and was defeated by his brother in a death fight decades later. Mythras, defying stereotype, answers quite a few of Perun's priests' prayers in honor of the sky god's sacrifice.

Pwiffle: A card game created by the Wise Man and the favorite of the gods after a board game from Earth involving dungeons.

Ratkin: A race created by Veles as cannon fodder and slaves for his goblins that was later given gifts by Svarog out of pity. They are still ill-treated by many other races.

Rus Kingdoms: Danish raiders had a history of getting transported to Mokosh due to their gods, the Aesir, hoping they'd conquer the place. Instead, they interbred with some of the Slavic folk to create the Rus kingdoms. They are a constantly feuding set of principalities and jarldoms that regularly try to invade Ledziana and Magyar. They occupy the north of the Southern Kingdoms, peculiar as that may be and still worship the Aesir but acknowledge the Ledzianan gods as real.

Star Bridge: A cross-planetary or dimensional gateway.

Southern Kingdoms: The former state of Ledziana that has been broken up into smaller states after the death of the old king. Confusingly, the Southern Kingdoms is also the name of the entire continent that once had another continent above it in ancient times. No one has any idea what happened to that.

Svarog: The god of creation and middle brother of the creator deities with Perun as well as Veles. He is the god of the dwarves.

The Thirteen: Veles' death lord lieutenants and generals.

Thor: The god of thunder in the Rus Kingdoms. He is far dumber and less heroic than his Marvel counterpart.

Triglav: The Divine Voltron. Triglav is a combination of Perun, Svarog, and Veles and is an overgod, AKA one of the most powerful beings even among the gods. The three can't combine without Perun and are now greatly weakened.

The Twisted Gods: Beings that are even worse than Veles and defeated by the creator gods at the start of creation. They're a little Lovecraft, a little Clive Barker, and a little "Oh my god, what the hell is that thing?" Veles works to keep them in the Underworld's Pit. They are also known as the Ungods, the Neverwere, the Curseborn and several other epithets.

Underworld: Veles' domain and where all mortals go when they die. Strangely, he's quite fair and the only mortals who go unpunished for their crimes are his followers, but even they don't go to the same place as heroes or the innocent.

Universal Magical Conductors (UMCs): Devices being used by Veles to channel magical energy into Earth as part of his plan to ascend to overgod status.

Veles: The god of the Underworld, death, evil, and wealth. Veles is a malevolent but congenial god that has decided that mortals must go. As a creator deity, he is one of the most powerful beings in the universe but limited by the fact he's stronger than almost all other gods individually but not all of them together. He looks like Peter Stormare from *Bad Boys* dressed as a Sith Lord.

Water Demon: The corrupted form of Belobog, the god of good fortune. He has assumed a squid-like kaiju-esque form. No, he doesn't look like Cthulhu. You're imagining things.

Wights: A type of undead that possesses the mindless malevolence of pure evil while remaining soulless. They are usually created by deathrot and are used as shock troops by the Twisted Ones. Veles finds them useless due to their lack of corruptibility.

Witch Queen of Angho'horak: The first death lord and Veles' chief disciple. She is the most powerful necromancer in the world.

AUTHOR'S NOTE

I'd like to thank you for reading this book. The publishing industry is changing dramatically since the advent of eBooks. It is now very difficult to get any book noticed, regardless of quality. If you enjoyed this book, you could do some very simple things to help me attract attention.

Word of mouth is the number one source of success for novels, so simply telling family and friends about the book is a great start. Here are a few other ways of helping, if you are so inclined:

* Post a rating or review where you purchased the eBook
* Post a rating or review on Goodreads
* Talk about the book or write a review on Facebook
* Tell folks about the book in a blog post.

If you like any of my other books, please feel free to check them out. A lot of my series are interlinked, and you never know when you'll find someone familiar showing up.

ABOUT THE AUTHOR

C. T. Phipps is a lifelong student of horror, science fiction, and fantasy. An avid tabletop gamer, he discovered this passion led him to write and turned him into a lifelong geek. He is a regular blogger and also a reviewer for The Bookie Monster.

Bibliography

Novels

The Rules of Supervillainy (Supervillainy Saga #1)
The Games of Supervillainy (Supervillainy Saga #2)
The Secrets of Supervillainy (Supervillainy Saga #3)
The Kingdom of Supervillainy (Supervillainy Saga #4)
The Tournament of Supervillainy (Supervillainy Saga #5)
The Future of Supervillainy (Supervillainy Saga #6)
The Horror of Supervillainy (Supervillainy Saga #7)
Tales of Supervillainy: Cindy's Seven (Supervillainy Saga #8)
The Fall of Supervillainy (Supervillainy Saga #9)

I Was a Teenage Weredeer (The Bright Falls Mysteries, Book 1)

An American Weredeer in Michigan (The Bright Falls Mysteries, Book 2)
A Nightmare on Elk Street (The Bright Falls Mysteries, Book 3)

Esoterrorism (Red Room, Vol. 1)
Eldritch Ops (Red Room, Vol. 2)
The Fall of the House (Red Room, Vol. 3)

Agent G: Infiltrator (Agent G, Vol. 1)
Agent G: Saboteur (Agent G, Vol. 2)
Agent G: Assassin (Agent G, Vol. 3)

Cthulhu Armageddon (Cthulhu Armageddon, Vol. 1)
The Tower of Zhaal (Cthulhu Armageddon, Vol. 2)
The Tree of Azathoth (Cthulhu Armageddon, Vol. 3)

Lucifer's Star (Lucifer's Star, Vol. 1)
Lucifer's Nebula (Lucifer's Star, Vol. 2)

Straight Outta Fangton (Straight Outta Fangton, Vol. 1)
100 Miles and Vampin' (Straight Outta Fangton, Vol. 2)
Vampiraz4Life (Straight Outta Fangton, Vol. 3)

Wraith Knight (Wraith Knight, Vol. 1)
Wraith Lord (Wraith Knight, Vol. 2)
Wraith King (Wraith Knight, Vol. 3)

Dark Destiny (Dark Destiny, Vol. 1)
Destiny's Paradox (Dark Destiny, Vol. 2)

Brightblade (The Morgan Detective Agency, Book 1)
Brighteyes (The Morgan Detective Agency, Book 2)

Daughter of the Cyber Dragons (The Cyber Dragons Series, Book 1)
Revenge of the Cyber Dragons (The Cyber Dragons Series, Book 2)
End of the Cyber Dragons (The Cyber Dragons Series, Book 3)

Space Academy Dropouts (The Space Academy Series, Book 1)
Space Academy Rejects (The Space Academy Series, Book 2)
Space Academy Washouts (The Space Academy Series, Book 3)

Moon Cops on the Moon (Moon Cops, Book 1)
Moon City Vice (Moon Cops, Book 2)

Lords of Dragon Keep (Dark Undermaster, Book 1)
Guardians of Dragon Keep (Dark Undermaster, Book 2)
Wizards of Dragon Keep (Dark Undermaster, Book 3)

Psycho Killers in Love

Tales of an Eldritch Wasteland

Anthologies (as editor)
Blackest Knights
Blackest Spells
Tales of Capes and Cowls
Tales of the Al-Azif
Tales of Yog-Sothoth

Curious about other Crossroad Press books? Stop by our website:
http://crossroadpress.com
We offer quality writing
in digital, audio, and print formats.

Subscribe to our newsletter on the website homepage and receive a
free eBook.

www.ingramcontent.com/pod-product-compliance
Lightning Source LLC
Chambersburg PA
CBHW051527250626
47156CB00001B/262